DAVID BALDACCI

THE HIT

GRAND CENTRAL
PUBLISHING

LARGE PRINT

Copyright © 2013 by Columbus Rose, Ltd.
All rights reserved. In accordance with the U.S. Copyright Act of 1976, the scanning, uploading, and electronic sharing of any part of this book without the permission of the publisher is unlawful piracy and theft of the author's intellectual property. If you would like to use material from the book (other than for review purposes), prior written permission must be obtained by contacting the publisher at permissions@hbgusa.com. Thank you for your support of the author's rights.

Grand Central Publishing
Hachette Book Group
237 Park Avenue
New York, NY 10017

www.HachetteBookGroup.com

Printed in the United States of America

RRD-C

First Edition: April 2013
10 9 8 7 6 5 4 3 2 1

Grand Central Publishing is a division of Hachette Book Group, Inc.
The Grand Central Publishing name and logo is a trademark of Hachette Book Group, Inc.

The Hachette Speakers Bureau provides a wide range of authors for speaking events. To find out more, go to www.hachettespeakersbureau.com or call (866) 376-6591.

The publisher is not responsible for websites (or their content) that are not owned by the publisher.

LCCN: 2013932590

To the cast and crew of
Wish You Well,
thanks for an incredible ride

THE HIT

CHAPTER

1

FEELING ENERGIZED BY THE DEATH that was about to happen, Doug Jacobs adjusted his headset and brightened his computer screen. The picture was now crystal clear, almost as if he were there.

But he thanked God he wasn't.

There was thousands of miles away, but one couldn't tell that by looking at the screen. They couldn't pay him enough to be *there*. Besides, many people were far better suited for that job. He would be communicating shortly with one of them.

Jacobs briefly glanced around the four walls and the one window of his office in the sunny Washington, D.C., neighborhood. It was an ordinary-looking low-rise brick building set in a mixed-use neighborhood that also contained historical homes in various states of either decay or restoration. But some parts of Jacobs's building were not ordinary at all. These elements included a heavy-gauge steel gate out front with a high fence around the perimeter of the property. Armed sentries patrolled the interior halls and surveillance cameras monitored the exterior. But there was nothing on the outside to clue anyone in to what was happening on the inside.

And a lot was happening on the inside.

Jacobs picked up his mug of fresh coffee, into which he had just poured three sugar packets. Watching the screen required intense concentration. Sugar and caffeine helped him do that. It would match the emotional buzz he would have in just a few minutes.

He spoke into the headset. "Alpha One, confirm location," he said crisply. It occurred to him that he sounded like an air traffic controller trying to keep the skies safe.

Well, in a way that's exactly what I am. Only our goal is death on every trip.

The response was nearly immediate. "Alpha One location seven hundred meters west of target. Sixth floor of the apartment building's east face, fourth window over from the left. You should just be able to make out the end of my rifle muzzle on a zoom-in."

Jacobs leaned forward and moved his mouse, zooming in on the real-time satellite feed from this distant city that was home to many enemies of the United States. Hovering over the edge of the windowsill, he saw just the tip of a long suppressor can screwed onto a rifle's muzzle. The rifle was a customized piece of weaponry that could kill at long distances—well, so long as a skilled hand and eye were operating it.

And right now that was the case.

"Roger that, Alpha One. Cocked and locked?"

"Affirmative. All factors dialed in on scope. Cross-hairs on terminal spot. Tuned frequency-shifting suppressor. Setting sun behind me and in their faces. No optics reflect. Good to go."

"Copy that, Alpha One."

Jacobs checked his watch. "Local time there seventeen hundred?"

"On the dot. Intel update?"

Jacobs brought this information up on a subscreen. "All on schedule. Target will be arriving in five minutes. He'll exit the limo on the curbside. He's scheduled to take a minute of questions on the curb and then it's a ten-second walk into the building."

"Ten-second walk into the building confirmed?"

"Confirmed," said Jacobs. "But the minute of interview may go longer. You play it as it goes."

"Copy that."

Jacobs refocused on the screen for a few minutes until he saw it. "Okay, motorcade is approaching."

"I see it. I've got my sight line on the straight and narrow. No obstructions."

"The crowd?"

"I've been watching the patterns of the people for the last hour. Security has roped them off. They've outlined the path he'll take for me, like a lighted runway."

"Right. I can see that now."

Jacobs loved being ringside for these things, without actually being in the danger zone. He was compensated more generously than the person on the other end of the line. At a certain level this made no sense at all.

The shooter's ass was out there, and if the shot wasn't successful or the exit cues made swiftly, the gunner was dead. Back here, there would be no acknowledgment of affiliation, only a blanket denial. The shooter had no documents, no creds, no ID that would prove otherwise. The shooter would be left to hang. And in the country where this particular hit was taking place, hanging would be the shooter's fate. Or perhaps beheading.

All the while, Jacobs sat here safe and drew bigger money.

But he thought, *Lots of folks can shoot straight and get away. I'm the one doing the geopolitical wrangling on these suckers. It's all in the prep. And I'm worth every dollar.*

Jacobs again spoke into his headset. "Approach is right on target. Limo is about to stop."

"Copy that."

"Give me a sixty-second buffer before you're about to fire. We'll go silent."

"Roger that."

Jacobs tightened the grip on his mouse, as though it were a trigger. During drone attacks he had actually clicked his mouse and watched a target disappear in a flame ball. The computer hardware manufacturer had probably never envisioned its devices being used for *that*.

His breathing accelerated even as he knew the shooter's respiration was heading the other way, achieving cold zero, which was what one needed to make a long-range shot like this. There was no margin of error at all. The shot had to hit and kill the target. It was that simple.

The limo stopped. The security team opened the door. Bulky, sweaty men with guns and earwigs looked everywhere for danger. They were pretty good. But pretty good did not cut it when you were up against outstanding.

And every asset Jacobs sent out was outstanding.

The man stepped onto the sidewalk and squinted against the sun's dying glare. He was a megalomaniac named Ferat Ahmadi who desired to lead a troubled, violent nation down an even darker road. That could not be allowed to happen.

Thus it was time to nip this little problem in the bud. There were others in his country ready to take over. They were less evil than he was, and capable of being manipulated by more civilized nations. In today's overly complex world, where allies and foes seemed to change on a weekly basis, that was as good as it got.

But that was not Jacobs's concern. He was here simply to execute an assignment, with emphasis on the "execute" part.

Then over his headset came two words: "Sixty seconds."

"Copy that, Alpha One," said Jacobs. He didn't say anything as stupid as "good luck." Luck had nothing to do with it.

He engaged a countdown clock on his computer screen.

He eyed the target and then the clock.

Jacobs watched Ahmadi talk to the reporters. He took a sip of coffee, set it down, and continued to watch as Ahmadi finished with his prearranged questions. The man took a step away from the reporters. The security team held them back.

The chosen path was revealed. For the photo op it would present, Ahmadi was going to walk it alone. It was designed to show his leadership and his courage.

It was also a security breach that looked trivial at ground level. But with a trained sniper at an elevated position it was like a fifty-yard gash in the side of a ship with a billion-candlepower beacon lighting it.

Twenty seconds became ten.

Jacobs started counting the last moments in his head, his eyes glued to the screen.

Dead man arriving, he thought.

Almost there. Mission nearly complete, and then it was on to the next target.

That is, after a steak dinner and a favorite cocktail and trumpeting this latest victory to his coworkers.

Three seconds became one.

Jacobs saw nothing except the screen. He was totally focused, as though he were going to deliver the kill shot himself.

The window shattered.

The round entered Jacobs's back after slicing through his ergonomic chair. It cleared his body and thundered out of his chest. It ended up cracking the computer screen as Ferat Ahmadi walked into the building unharmed.

Doug Jacobs, on the other hand, slumped to the floor.

No steak dinner. No favorite cocktail. No bragging rights ever again.

Dead man arrived.

CHAPTER

2

HE JOGGED ALONG THE PARK trail with a backpack over his shoulders. It was nearly seven at night. The air was crisp and the sun was almost down. The taxis were honking. The pedestrians were marching home from a long day's work.

Horse-drawn carriages were lined up across from the Ritz-Carlton. Irishmen in shabby top hats were awaiting their next fares as the light grew fainter. Their horses pawed the pavement and their big heads dipped into feed buckets.

It was midtown Manhattan in all its glory, the contemporary and the past mingling like coy strangers at a party.

Will Robie looked neither right nor left. He had been to New York many times. He had been to Central Park many times.

He was not here as a tourist.

He never went anywhere as a tourist.

The hoodie was drawn up and tied tight in front so

his face was not visible. Central Park had lots of surveillance cameras. He didn't want to end up on any of them.

The bridge was up ahead. He reached it, stopped, and jogged in place, cooling down.

The door was built into the rock. It was locked.

He had a pick gun and then the door was no longer locked.

He slipped inside and secured the door behind him. This was a combination storage and electrical power room used by city workers who kept Central Park clean and lighted. They had gone home for the day and would not be back until eight the next morning.

That would be more than enough time to do what needed doing.

Robie slipped off the knapsack and opened it. Inside were all the things he required to do his work.

Robie had recently turned forty. He was about six-one, a buck eighty, with far more muscle than fat. It was wiry muscle. Big muscles were of no help whatsoever. They only slowed him down when speed was almost as essential as accuracy.

There were a number of pieces of equipment in the knapsack. Over the course of two minutes he turned three of those pieces into one with a highly specialized purpose.

A sniper rifle.

The fourth piece of equipment was just as valuable to him.

His scope.

He attached it to the Picatinny rail riding on the top of his rifle.

He went through every detail of the plan in his head twenty times, both the shot he had to make and his safe exit that would hopefully follow. He had already memorized everything, but he wanted to arrive at the point where he no longer had to think, just act. That would save precious seconds.

This all took about ninety minutes.

Then he ate dinner. A bottle of G2 and a protein bar.

This was Will Robie's version of a Friday night date with himself.

He lay down on the cement floor of the storage room, folded his knapsack under his head, and went to sleep.

In ten hours and eleven minutes it would be time to go to work.

While other people his age were either going home to spouses and kids or going out with coworkers or maybe on a date, Robie was sitting alone in a glorified closet in Central Park waiting for someone to appear so Robie could kill him.

He could dwell on the current state of his life and arrive at nothing satisfactory in the way of an answer, or he could simply ignore it. He chose to ignore it. But perhaps not as easily as he once had.

Still, he had no trouble falling asleep.

And he would have no trouble waking up.

And he did, nine hours later.

It was morning. Barely past six a.m.

Now came the next important step. Robie's sight line. In fact, it was the most critical of all.

Inside the storage room, he was staring at a blank stone wall with wide mortar seams. But if one looked more closely, there were two holes in the seams, which had been placed at precise locations to allow one to see outside. However, the holes had been filled back in with a pliable material tinted to look like mortar. This had all been done a week ago by a team posing as a repair crew in the park.

Robie used a pincers to grip one end of the substance and pull it out. He did this one more time and the two holes were now revealed.

Robie slid his rifle muzzle through the lower hole, stopping it before it reached the end of the hole. This configuration would severely restrict his angle of aim, but he could do nothing about that. It was what it was. He never operated in perfect conditions.

His scope lined up precisely with the top hole, its leading edge resting firmly on the mortar seam. Now he could see what he was shooting at.

Robie sighted through it, dialing in all factors both environmental and otherwise that would affect his task.

His suppressor jacket was customized to fit the

muzzle and the ordnance he was chambering. The jacket would reduce the muzzle blast and sonic signature, and it would physically reflect back toward the gun's stock to minimize the suppressor's length.

He checked his watch. Ten minutes to go.

He put in his earwig and clipped the power pack to his belt. His comm set was now up and running.

He sighted through the scope again. His crosshairs were suspended over one particular spot in the park.

Because he couldn't move his rifle barrel, Robie would have a millisecond's glimpse of his target and then his finger would pull the trigger.

If he was late by a millisecond, the target would survive.

If he was early by a millisecond, the target would survive.

Robie took this margin of error in stride. He had had easier assignments, to be sure. And also tougher ones.

He took a breath, and relaxed his muscles. Normally he would have someone acting as a long-distance spotter. However, Robie's recent experiences with partners in the field had been disastrous, and he had demanded to go solo on this one. If the target didn't show, or changed course, Robie would get a stand-down signal over his comm pack.

He looked around the small space. It would be his home for a few minutes more and then he would never see it again. Or if he screwed up, this might be the last place he ever saw.

He checked his watch again. Two minutes to go. He didn't return to his rifle just yet. Taking up his weapon too early could make his muscles rigid and his reflexes too brittle, when flexibility and fluidity were needed.

At forty-five seconds to target, he knelt and pressed his eye to the scope and his finger to the trigger guard. His earwig had remained silent. That meant his target was on the way. The mission was a go.

He wouldn't look at his watch again. His internal clock was now as accurate as any Swiss timepiece. He focused on his optics.

Scopes were great, but they were also finicky. A target could be lost in a heartbeat and precious seconds could pass before it was reacquired, which guaranteed failure. He had his own way of dealing with that possibility. At thirty seconds to target he started exhaling longer breaths, walking his respiration and heart rate down notch by notch, breath by elongated breath. Cold zero was what he was looking for, that sweet spot for trigger pulls that almost always ensured the kill would happen. No finger tremble, no jerk of the hand, no wavering of the eye.

Robie couldn't hear his target. He couldn't yet see him.

But in ten seconds he would both hear and see him.

And then he would have a bare moment to acquire the target and fire.

The last second popped up on his internal counter.

His finger dropped to the trigger.

In Will Robie's world once that happened there was no going back.

CHAPTER

3

THE MAN JOGGING ALONG did not worry about his security. He paid others to worry for him. Perhaps a wiser man would have realized that no one valued a specific life more than its owner. But he was not the wisest of men. He was a man who had run afoul of powerful political enemies, and the price for that was just about to come due.

He jogged along, his lean frame moving up and down with each thrust of hip and leg. Around him were four men, two slightly in front and two slightly behind him. They were fit and active, and all four had to slow down their normal pace a bit to match his.

The five men were of similar height and build and wearing matching black running suits. This was by design because it resulted in five potential targets instead of one. Arms and legs swinging in unison, feet pounding the trail, heads and torsos moving at steady but still slightly different angles. It all added up to a nightmare for someone looking to take a long-distance shot.

In addition, the man in the center of the group wore lightweight body armor that would stop most rifle rounds. Only a head shot would be guaranteed lethal, and a head shot here over any distance beyond the unaided eye was problematic. There were too many physical obstacles. And they had spies in the park; anyone looking suspicious or carrying anything that might be out of the ordinary would be tagged and sat on until the man had passed. There had been two of those so far and no more.

And yet the four men were professional, and they anticipated that despite their best efforts, someone might still be out there. They kept their gazes swiveling, their reflexes primed to move into accelerated action if necessary.

The curve coming up was good in a way. It broke off potential sniper sight lines, and fresh ones would not pick up for another ten yards. Though they were trained not to do so, each man relaxed just a fraction.

The suppressed round was still loud enough to catapult a flock of pigeons from the ground to about a foot in the air, their wings flapping and their beaked mouths cooing in protest at this early morning disturbance.

The man in the center of the joggers pitched

forward. Where his face had once been was a gaping hole.

The long-distance flight of a 7.62 round built up astonishing kinetic energy. In fact, the farther it traveled the more energy it built up. When it finally ran into a solid object like a human head the result was devastating.

The four men watched in disbelief as their protectee lay on the ground, his black running suit now mottled with blood, brain, and human tissue. They pulled their guns and looked wildly around for someone to shoot. The security chief spoke into his phone, dialing up reinforcements. They were no longer a protection detail. They were a revenge detail.

Only there was no one on whom to exact that revenge.

It had been a scope kill, and all four men wondered how that was possible, on the curve of all places.

The only people visible were other joggers or walkers. None could have a rifle concealed on them. They all had stopped and were staring in horror at the man on the ground. If they had known who he was, their horror might have turned to relief.

Will Robie did not take even a second to relish the exceptionally fine shot he had just made. The constraints on his rifle barrel and thus his shot had been enormous. It was like playing a game of Whac-A-Mole. You never knew where or when the target would pop out of the hole. Your reflexes had to be superb, your aim true.

But Robie had done it over a considerable distance with a sniper rifle and not a child's hammer. And his target wasn't a puppet. It could shoot back.

He hefted the tubes of pliable material that had been used to replace the mortar. From his knapsack he took a hardening solution from a bottle and mixed it with some powder he had in another container. He rubbed the mixture on one end and the sides of the two tubes and eased them through the open holes, lining the edges up precisely. Then he rubbed the mixture on the other end of the tubes. Within two minutes the mixture would harden and blend perfectly with the mortar, and one would be unable to slide the tubes out anymore. His sight line had, in essence, vanished, like a magician's assistant in a box.

Knapsack on his back, he was disassembling his weapon as he walked. In the center of the room was a manhole cover. Underneath Central Park were numerous tunnels, some from old subway line construction, some carrying sewage and water, and some just built for now unknown reasons and forgotten about.

Robie was about to use a complicated combination thereof to get the hell out of there.

He slid the manhole cover into place after he lowered himself into the hole. Using a flashlight, he navigated down a metal ladder and his feet hit solid earth thirty feet later. The route he had to follow was in his head. Nothing about a mission was ever written down. Things written down could be discovered if Robie ended up dead instead of his target.

Even for Robie, whose short-term memory was excellent, it had been an arduous process.

He moved methodically, neither fast nor slowly. He had plugged the barrel of his rifle with the quick-hardening solution and pitched it down one tunnel; a constant flow of fast water would carry it out to the East River, where it would sink into oblivion. And even if it were found somehow the plugged barrel would be ruined for any ballistics tests.

The stock of the weapon was dropped down another tunnel under a pile of fallen bricks that looked like they had lain there for a hundred years and probably had. Even if the stock was discovered it could not be traced back to the bullet that had just killed his target. Not without the firing pin, which Robie had already pocketed.

The smells down here were not pleasant. There were over six thousand miles of tunnels under Manhattan, remarkable for an island without a single working mine of any kind. The tunnels carried pipes that transported millions of gallons of drinking water a day to satisfy the inhabitants of America's most populous city. Other tunnels carried away the sewage made by these very same inhabitants to enormous treatment plants that would transform it into a variety of things, often turning waste into something useful.

Robie walked at the same pace for an hour. At the end of that hour he looked up and saw it. The ladder with the markings *DNE EHT.*

"The End" spelled backward. He did not smile at someone's idea of a lame joke. Killing people was as serious as it got. He had no reason to be particularly happy.

He put on the blue jumpsuit and hard hat that were hanging on a peg on the tunnel wall. Carrying his knapsack on his back, he climbed the ladder and emerged from the opening.

Robie had walked from midtown to uptown entirely underground. He actually would have preferred the subway.

He entered a work zone with barricades erected around an opening to the street. Men in blue jumpsuits just like his worked away at some project. Traffic moved around them, cabs honking. People walked up and down the sidewalks.

Life went on.

Except for the guy back at the park.

Robie didn't look at any of the workers, and not

a single one of them looked at him. He walked to a white van parked next to the work zone and climbed in the passenger side. As soon as his door thunked closed, the driver put the van in gear and drove off. He knew the city well and took alternate routes to avoid most of the traffic as he worked his way out of Manhattan and onto the road to LaGuardia Airport.

Robie climbed into the back to change. When the van pulled up to the terminal's passenger drop-off, he stepped out dressed in a suit with briefcase in hand and walked into the airport terminal.

LaGuardia, unlike its equally famous cousin, JFK, was king of the short-haul flights, handling more of them than just about any other airport outside of Chicago and Atlanta. Robie's flight was very short, about forty minutes in the air to D.C.—barely enough time to stow your carry-on, get comfortable, and listen to your belly rumble because you weren't going to get anything to eat on a flight that brief.

His jet touched down thirty-eight minutes later at Reagan National.

The car was waiting for him.

He got in, picked up the *Washington Post* lying on the backseat, and scanned the headlines. It wasn't there yet, of course, although there would be news online already. He didn't care to read about it. He already knew all he needed to know.

But tomorrow the headline on every newspaper in the country would be about the man in Central Park who had gone out to jog for his health and ended up dead as dead could be.

A few would mourn the dead man, Robie knew. They would be his associates, whose opportunity to inflict pain and suffering on others would be gone, hopefully forever. The rest of the world would applaud the man's demise.

Robie had killed evil before. People were happy, thrilled that another monster had met his end. But the world went on, as screwed up as ever, and another monster—maybe even worse—would replace the fallen one.

On that clear, crisp morning in the normally serene Central Park his trigger pull would be remembered for a while. Investigations would be made. Diplomatic broadsides exchanged. More people would die in retaliation. And then life would go on.

And serving his country, Will Robie would get on a plane or train or bus or, like today, use his own two feet, and pull another trigger, or throw another knife, or strangle the life out of someone using simply his bare hands. And then another tomorrow would come and it would be as though someone had hit a giant reset button and the world would look exactly the same.

But he would continue to do it, and for only one reason. If he didn't, the world had no chance to get better. If people with some courage in their hearts stood by and did nothing, the monsters won every time. He was not going to let that happen.

The car drove through the streets, reaching the western edge of Fairfax County, Virginia. It pulled through a guarded gate. When it stopped Robie got out and walked into the building. He flashed no creds, and didn't stop to ask permission to enter.

He trudged down a short hall to a room where he would sit for a bit, send a few emails, and then go home to his apartment in D.C. Normally after a mission he would walk the streets aimlessly until the wee hours. It was just his way of handling the aftermath of what he did for a living.

Today he simply wanted to go home and sit and do nothing more exacting than stare out his window.

That was not to be.

The man came in.

The man often came in carrying another mission for Robie in the form of a USB stick.

But this time he carried nothing except a frown.

"Blue Man wants to meet with you," he said simply.

Nothing much the man could have said would have intrigued or surprised Robie.

But this did.

Robie had seen a lot of Blue Man lately. But before that—for twelve years before that, to be precise—he hadn't seen him at all.

"Blue Man?"

"Yes. The car's waiting."

CHAPTER

4

JESSICA REEL SAT ALONE AT a table in the airport lounge. She was dressed in a gray pantsuit with a white blouse. Her flat shoes were black with a single strap over the top of each foot. They were lightweight and built for speed and mobility if she had to run.

Her only nod to eccentricity was the hat that sat on the table in front of her. It was a straw-colored panama with a black silk band, ideally suited for traveling because it was collapsible. Reel had traveled much over the years, but she had never worn a hat during any of those previous trips.

Now had seemed like a good time to start.

Her gaze drifted over thousands of passengers pulling rolling luggage and carrying laptop cases over their shoulders with Starbucks cups cradled in their free hands. These travelers anxiously scanned electronic marquees for gates, cancellations, arrivals, departures. And minutes or hours or days later if the weather was particularly uncooperative, they would climb into silver tubes and be flung hundreds or thousands of miles to their destination of choice, hopefully with most of their bags and their sanity intact.

Millions of people did this same little thirty-thousand-foot-high dance every day in nearly every country on earth. Reel had done it for years. But she had always traveled light. No laptop. Enough clothes for a few days. No work went with her. It was always waiting for her when she got there. Along with all the equipment she would need to complete her designated task.

And then she would make her exit, leaving behind at least one person dead.

She fingered her phone. On the screen was her boarding pass. The name on the e-ticket was not Jessica Reel. That would have been a little inconvenient for her in these suddenly troubled times.

Her last task had not gone according to plan—at least not according to the plan of her former employer. However, it had been executed exactly as Reel had envisioned it, leaving a man named Douglas Jacobs dead.

Because of this Reel would be not only persona non grata back home, but also very much a wanted person. And the people she used to work for had an abundance of agents who could be called up to hunt her down and end her life as efficiently as she had Jacobs's.

That scenario was definitely not in Reel's grand scheme, and thus the new name, fresh documents, and panama hat. Her long hair was colored blonde from the natural brown. Tinted contacts transformed greenish eyes to gray. And she had been given a modified nose and a revised jawline courtesy of a bit of ingenious plastic surgery. She was, in all critical respects, a new woman.

And perhaps an enlightened one as well.

Her flight was called. She rose. In her flats she was five-nine—tall for a woman—but she blended in nicely with the bustling crowd. She donned her hat, purchased her Starbucks, and walked to the nearby gate. The flight left on time.

Forty somewhat bumpy minutes later it landed with a hard jolt on the runway tarmac minutes ahead of a storm's leading edge. The turbulence had not bothered Reel. She always played the odds. She could fly every day for twenty thousand years and never be involved in a crash.

Her odds of survival on the ground would not be nearly as good.

She walked off the plane, made her way to the cabstand, and waited patiently in a long line until her turn came up.

Doug Jacobs had been the first but not the last. Reel had a list in her head of those who would, hopefully, join him in the hereafter, if there was such a place for people like Jacobs.

But the list would have to wait. Reel had somewhere

to go. She climbed into the next available cab and set off for the city.

The cab dropped her near Central Park. The park was always a busy place, full of people and dogs and events and workers, controlled chaos if ever there was such a thing.

Reel paid the cabbie and turned her attention to the closest entrance to the park. She walked through the opening and made her way as close as possible to where it had happened.

The police had taped off great chunks of the area so they could perform their little forensics hunt, collect their evidence, and hopefully catch a killer.

They would fail. Reel knew this even if New York's Finest didn't.

She stood shoulder to shoulder with a crowd of people just beyond the official barricades. She watched the police methodically working, covering every inch of ground around where the body had fallen.

Reel looked at the same ground and her mind started to fill in blanks that the police didn't even know existed.

The target was what it was. A monster who needed killing.

That didn't interest Reel at all. She had killed many monsters. Others took their place. That was how the world worked. All you could do was try to keep slightly ahead in the count.

She was focused on other things. Things the police could not see.

She lined up the taped outline of the body on the trail with trajectory patterns in all directions. She was sure the police had already done that, Forensics 101 after all. But soon thereafter, their deductive ability and even their imagination would reach their professional limits, and thus they would never arrive at the right answer.

For her part, Reel knew that anything was possible. So after exhausting all other possibilities and performing her own mental algorithms to figure the shooter's position, she focused on a stone wall. A seemingly impenetrable stone wall. One could not fire through such an obstacle. And the doorway into the place that was surrounded by the stone wall had no sight line to the target. And it was no doubt securely locked. Thus the police would have discounted it immediately.

Reel left the crowd and started a long sweeping walk that angled her first to the west, then north, and finally east.

She drew out a pair of binoculars and focused them on the wall.

One would have to have two holes. One for the muzzle allowing for the greater width of the suppressor sleeve. And one for the scope.

Reel knew precisely where and how large those holes would need to be.

She worked the thumbwheel on her optics. The

wall came into sharper focus. Reel looked at two areas of the wall, one higher than the other, both located in mortar seams.

The police would never see it because they would never be looking for it.

But Reel was.

There was no surveillance camera that she could see pointed at the wall. Why would there be? It was simply a wall.

Which made it perfect.

And on that wall were two patches of mortar that were a slightly different color, as though they had been more recently applied than their neighbors. And they had been, Reel knew.

As soon as the shot was fired the holes would be refilled. The hardening compound would work its magic. For some hours, even some days afterward, the coloration would be slightly, ever so slightly, different. And then it would look just like the rest.

The shot had come from there.

The escape would have also come from there.

Reel looked down at the ground.

Maintenance shed. Pipes, tunnels.

Underneath the park was a maze of tunnels— water, sewer, and abandoned subway tracks. Reel knew this for a fact. It had figured into one of her kills years ago. So many places to run and hide under America's largest city. Millions of people above were jostling for space, while down below you could be as alone as though you were on the surface of the moon.

Reel began to walk again after putting her binoculars away.

The exit would have probably been in some far-off part of the city. Then the shooter would rise up to street level. A quick ride to the airport or train station and that would be it.

The killer goes free.

The victim goes to the morgue.

The papers would cover it for a while. There might be some geopolitical retaliation somewhere, and then the story would die. Other stories would take its place. One death meant little. The world was too big. And too many people were dying violent deaths to focus for long on any one of them.

Reel walked toward a hotel where she had reserved a room. She would hit the gym to work the kinks out, sit in the steam shower, have a bit of supper, and think about things.

The jaunt to Central Park had not been without purpose.

Will Robie was one of the best, if not the best they had.

Reel had no doubt that Robie had pulled the trigger that morning in Central Park. He had covered his tracks. Made his way aboveground. Taken a plane to D.C. Checked back in at the office.

All routine, or as routine as things got in Robie's world.

In my world too. But not anymore. Not after Doug Jacobs. The only report they'll want about me now is my autopsy results.

Reel was fairly sure Robie would be summoned for another mission.

His mission will be to track me down and kill me.

You send a killer to catch another killer.

Robie versus Reel. Nice ring to it.

It sounded like the fight of the century.

And she was certain it would be.

5

I T W A S R A I N I N G O U T S I D E. There was no window in the room, but Robie could hear the drops hitting the roof. The weather had turned chilly in the last twenty-four hours. Winter was not here yet, but it was knocking on the door.

Robie put one palm on the table and continued to stare at Blue Man.

Obviously, Blue Man was not his real name. It was Roger Walton, but Blue Man would be the only way Robie would ever refer to him. It had to do with the man's high-level position—in the Blue Ring, to be precise. There were rings above Blue, but not many.

He looked like a grandfather. Silver hair, lengthening jowls, round glasses, immaculate suit, red paisley tie, old-fashioned collar pin, shined wingtips.

Yes, Blue Man was indeed high up in the agency. He and Robie had worked together before. Robie trusted Blue Man more than he trusted most folks here. The list of people Robie trusted was quite short.

"Jessica Reel?" said Robie.

Blue Man nodded.

"We're sure?"

"Jacobs was her handler. Jacobs was carrying out a mission with Reel. But Jacobs was shot instead of the target. We subsequently determined that Reel was not even in the vicinity of the target. It was all a sham."

"Why kill Jacobs?"

"We don't know that. What we do know is Reel has gone off the grid."

"You have proof she killed Jacobs? Maybe she's dead and someone else did it."

"No. It was Reel's voice on the line with Jacobs right before the shot was taken. Jacobs would have had no idea where in the world she was. She would sound the same whether she was a thousand feet or a thousand miles away." He paused. "We performed a shot trajectory analysis. Reel made the kill shot from an old town house down the street from where Jacobs was working."

"No bulletproof windows in the place?"

"There will be now. But the blinds were drawn and the building is protected against electronic sur-veillance. The shooter had to know the exact layout of Jacobs's office to make that hit, because otherwise they were shooting blind."

"Any evidence at the town house?"

"Not really. If Reel was there she policed her brass."

Well, she would, wouldn't she, thought Robie. *That's what we're trained to do, if we have the chance.*

Blue Man tapped his finger on the table. It seemed to be in rhythm with the raindrops. "You knew Reel?"

Robie nodded. He knew that question was going to come up and was surprised it hadn't already. "Came up through the ranks together, so to speak. Did a few missions with her early on."

"And your thoughts on the woman?"

"She didn't talk a lot, which was okay with me because I didn't either. She did her job and she did it well. I never had any concerns with her covering my back. I believed she would go on to do first-rate work."

"She did, until this," noted Blue Man. "She's still the only female operative we've ever had."

"Out there gender doesn't mean anything," replied Robie. "So long as you can shoot straight under pressure. So long as you can do your job."

"What else?"

"We never shared anything personal about each other," said Robie. "It was not a bonding experience. We weren't in the military. We knew we would not be working together long-term."

"How long ago was this?"

"Last mission was well over ten years ago."

"Did you ever doubt her patriotism?"

"I never really thought about it. I figured if she had

gotten that far the question of her loyalty would have been settled."

Blue Man nodded thoughtfully.

Robie said, "So why am I here? Just gathering intel on Reel from the people who knew her? You'll find others hopefully who knew her better than I did."

"That's not the only reason," said Blue Man.

The doorknob turned and another man entered the room.

Blue Man was near the top of the agency food chain. This man was even more highly situated than that. Robie would not refer to him by a color.

Jim Gelder was the number two man here. His boss, the director of central intelligence, testified before Congress, went to all the parties, did the D.C. song and dance, and fought for more budget dollars.

Gelder did everything else, meaning he basically ran the place, or at least the clandestine operations part of it, which many considered the most important.

He was in his late forties, but looked older. He had once been trim but had become thick around the middle. His hair was thinning rapidly and his face bore extensive sun damage. Not unusual for a man who had started out in the Navy, where an overabundance of wind, sun, and salt was an occupational hazard. He was as tall as Robie, but seemed larger still.

He glanced at Blue Man, who nodded back deferentially.

Gelder fell into a chair opposite Robie, sat back, unbuttoned his off-the-rack suit, and slid a hand through his graying hair. He cleared his throat and said, "Have you been brought up to speed?"

"For the most part," said Robie.

He had never been in Gelder's presence before. He didn't feel intimidated, only curious. Robie never felt intimidated by anyone unless the person had gotten the drop on him with a weapon. And that almost never happened.

"Jessica Reel," said Gelder. "Shitstorm."

"I've told what I know about her. And it's not much."

Gelder picked at a bit of jagged nail on his right thumb. Robie noted that the other nails were bitten down to the quick. Not a comforting feeling since he was the number two intelligence man in the country. But Robie knew the man had a lot to worry about. The world was one catalyst away from blowing up.

Gelder had risen to lieutenant commander in the Navy before transferring over to the spy side. It had been a springboard for a fast-rising career, culminating in his current position. It was widely known that he could have had the number one slot but didn't want it. He liked to do things, but kissing Congress's ass was not one of them.

"We have to get her," said Gelder. "Alive or dead. Alive, preferably, so we can find out what the hell happened."

"I can see that," said Robie. "I'm sure you have a plan to do just that."

Blue Man looked at Gelder. Gelder glanced up at Robie.

"Well, actually, *you're* the plan, Robie," said Gelder.

Robie did not look at Blue Man, though he could feel the man's gaze now on him. "You want me to go after Reel?" he said slowly. This scenario had never occurred to him and he suddenly wondered why not.

Gelder nodded.

"I'm not a detective," said Robie. "That's not my strength."

Blue Man looked at him. "I would disagree with you on that point, Robie."

"But regardless, send a killer to find a killer," said Gelder simply.

"You have lots of them on the payroll," Robie replied.

Gelder stopped picking his nail. "You come highly recommended."

"Why? Because of what happened recently?"

"We would be derelict in our duties if we ignored that," said Gelder. "You're just coming off an assignment. I think you can be better deployed tracking down Reel."

"Do I have a choice?"

Gelder stared across at him. "Is there a problem?"

"Despite what you said, I don't think I'm the right man for the job."

In answer Gelder slipped a small square electronic tablet from his inside jacket pocket. He scrolled down some screens, reading as he did so.

"Well, let me give you some 'specifics' as to why you are the right man for the job. You graded first in your class with record marks. Two years later Jessica Reel was first in her class with a score that would have been a record but for yours."

"Yes, but—" Robie began, but Gelder put up a hand.

"In a practice scenario you were the only one to track her down and capture her."

"That was a long time ago. And it wasn't the real thing."

"And finally, you saved her life once."

"Why does that matter?" asked Robie.

"It might make her hesitate for a second, Robie. And that should be all you need." He added, "Not that I was required to provide an explanation for you to follow a *direct order*, but there you are. Consider it a gift under extraordinary circumstances."

He rose and glanced at Blue Man. "Keep me informed." He looked back at Robie. "As always, failure is not an option, Robie."

"And if I do fail I better die in the process, right?" said Robie.

Gelder looked at him as though he had merely stated the obvious.

The next moment the door opened and the number two man walked out through it. He closed the door behind him with the finality of a coffin lid shutting.

Blue Man glanced nervously at Robie, who was still staring at the door. Then Robie slowly looked over at Blue Man.

"You knew about this?" Robie asked.

Blue Man nodded.

"And what do you think about it?"

"I think you are ideally suited for it."

"Dead or alive? Was that bullshit or code or both?"

"I truly think they want her alive. She needs to be interrogated. She was one of our top operatives. We've never had one of them turn before."

"Well, you know that's not true. There seems to be a run on turncoats in the agency lately."

Blue Man looked pained by this statement, but he could hardly dispute it in light of recent events.

"So that's what you think this is? She was turned? So why kill Jacobs? Now we know she's gone bad. It's not like she can walk back into the job and start collecting valuable intel for her new employer. Doesn't make sense."

"It has to make sense in some way. Because it's happened."

Robie said, "Jacobs is dead. Reel is nowhere to be

found. Her being turned is only one possibility. There are others."

"Her voice was on that secure operations line along with Jacobs's."

"Still other possibilities."

"And now you have the chance to explore them, Robie."

"I'm assuming there is no opportunity to decline the assignment?"

Blue Man did not even bother to answer.

"The target left standing in the Middle East. It would seem that maybe he did the turning. Why not start there?'

"Tricky situation. Ferat Ahmadi is vying to fill the power vacuum in Syria. He has a lot of support on the ground. Unfortunately, he is a terrible choice as far as we are concerned. We've had a lot of that happening with the Arab Spring. Those countries are electing people who hate us to lead them."

"Okay, but I take it the Chinese and Russians would not be happy that we're picking winners and losers over there again," commented Robie.

"The assassination attempt coming out would not be in our interests, no."

"If it had gone according to plan, how was it going to be covered up?"

"Standard procedure. Blame it on opposition leaders

to Ahmadi. Not a stretch by any means. They've tried to kill him twice. They're just not very good at it. We were going to leave evidence behind that would lead back to one of them."

"Two birds with one stone?"

Blue Man nodded. "We try to be efficient. That would leave a third party standing who we can at least attempt to talk sense to."

"But that's all been shut down now."

"Yes, it has."

Robie stood. "I'll need whatever you have on Reel."

"Being assembled as we speak."

"Okay," said Robie, but for him, right now, nothing was okay.

"What did you really think of Reel when you worked with her?"

"I already told you."

"The unvarnished version."

"She was as good as me. Maybe now she's better. I don't know. But it looks like I might find out."

As he turned to leave Blue Man said, "We've had a run of bad luck lately, Robie."

"Yeah, I guess you could say that."

"I suppose that the longer you stay in service the greater the chance that someone will try and turn you," said Blue Man. He tapped his fingers on the table and looked off.

"The more years of service, the more value you might have."

Blue Man glanced over at him. "Others have been tempted. Successfully."

"A few out of many."

"Still a problem."

"Is it a problem for you?" asked Robie.

"No more than it is for you, I'm sure."

"Glad we got that straight." Robie walked out to begin his new assignment.

6

ROBIE DROVE THROUGH THE STREETS of D.C. with a USB stick in his coat pocket. On it was the career of Jessica Elyse Reel. Robie already knew some of it. By tomorrow he would know all of it, except for the parts yet to be filled in.

The rain was falling more steadily. D.C. in the rain was a curious spectacle. There were of course the monuments, the popular target of busloads of tourists, many of whom probably despised much about the federal city. But they came to gawk at the pretty structures, figuring their tax dollars had paid for them.

In the gloom the mighty Jefferson and Lincoln and Washington memorials and monument, respectively, seemed diminished to a grainy outline one would see on an aged, tattered postcard. The Capitol dome loomed large, towering over all other nearby structures. It was the place where Congress did—or increasingly did not do—its work. But even the enormity of the colossal dome seemed lessened in the rain.

Robie steered his Audi toward Dupont Circle. He had lived in an apartment near Rock Creek Park for years. Less than a month ago he had moved out. That had everything to do with one of his previous assignments. He simply couldn't stay there anymore.

Dupont was in the middle of town, full of nightlife, dozens of hip restaurants offering cuisines from around the world, esoteric retailers, highbrow booksellers, and retail shops that one could find nowhere else. It was exciting and energizing and a real asset to the city.

But Robie didn't crave the nightlife. When he ate out, he ate alone. He didn't shop in the hip shops. He didn't browse through the highbrow bookstores. When he walked the streets, which he often did, particularly later at night, he didn't seek out contact with others. He didn't welcome companionship at any level. There would have been little point to it, especially now.

He parked in the underground garage of his apartment building and took the elevator up to his floor. He inserted two keys into the twin locks—both deadbolts—on his apartment door. The alarm system beeped its warning. The beeps stopped when he disarmed it.

He took off his coat but didn't remove the USB stick. He walked to the window and stared down at the wet streets. Rain cleansed, or at least that was the theory. There were parts of this town that could never be clean, he thought. And not just the high-crime areas. He operated in the world of government power, and it was as dirty as the grimiest alley in the city.

He'd had a brush with normalcy recently. But it was just a brush. It hadn't stuck to him, and had eventually fallen away.

But it had left remnants.

He pulled out his wallet and removed the photo.

The girl in the picture was fourteen going on forty. Julie Getty. Small, skinny, straggly hair. Robie didn't care about her appearance. He admired her for her courage, her intelligence, and her spunk.

She had given him this photo of her when they had parted ways. He should never have kept it. It was too dangerous. It could lead back to her, yet Robie had still kept it. He simply didn't seem able to part with it.

Robie had never had children, and never would. If he had, Julie Getty would have been a daughter of whom he would have been proud. However, she wasn't his daughter. And she had a new life to lead. A life that he could not really be part of. That's just the way it was. It was not his choice.

He put the photo back in his wallet at the same time his cell phone buzzed.

At first he smiled when he saw who was calling, and then the smile turned to a frown. He debated whether to answer, but decided if he didn't she would just keep calling.

It was simply how she was wired.

"Hello?"

"Robie. Long time."

Nicole Vance was an FBI special agent. A super agent according to Julie Getty. Julie had also thought that Vance had a thing for Robie. In fact, she'd been sure of it.

Robie had never found that out for certain and wasn't sure he wanted to. Something in the recent past had turned him off to anything remotely resembling a relationship with a woman. It wasn't an issue of desire. It was one of trust. Without that, Robie couldn't muster the desire.

Robie was trained never to be deceived. Never to be played for a fool. Never to be left without a seat when the music stopped. And yet he had been deceived. It had been a humbling experience that he didn't care to repeat.

Vance's voice sounded the same. A little too amped up for Robie right now, but he had to admire the woman's energy.

"Yeah, it has been."

"You been traveling lately?"

He hesitated, wondering whether she had put the events in Central Park together with him.

Vance had a good idea of what Robie did professionally. As an FBI agent sworn to uphold and protect, she couldn't be privy to any more than she already knew. They operated in two distinct worlds, both necessary, both not mutually exclusive.

But both incompatible nonetheless. And if their jobs were incompatible, then so were they as individuals. Robie clearly saw that now. In fact, he had always known it.

"Not much. You?"

"Just the mean streets of D.C."

"So what's up?"

"You free for dinner?"

Robie again hesitated. He hesitated so long, in fact, that Vance finally said, "It's not that complicated, Robie. Either you are or you aren't. No skin off here if you say no."

Robie wanted to say no. But for some reason he said, "When?"

"Around eight? I've been wanting to try this new place over on Fourteenth." She told him the name. "I hear they strain their tomatoes through linen cloths to make their cocktails."

"You like cocktails that much?" he asked.

"Tonight I do."

Robie knew there had to be an ulterior reason for Vance to be calling him to go to dinner. Yes, he believed that she liked him. But she was super agent Vance for a good reason. She never turned it off.

"Okay," he said.

"Just like that?"

"Just like that."

"I'm officially surprised."

So am I, thought Robie.

"Any interesting cases you're involved with?" she asked. "It's just a rhetorical question, of course."

"How about you?"

"Oh, this and that."

"Care to elaborate?"

"Maybe I will at dinner. Or maybe I won't. Depends on the quality of those cocktails."

"See you then."

He put the phone away and watched out the window again as people scurried along the streets trying to escape a rain that seemed to have settled into the bones of the area, making things as wet and chilly and miserable as possible.

Robie slowly moved through the eleven hundred square feet of his apartment. The place was where he lived, but it seemed to be uninhabited. There was furniture, to be sure. And food in the fridge. And clothes in the closet. But other than that there were no personal effects whatsoever, principally because Robie had none to bring here.

He had traveled the world, but had never purchased a souvenir to bring back. The only thing he had to bring home on his return trips was himself, surviving to do what he did another day. He'd never purchased a postcard or snow globe after ending someone's life. He just got on a plane, or train, or sometimes drove or walked home. That was it.

He took a nap and when he woke he showered and changed into fresh clothes. He had a few hours to kill before going to meet Vance.

He opened his laptop, inserted the USB stick, and the life of Jessica Elyse Reel came to life in all its megapixel glory.

But before he could start reading his phone buzzed.

He looked at the email that had just popped into his box. It was quite to the point.

Sorry it's come to this, Will. Only one can survive, of course. Selfishly, I hope it's me. Respectfully, JR.

CHAPTER

7

Robie immediately contacted Blue Man and told him what had happened. A trace was put on the email Robie had received. The report came back thirty minutes later and it was not good.

Untraceable.

For Robie's agency to concede something was untraceable was a big deal. Whoever Reel was working with, they weren't slackers.

The other point to consider was how Reel had gotten Robie's email address. It certainly wasn't public knowledge. Blue Man was probably thinking the same thing.

Reel might have a confederate in the ranks of the agency. A leave-behind who was feeding information to the woman. That information might include that Robie had been assigned to track her down, a fact that was only hours old. Whoever the insider was, he had access to a lot.

Robie once more began reading the file on Jessica Reel contained on the USB stick. Reel had had some

impressive hits over the years. She, like Robie, operated at the highest level and had taken down people
in situations that would have challenged Robie to the
fullest.

He'd never doubted that Reel was good. But he
was a little surprised that she was *that* good.

*And she may have a spy on the inside telling her all
she needs to know to get enough of an advantage to take
me out before I get to her. Which means my own agency
is a threat.*

Robie kept reading until he came to the hit on
Doug Jacobs. Quick, clean, ingenious really. Nail
the handler while he thinks you're about to take out
someone else.

And a sniper's nest had been found in the hotel in
the Middle East. The gun muzzle had been placed
perfectly so that when Jacobs did the satellite zoom
Reel had suggested, he could see the gun barrel. But
there had been no sniper.

There was no evidence that Reel had been the
shooter who had ended Jacobs's life. But the email
Robie had just received left no doubt that she was
involved somehow.

So the woman was supposed to be in the Middle
East, but she might have been in D.C. drawing a bead
on the man talking to her through a headset. Other
things being equal, it probably was Reel who took the
shot on Jacobs. If it were Robie, he would want to

make sure the kill was done correctly. He wouldn't have wanted anyone else pulling the trigger.

Which meant he had to go somewhere right now, before he met Vance for dinner.

Robie barely glanced at the three-story building where Jacobs's life had ended. He knew what had happened there, at the end of the bullet's path. Now he needed to understand the beginning of that path.

The old town house was only a few failed support columns from collapsing. Built in the late 1800s, the five-story building had been used for many different purposes over the years. These included a private school and a men's club that had ceased to exist over fifty years ago. But no one famous had ever lived there, so it would never become a historical registry building. In the coming years it would probably be knocked down if it didn't tumble down on its own first.

Robie gazed up at the building's front. Staring back at him were aged brick, scraggly vines clinging to the walls, dead grass, and a rotted front door. He walked gingerly up the steps, avoiding the holes in the porch planks. The building had been secured, but stealthily. There were watchful eyes that had already cleared Robie to enter the premises. He used a key he had been given to open the front door and entered. The electricity had long since been turned off, so he pulled a flashlight from his pocket and walked on, clearing piles of rubble and giving a wide berth to missing floorboards.

The building was hundreds of yards from the agency outpost where Jacobs had been working. It was a long-distance shot certainly, but manageable ten times out of ten by a capable shooter.

Robie took the stairs up to the fifth floor. He had already been told that that was from where the shot had come. It was the only position in the town house that provided a clear sight line to Jacobs's office.

He heard raindrops starting to fall more heavily as he reached the fifth floor landing. He walked down the hall. He felt the chill from the outside reach him through innumerable chinks in the building's walls. He might be able to see his breath if it weren't so dark.

He shined his light ahead of him, taking care to avoid weak spots in the floor. It would have been dicey setting up your shot from here, despite the clear sight line. You had no way to know if the floor would collapse under you.

But it hadn't and Jacobs had died.

Robie slowed his walk as he approached the room. It was in a turret on the right side of the building.

He knew the place had already been gone over by agency personnel, but he also had been told that nothing had been disturbed. And the police hadn't been told about this building yet, but no doubt their investigation would get here at some point. But for now Robie had a small window of opportunity.

He opened the door and stepped inside.

There was only one spot in the room from where the shot really could have been made. The turret room had three south-facing windows. The one in the middle had the truest sight line to Jacobs.

Robie drew nearer and shined his light around. On the windowsill was a narrow disturbance in the dust pattern. That was where the rifle muzzle had rested. Another disturbance of dust on the floor represented the shooter's knee.

There was a slight discharge from the rifle on both the sill and the floor. The suppressor would have vented the propellant gas out just about there.

No shell casing had been found, so the brass had been policed, as Blue Man had pointed out. But the dust disturbances could easily have been covered up as well.

Only they weren't, which told Robie that the shooter didn't care if the sniper's nest was discovered.

He picked up a long piece of shoe molding that had broken off, knelt down, and, using the molding as an imaginary weapon, drew a bead on Jacobs's office.

Fifth floor looking down on third floor. The reverse wouldn't work, of course, because of the angle of the shot. You couldn't fire up and nail your target. You had to fire down. If Jacobs's building had been taller than five stories and he had been on a higher floor, the old town house would not have worked as a shooting nest.

But they would have just found another place that did work.

Robie assumed that bulletproof glass was being added to the windows of many agency buildings right this second.

It was clear that Reel, or whoever the shooter had been, was in possession of the layout of Jacobs's office. Back to the window, computer screen in front. No obstructions to the flight path of the killing round. Chest shot, wrecked the heart, clanged off a rib, and exited the body, hitting the computer.

Robie was guessing about the collision with the rib. If the bullet had passed right through the body it would have hit the top of the desk most likely, not the computer. The angle was too extreme. Ribs were hard enough to change a bullet's flight path. He hadn't seen Jacobs's autopsy results, but he wouldn't be surprised to see that sort of internal damage.

So the shot was fired. Jacobs was dead. If Reel were the shooter she would have heard through her headset the window breaking, the impact of her round with Jacobs, and Jacobs dying. Confirmation of a kill. It was always nice to have when you were firing blind through a window.

And she would have had possession of the layout

of Jacobs's office. Reel wouldn't have actually been shooting "blind."

Inside info again.

Like my email address.

She might be following me right now. Or she might be here waiting for me, figuring I would come to the town house at some point.

Robie scanned the street below, but saw nothing other than people scurrying along to get out of the rain. But people like Reel wouldn't show themselves so carelessly. Robie looked down at his shoe. Something white was sticking out from under the sole. He picked the item off. It was soft, falling apart. He held it to his nose. It had a scent.

Then Robie forgot about that when he heard a disturbance outside the house. Raised voices. Sounds of footsteps on the front porch.

He raced out of the room and down the hall. He reached a window where he could see the front door. There were people clustered out there. An argument was going on. Robie could see people he assumed were from his agency.

And he could see other people who were not.

They were easy to tell apart. The ones *not* from his agency were wearing blue windbreakers with gold lettering on the back.

There were only three gold letters. But they were three letters Robie did not want to see.

FBI.

And when he saw who was heading up the FBI agents he turned and moved as quickly as he could toward the rear of the house.

He was meeting Nicole Vance for dinner at eight.

He did not want to meet her inside this town house in the next two minutes.

CHAPTER

8

ROBIE KNEW HOW TO EXIT QUIETLY. He did so now, coming around the corner and watching from behind some bushes as Vance continued to argue with the other men.

He pulled his phone and sent a text to Blue Man.

A minute later Robie saw one of the men arguing with Vance touch his ear.

Message communicated.

He stopped arguing and Robie heard him say, "The place is yours to search, Agent Vance. We'll leave you to it."

Vance halted in midsentence and stared at the man.

Robie ducked down as she swiveled her head, looking in all directions. He could tell she knew exactly what had just happened. The dogs had been called off. The place was open to her now. That order had come from high up. Some condition had changed in the last few seconds.

Robie was on the move, because he knew that Vance's next tactic might be to send her men rushing in all directions to look for the source of the change on the ground. He didn't want her to discover that the source was him. It would make dinner later even more uncomfortable than it was already shaping up to be.

Robie reached his car and drove off. He punched in a number and Blue Man answered almost immediately.

"Thanks for the assist back there," said Blue Man.

Robie snapped, "I'm meeting with Vance tonight. Agreed to it before I knew she was involved in this. Would have been nice to know before. Getting blindsided like that out of the gate does not inspire confidence."

"We didn't know she had been assigned to it. We don't run the FBI. I suppose that her success last time has lifted her up in the eyes of the Bureau."

"Exactly how much does the Bureau know?" Robie asked. "Your guys being outside that building tells her that it's not a routine murder."

"We couldn't completely cover up what happened to Doug Jacobs. FBI involvement was inevitable. But it's up to us to manage it properly."

"So, again, how much do they know?" Robie asked.

"They know that Doug Jacobs was a federal employee. They do not and will not know that he works for our agency. He is officially a member of DTRA."

"Defense Threat Reduction?"

"More specifically in their Information Analysis Center. The building Jacobs was in is leased by the Center. It provides good cover for us. Not that we ever expected Jacobs to be shot dead in his office."

"And DTRA will play the game?" Robie queried.

"They think big picture, just like we do. They're part of DoD, after all."

"Do they know what Jacobs was doing in that office when he was shot?"

"There would be no possible good coming from my answering that question. Suffice it to say that ignorance is bliss."

"Meaning DTRA won't have to technically lie to the FBI when they come calling?"

"They have already come calling."

"And what is the official line?" Robie said.

"Jacobs was shot while performing his mundane job, possibly by a rogue gunman targeting the federal government."

"And you think the FBI will buy that?"

"I don't know if they will or not," replied Blue Man. "That's not my concern."

"But you can't let the FBI find out that Jacobs was actually orchestrating the assassination of a foreign leader."

"He wasn't a foreign leader *yet*. We do our best to be proactive. Eliminating those already in power is a tricky thing. Sometimes necessary but to be avoided if possible since it's technically illegal."

"Vance is tenacious as hell."

"Yes, she is," agreed Blue Man.

"She might get to the truth."

"That is not an option, Robie."

"Like you said, you don't run the FBI."

"What will you talk about with her tonight?" asked Blue Man.

"I don't know. And if I cancel she might get suspicious."

"Do you think she suspects your involvement in any of this?"

"She's smart. And she sort of knows what I do for a living."

"That was a mistake, Robie, it really was, letting her know that."

"I really didn't have a choice, did I?"

"What if she starts asking questions?"

"Then I'll answer them. In my own way."

Blue Man seemed about to continue this line of questioning, but then said, "What's your next step on Reel?"

"Any way to trace her movements leading up to the shooting? I mean, do we know for certain if she was in the country and pulled the trigger? Her voice over the headset doesn't prove she was actually the shooter."

"Reel went silent before the shot, so we didn't pick up any sounds on her end, just on Jacobs's. But her voice means she was involved somehow."

Robie said, "The sniper nest was set up overseas. Any clues there?"

"Nothing. We confirmed that she was seen there, but two days before. Plenty of time to get back here and shoot Jacobs."

"What's the latest on Ahmadi?"

"Business as usual. We removed all traces of the sniper nest, of course."

"Planning another hit on him?" asked Robie.

"Well, if he was aware of the first try and foiled it, turning it back on us, I would imagine he would be ultra-cautious now. We might not see his face again until he's Syria's new leader."

"I don't like it that Reel had my email address."

"I don't like it either," agreed Blue Man.

"We have a mole. A leave-behind."

"Possibly. Or she might have gotten that information beforehand."

"How would she know I'd be the one going after her?"

"A calculated assumption?" suggested Blue Man.

"She might be tailing me right now."

"Don't get paranoid on me, Robie."

"You missed that window by a few years. My paranoia knows no bounds now."

"Where are you off to now?"

"To get ready for my dinner."

Robie clicked off and accelerated. He checked his rearview for Vance, Reel, and assorted bogeymen.

I'm not growing paranoid. I am paranoid. And who could blame me?

He punched the gas harder.

Sending a killer to catch a killer actually made sense.

We talk a different language and we see the world through a separate prism that no one else could possibly understand.

But it worked both ways. Reel would understand him as much as he would understand her.

So Reel dead.

Or me.

It really was that simple.

And also that complicated.

CHAPTER

9

JESSICA REEL SAT ON HER bed in her hotel room. Her sweat-drenched exercise clothes lay on the floor. She was naked and looking down at her toes. The rain was hitting with increased velocity outside.

Like bullets. But unlike bullets rain leaves you alive.

She rubbed her hand over her flat belly. Her firm core had come from agonizing exercise and careful diet. It had nothing to do with appearance. The core was power central. And fat slowed you down. In her world that was poison. She was also proficient in every martial art worth anything in close-quarter combat.

She had had to use her fitness and fighting skills to survive many times. She didn't always kill with a gun from long range. Sometimes her targets were right in front of her, trying to murder her as fiercely as she them. And they were almost always men. That gave them a genetic advantage in size and strength.

Still, up to this point, she had always been the winner. But that was only until the next time. In her field, you only lost once. After that, no one bothered to keep score anymore.

You just got eulogized. Maybe.

She debated whether to send Robie another message. But she decided that would be overplaying her hand. She didn't underestimate anyone. And though her cell was presumably untraceable, the agency might buck those odds, track her back through communication channels and find her.

And what more was there left to say anyway? Robie had his assignment. He would do his best to carry it out.

Reel would do her best to make sure he failed. One or both of them might end up dead. That was the nature of the beast. There was nothing fair about it. It was just the way it was.

Reel slipped on a robe, crossed the room, and pulled her phone from her jacket hanging on the door. She began hitting keys. It truly was amazing what these devices could do. Trace your every step. Tell you exactly how to get to somewhere else. With a flick of a key Reel could get the most esoteric information in a matter of seconds.

But there was a flip side to all this freedom.

People had trillions of eyes now with which to watch you. And it wasn't just the government. Or big business. It could be the man on the street with the latest gadgetry and a modicum of technical savvy.

That made Reel's job harder. But it was hard to begin with.

She digested the information that had come up on the screen. She put it away, slipped into the bathroom, and took off her robe. The hot water in the shower felt good. She was tired, her muscles weary from a workout that had pushed her harder than ever.

There had been a couple of young guys in the gym doing one-armed curls while preening in the mirror. Another had put in twenty moderately active minutes on the elliptical and obviously thought that qualified him as a stud. She had gone into an adjoining room and begun her exercise. She had sensed two of them watching her after a few minutes. It wasn't the way she was dressed. She didn't wear tight-fitting spandex. Loose, baggy clothing that covered her completely was her thing. She was there to sweat, not find a husband or a one-night stand.

She sensed they weren't a threat. They were simply astonished at what she was doing with her body. Thirty minutes later, when she was barely a third of the way through her routine, they turned and left, shaking their heads. She knew what they were thinking:

I couldn't last five minutes at that pace.

And they would be right.

She turned off the shower, dried off, and put her robe back on, her hair wrapped in a towel. She scanned the room service menu and selected a salad and indulged herself with a glass of a California zinfandel.

When the young, good-looking man brought the tray in she caught his reflection in the mirror. He was checking her out.

Reel had slept with men on several different continents. All had been in connection with a job. A means to an end. If she could use sex to get her where she needed to go, so be it. She assumed that was one reason the agency had employed her. And they had encouraged her to use that weapon in her arsenal, with the caveat that she was never to become personally involved with any of them. Which translated into never feeling anything for them at all. She was a machine and they were simply convenient for the mission.

In that regard men were decidedly the weaker sex. Women could get them to do anything with a promise of action under the sheets, up against a wall, or on their knees, as the case might be.

She signed the bill and gave him a generous tip.

His eyes asked her for more.

She denied the request simply by turning away.

Once the door closed behind her she took off her robe, freed her hair, and put on a pair of shorts and a T-shirt. She pushed a table against the door, sat down to her meal, and slowly sipped her wine as the rain pounded away outside.

She would soon have somewhere to go. It was

always important to keep going. Stationary objects tended to get run over.

At some point soon Will Robie would come after her in earnest. That would then occupy much of Reel's time and energy. Until that point, she would have a window of opportunity.

She intended to make the most of it.

Doug Jacobs was one level.

Now Reel was moving to the next level.

It wouldn't be easy. By now they were forewarned.

Doug Jacobs had a wife and two young children. Reel knew what they looked like. She knew their names. She knew where they lived. She knew they were now suffering tremendous grief. Because of what Jacobs did, his family couldn't be told the exact circumstances of his death.

It was just company policy. And that policy never varied.

Secrets to the last.

There would be a funeral and Jacobs would be laid to rest. And that would be the only normal thing about his passing. His young widow would go on with her life, probably remarry. Perhaps she would have more children. Reel would suggest that she marry a plumber or a salesman. Her life would be far less complicated.

Jacobs's children might or might not remember their father.

For Reel, that wasn't such a bad thing.

In her mind Douglas Jacobs wasn't all that memorable.

Reel finished her meal and slipped under the covers.

She remembered as a child listening to the rain beating outside as she lay in bed. No one had come to check on her. It wasn't that sort of a home. People who came to you in the night where Reel had grown up usually had ulterior motives, motives that were not benign in the least. This had made her suspicious and hardened from an early age. This had made her want to be alone, only summoning companionship on her terms.

When people came for you in the night the only response was to hurt them before they could hurt you.

In her mind's eye she conjured the image of her mother—a frail abused woman who on her last day on earth looked forty years older than she actually was. Her death had been violent, wrenching. She had not gone quietly, but she had, eventually, gone. And Jessica Reel, then only seven years old, had watched it all happen. It had been traumatic in ways that even now Reel didn't fully understand or appreciate. The experience had come to define her, and guaranteed that many normal things people did in life would never be part of hers.

What happened to you as a child, particularly something bad, changed you, absolutely and completely.

It was like part of your brain became closed off and refused to mature any further. As an adult you were powerless to fight against it. It was simply who you were until the day you died. There was no "therapy" that could cure it. That wall was built and nothing could tear it down.

Maybe that's why I do what I do. Engineered from childhood.

Her gun was under her pillow, one hand clenching it, and the table still against the door.

She would sleep well tonight.

It might be the last time she ever did.

CHAPTER

10

ROBIE SAT AT A TABLE in the restaurant that allowed him to see out onto the street. He alternated between looking out at the street and at the TV that was mounted on a wall behind the bar. On the TV was a news report about an upcoming Arab summit that was scheduled to occur in Canada. Apparently it was felt that the neutral setting, far away from terrorist acts and wars, might shorten the odds of a breakthrough occurring. Sponsored by the UN, it hoped, the news anchor said, to usher in a new age of cooperation among countries that had for too long been at war with one another.

"Good luck on that," Robie said to himself.

The next instant the channel was changed and Robie was watching an ad for Cialis with an older man and woman in bathtubs that were set outside. It was apparently a sexual metaphor he had never figured out. Then the bathtubs vanished and another news anchor was talking about an upcoming trip by the president to Ireland where he was hosting a symposium on the threat of international terrorism and ways to stop it.

"Good luck on that too," muttered Robie.

He glanced away from the TV in time to see Nicole Vance walking down the street at a hurried pace. He glanced at his watch. She was about fifteen minutes late. She was applying a touch of makeup and lipstick and checking the results in a small mirror she carried. He noted that she had changed from her working clothes into a dress, stockings, and heels. Maybe the reason for the lateness.

She fortunately did not see him watching her as she hurried past him to the door of the restaurant, slipping her makeup kit back into her small purse. Robie doubted Vance would have wanted to be spotted "checking her face" before their dinner.

"You look thinner."

Robie glanced up as Nicole Vance sat across from him. "And you look harried," he replied.

"Sorry about being late. Got stuck on a case."

The waiter came and took their drink orders. When he departed Robie broke a breadstick in half, ate part of it, and said, "Something new?"

"Something interesting at least."

"I thought all of your cases were interesting."

"The bad guys are usually pretty obvious. It just

becomes a matter of evidence collection. And that tends to get very boring very fast."

"Care to talk about it?"

"You know better than that, Robie. Ongoing investigation. Unless you got transferred to the FBI and nobody told me." She stared across at him. "So, have you been out of town?"

"You already asked me that."

"You didn't answer me."

"Yeah, I did. I said, not much."

"But some?"

"And you're concerned about my travel schedule why?" he asked.

"Some interesting things going on in the world. Right in our backyard, even."

"They always are. So what?"

"I'm not entirely unfamiliar with what you do for a living."

Robie looked right and then left and then back at Vance.

Before he could speak she said, "I'm sorry. I shouldn't have gone there."

"No, you shouldn't."

"We got off on the wrong foot."

Robie said nothing.

"Okay, *I* got off on the wrong foot. How have you been?"

"Busy, just like you." He paused. "I thought about

calling you a few times. Just never got around to doing it. I'm sorry. Things got a little crazy for me."

"I have to say I'm surprised you even thought about calling me."

"Why? We'd agreed to keep in touch."

"I appreciate that, Robie. But I don't think your job allows for a lot of downtime."

"Neither does yours."

"It's a different sort of thing. You know that."

Their drinks came and Vance gratefully took a sip of hers. "Omigod that is good."

"Can you taste the linen?"

She set her glass down and smiled. "Every single thread."

"Sense of humor will get you through a lot."

"That's what people keep telling me. But I keep finding fewer things to laugh at."

"Which brings us back to tonight. Why the call for drinks and dinner? Really?"

"Two friends getting together."

"A busy FBI agent working long hours? Don't think so."

"I have no agenda, Robie."

Robie just looked at her.

"Okay, I sort of have an agenda."

"Then let me sort of hear it."

She sat forward and lowered her voice. "Douglas Jacobs?"

Robie's face was impassive. "Who is he?"

"Who *was* he. Jacobs is dead. Shot at his office."

"Sorry to hear that. What happened?"

"Not sure. He apparently worked for DTRA. Do you know them?"

"I know of them."

"I say 'apparently' because I'm pretty sure everyone I've spoken to is lying his ass off."

"Why?"

"You know why, Robie. This is spook territory. I'm sure of it. And they always lie."

"Not always," he reminded her.

"Okay, but most of the time they do." She took another sip of her cocktail and eyed him keenly. "You're sure you didn't know Jacobs?"

"I never met the man," Robie said truthfully.

Vance sat back and looked at him skeptically.

"Do you know everyone at the FBI?" he said.

"Of course not. It's too big."

"Okay, proves my point."

"My gut tells me that Jacobs was involved in something really important. And what happened to him has scared the crap out of certain highly placed people."

Yes he was and yes it has, thought Robie.

"Even if I knew anything, Vance, I couldn't tell you. You know that."

"A girl can always hope," she said sweetly, draining her glass and lifting her hand to order another.

They ate their meal mostly in silence. When they were done Vance said, "I never was fully briefed on what happened after Morocco."

"I'm sure you weren't."

"Did it all turn out okay for you?"

"Sure. Everything's fine."

"He lied," added Vance. "The thing at the White House?"

"What about it?"

"You were in the middle of it."

"Not officially, no."

"But in all important respects, yes."

"It's ancient history. I'm not much into history. I try to be more of a forward thinker. "

"Your compartmentalization skills are amazing, Robie."

He shrugged. "Necessary part of the job. Hindsight might be twenty-twenty. You learn from mistakes, and you move on. But every situation is different. One size does not fit all."

"A lot like working cases. So how much longer are you going to be doing what you're doing?"

"How long are you going to be doing what you're doing?"

"Probably till I drop."

"You really think so?"

"I don't know, Robie. You said you're a forward thinker. I'm more of a live-in-the-present kind of person. So when are you going to call it quits?"

"I probably won't be the one making that decision."

She sat back, took in the meaning of his words, nodded. "Then maybe you should try to make sure you're the one deciding."

"Doesn't go with the territory, Vance."

They said nothing for about a minute. Each played with the drink in front of them.

Finally Vance asked, "Have you seen Julie?"

"No," he replied.

"Didn't you promise her you'd keep in touch?"

"I promised you too and look what happened."

"But she's just a kid," countered Vance.

"That's right. She has a long life ahead of her."

"But a promise is a promise."

"No, not really," answered Robie. "She doesn't need me anywhere near her. She's got a decent shot at a normal life. I'm not going to screw that up for her."

"Noble of you."

"Whatever you want to label it."

"You're a really hard person to relate to."

Robie again said nothing.

"I guess as long as you do what you do this is how it'll be."

"It is what it is."

"Do you wish it could be different?"

Robie started to answer this seemingly simple question and then realized it was not nearly as simple as it appeared to be. "I stopped wishing a long time ago, Vance."

"Why keep doing it, then? I mean, I have a crazy-ass life, though nothing like yours. But at least I have the satisfaction of putting slime away."

"And you think I don't?"

"I don't know. Do you?"

Robie put some cash down on the table and rose. "Thanks for the call. It was nice catching up. And good luck on your case."

"Do you really mean that?"

"Probably more than you know, actually."

CHAPTER

11

JESSICA REEL HAD LEFT New York and flown to D.C. She had done this because what she had to do next had to be done here.

There were three ways to approach the mission. For a mission was what Jessica Reel was on.

You could start from the bottom and move to the top.

Or start at the top and move to the bottom.

Or you could mix it up, be unpredictable, go in no particular order.

The first option might be more symbolically pure.

The third approach greatly improved Reel's odds of success. And her ability to survive.

She opted for success and survival over symbolism.

This area of D.C. was full of office buildings, all empty at this late hour. Many high-level government executives worked here, along with their even more affluent private-sector counterparts.

That didn't matter much to Reel. Rich, poor, or in

between, she just went to where she needed to go. She had killed whoever they had tasked her to eliminate. She had been a machine, executing orders with a surgical efficiency.

She placed an earwig in her left ear and ran the cord to the power pack attached to her belt. She smoothed down her hair and unbuttoned her jacket. The pistol sat ready in her shoulder holster.

She looked at her watch, did the math in her head, and knew she had about thirty minutes to think about what she was going to do.

The night was clear, if cool, the rain having finally passed. That was expected this time of year. The street was empty of traffic, also expected at this hour of the night.

She walked to a corner and took up position next to a tree with a bench below. She adjusted the earwig and looked at her watch again.

She was a prisoner not only to time but also to *precise* time, measured in seconds. A sliver off here or there and she was dead.

Through her earwig she learned that the man was on the move. A bit ahead of schedule, he would be here in ten minutes. Knowing her agency's communication frequencies was a real advantage.

She pulled the device from her pocket. It had a black matte finish, measured four by six inches, two buttons on top, and was probably—aside from her gun—the most important thing she carried. Without this, her plan could not work barring a major piece of luck.

And Reel could not count on being that lucky.

I've already used up all of my luck anyway.

She looked up as the car came down the street.

A Lincoln Town Car.

Black.

Do they make them in any other color?

She needed confirmation. After all, in this city black Town Cars were nearly as plentiful as fish in the ocean. She raised the night optics to her eyes and looked through the windshield. All the other windows were tinted. She saw what she needed to see. She lowered the optics and put them in her pocket. She took a penlight from her pocket and flashed it one time. A beam of light answered her. She put the light away and fingered the black box. She looked up and then across the street.

What was about to happen next had cost her a hundred bucks. She hoped it was money well spent.

She pushed the right-side button on the black box.

The traffic light immediately turned from green to yellow to red. She put the box away.

The Lincoln pulled to a stop at the intersection.

The figure darted out from the shadows and approached the Lincoln. He held a bucket in one hand, something else in the other. Water splashed on the windshield.

"Hey!" yelled the driver, lowering his window.

The kid was black, about fourteen. He used a squeegee to get the soapy water off the glass.

The driver yelled, "Get the hell out of here!"

The light stayed red.

Reel had her gun out now, its barrel resting on a low branch of the tree she was standing beside. On the gun's Picatinny rail was a scope. The pistol's barrel had been lengthened and specially engineered for a longer-range shot than most handguns could accomplish.

The kid ran around to the other side and used the squeegee to whisk off the water from that side.

The passenger-side window slid down.

That was the key for Reel, the passenger window coming down, because the man in the back was riding behind the driver. Angle of shot was the whole ballgame.

She aimed, exhaled a long breath, and her finger moved to the trigger.

Point of no return.

The black kid ran back to the driver's side and held out his hand. "Super clean. Five bucks."

"I said get out of here," shouted the driver.

"My momma needs an operation."

"If you're not gone in two seconds—"

The man never finished because Reel fired.

The round zipped in front of the man in the passenger

seat, cut a diagonal between him and the driver, and slammed into the forehead of the man in the back.

Reel put the weapon in her pocket and hit the other button on the black box.

The light turned green.

The Lincoln did not go.

The driver and the passenger started shouting. They jumped out of the car.

The squeegee kid was long gone. He had started to run as soon as the gun fired.

The men were covered in blood and brains.

Reel slipped away into the night. She was already disassembling, with one hand, the pistol where it was concealed in her pocket.

In the car Jim Gelder slumped forward, held in his seat only by his seat belt. A chunk of his brain lay against the back window.

The agency would have to find a new number two man.

As the twin security guards raced around looking for the shooter, Reel walked down into a nearby Metro entrance and boarded a train. Within a few minutes she was miles away.

She forgot about Jim Gelder and moved to the next target on her list.

CHAPTER

12

In Robie's world there wasn't much difference between day and night. He didn't work nine-to-five, and so seven p.m. was as good a time as any to start his next task.

The Eastern Shore of Virginia was not an easy place to get to by car, bus, or plane. And no train went there.

Robie opted to drive. He liked the control.

He drove south until he got to the Norfolk, Virginia, area. From there he headed north across the Chesapeake Bay Bridge-Tunnel that connected the Eastern Shore to the rest of the commonwealth. The bridge-tunnel's low trestle bridges dipped down into mile-long tunnels running inside man-made islands and then back onto high-level bridges soaring over a couple of navigation channels. Sometime after eleven, Robie finally left the bridge-tunnel behind and drove onto firm land.

Virginia's share of the Eastern Shore was comprised of two rural counties, Accomack and Northampton.

They were as flat as a table and made up the "-va" in the Delmarva Peninsula. The two counties had a combined population of about forty-five thousand hardy souls, whereas the geographically smaller Fairfax County, Virginia, alone had over a million. It was nearly all farmland: cotton, soybeans, and chickens on a large scale.

The Eastern Shore also was home to a NASA installation, Wallops Flight Facility, and a place for wild ponies to roam, Chincoteague Island.

Robie was looking for something wild tonight, a rogue assassin who was working for someone else.

Or maybe herself.

Robie drove for another ten miles until rural became seemingly uninhabited. In the distance, very near the coastline, he saw a black speck that was darker than the night around him. He turned down a dirt road, drove on, and then stopped in front of the speck, which up close was revealed to be a cottage with shingle siding turned gray by the sun and the salty air. Behind it was the Atlantic, pounding the shore, sending up sprays of water as it collided with large boulders that formed a crude bulwark.

This was oceanfront all right, but Robie did not think it would be a tourist destination anytime soon. He could understand why Jessica Reel would want to live here. The isolation was complete. To her, companionship must have seemed highly overrated.

He sat in the car and took it all in, side to side and up and down.

Up revealed a storm coming. Down was loamy soil, good for growing things, not so good for building homes. No basements here, he concluded. Robie imagined that at some point the ocean might reclaim this spit of land.

Side to side revealed only a small outbuilding. There was no garden, no lawn really.

Reel must live simply. Robie had no idea where she would even go to get her provisions. Or a plumber. Or an electrician. Maybe she didn't need any of those things.

He didn't even know how often she was here. He certainly didn't expect her to be here now. But expectations were not the same things as facts.

He climbed from his car. His gun was already out. He moved away from every sight line the door or windows in the cottage would provide. There were no trees around for someone to line up a shot. It was flat land, no place to set up a clandestine nest and wait until he walked into the crosshairs.

All that should have made Robie feel good.

It didn't. Because there was also no cover for him.

And because it meant he was missing something.

A place like this, you had to have some plan. A defensive bulwark even if it didn't look like one. If this had been his place he would have. And he didn't think he and Reel were all that different when it came to survival measures.

He crouched down and looked around. The cottage was dark. It was probably empty. But that was not the same as being safe to enter.

Jessica Reel did not have to be at home in order to kill an intruder.

He circled the cottage twice, moving closer with each sweep. There was a pond on the ocean side thirty yards away on a ruler-straight line off the back door. As he shined his light on it he could see that its surface was clear, although the ground around was slicked with a slimy coating of algae.

Other than that, there was not a single element to capture his interest.

Except for the cottage.

Robie squatted in the middle of a field and mulled over the situation.

He finally arrived at a plan of attack and went back to his car to get what he needed. He collected these items in a long brown leather pouch that he slung over his shoulder. He crept within a hundred feet of the front door of the cottage and stopped.

He took out a short-barreled rifle and slipped in a round. He took aim and fired at the front door. The round passed through the wood and entered the cottage.

Nothing else happened.

He slipped a second round in and aimed at the front-porch floorboards. He fired. Wood shot into the air.

Nothing else happened.

He loaded a third round, took aim, and shot the front-door lock off. The door swung open.

But that was all.

He put the rifle away in his bag and put it back in the car. But he slipped another device from the bag into his jacket pocket.

He took out his pistol and moved forward but keeping low. When he reached the cottage he took the device out of his pocket and aimed it at the building. He looked at the readout screen on the device.

No thermal images appeared.

Unless Reel had managed to freeze herself, she was not in the cottage, nor was anyone else.

But that still didn't mean it was safe.

Robie couldn't scan the entire place for bombs like at the airport. There were no explosives-sniffing dogs handy. At some point he would have to risk it. And that point was upon him. He put the thermal imager away and pulled from his pocket a short metal object and turned it on.

He opened the door and entered, placing his feet carefully and using the electronic device to reveal any invisible-to-the-naked-eye trip wires. He also scrutinized each section of the floor before stepping on it to see if the wood looked new. Pressure plates under floorboards could not be detected by his device.

He moved through each room, finding nothing. It didn't take long because the place was not very large. What struck him was it looked just like his apartment—not in size and design, but in what was in it.

Or rather what wasn't in it. No personal effects. No photos. No souvenirs, no knickknacks. Nothing that showed Reel belonged to anyone or to anywhere.

Just like me.

He moved into the kitchen at the same instant his phone buzzed.

He looked down at the screen.

The text on the screen was in all caps:

GELDER SHOT DOWN IN CAR IN D.C. REEL SUSPECTED.

Robie put the phone away and considered this.

Alarming news under any circumstances, but he had been trained not to overreact to anything. His primary thought was to get out of here. He had risked much and gotten little.

He looked to his right and saw a door. It looked like a pantry or storage closet. He wondered why he hadn't noticed it before, and then saw that it was painted the same color as the wall of the kitchen.

It was imperfectly closed, leaving an inch gap. He nudged it open with his foot while his pistol was trained directly on it.

The pantry was empty.

The trip had been a waste of time.

And while he'd been down here, Reel had likely killed the number two man in the agency. She was scoring touchdowns and he didn't even have a first down yet.

He shined his light inside the space for a better look, although it was obviously empty. That's when he saw the word written on the rear wall:

SORRY.

Robie kicked open the back door, figuring this was the easiest way out and would allow him to exit without retracing his path through the cottage.

Seemed like a good idea. Safer.

But then he heard the click and the whoosh, and the good safe idea instantly became a nightmare.

CHAPTER

13

THE DARK, calm night over the Eastern Shore was disrupted by a flame ball.

The little cottage disintegrated in the fire, the dry wood providing a perfect fuel for the inferno. Robie leapt from the back porch, rolled, and came up running.

In disbelief he watched as a wall of flames rose on either side of him, forming a straight corridor that he had to run down.

This was all by design, of course. The fuel for the fire had to have been carefully piped under the dirt, and the trigger for it must have been tied to the same one that had erupted in the cottage.

Robie sprinted ahead.

He had no choice.

He was heading right toward the small pond that he had seen before. The walls of fire ended there.

An instant later the remains of the cottage exploded. He ducked and rolled again from the concussive force, almost pitching into the right side of the wall of fire.

He rose and redoubled his efforts, thinking that he would reach the water.

Water was a great antidote to fire.

But as he neared the edge of the pond, something struck him.

No scum. No algae on the surface although the ground around was full of it.

What could kill green scum?

And why was he being forced to run right toward the one thing that could possibly save him?

Robie tossed his gun over the top of the wall of flames, pulled off his jacket, covered his head and hands with it, and threw himself through the wall of flames on the left side. He could feel the fire eating at him like acid.

He cleared the flames, and kept rolling, over and over, to beat out any fire that might have attached itself to him. He stopped and looked up in time to see the flames reach the pond.

The resulting explosion threw Robie through the air, and he landed on his back, thankfully in about an inch of water that softened the impact.

He rose on shaky legs, his shirt shredded, his jacket gone. He had no idea where his gun had landed. Thankfully, he still had his pants and shoes.

He looked in his pocket and snagged his car keys. Immediately he dropped them, because the plastic top was searing to the touch.

He gingerly picked the keys up and stood there mutely watching the pond burn.

No algae—although it was growing everywhere else—because of the fuel or accelerant that had been placed in the pond. He wondered why he hadn't smelled it when he'd made his recon around the small body of water. But then there were many ways to mask such odors. And the smell of the nearby ocean was pungent.

He looked back at where Reel's cottage had once stood.

Sorry.

Are you sorry, Jessica? Somehow Robie didn't think so.

The lady was definitely playing for keeps. Robie would have expected nothing less.

He found his jacket and his gun. The gun was okay. It had missed a puddle of water and landed on a pebble path. His jacket was burned up. He felt the lump of metal and plastic inside.

His phone. He doubted the manufacturer's warranty would cover this sort of mishap.

His wallet was luckily in his pants and not damaged.

He limped back to the car. His right arm and left leg felt so hot they seemed frozen. He got into the car and closed the door, locking it, though he was probably the only human being for miles. He started the car and turned on the interior light. He checked his face in the rearview mirror.

No damage there.

His right arm had not been so lucky. Bad burn there.

He slipped his burned trousers down and examined his left leg: red and slightly blistered near his upper thigh. Some of the pants fabric was embedded in the burn.

He kept a first aid kit in the car. He pulled it out, cleaned the burns on his thigh and arm as best he could, applied salve to the damaged areas, covered them with gauze, and then threw the first aid kit on the floorboard.

He turned the car around and headed back the way he had come. He had no way to contact Blue Man or anyone else. He couldn't stop to get medical care. Too many explanations and reports filed.

As isolated as the Eastern Shore was, flame balls rising twenty feet in the air would attract notice. He passed a police car, rack lights blazing and siren blasting, on his way back. They wouldn't find much left, he knew.

He made it back to D.C. in the wee hours of the morning, reached his apartment, retrieved a spare phone, and called Blue Man. In succinct sentences he told him what had happened.

"You're lucky, Robie."

"I feel lucky," he replied. "Part good, part bad. Fill me in on Gelder."

Blue Man took a few minutes to do so.

Robie said, "So that's all. Just where and how? No eyes on Reel anywhere?"

"Come in and we'll see to your injuries."

"No theories on why she would target the number two?" Robie persisted.

"That's all they would be right now, just theories."

There was something in Blue Man's voice that began to concern Robie. "Something going on between the lines here?" Robie asked.

Blue Man didn't answer.

"I'll be in in a few hours. Want to check some things out."

"Let me give you another location to go to."

"Why is that?" asked Robie.

Blue Man gave him the address without elaboration.

Robie put down the phone and walked over to the window.

Reel had been in town last night to gun down Gelder. That was officially speculation, but something in Robie's gut told him it was true.

If so, she could still be out there. Why she would hang around was not easy to answer. Typically, whenever Robie had killed he had left wherever he was immediately, and for obvious reasons.

But this wasn't typical, was it?

Not for me and not for her.

Robie took off the gauze around his burns, showered, put on fresh dressings and fresh clothes.

Blue Man had told him where the shooting had taken place. The area would be full of cops. Robie couldn't do much more than observe. But sometimes observations led to breakthroughs. He would have to hope that would be the case here.

As he walked down to his car he knew one thing. He would not be able to survive many more nights like the last one. Reel seemed to be one step ahead at all times. That was often the case with the person being chased and the one doing the chasing.

Reel knew why she was doing what she was doing.

Robie was still playing catch-up.

Maybe that's all I'll be doing on this one.

So right now the odds were definitely stacked in Jessica Reel's favor. Robie couldn't see any development that would easily or quickly change that state of affairs.

He drove off right as the sun was starting to rise.

Just another beautiful day in the capital city.

He was glad he was still alive to see it.

CHAPTER

14

HE HAD LIVED. Reel had watched it on her laptop.

Inside the outbuilding near her cottage was a camera on a tripod pointed at the cottage and uplinked to a satellite. Through it she had seen Robie drive up, get out, and recon the property.

He hadn't looked inside the outbuilding, which had been a mistake on his part.

It was gratifying to her that Robie made mistakes.

But then he had done the remarkable. He had figured out that the pond was a trap and risked throwing himself through a wall of fire to survive.

She clicked some computer keys and watched it again, in slow motion.

Robie burst from the house and then her view of him was gone, blocked by the wall of flames. It was designed to lead him right to the pond, which looked like a safe harbor but would be his grave.

Yet under the most intense pressure he had kept

his wits, deduced the safe harbor was a trap, and executed on the fly a maneuver designed to keep him alive.

And he had succeeded.

She froze the screen on the image of Robie walking back to his car.

Could I have just done what he did? Am I as good as he is?

She stared at the screen, looking into Robie's face, trying to read the man's mind, to delve into what he was thinking at just that moment in time.

But the face was inscrutable.

A good poker player.

No, a great poker player.

She closed the laptop and sat back on her bed. She pulled a Glock nine-millimeter from her belt holster and started disassembling it. She did it without looking, as she had been trained to do.

Then she started to put it back together, again without looking.

This exercise always served to calm her, make her think more clearly. And she needed to think as clearly as possible right now.

She was fighting an engagement on two flanks.

She had her list with more names on it. These people were now forewarned. Their protective shells were being hardened as she sat there.

And she had Will Robie, who was now more than a little angry at almost being killed by her. He would be coming hard on her rear flank.

That meant she had to have eyes in the back of her head, see both combat fronts at the same time. Difficult, but not impossible to do.

Robie had gone to her cottage on the Eastern Shore to learn more about her. He had found nothing except an attempt on his life.

But now Reel needed more information on Robie. She had thought he would be the one to come after her. The episode at the cottage had confirmed this.

She rose, made a phone call, and then slipped into jeans, sweater, boots, and a hoodie. Her gun rested in her belt holster. A Ka-Bar knife rode in a leather sleeve wrapped around her left arm and hidden under the hoodie. She could pull it free in a second if need be.

Her main problem was that despite her changed appearance there were eyes everywhere. Much of the United States and the civilized world was now one big camera. Her former employer would be using sophisticated search and facial recognition software, going through databases housing billions of images, in a 24/7 attempt to track her down.

With that many resources leveled against her, Reel had no margin of error. She had built a nice bulwark of defenses, but nothing was perfect. Nearly every defensive line in every war had been pierced at some point. And she was under no delusions that she would be one of the rare exceptions.

She took a cab to a major intersection and then got out. The rest of the way would be on foot. It took her thirty minutes to walk it, unhurried, seemingly out for a casual stroll. Along the way she used every skill she possessed to attempt to see anyone watching her. Her antennae never quivered.

She reached the spot ahead of schedule and surveyed it from a hidden observation point. If something were going to happen, here was where it would transpire.

Twenty minutes passed and she saw him approach. He was dressed in a suit and looked like a bureaucrat. Which he was. He didn't carry a bulky manila file with him. That would have been the old days.

And I'm old enough to remember some of the "old days," she thought.

He bought a newspaper from a machine and clanged the metal and glass door shut, checking it once to make certain it had closed properly. It was a routine sort of thing and would not warrant any attention from anyone.

He turned and walked away.

Reel watched him go and then strolled over to the machine, inserted her coins, opened the door, and withdrew the next paper that sat on top of the pile. At the same instant her hand closed around the black thumb drive the man had placed there.

It was an old-fashioned drop procedure to retrieve modern-day digital info. Her informant was an old friend who owed her a favor and was not yet aware that others in the intelligence field were after her. It had worked to her advantage that the agency had chosen to close ranks on her little detour from duty. This she had confirmed by using electronic back doors into the agency's databases, back doors she had set up a long time ago. Soon these back doors would be firmly closed and her old friends would be doing their best to kill her. But for now, she had access.

Reel turned and walked away, her steps unhurried, but every sense on alert. She slipped inside a fast-food restaurant and made her way to the ladies' room. She took out the drive and a device in her other pocket, which enabled her to check the drive for malware or an electronic tracker. An old friend was an old friend, but in the spy business you really didn't have any friends, just enemies and people who could become your enemy.

The thumb drive was clear.

She took a circuitous route back to her hotel, using a cab, a bus, the Metro, and finally her feet. Two hours later she was back in her room, nearly certain that all that had elapsed during the last three hours had passed by unobserved by anyone looking for her.

She kicked off her shoes and sat at the desk set against one wall. She opened her laptop and plugged the drive into the USB slot. She opened the file on the drive and the information started to spread across her screen.

This was Will Robie's life—well, as much as his employer knew of it. Some she was already aware of, but there was much fresh information on here. In many profound ways, his early life mirrored her own.

Neither had had a real family growing up.

Both had been loners.

Both had gone down certain paths in life, only to be pulled from what would probably have been early deaths, to serve on behalf of their country.

Both had problems with authority.

Both liked to go their own way.

Both were extremely good at their job.

Neither had ever failed.

Now one of them would be guaranteed to do so.

Only one winner per contest.

No ties allowed.

She scrolled down until she came to two photos on the screen.

The first was an attractive, tenacious-looking woman in her late thirties. Even if Reel hadn't known she was a federal cop, she would have assumed it from the look.

Special Agent Nicole Vance, known as Nikki to her friends, of which she didn't appear to have many, according to the notes accompanying the picture.

She was a die-hard FBI agent. She had bucked the gender bias that lived in every agency and workplace. Her professional star had risen like a shuttle rocket blasting off from Florida, all based on pure merit and sheer guts.

She was the one investigating the death of Doug Jacobs.

She knew Robie. They had worked together.

She could be a problem. Or an unlikely asset. Only time would tell.

Reel memorized every feature of Vance's face and all the accompanying information as well. Memorization was a skill that one grew adept at in this field, or one did not survive in this field.

She focused on the second photo.

The girl was young, fourteen, the notes said.

Julie Getty.

Foster care. Parents murdered.

She had worked with Robie, in an unofficial capacity of course. She had shown herself to be resilient, quick-witted, and adaptable. She had survived things most adults would have succumbed to. Most importantly, Robie seemed to care about her. He had risked a lot to help her.

Reel rested her chin on her knuckles as she gazed into that youthful countenance. In its depths she saw age beyond the official years. Julie Getty had clearly suffered much. She had clearly survived much. But the suffering never really left you. It became a part of you, like a second skin that you could never shed no matter how much you wanted to.

It was the shell one showed to the world every day, hardened, nearly puncture-proof, yet nothing really could be. That was not how humans were built.

We have a heart. We have a soul. And they can be obliterated at any time.

Reel ordered some room service. After it came she ate her food, drank her coffee, and stared at that photo.

The facts behind the face she had already memorized. She knew where Julie Getty lived, whom she lived with, and where she went to school. She knew that Robie had not once visited her.

And she knew why.

He's protecting her. Keeping her separate from his world.

My world.

It was no place for amateurs, capable or not.

But she wasn't separate.

She had ceased to be separate from the moment she met Will Robie.

Julie was an only child. An orphan now, with her parents killed. That was something Reel could relate to. Being on your own.

She had really been on her own since she was younger than Julie. One didn't do what Reel did for a living by growing up in ordinary ways. There had to be a hurt present, a pain that never left you, to make you take a gun or a knife or your hands and force the life out of another human being over and over and over. You didn't go to school and play sports and join debate team or become a cheerleader and then go home to a loving mom and dad and end up doing what Reel had spent most of her adult life doing.

Reel took another sip of coffee and cocked her head as the rain started up outside. As it pelted against the windows she kept looking at the image of Julie Getty.

You could be me like me, she thought.

And like Robie.

But if you have to make the decision, if the opportunity presents itself… Walk away.

No, run away, Julie.

Reel closed the laptop and the image of Julie vanished.

But not really. It was still there. Burned right into her brain.

For in some ways, when she looked at Julie Getty, it seemed Jessica Reel was simply staring at herself.

CHAPTER

15

MORE POLICE TAPE. IN THE wind and rain it looked like golden strands of rope shimmying against the dark. FBI vans, police cars, barricades, press people trying to push through, uniforms pushing them back.

It was always the same.

At the center of it was always at least one dead body, usually more. It was getting to the point that every day brought a new slaughter for people to dissect.

Robie watched all of this activity with an informed eyed as he stood behind the barricades. He had thought about many things since nearly dying on the Eastern Shore. One in particular was nagging at him.

I didn't clear the outbuilding before going into the cottage.

He imagined there might have been some interesting things in that outbuilding. But there was no way to go back there now. The police would be all over the place. He wondered what they might find.

He called Blue Man and asked that very question.

"The outbuilding is no longer there," Blue Man said.

"What do you mean it's no longer there?"

"About two minutes after you left, it disintegrated into flames. Accelerant plus perhaps a phosphorus-based incendiary component. The temperature would have been so hot it would turn metal to liquid. I just watched the feed from one of our satellites. The police are there now, but finding nothing."

"She covered her tracks well."

"Did you expect anything less?"

"I guess not."

"Don't forget to come in," said Blue Man.

"You'll see me at some point."

Robie clicked off and watched the police and FBI go about finding nothing.

The Town Car sat in the same spot, but it was partially blocked from view by a blue plastic tarp shield that had been erected around it.

Blue Man earlier had filled Robie in on the details of the execution, for that's what it had been. Some kid had come to clean the windshield. First the driver's-side and then the passenger-side windows had come down, through which the security agents had warned the kid off.

The shot had come through the passenger side, hit Gelder in the forehead, and ended his life. Neither of the security guys had been touched.

It was only Gelder she had been after. That made

sense. He was number two. If he were the number one guy at the agency, Robie would have started to feel more than a little nervous, because he might be next on the list.

The kid had run off. They were looking for him, but even if they found him Robie was certain he would have nothing to tell them. He'd been paid to do what he'd done. But there was no way he ever would have seen who paid him.

To go from a desk banger like Douglas Jacobs and leapfrog all the way up to the man holding down the number two slot at the agency was a jump of impressive length. Robie wondered about the rationale behind it. For he figured Reel had to have some reason. He didn't think she was simply picking her targets out of a jar.

And that meant that Robie had to come to understand her logic. And to do that he had to come to understand not just Reel, but also the men she had killed.

He figured Gelder's file would be much thicker than Jacobs's, and most of it would be classified. Robie wondered how much of it would be kept from him. At some point he might have to start pushing back against the natural secrecy that the personnel of the agency carried in their DNA. He couldn't solve what he couldn't understand.

He glanced up at the traffic light. It was green

now, but no cars moved through because the road had been closed down.

He looked back at the car and then at the traffic light.

He nodded. She'd covered that as well.

He made another call to Blue Man. "Have someone check the cycles on the traffic light the car was stopped at. I'm betting she interfered with it to get the car to stop where it did when it did. Otherwise, she's shit out of luck if the light was green."

"We already did. And they were manually overridden, presumably by her."

Robie put his phone away and started walking off. But he kept looking back over his shoulder to judge the likely path of the bullet, reversing that route to get where he needed to go.

He stopped near a tree. It was far away from the crime scene, so the police had not gotten to it yet, but they would.

He eyed the lowest branch, looking for any recent marks where a gun barrel had been laid. He saw none, but that meant nothing. He next examined the little dirt patch the tree was set in and the sidewalk around it.

Blue Man had said there were no witnesses. Well, actually there were three: the two security agents and the kid. But the guards had seen nothing. Didn't even know really from precisely which direction the shot had come. The kid would be of no help because he would know nothing.

Robie did a sight line to the car window. A fine shot on a diagonal line between two stationary objects at distance.

At night.

In less than ideal conditions.

The margin of error he calculated to be nonexistent.

She had to have used a scope and a hybrid weapon, something between a pistol and a rifle. This was not the Eastern Shore, after all. There were potential witnesses everywhere. Pulling out a long-barreled rifle was problematic at best.

She'd gotten the shot off and then was gone. Like smoke. That didn't just happen. You had to make it happen.

His gaze went to the bushes surrounding the tree, and he saw it on his second pass. He knelt down and picked it up. It was white, falling apart. He put it to his nose. It had a scent.

His mind went back to the town house where the kill shot on Jacobs had come from. Same thing.

He put it in his pocket. It was the only clue he could see and he was not going to leave it for the police to find. They were not his ally in this.

He looked around. There were four directions on

the compass, and they translated into thousands of potential escape routes for Reel to take.

His phone buzzed again.

He hoped it was Blue Man, maybe to finally tell Robie why he was acting so funny.

Only it wasn't Blue Man.

It was Jessica Reel.

CHAPTER

16

NOTHING PERSONAL.

Robie stared at the two words on the tiny screen. Then he stared even harder when the next words appeared:

Part of me is glad you made it.

Without really thinking, he thumbed a response:

Which part?

She didn't answer the question, but her next text was even more surprising:

When things look simple they're usually not. Right and wrong, good and bad are in the eyes of the definer. Understand the agenda, Will. And watch your back.

His phone buzzed again. He knew it would. It wasn't another text from Reel. It was a phone call.

He answered. "Robie."

"You need to come in. Now."

"Who is this?"

"The office of Director Evan Tucker."

Okay, thought Robie. They had seen the texts from

<u>Reel,</u> because they'd been monitoring his phone ever since she emailed him the first time. *He's the number one at the agency and is obviously feeling a little stressed out. Can't blame him there.*

"Where? Langley?"

"The director is at home. He will meet you there."

Five minutes later Robie was in his car and heading to Great Falls, Virginia. The roads were narrow and winding, but in this heavily wooded, rural-looking suburb lived some of the richest, most powerful people in the country.

Director Tucker lived at the end of a cul-de-sac. There was a concrete barricade set up fifty feet before the home and spanning the entire road, interrupted only by a lift gate in the center that allowed vehicles to pass in single file. Tucker lived in a substantial brick-and-siding center-hall colonial with a cedar shake roof set on a total of five acres with a pool and tennis court and about two acres of woods.

Robie pulled his car to a stop at the improvised guard shack set up at the barricade. He and his car were searched and his appointment verified. He had to leave his car and walk the rest of the way.

He eyed one of the grim-faced agents. "I'm very partial to that Audi. Make sure it's here when I get back."

The man didn't even crack a smile.

They had taken Robie's gun, which was not

unexpected. Still, he felt naked as he made his way up the sidewalk to the front door.

Other guards were there. He was searched once more, as though he could have somehow acquired a weapon in the preceding fifty feet. The door was opened and he was escorted inside.

It was still fairly early but he figured the DCI had been up ever since his second in command had gone down with a single round to the forehead.

It would have made Robie sleepless too.

The paneled library he was led into was filled with books that looked like they had actually been read. A rectangular-shaped rug partially covered the plank floor. There was a desk at one end with a banker's lamp turned on. A chair was positioned in front of the desk.

Behind the desk sat Evan Tucker. He was in a white shirt, sleeves rolled up, and dark slacks. His overly starched collar was undone, and there was a cup of coffee perched on the desk within easy reach.

He motioned Robie to the chair and said, "Coffee?"

"Thanks."

The escort disappeared, presumably to fulfill this request. In the meantime Robie sat back and took in the man who led his agency.

He looked older than his fifty-four years. His hair was all gray, his waist was thick, and his hands were dotted with age spots. But it was the face that really told the story: lined, jowly, with eyes that were ensnared in deep pockets of flesh. They looked like miniature sinkholes swallowing the man whole. The lips were narrow and cracked. The teeth behind were yellowed and irregular in shape. He made no attempt to conceal them. But then again, Robie figured Evan Tucker had very little reason to smile in his job.

The coffee came and the aide departed, closing the door behind him.

Tucker pushed a button hidden in the kneehole of his desk and Robie heard a sudden hum of power. He looked at the windows as thick panels slid across them. He looked at the door as the same thing happened there.

It was all very James Bond–like, but it had a legitimate and tangible purpose. The room had just been turned into a SCIF, or sensitive compartmented information facility. Obviously, what Robie was about to hear was considered to be intelligence residing at the very highest levels of the clandestine community.

Tucker sat back in his chair and continued to look at Robie. "She's been communicating with you," he said. The tone was slightly accusatory. "Sending you these stupid messages. Like it's some sort of game. And telling you she doesn't really want to blow your head off. It's all bullshit, I trust you know that."

Robie didn't flinch. He never flinched. It took your

mind off the game. "I know it. But there's also nothing I can do about that. Your people say they can't track her."

"They tell me she's using encryption levels above the NSA's standard platform. She's obviously planned this out well."

"But if she keeps texting me, it gives us some information. And she might make a mistake. In fact, I think she's already made a mistake by communicating with me."

"She's playing head games with you, Robie. She's really good at that. I've seen the reports on her. She's a manipulator. She can get people to do things by worming her way into their confidence."

"She tried to burn me alive. Funny way to gain my confidence."

"But then she tells you she's sorry? No harm, no foul? And telling you to watch your back? Right and wrong? She's doing her best to flip this whole thing to where she comes out innocent and misjudged. Makes me sick to my stomach."

"She can say whatever she wants to. It doesn't change my task, does it?" Robie took a sip of his coffee and then put it back down.

Tucker kept looking at Robie like he was trying to discern the slightest uncertainty in his words. "Gelder was a good man. So was Doug Jacobs."

"So you knew Jacobs too?" asked Robie.

"No, but he certainly didn't deserve to be shot in the back by a traitor."

"Right," said Robie.

"You do what she does, Robie," said Tucker. "Walk me into her mind."

Robie didn't answer right away, because he wasn't exactly sure what the man was asking. "I can tell you technically how she would approach her tasks. I can't tell you why she's turned traitor. I don't know enough about her yet. I was just assigned this."

"She's not letting the grass grow under her feet. You can't either."

"I've been to the scene of both shootings."

"And almost run into an FBI agent in charge of the investigation. You later had dinner with the woman. Is there a conflict there that *you're* not seeing?"

"I didn't volunteer for this mission, sir. And I had no way to control who was assigned by the FBI to investigate."

"Go on."

"I've also been to Reel's cottage on the Eastern Shore."

Tucker nodded. "And almost gotten burned to death for your trouble. I've watched the SAT footage. I think you need to elevate your game, Robie. Or else she's going to kill you too. You come highly recommended. But we don't need to find out down the road that she's better than you are."

Robie coolly appraised the man sitting behind his

desk in his fine house with his guards and barricades all around. Robie knew about Tucker. He'd been a politician, then came over to the intel side. He'd never been a field agent. Never worn the uniform. Like Jacobs he was never *there*. He got to watch long-distance on SAT screens as others died violently.

Robie knew that drone technology ended up saving lives because you didn't need to send in an entire team and put them in harm's way. It was only the target at risk of dying. But sometimes computers and satellites and drones weren't enough. That's when Robie got called up. And he did his job. What bugged him was the desk grunts thinking that what they did was exactly what he did. It wasn't. Not by a long shot.

"You think I'm being unfair?" said Tucker in a patronizing tone.

"The issue of fairness has nothing to do with what I do," replied Robie.

"That's good to hear. It saves us time."

Robie looked around. "Since we're in a SCIF, sir, perhaps you can give me your opinion of why this is happening."

"Reel has turned. Someone turned her."

"Who do you think that is? The agency must have some idea."

"You have info on her last four missions. They took place over the better part of a year. I would say the answer would lie there."

"Might the answer lie with the man she *didn't* kill?"

"Ferat Ahmadi, you mean?"

Robie nodded. "Sometimes the simplest answers are the right ones."

"That explains Jacobs. It doesn't explain Gelder."

"Let's explore that. Did Gelder have a role in the hit on Ahmadi?"

Tucker looked around, his expression saying the SCIF wall suddenly wasn't sturdy enough to contain the weight of this conversation.

Robie said, "If you don't think I'm cleared for it, we can discontinue the discussion."

"It would be quite stupid to bring you into this and not think you're cleared for it."

"So did Gelder have a role?"

"To my knowledge—" began Tucker, but Robie held up a hand like a cop directing traffic, which was actually what he felt like right now.

"With all due respect, sir, prefaces like that do me no good. You're not testifying on the Hill. I need a complete answer or none at all."

"Gelder headed up the clandestine operations, but he had no direct involvement in the Ahmadi mission," said Tucker as he sat up straighter and seemed to look at Robie in a new light.

"So if we discount Ahmadi, where else do we look? We need some connecting dots between Jacobs and Gelder."

"Has it occurred to you that Reel might just be targeting individuals at the agency based on some paranoid template in her own mind? She was working with Jacobs. She could set him up easily. He's dead. Gelder is the number two man. She takes him down and it does catastrophic damage to the agency and helps our enemies. There could be no more rhyme or reason to it than that."

"Don't think so."

"Why not?" Tucker said sharply.

"Anybody could do that. Reel isn't just anybody."

"I didn't think you knew her that well. The file says you've had no contact with her for over a decade."

"That's true. But the contact I did have with her was pretty intense. You get to know a person under conditions like that. It's like you've known them your whole life."

"People change, Robie."

"Yes, they do."

"So what exactly is your point?"

"She has a plan. And the plan is of her own making."

"And you're basing that on what? Your gut?"

"If she were working for someone else, she would not be communicating with me. The standard rules of engagement preclude that. Her employers would be monitoring that, just as you are monitoring my communications. She wouldn't risk that. I think this is personal."

"She could be playing you. Taking you off your game. She's an attractive woman. Her record indicates that she's used *all* her assets to successfully complete her missions in the past. Don't get sucked in."

"I've taken that into account, sir. Still doesn't add up."

"Then if she has an agenda, what is it? We're talking in circles."

"I have more homework to do. The connection between Gelder and Jacobs is where I'll start."

"If there is one."

"A word of caution, sir."

Tucker looked at him. "I'm listening."

"Reel has gone from low-level to high in one step. She could be doing a zigzag route to throw us off."

"That presumes she has more targets."

"I don't think there's any doubt of that."

"I hope you're wrong."

"I don't think I am."

"And your word of caution?"

"What if she decides to keep moving up the agency's hierarchy?"

"Then there's only one slot left. Me."

"Right."

"I have security."

"So did Jim Gelder."

"My security is better."

"But so is Jessica Reel," replied Robie.

"Pretty damn ironic that this country gave her the skills she's now using against us," grumbled Tucker.

"You gave her *another* set of skills, sir. The most important one she already had."

"And what skill was that?"

"Nerve. Most people think they have it. Almost all of them are wrong."

"You have that skill too, Robie."

"And I'm going to need it now. Every bit I've got."

CHAPTER

17

THE DRIVE BACK TO HIS apartment took Robie only about thirty minutes at this time of the morning, but it felt like thirty hours.

He had a lot on his mind.

What he had said to Tucker and what Tucker had said back to him had commingled in his brain like a soupy mess. He really didn't know what to make of the meeting with the DCI.

The texts from Reel had convinced Robie that she was working alone. This was personal to the woman. You don't miss your adversary and then say you're half glad that was the case. It was clear, though, that she was trying to get inside his head. Her subtle references to right and wrong, advising him to watch his back, were classic manipulation techniques to make him doubt both his mission and his trust in the agency. She was good—there was no question about that.

Robie and Reel had received the same level of

training, come up through the same systems, the same ranks, had the same protocols grafted onto their professional souls. But they were different. Robie would have never once thought of texting an opponent like that. He usually took the more direct route to his goal. Whether it was a gender thing or not he didn't know and didn't care. The differences were real, that's what was important.

It was possible Reel could have changed. But then it was also possible she was exactly who she had always been.

He got back to his apartment building, parked in the underground garage, and rode the elevator up to his floor. He checked the hallway for anything unusual, then unlocked the door and punched in the disarming code on the security panel.

He put on a pot of coffee, made a peanut butter and honey sandwich, and sat in the window seat of his living room. He drank the coffee, ate the sandwich, and studied the rain that had started to pour outside. It was surely fouling a rush hour into the city that was miserable in the sunshine, much less with slicked roads and buckets of water falling on windshields.

He reached into his pocket and pulled out the tiny white object. It had disintegrated more in his pocket, but it was still there. He needed to find out exactly what it was. He had found it at both kill sites.

Once could be a coincidence. Twice was a pattern.

And if Reel had left this, there had to be a reason.

He poured a second cup of coffee, sat at his desk, and clicked the keys on his laptop. Doug Jacobs's life spread across his screen like blood on a test strip.

It would have been an interesting life to the layman, but a rather ordinary one by Robie's standards. Jacobs had been an analyst and then a handler. He had never fired a weapon on behalf of his country. Until his violent death he had never been wounded in his line of work.

He had killed many—from a distance and using people like Robie to pull the actual trigger. There was nothing wrong with that. Men like Robie needed people like Jacobs to accomplish their missions as well.

Jacobs had worked with Reel on five different occasions over three years. No problems, not even the slightest execution hiccup. All targets had been eliminated and Reel had come home safe to be deployed again.

He wasn't sure the pair had ever met face-to-face. There wasn't anything in the record to show they had. That was not unusual. Robie had never met any of his handlers. The agency subscribed to the Chinese wall policy on operatives. The less people knew about each other, the less they could tell if they were captured and tortured.

Robie discounted any issues in Jacobs's personal life. With Reel's being involved, this had to emanate from his professional life.

So many successful missions. No problems. Then Reel had shot Jacobs in the back while she was supposedly on a mission in the Middle East to end the life of someone America could not tolerate being in power.

Finding nothing in Jacobs's file, Robie opened the far larger digital history of James Gelder.

Gelder had been a lifelong public servant starting in the military, all in the intelligence sector. He had risen quickly and was seen as a likely successor to Evan Tucker—unless the president decided to make a political statement and appoint some Capitol Hill banger whose only connection to intelligence was that he had none.

Evan Tucker was the public face of the agency, to the extent it had one. He was more hands-on than some of his predecessors, but at the operations level it was Gelder's ball to carry across the goal line.

Robie wondered who would replace him. Would anyone want the job, seeing how it had ended for Gelder?

Robie started way back at the beginning, before Gelder had even joined the agency and was still in the Navy. Then he methodically worked his way forward. The man had had an exemplary career and the respect that Robie had for him only increased.

He came to the end of the file and sat back.

So why would Jessica Reel kill him? If this was personal, what would the reason be? Robie could find no connection between Reel and Gelder. As Evan Tucker had said, Gelder had had no direct hand in the Ahmadi mission other than to give it his official blessing. And Robie could find no other evidence that Gelder had worked with Reel either directly or indirectly.

He hit some computer keys to exit out of the file, but a crack of thunder distracted him and he hit a couple of other keys by accident. The page he was looking at was instantly reformatted. Headers and footers and other electronic gibberish sprang forth.

Shit.

He couldn't change the page; it was a read-only document, of course.

He hit some keys to try and get out of this new, if accidental, format, but nothing seemed to work. He was about to try again when he looked down at the bottom of the page. In a very faint font, so faint he needed to turn on his desk lamp to see it better, was one word in brackets.

[Deleted]

Robie stared at the faded word like it was a ghost appearing on his screen.

Shit again.

He immediately paged back through Gelder's file and found twenty-one instances of *[Deleted]*.

He went back through Jacobs's file, hit the same key combo, and found nineteen such deletions.

He sat back.

He had expected some censorship, but they had basically electronically redacted the whole damn thing. Who "they" were could include either only certain unknown persons, or the entire agency from Tucker on down.

He opened Reel's official file, and after performing the same keystrokes on this document, he found it littered with the *[Deleted]* mark.

They want me to investigate this, but they've tied my arms and my legs together. They've lied to me by not telling me the whole story.

He grabbed his phone to call Blue Man, but stopped, his finger hovering over the keypad.

Blue Man had sounded very unusual during their last call. He had wanted Robie to come in, ostensibly so his burns could be attended to. But he had given Robie another location, and this made him wonder if the burns were uppermost on Blue Man's agenda.

There was clearly something going on here to which Robie was not attuned.

He rose and went to the window and stared out at the rain, as though the messy weather would somehow clear his thinking.

It did and it didn't.

It did in that Robie decided he would go in to see Blue Man. But he would not mention what he had just discovered. He would see how it played out. He would see if Blue Man brought it up or whether he was playing for a side other than Robie's. Yesterday this would have been unthinkable. But yesterday what Robie had just seen on the screen would have been unthinkable too.

His thinking was far less clear when it came to Jessica Reel. He was beginning to have doubts there. Severe ones.

Nothing personal, she had said.

Yet Robie was beginning to think that somehow this couldn't get any *more* personal for the woman. And if that were the case he had to find out why.

18

As HE WAS PULLING OUT of his garage Robie heard ~~his~~ phone ring. He looked at the screen and groaned. She had called many times and he had never called back. He was hoping she would just stop phoning. But it didn't seem she was getting the message.

On impulse he hit the answer button. "Yeah?"

"What the hell game are you playing, Robie?"

Julie Getty sounded just like she had the last time they had spoken. Slightly ticked off. Slightly mistrustful. Well, she actually sounded really pissed off and vastly mistrustful.

And he couldn't really blame her.

"Not sure what you mean?"

"I mean, when someone leaves you twenty-six voice mails, it 'might' be a sign they want to talk to you."

"So how's life treating you?"

"Shitty."

"Seriously?" Robie said cautiously.

"No, not seriously. Jerome's been everything as

advertised. In fact, maybe too good. I feel like I'm Huck Finn back living with the Widow Douglas."

"I wouldn't hold that against him. A normal, boring life is severely underrated."

"But you'd know all about how I was doing if you'd called me back!"

"I've been busy."

"You wimped out on me and you know it. I even went by your place, but you moved out. I waited for hours five separate times until I figured that out. Then I kept looking in the obits for your picture because I figured you were a man who kept his word. And if you didn't contact me it was because you must be dead. I only tried to call one more time for the hell of it."

"Look, Julie."

She snapped, "You promised me. I normally discount shit like that, but I trusted you. I really trusted you. And you let me down."

"You do not need someone like me in your life. I think past events showed you that was the case."

"Past events showed me that you were a man who did what he said he would do. Only then you stopped."

"It was for your own good," Robie said.

"Why don't you let me decide stuff like that?"

"You're fourteen. You don't get to make those sorts of choices."

"So you say."

"You can hate me and curse me and think I'm a pile of shit. But in the end it's for the best."

"No thinking needed. You *are* a pile of shit."

The line went dead and Robie dropped the phone on the seat.

He shouldn't feel bad about this, he really shouldn't. Everything he had told Julie Getty was the truth.

So why do I feel like the world's biggest asshole?

A half mile from his apartment he pulled to the curb and got out. He opened the door of the shop and went inside. He was instantly hit by a thick wall of scents. If he'd had allergies he would have started sneezing.

He walked to the counter where a young woman was working. He pulled out the tiny white fragments and set them on the counter as she turned to him.

"Strange question, I know," he began. "Could you tell me what kind of flower this is?"

The young woman peered down at the fragments of petals. "That's not really a flower, sir."

"It's all that was left."

She poked it with a finger and held it up to her nose. She shook her head. "I'm not sure. I only work here part-time."

"Is there anybody else who can help me?"

"Give me a sec."

She stepped into a back room and a few moments later a woman wearing spectacles came out. She was

older and heavier and for some reason Robie concluded that she was the owner of this florist shop.

"Can I help you?" she asked politely.

Robie repeated his question. The woman picked
up what remained of the petal, held it close to her
eyes, took off her glasses, examined it more closely,
and then took a whiff.

"White rose," she said decisively. "A Madame
Alfred Carriere." She pointed to a spot on the petal.
"You can see just a hint of pink blush there. And
the smell is strong spicy-sweet. The Madame Plan-
tier by comparison is all white and the smell is quite
different—at least it is to someone who knows roses.
I've got some Carriere in stock if you'd like to see
them."

"Maybe another time." Robie paused, thinking
how best to phrase this. "What would you buy white
flowers for? I mean, what sort of an occasion?"

"Oh, well, white roses are a traditional wedding
flower. They symbolize innocence, purity, virginity,
you know, those sorts of things."

Robie glanced over at the young woman and found
her rolling her eyes.

"Although it is interesting," said the older woman.

Robie refocused on her. "What is?"

"Well, white roses are often used at funeral ser-
vices too. They represent peacefulness, spiritual love,
that sort of thing." She glanced down at the petal

Robie had brought in. She put her finger on the pink-ish smudge. "Although that's another sort of symbol that I wouldn't associate with peace."

"The pink part? What do you mean?"

"Well, some people associate it with something entirely different from peace and love."

"What?"

"Blood."

CHAPTER

19

ROBIE LEFT THE FLOWER SHOP and headed on. He had a lot to think about. And he was angry. Flowers at both scenes. No, actually *remnants* of flowers at both scenes. The files he had been given were not the only thing his agency had redacted. They had policed the crime scenes and removed the white roses that Reel had left there, but they had missed a couple petals.

In her message Reel had suggested that he watch his back. That there were other agendas on the table. Now he was thinking she was more right than wrong about that.

The new location Blue Man had directed him to was west of D.C. in Loudoun County, Virginia. This was horse country, big estates behind miles of fencing, mingled with more modest homesteads. Interspersed throughout were small towns with upscale shopping and restaurants that catered to the well-heeled playing at being country squires. Alongside those establishments were stores that sold things people actually needed, like crop seed and saddles.

Eventually Robie turned down a graveled lane bracketed by dense pines that had turned the ground underneath them orange with their fallen needles. There was a sign at the entrance to the lane that warned folks who did not have business down here not to make the turn.

He came to a steel gate manned by two men in cammies and holding MP5s. He and his car were searched and his invitation to be here confirmed. The steel gate slid open on motorized tracks and he drove on.

The complex was sprawling and all on one story. It looked like a well-funded community college.

He parked and walked to the front door, was buzzed in, and a woman in a conservative navy blue pantsuit escorted him back. On her hip rode her security creds. Robie eyed them. When she glanced up at him and saw what he was doing she admonished, "I wouldn't commit them to memory."

"I never do," replied Robie.

He was left in a sterile examination room by the woman, who closed the door behind her. He assumed it would lock automatically. He doubted they wanted him wandering the halls unaccompanied.

A minute later the door opened and another

woman came in. She was slender, in her late thirties, with long dark hair tied back, glasses, and red lipstick. She wore a white doctor's coat.

"I'm Dr. Karin Meenan, Mr. Robie. I understand you've sustained some injuries?"

"Nothing too serious."

"Where are they located?"

"Arm and leg."

"Can you disrobe and get up on the table, please?"

She prepared some medical devices while Robie took off his jacket, shirt, pants, and shoes. He perched on the table while Meenan sat on a stool with rollers and moved closer to him.

She looked at the burns. "You think these aren't serious?" she said, her eyebrows hiked.

"I'm not dead."

She continued to examine him. "I guess you have a different set of standards than most."

"I guess."

"Did you clean these?"

"Yes."

"You did a good job," she noted.

"Thanks."

"But they need some more work."

"That's why I'm here."

"I'm also going to give you some meds to prevent infection. And a shot."

"Whatever you think best," replied Robie.

"You're a very cooperative patient."

"Do you get any other kind here?"

"Not really. But I didn't always work here, either," said Meenan.

"Where before?"

"Trauma center, southeast D.C."

"Then you've seen your share of gunshot wounds."

"Yes, I have. Speaking of which, you have your share." She eyed two spots on Robie's body. She placed her finger in a divot on Robie's arm. "Nine-mil?"

"Three-fifty-seven, actually. Shooter was using an off-brand that luckily jammed on him the second time around, or else I might not be here talking to you."

Her gaze flicked up at him. "Are you often lucky in your work?"

"Almost never."

"It's not about luck, is it?"

"Almost never," he repeated.

She spent the next hour thoroughly cleaning and then bandaging his wounds. "I can give you the first round of meds in the butt or the arm. The injection spot will be sore for a while," she said.

Robie immediately held out his left arm.

"You shoot right-handed, I take it."

"Yes," he answered.

She stuck the syringe into his arm and depressed the plunger. "There will be a bottle of pills waiting for you in the lobby. Follow the directions and you shouldn't have any problems. But you *were* lucky. You came close to requiring skin grafts. As it is the skin may not heal completely without plastic surgery."

"Okay."

"I don't suppose I'll see you again."

"Do you do autopsies here?"

She looked surprised. "No, why?"

"Then you probably won't see me again."

Robie slipped his clothes back on. "Can you direct me to where I need to go next?"

"Someone else will come in to do that. There aren't many places here I'm cleared to go."

"Glad you signed up?"

"Are you?" she shot back.

"Keep asking myself that every day."

"And your answer?"

"It changes depending on the day."

She held out her card. "My contact info is on there. Burns are not to be messed with. And you really need to take it easy. I would limit strenuous exercise, travel, and..." Her voice trailed off as he stared at her. "And none of that is possible, right?"

He took the card. "Thanks for fixing me up."

She walked to the door and then turned back. "For what it's worth, good luck." And then she was gone.

Robie waited there for another five minutes.

The door opened.

Blue Man stood there. Suit, modest tie, polished shoes, hair perfect.

But his face was not.

In those features Robie could see that Blue Man was not himself at all today.

Which meant that things were about to change for Robie.

CHAPTER

20

JESSICA REEL WAS ONCE MORE on the move.

She had never liked to stay in one place for too long.

She had taken a cab and then she had walked. She liked to walk. When you were being driven in a cab you gave up some measure of control. She never liked to do that.

This day was cooler than the day before. The rain had come and gone yet it was overcast and still felt damp. But it wasn't a humid damp. It was a chilly one.

She was glad of the long trench coat. And the hat.

And the sunglasses, despite the weak light.

The car came down the street. It was a late-model hunter green Jag convertible. A man was driving. He looked to be in his late forties. His hair was short and he sported a small graying goatee.

His name was Jerome Cassidy. He had overcome alcohol addictions and other problems to become a self-made millionaire. There were many lessons to be learned from the man's personal triumph.

But the person sitting next to Cassidy interested Reel far more.

Fourteen, small for her age, with messy hair.

When the car stopped and she got out, Reel saw that she wore torn jeans, cheap sneakers, and a sweatshirt. A large backpack was over one shoulder. It looked like it weighed as much as she did.

Julie Getty looked like a typical urban teen going to school.

A few words were exchanged between the two and then the Jag drove off.

Reel knew that Jerome Cassidy loved Julie Getty as a father did a daughter, though they had just recently become acquainted.

Now she forgot about Cassidy and focused on Julie.

The first thing she did was scan the area. She doubted they would have thought that far ahead, but one never knew.

She saw no one watching Julie, and she was confident she would have if they had been there. She slipped her phone from her pocket and took some pictures of Julie and the school she was now heading into.

School was out at three-fifteen.

She knew that Julie did not ride in the Jag for the trip back home. She took the bus.

Reel would be back at three-ten.

She watched Julie disappear through the doorway

of the school building and then turned and walked down the street.

Killers sometimes returned to the scene of the crime. That was next on her agenda this morning. She wasn't interested in the crime scene itself. She was more interested in someone who she knew would be there.

When she arrived at her destination, Reel saw that the barricades had been pulled back until only the two buildings in question were still off-limits.

She stepped inside a shop, bought a coffee and newspaper, and stepped back out. She sat on a bench, read her paper, drank her coffee, and waited.

It took one hour before the woman came out. Reel had long since finished her coffee and the paper. She now just sat there looking idly around. Or so it seemed.

She made no visible reaction to the woman's appearance on the scene.

Nicole Vance talked to one of her agents and signed off on a document. She stepped back and took a long look at the building from where the shot had been fired that had killed Doug Jacobs. Then she gazed toward the building where Jacobs's life had ended.

Reel knew that Vance was very good at her job. She knew that the woman had probably gathered all the evidence that was collectible at both sites. She would go over it and then look for the killer. She wouldn't find the killer. Not because she wasn't good enough, but because it just wasn't the sort of crime that the police ever solved.

Reel knew that either the people after her would get to her first, long before the police would be made aware of her presence, or else she would finish her work and disappear forever.

Reel was not afraid of much. She was not afraid of the police. Or the FBI. Or Special Agent Vance.

She was afraid of her former employer.

She was afraid of Will Robie.

But she was most afraid of failing at the one mission that had come to define her perhaps as she truly was.

She took some photos of Vance with her phone while pretending to make a call.

She knew where Vance lived. A condo in Alexandria. She'd been there quite some time. Never married. Never close to being married. Her career apparently was her perfect soul mate.

But she liked Robie. That was obvious.

That could help Reel. And hurt Robie.

She thought things through. Robie had sustained burns. That meant getting treatment at an agency facility. And with Jim Gelder dead, Robie almost certainly would have been summoned to meet with the one man above Gelder: Evan Tucker.

She took a cab to a Hertz dealer, rented a car,

and drove off, merging into traffic and, in her mind, merging the possibilities of the young teen and the FBI agent. There was nothing fair about what Reel was thinking about doing. Yet when one had few options, one had to go with them.

She drove to Virginia and stopped in front of an imposing building that was relatively new.

United States Courthouse.

It was inside here that justice was supposed to be accomplished. It was inside here that wrongs were supposed to be righted. The guilty punished. The innocent absolved.

Reel didn't know if any of that happened in courthouses anymore. She wasn't a lawyer and didn't understand the intricacies of what lawyers and judges did.

But she did understand one thing.

There were consequences to choices.

And a choice had been made by someone in that building and she happened to be the consequence of that choice.

She waited for another hour, her car parked on the street, its engine running. There was virtually no parking around here. She had been lucky enough to snag a spot and didn't want to give it up.

The clouds had steadily moved back up the river and thickened. A few drops of rain plopped onto her windshield. She didn't notice; her attention was riveted on the front steps of the courthouse. Finally, the doors opened and four men walked out.

Reel was only interested in one of the four. He was older than the rest. He should have known better. But perhaps with age, at least in his case, did not come wisdom.

He was white-haired, tall, and trim, with a tanned face and small eyes. He said something to one of the other men and they all laughed. At the bottom of the stairs they parted company. The white-haired man went to the left, the others to the right.

He opened his umbrella as the rain became steadier. His name was Samuel Kent. His intimates called him Sam. He was a federal judge of long standing. He was married to a woman who came from money. Her trust fund fueled a lavish lifestyle with an apartment in New York, a historically important eighteenth-century town home in Old Town Alexandria, and a horse farm in Middleburg, Virginia.

A year ago, the chief justice of the U.S. Supreme Court had appointed Sam Kent to the FISC, which stood for Foreign Intelligence Surveillance Court, the most clandestine of all federal tribunals. It operated in absolute secrecy. The president had no authority over it. Neither did Congress. It never published its findings. It was really accountable to no one. Its sole purpose was to grant or reject surveillance warrants for foreign agents operating in the United States. There were only eleven FISC judges, and Sam Kent was thrilled to be one of them. And he never rejected a warrant request.

Reel watched Kent walk down the street. She knew his Maserati convertible was parked in a secure section of the courthouse garage, so he wasn't driving anywhere. His town home would have been within walking distance of the old federal courthouse in Old Town, which was now used by the bankruptcy court. But it was too far to walk from this courthouse. There were two Metro stops in the area, but Reel doubted he would be taking public transportation. He just didn't seem the sort to mix with regular people. At this hour of the day she assumed he might be going to grab a bite to eat at one of the nearby restaurants.

She pulled out onto the street and followed the judge at a discreet distance.

In her head Reel had her list. There were two crossed off.

Judge Kent was the third name on that list.

She had covered the intelligence sector. Now it was time to move on to the judiciary.

Kent was very foolish for walking alone even in daylight, she thought. With Gelder and Jacobs dead he would have to know.

And if he knew, he should be aware that he was on the list.

And if he didn't know, he was not nearly as formidable an opponent as she thought.

And I know that's not the case.

Something was off here.

Her gaze hit the rearview mirror.

And that's when Jessica Reel realized that she had just made a very costly mistake.

CHAPTER

21

"You look like your government pension got shit-canned," said Robie as he walked next to Blue Man down the hallway.

"It did. But that's not why I'm upset."

"I didn't think they could take pensions away from federal employees."

"We're not the Department of Agriculture. It's not like we can write an op-ed in the *Post* because we're upset."

"So where are we going?"

"To talk."

"Just you and me?"

"No."

"Who else? I've already spoken with Evan Tucker. And number two is no longer with us."

"There's a new number two. At least an interim one."

"That was fast."

"Never let it be said that government bureaucracy doesn't move fast when it has to."

"So who is he?"

"*She.*"

"Okay. Glad to see the agency is progressive. What's her name?"

"I'm sure she'll introduce herself."

"And you can't tell me because...?"

"It's a new paradigm, Robie. Everyone is feeling their way."

"New paradigm? Because of what happened to Jacobs and Gelder?"

"Not just that, no."

"What else is there?" asked Robie.

"I'm sure that will be explained."

Robie didn't ask another question, because it was clear that Blue Man was not in the mood to answer. And Blue Man was not the one to question about the crime scenes being policed and the roses taken. Robie wondered if the interim number two would be the one to talk to about that.

The door at the end of the hall opened, Robie was ushered in, and Blue Man left, closing the door behind him. Robie looked around the room. It was large but with minimal furniture. A round table with two chairs. One was empty. The other was not.

The woman was in her late fifties, about five-five, stout, with a heavily wrinkled face and graying hair that hung straight to her shoulders. Big round glasses partially obscured her plump face. She looked like the smartest girl in high school who had aged badly.

Robie didn't recognize her. But it was a clandestine agency after all. It didn't advertise its personnel.

"Please sit, Mr. Robie."

Robie sat, unbuttoned his jacket, and put his hands on his stomach. He wasn't planning on starting the conversation. She had summoned him. It was her show to run.

"My name is Janet DiCarlo. I have assumed Mr. Gelder's duties."

Not "the deceased Mr. Gelder." Not "the unfortunate Mr. Gelder." Not "the murdered Mr. Gelder." Apparently no time for sympathy.

"That's what I understand."

"I have reviewed the files and your recent steps."

Robie wanted to say, *You mean my missteps.*

Something was not making sense here. He was wondering why the one-two punch. First Tucker at home. Now his new lieutenant. Had this been planned out in advance?

DiCarlo stared across the width of the table at him. "How are the injuries?"

"Fixed."

"It was close," she noted.

"Yes, it was."

"I saw the satellite feed. I don't think you'll survive another one like that."

"Probably not."

"You haven't found out much."

"I'm working it. Takes time."

"But we're running out of time."

He said, "Well, you folks are making it harder."

She leaned forward. "Well, perhaps I can make it a little easier. Jessica Reel?"

"What about her?"

"I think I can help you with her."

"I'm listening."

"You need to listen very carefully," said DiCarlo.

"I am."

"There is a reason why I have been elevated to this spot at this point in time."

"I'd like to hear it."

"I can tell you things about Reel that you might find helpful."

"How is that?"

"I helped train her."

CHAPTER

22

REEL DID NOT DO THE OBVIOUS. The obvious would have been to speed up or otherwise take evasive action. She did neither after processing the ground conditions in her mind and arriving at the best scenario for her survival.

There were two cars. One SUV, one sedan. Both were black. Both had tinted windows all around. Reel figured they were full of men with weapons. They were no doubt in communication with one another.

As though she were competing in a chess match, she jumped four moves ahead, retraced each link in that mental chain, and decided it was time.

She still didn't punch the gas. She didn't try to turn down a side street. That was too predictable. She calmly eyed the rearview mirror, looked at the rain-slicked streets, glanced at the traffic around her, and finally noted Judge Kent's position on the street.

She counted to three and slammed not the gas, but the brakes.

Smoke poured from her rear wheels as traffic veered around her.

She counted to three again and hit the gas. But only after putting the car in reverse.

She surged backward, right at the SUV and the sedan.

In her mind she could hear the communications going back and forth between the two attack units: *She's trying to ram us. Disable us.*

She angled her car's rear at the grille of the smaller sedan. It was the game of chicken played at speed and partially in reverse.

The sedan blinked. It veered a foot to the left. But the bigger SUV instantly filled this gap.

In her mind Reel imagined the next communication.

The far heavier SUV would take the impact, while the sedan stayed clear. She could almost see the men in the SUV checking their seat belts, getting ready for the impact. After the collision, the men in the sedan would perform the execution on Reel.

What the SUV could not do, however, was match the agility of a smaller car, especially with someone as skilled as Jessica Reel behind the wheel.

She timed it perfectly, cutting the wheel hard and instantly pointing her car's rear at the gap created by the SUV's move, like a running back executing a cutback at the line as a hole appeared. At the same time as she pulled her pistol, she used her elbow to hit the button to roll down her window.

One would think that a car moving backward could not be as efficient as one moving forward. But the key was that Reel was moving in the direction she wanted to go, which was behind her. The SUV and sedan weren't. Because where they wanted to go was where Reel was going, which was in the opposite direction.

Reel flew through the gap, aimed her gun, and fired. The rear tire of the SUV exploded and the tread unraveled, launching rubber crocodile hides off into the roadway. It swerved and collided with the sedan.

Clear of both vehicles, Reel let go of the gas, spun the wheel, executed a seamless J-turn that the Secret Service would have given her full marks for, and ended up with the front of her car pointed in the opposite direction.

She punched the gas once more, turned down a side street, and was gone.

Five minutes later she abandoned the car and walked away with a small bag containing clothes and other necessities that she always carried for just this sort of scenario. There was no need to wipe the car for her prints. She always wore gloves.

She entered a nearby Metro station, boarded a train, and within a few minutes was hurtling miles away from the two cars, the targeted federal judge, and her nearly premature death.

Still, with all that accomplished she gave herself a failing grade, and with good reason. Reel had always been her own harshest critic, and today she was brutal. She had committed at least five mistakes, any one of which could have led to her death.

Should have led to my death.

In addition to that, she would have to change her identity yet again.

They knew her car. They would trace it back to the rental place. They would know her new name and her credit card number and her driver's license. These were all ways to trace her. Thus those items were now useless to her.

Fortunately, she had planned for that and had backups. But she had not planned for them to be corrupted so soon. This was clearly a setback.

Even more critically, Judge Kent had been fully alerted.

It was a screwup of regrettable proportions.

She took a cab to a bank and gained entry to a safety deposit box she had rented there under the ID that had just been put at risk. There she kept additional IDs, credit cards, passports, and other documentation she would now need. She did this as quickly as possible because they were probably on their way right now.

She left the bank and walked to a cabstand. She could not stay at a hotel near the bank. That would make it far too easy for them. She took the taxi to another cabstand, got out, and waited in line for another cab. She didn't take the first one that came through and took a long, hard look at the second.

She gave the cab an address across town. After he dropped her off, she walked for a mile in the opposite direction.

These were all extraordinary measures to a layperson, she knew. But they were actually a bare necessity in her field.

She checked into another hotel under the new identity, went to her room, and put the few things in her bag away. She cleaned and fully loaded her gun as she sat at a table by the window looking for black vehicles with tinted windows pulling up in front.

A moment later she glanced at her shirtsleeve.

She had not gotten out of the predicament entirely unscathed. The bullet had ripped through her shirt, burning her skin before embedding in the passenger door.

She rolled up her sleeve and looked at the wound. The heat from the shot had cauterized the ridge in her skin. It didn't worry her—she had scars from past missions that made this one look lightweight by comparison.

She supposed Will Robie had his share of mementos from his missions. And he would have some fresh ones thanks to her trap on the Eastern Shore. If they ever faced off she had to hope those wounds would slow him down enough to give her an edge.

She looked at her watch. She would have to leave soon. To get to the school on time.

For now, Reel continued to stare outside as the rain fell.

It was a gloomy day. It perfectly matched her life.

They had clearly won this round. She had to hope it would be their only victory against her.

CHAPTER

23

Janet DiCarlo stared across at Robie, but didn't appear to be actually focused on him. Robie wondered if the woman was even aware he was still in her presence. It had been at least two minutes since she had dropped the bombshell on him.

"Ma'am?" said Robie gently but firmly. "You said you trained her?"

DiCarlo blinked, shot a glance at Robie, and sat back, looking slightly embarrassed.

"She was the first and only female field operative recruited to the division. I was one of the few female handlers who worked with people in your division. People at the agency thought it would be a good idea to put the two of us together. I had years of experience and she a ton of potential. She bested every man in the class that year."

"I worked with her on some assignments early on in our careers."

"I know," responded DiCarlo.

Robie looked surprised by this, but DiCarlo's expression showed he shouldn't have been.

"We keep score, Mr. Robie. People do, you know. In everything. Sports, business, relationships."

"And killing people," said Robie.

"Terminating problems," corrected DiCarlo.

"My mistake," he said dryly.

"We admired your record," said DiCarlo. "Jessica in particular was an admirer of yours. She often said you were the best of all of them. You graded higher than her head-to-head. You were the only one to do so."

"Since she almost killed me I think she might have to reevaluate her opinion."

"The key word being 'almost.' The fact is she didn't kill you. You escaped from her attempt."

"Part luck, part instinct. But that doesn't help us get to her."

"It may, in a way."

DiCarlo sat forward and steepled her hands in front of her. "I have evaluated both of you as objectively as I can. I think you are equally gifted, in both similar and dissimilar ways. You think alike. You adapt well. You have ice in your veins. You pride yourselves on being one step ahead, and if the other side catches up, you can still win by changing tactics on the fly."

"Again, how does that help me get to her?"

"It doesn't. Not directly. I'm telling you this so

that you will better know how to confront and beat her when the time comes."

"*If* the time comes. I have to find her first."

"Which leads us to the question of why she's doing what she's doing. That may well take us to the next target before she gets there. I see that as your best chance to catch up, so to speak. In fact, it's probably the only way. Otherwise, you'll always be one step behind."

"So why do you think she's doing it?" asked Robie.

"When I was first told that Jessica was suspected in her handler's murder, I refused to believe it."

"Do you still not believe it?"

DiCarlo laid her hands flat on the table. "It's ultimately unimportant what I believe, Mr. Robie. I have been tasked to aid you in finding Jessica Reel."

"And killing her?" Robie said. He wanted to see her reaction, because only Blue Man had expressly said they wanted her for interrogation. Everyone else, including Jim Gelder and Evan Tucker, had been either vague or silent on that point.

"You've been assigned to this mission long enough to know what results are desired."

"You would think. But nothing about this task has been made clear."

DiCarlo sat back in her chair and stared off. She finally regrouped and said, "Be that as it may, it doesn't really impact you and me and why we're here."

Robie nodded. "We can agree on that, for the time being. So that gets us back to the question: why is she doing this?"

"I think it might be beneficial for you to hear some of her history, Robie. Using the skills that I know you possess, one or more of these facts might aid you down the road."

Robie mulled over this for a few moments. "Okay. Let's take a trip down Jessica Reel's life."

She began, "Reel came to the agency under what I would say are unique circumstances, that is, not through traditional routes."

"So she wasn't former military? Most of the people who do what we do are."

"No. Nor was she in the intelligence field."

"She never talked about herself to me."

"I'm sure she didn't. Jessica Reel was born in Alabama. Her father was a white supremacist who led an antigovernment group for years. He was also a drugs and explosives trafficker. He didn't like the color black, but he apparently loved the color green. He was arrested in a shootout with the DEA and ATF and is now serving a life sentence in a federal penitentiary."

"And her mother?"

"Killed by her father when Jessica was seven. After he was arrested, her remains were found in the basement of their home. They'd been down there for quite some time."

"So you're sure he killed his wife?"

"Jessica witnessed the execution, for that's what it was. Mrs. Reel did not share her husband's views and was thus a liability to him. By the way, all of the facts I'm telling you we have independently verified. We didn't simply take the word of a little girl for it. And the authorities had plenty of other evidence tying the husband to the crime. It was just a matter of finding the body. Not that it mattered, really, since he was in prison for life on the other charges, but it was a semblance of justice for Jessica and her poor mother."

"Okay. And what happened to little Jessica after that?"

"Shuttled to relatives in other states who either didn't want her or couldn't afford another mouth to feed. She ended up in the foster care system in Georgia. Some really bad people got hold of her. Forced her to do things she didn't want to do. She escaped from them and started living on the streets."

"She doesn't sound like the sort of person the agency would ever consider recruiting. How was the connection made?"

"I'm getting to that, Mr. Robie," DiCarlo said, frowning.

"Sorry, ma'am, go ahead."

Robie sat back, his full attention on the woman.

"When she was sixteen, Reel did something that

would later lead her to be put in the Witness Protection Program."

"What?" said Robie in surprise.

"She became an inside informant against a neo-Nazi group that was planning a mass attack against the government."

"How did a sixteen-year-old girl manage that?"

"One of the foster parents she was taken in by had a brother who was in the Nazi group. He and some of his friends would use their house as a base when they were in town recruiting in Georgia. Reel went to the FBI and offered to wear a wire and take other steps to help build a case against them."

"And the Bureau let her?"

"I know it sounds extraordinary. But I read the special agent in charge's report on the initial meeting with Reel. He couldn't believe she was sixteen. Not just in looks. His notes said he thought he was interviewing a hardened combat veteran. The girl was unshakable. She had an explanation for everything. Whatever the Bureau threw at her she flicked it off. She really wanted to nail those guys."

"Because of her old man? And her mother?"

"I thought that too. But you're never sure where you stand with Reel. She does things for purposes that seem clear only to her."

"So she helped nail the neo-Nazis?"

"Not only that, she killed one of them. This was after she had taken his weapon from him."

"At sixteen?"

"Well, she was seventeen by then. She spent a year infiltrating the organization. She gained their trust, cooked their meals, wrote their disgusting hate pamphlets, washed their filthy uniforms. By the end she was helping them plot out their master attack. And of course feeding the Bureau all the details."

"I can think of only a handful of undercover agents at the FBI who could have pulled that off. And none of them were teenagers."

"When they mounted their attack, the Bureau was waiting, with force. But there was still a battle. The man Reel killed was in the process of ambushing several FBI agents. She saved their lives."

"And was put in Witness Protection?"

"The neo-Nazi organization is a labyrinth in this country. Their reach is far. With Reel's help they wiped out part of it, but the monster still lived."

"And how did she go from Witness Protection to the agency?"

"Through the Bureau we learned what Reel had done. It occurred to us that she had a skill set that was going to waste. And we could protect her as well as the U.S. Marshals could. And with her new job she would be invisible. New identity, traveling all the time, and she would gain personal protection skills that would make it very hard for anyone, even the skinheads, to get to her and kill her. We approached Reel about coming to work for us. She accepted on the spot. No second-guessing. We spent years educating and training her. As we did you."

"That qualifies as a unique way into the agency, I'll give you that."

DiCarlo didn't say anything for a few moments. "Not so different from how you came to us, Mr. Robie."

"This isn't about me. It's about her. And from what you've just told me I could go in either direction on Reel."

DiCarlo looked puzzled. "Explain that."

"I'm assuming that because of her traumatic childhood you gave her a series of psychological tests to see if she was mentally up to the demands of the job?"

"Yes, and she passed all of them with flying colors."

"Either because she was okay mentally or she's a great liar."

"She *is* a great liar. She fooled the skinheads for over a year."

"And it sounds like she's patriotic, which gets us back to the question of why she's turned on us. So either something happened and she's doing this for reasons we don't as yet understand, or she's been turned in the traditional way, which means she fooled all of you and wasn't as patriotic as you believed."

"I follow your reasoning."

"And while I appreciate better understanding her history, what I need to know more about is her missions from the last two years."

"Why two years?"

"That to me is the outer reaches of how long she would carry something around inside her and then lay the plans necessary to execute her response. That's only in the case of her not being turned in the traditional sense, which could be simply about money."

"I would never believe that about Jessica."

Robie cocked his head and stared at her. "Would you believe it about me?"

"I don't know you the way I do her."

"The fact is, ma'am, you don't really know either one of us. That's why people like Reel and me are so good at what we do. It's why you approached us in the first place. You don't get to be like us if your childhood was normal. We're not Beaver Cleavers with a stay-at-home mom in pearls making us pies and pouring us milk after school."

"I understand that."

"Until I'm proved wrong I will assume that Jessica Reel is doing this for some reason unrelated to being bought off. To better understand that I need to know what she was involved with in the last two years."

"I would have assumed that you were given her files."

"I require *all* of her files. Not just the redacted ones."

DiCarlo looked startled. "What are you talking about?"

"The electronic files I was given were censored. Some information was deleted. There were time gaps. I need the whole picture if I'm going to be able to do my job." Robie paused and then decided to say it. "And the crime scenes were tampered with. Things were removed. Not by the police. By our people. I need to know what was taken, and why."

DiCarlo glanced away. But before she did so Robie saw in the woman's eyes an apprehensive look.

When she looked back she had composed herself. "I will look into that matter immediately and get back to you."

Robie nodded, not trying all that hard to disguise his look of skepticism.

He stood. "So do you want me to kill Jessica Reel?" he asked.

DiCarlo stared up at him. "I want you to find the truth, Mr. Robie."

"Then I better get to it."

CHAPTER

24

Robie drove back into D.C., but he didn't return to his apartment. Instead, he drove to a school.

He parked at the curb and looked around. This was a nice section of D.C. The school Julie Getty attended was one of the best. But it was not one where uniforms were issued and all the students were the progeny of the upper crust. Kids got in here solely on their merits, not based on their parents' ability to pay the tuition or donate to the school. Once you got in the tuition was taken care of. The place was based on individuality. There were rules, of course, but the students at the school were expected to march to the beat of a different drummer.

Robie assumed that Julie Getty was thriving in such an environment. He had discovered that her beat and her drummer were as individual as was humanly possible.

He thought about how he would handle this first

encounter with her. And then he stopped thinking about it. There was no good way to approach this.

I'm going to take my lumps and maybe that's best.

The rain seemed to want to linger, and Robie turned on his windshield wipers and watched them shove the water off the glass. He looked at his watch. Anytime now. There was a line of cars waiting to pick up students. There was no bus service at the school, although there was a stop across the street for a public bus.

A few seconds later the doors to the school opened and the students started to stream out. Robie got out of the car when he saw her, turned up his collar against the light rain, and jogged across the street.

Julie was walking near the back of a group of girls. She had her earbuds in and was pecking away on her smartphone. She had come a long way in a short time, thought Robie. When he first met her she couldn't afford a phone of any kind.

He let the group of girls pass and then stepped forward.

Julie stopped, looked up, and Robie could see first happiness and then anger on her features.

"What are you doing here?" she demanded.

"Fulfilling my promise to come and see you."

"Little late for that."

"Is it?"

The rain started to fall harder.

"You need a ride home?" he asked as he saw her shiver.

"I take the bus across the street."

Robie turned to see a bus gliding to a stop at the far curb. "I thought after last time you'd never get on another bus."

Robie could see a glimmer of a smile on her face and sought to press this advantage. "I can drive you. We can talk. I can check up on Jerome. Make sure he's being a good guardian."

"He's fine. I told you."

"Nothing like seeing it for myself."

"I don't want you to be here just because you feel shitty about how you've treated me."

"I do feel shitty, but that's not why I'm here."

"Why, then?"

"Can we get out of the rain?"

"Afraid of melting?"

He pointed to her earbuds and phone. "Don't want you to be electrocuted."

"Right," she said sarcastically.

But she followed him over to his car. They slid in and Robie started the engine and drove off.

Julie pulled on her seat belt. "So why are you really here?" she asked again.

"Unfinished business."

"That doesn't mean anything to me."

"You're not making this easy."

"Why should I? You dissed me, but I bet you've seen super agent Vance plenty of times."

"I have, but only once and it was for professional reasons. She was trying to pick my brain on something."

"More murders?"

"Why do you say that?"

"What else could it be? You and Vance deal in dead bodies. Lots of them."

"I guess I can see that."

"But you still got together with her."

"It's different."

"Not to me."

Robie frowned. "Is this a competition?"

"It's about being a man of your word, Robie. I don't like people lying to me. If you didn't want to see me again all you had to do was say so. No sweat."

"You think it's that simple?"

"It should be."

"I'm here because I was wrong."

"About what?" she asked.

"I wanted to protect you. I should have known better."

"What do you mean?"

"In my line of work you make enemies. I wanted to keep those people away from you. I wanted you to have a fresh start. All old ties gone. I wanted you to have a shot at happiness."

"Are you bullshitting me?" she said.

"Happiness is elusive. I wanted a clean break for you. You almost died with me. I didn't want that to happen again."

"So why not tell me that up front?"

"Because I was an idiot."

"I don't think so, Will," she said in a softer tone.

"You know you call me Robie when you're pissed at me and Will when you're not?"

"Then try not to make me go back to calling you Robie."

He slowed for a red light and glanced over at her. "Maybe I wanted to do exactly what I told you I would. Maybe I wanted to keep in touch. Maybe…"

"Maybe you just wanted to be *normal*."

The light turned green and Robie started off again. He didn't speak for a few seconds.

"Maybe I did."

The rain started to come down more heavily.

"I think that was the most honest thing you've said to me."

"You're way too mature for fourteen."

"I'm fourteen in years. Not in experience. I wish I wasn't."

Robie nodded. "I understand that." He looked at her. "We cool now?"

"We're getting there. Maybe…Will."

Robie smiled and then eyed the rearview mirror.

He registered on the car not immediately behind him but the one behind that.

"What is it?"

He turned to see Julie staring at him.

She said, "I know that look. Is someone back there who shouldn't be?"

Robie thought quickly. It couldn't be. There was no way. But then again, why not? Everything that had happened so far had been totally unpredictable.

Now the problem was obvious. He had Julie with him. If he dropped her off she was vulnerable. If he kept her with him she was likely going to be in danger.

He glanced at her again and she seemed to pick up on the anxiety he was feeling.

"Look, when you get nervous, I get scared. What's going on?"

"I should have followed my gut, Julie, and just left you alone. This is exactly the reason I needed to stay away from you."

Julie started to look back, but Robie snapped, "Don't. They'll know we've spotted them."

"So what do we do?"

"We keep driving normally."

"That's it? That's the plan?"

"We keep driving normally until something happens to make us stop."

"Okay, that sounds more like it. Then what?"

"We just have to see what happens."

Robie tightened his grip on the wheel and cast another glance in the rearview. The car was still back there. It seemed to be driving normally too. Robie could be wrong. But he knew he wasn't. He'd been doing this too long.

So who was following him? His people or somebody else? And if somebody else?

It couldn't be Jessica Reel. That would break every rule in the book. But maybe that was her strategy. Breaking the rules made you unpredictable.

Well, he thought, *I can play that game too.*

CHAPTER

25

Robie kept at the pace of the traffic, making no sudden swerves and looking like any other motorist on the road. Then he decided to cut to the chase and see if the threat back there was real or imagined. It would only be a little feint, but it would draw a response if the threat was real.

He put on his right turn signal.

"Will, my house isn't that way," said Julie.

"Hold tight. Just doing a little test."

He glanced in the rearview. The third car was keeping directly behind the second one, so he couldn't see what he needed to. That in itself was telling. He swung the car out just a hair, to get it beyond the car in between.

Still nothing. The other car wasn't taking the bait.

Then he slowed and glanced back at a building across the street. In the reflection off the plate glass he saw the right turn signal illuminated on the third car.

Okay. Base established, he looked back up ahead as the intersection approached.

He started to turn right but then went straight through the intersection.

The car between them turned right. The second car was now exposed.

Its turn signal was no longer illuminated. It went straight ahead, but slowed to allow another car to pull in between.

Drivers in D.C. are not that nice, Robie thought.

And the decision to mimic his movements and go through the intersection had erased all doubt from his mind.

"Are we being followed?" asked Julie.

He glanced down at her. "Seat belt tight?"

She gave it a tug. "I'm good. You armed?"

He touched his chest. "I'm good."

"What's the plan?"

Robie didn't have time to answer. The car following them suddenly accelerated and came up next to them. Robie was about to hit the gas and take evasive action when he relaxed.

"Vance?" he exclaimed.

The FBI agent was indeed driving the other car.

Vance motioned to him to pull over. Robie turned down a side street and jacked the car into park. He was out of the car before Vance had a chance to take off her seat belt. He opened her car door.

"What the hell are you doing?" he snapped.

"Why so pissed?"

"I spotted a tail. You're lucky I didn't shoot you."

She slipped off her seat belt and got out. She looked over to see Julie standing next to Robie's car.

"Hi, Julie," she said.

Julie nodded at her and then looked tentatively at Robie.

He said, "Explain, Vance. Why were you following me?"

"Are you always this paranoid?"

"Yeah, I am. Especially these days."

"I wasn't tailing you."

"Oh, you just happened by here at the same time I was coming through?" Robie said skeptically.

"No. I saw you pick Julie up."

"And why were you here at all?"

Vance looked in Julie's direction and said in a low voice, "I think she might still be a target for some."

Robie took a step back. "What do you know that I don't?"

"Only that the Saudi had deep pockets and lots of allies. Julie is known to them. *I'm* known to them. But at least I have the Bureau covering my back. What does Julie have?" she added pointedly.

Robie took another step back and glanced in Julie's direction. He didn't know if Julie could hear them or not, but she was looking anxious.

"She's got me," he said quietly.

"Not until today. I was surprised to see you at the school waiting for her."

"Maybe I surprised myself," Robie said in a guilty tone.

Vance took a step toward him and her tone softened. "That's not a bad thing, Robie." She paused. "Who did you think I was?"

He glanced up. "It's sort of standard procedure in my line of work to be on the alert."

"Are you sure that's all?"

He shook his head wearily. "Why do I feel every time I'm around you it's an interrogation?"

"Because it's the only way I can ever get anything out of you," said Vance in exasperation. "And even then I always come away feeling like I know even less about you than I did before I asked. So if you're feeling frustrated, so am I." She paused and said in a calmer tone, "I know that your agency is on high alert after what happened to Jim Gelder."

Robie didn't respond to this.

"And add to that Doug Jacobs and maybe you guys have a shitstorm going on." She moved a step closer. "I didn't buy the DTRA cover. He was agency all the way. Probably a handler or an analyst."

"Will," called out Julie. "I'd like to get home. I've got a lot of home work to do."

Robie said, "One sec." He turned to Vance. "The

less you know about all of this, the better. I'm asking as a professional courtesy that you back off on this."

Vance was shaking her head before he'd finished speaking. "Doesn't work that way, Robie. You should know I can't back off. I've got a job to do. No punches pulled. Just the way it is."

She looked over at Julie before continuing. "And if it is a shitstorm then I'd follow your gut and keep far away from Julie. Taking out the number two at the agency? I don't think those types of people will balk at snuffing out the life of a fourteen-year-old."

She got back into her car and drove off. Robie watched her until she turned the corner and was gone.

Julie walked over to Robie. "What was that all about with super agent Vance?"

Robie said nothing, and Julie looked away in disappointment. "Just take me home, *Robie*," she said curtly.

They got into the car and drove off.

Behind them a car pulled around the corner from where it had been parked and started to follow them.

Jessica Reel was driving.

CHAPTER

26

REEL KEPT HER DISTANCE, figuring that Robie would still be on alert, but not as much as before. She had gotten quite a gift when Vance had shown up and started following Robie. That had allowed Reel to shadow him while he believed it was only Vance.

So now she had some breathing room and some observation time. She could find out things about Robie. More things.

As she followed him at a leisurely pace her mind drifted to the mental list of names.

Jacobs, done.

Gelder, done.

Sam Kent, a total disaster on her part.

She had one more name on the list. Kent would have communicated with the person by now. Gelder and Jacobs might have been chalked up simply as attacks on American intelligence. By missing Kent, she had clearly exposed her hand.

She had watched in admiration as Robie forced Vance to show her intentions with the traffic light feint. She would have done the same thing. Reel wondered if she could read Robie that easily by just assuming they would react to the same situation in the same way. Then she discarded that simplistic idea. Robie would probably figure that out soon enough and deliberately zig instead of zagging.

Then I'm dead.

About thirty minutes later she pulled to the curb as Robie stopped and Julie Getty climbed out of the car. She didn't look happy, thought Reel. Julie hurried up the steps to the most imposing four-story town home in the affluent neighborhood.

Reel nodded in approval as she looked around at the high-dollar homes. The foster care child had climbed far.

Then she returned her gaze to Robie. He was still in the car, still staring at Julie. When the door closed behind her, he pulled away.

Reel took a photo of the town home with her phone, waited for Robie to get a bit ahead of her, and then followed.

This was clearly Robie's Achilles' heel. He cared about somebody. He cared about this young woman. He had broken rule number one in their line of work.

You don't care about anyone. You have to be a

machine because you have to kill without remorse. And then move on to the next one after quickly forgetting the last.

Yet Reel could understand Robie making that mistake, for a very compelling reason.

I made it too.

She followed him back into D.C., where Robie pulled into the underground garage of an apartment complex.

Reel didn't go into the garage. That would be too obvious. She stared up at the nondescript eight-story building. It looked like a place where young people just starting out or older people downsizing might live mixed in with a healthy dose of middle-aged people who had simply never fully realized their goals in life.

It was totally unexceptional.

So that meant it was perfect for Robie.

He could hide in plain sight.

She had locked down his base and there was nothing more to be gained from staying here. Robie's place might be watched. There were enough traffic and pedestrians around that she wasn't overly worried about being spotted, but the longer she hung around the greater the risk.

And now Reel was confronted with a new problem.

She thought her list had been complete. But her gut was telling her there was someone else out there whom she hadn't accounted for.

Jacobs was a small fry.

Gelder was a big fish.

Kent was in the mix because he was a special sort of judge who perhaps wasn't simply a judge.

And there was a fourth person on her list.

But she sensed there was a fifth person, perhaps the most important one of all.

She needed more information. She needed to track the catalyst for all this right to its source. To do so she needed help.

A particular sort of help. And she knew right where to get it.

In the most unlikely of places.

Not the corridors of power.

She would find it at a local shopping mall.

CHAPTER

27

REEL DROVE OFF HEADING WEST. It would be tricky and delicate and perilous. But so was everything she did.

She gripped the steering wheel tighter. Not from nerves. She didn't really possess them, not like normal people. When she entered the danger zone she actually grew calmer, her heartbeat grew slower, and her limbs became supple. Her field of vision seemed to gain such clarity that everything around her slowed, allowing her to analyze every factor seemingly at her leisure.

And then it was usually over in a blink of an eye.

And someone lay dead.

The drive took over an hour. The traffic was bad, with rain that alternated between bucketing and merely falling.

She liked shopping malls, particularly because they were filled with people and had many entry and exit points.

She also hated shopping malls, particularly because

they were filled with people and had many entry and exit points.

She parked her car in an underground garage, then walked to a stairwell and up to the mall entrance. She moved past a group of teenage girls carrying multiple bags from a variety of stores. All were texting on their phones, oblivious to what was going on around them.

Reel could have killed them all before they could even hit send on their phones.

She walked into the mall and slowed her pace. She kept her glasses on, her ball cap pulled low. Her gaze darted everywhere, her mind a microprocessor clearinghouse of potential problems and what to do about them. She could never again simply go into a building, take a walk or a drive without engaging this part of her brain. It was like breathing. She couldn't not do it and expect to live.

She slowed even more as she neared the store she wanted. She walked past but not into the store. She made eye contact, flicked a finger under her chin, gave a slight nod, and kept going. She continued farther down the hall and then stopped, looking over some items in a kiosk. She looked up in time to see the person she had nodded at leave the store and turn in her direction.

Reel immediately walked in the opposite direction, eventually turning down a hallway toward the restrooms. She opened the door for the family restroom and closed it behind her. She entered the stall, pulled her gun, and waited. She didn't like cornering herself in this way, but there wasn't much choice.

The door opened a few seconds later. Peering through the space between the stall door and wall, she saw who it was.

"Lock the door," Reel said.

The person locked the door.

Reel came out, gun in hand.

The man looked up at her. He was short, maybe five-six and a hundred and thirty skeletal pounds. Physically he would have no chance against her, even without the gun. But she hadn't come here to pick a fight. She needed information.

The man's name was Michael Gioffre. He worked in a GameStop store at the mall, principally because he was an expert gamer and loved the thrill of the competition. He was in his early forties and had never really grown up. He wore a T-shirt stenciled with the title "Day of Doom."

He also had been a spy. He could talk out of both sides of his mouth glibly and could sell sand to a man dying of thirst. Now retired, he looked out only for himself.

And for Jessica Reel.

Because she had saved his life, not once but twice.

He was her gold card, one of the few she possessed.

Gioffre eyed the gun. "Serious shit?"

She nodded. "Is there any other?"

"Wouldn't have recognized you without the chin flick signal. Nice plastic surgery, by the way. Very becoming."

"When someone's cutting you, only go with the best."

"I've heard the official story. Gelder and another guy dead."

"That's right."

"Your doing?" His expression showed he did not expect an answer. "What can I do for you, Jess?"

Reel put her gun away and leaned against the sink. "I need information."

"Big risk you coming here."

"Not as big as three years ago. You've been off the grid for a while, Mike. I know where your cover team sets up. They're not there. In fact, they haven't been there for six months."

Gioffre folded his arms and leaned back against the door. "I *have* been feeling a little naked out there. But I guess they figured I was really retired after all and am officially into my retail gaming career. So no more cover. What information?"

"You knew Gelder?"

He nodded. "Lots of us did. He'd been there a long time."

"What about the other dead guy, Doug Jacobs? Cover was at DTRA?"

He shook his head. "No."

"They knew each other. And not just in agency circles."

"How do you know that?" asked Gioffre.

"Not relevant. But it's true."

"What's that got to do with me?"

"Nothing, but I need you to do something for me," said Reel.

"What?"

"Like I said, information. Not anything you know. Something you have to find out for me. And I need it right away."

"I don't have many contacts left inside."

"I didn't say it was on the inside. At least not anymore."

CHAPTER

28

ROBIE SAT BACK AND RUBBED his eyes. Janet DiCarlo hadn't yet sent him new files electronically, so he had gone over the redacted ones several times looking for things that might have escaped his notice before.

But there was nothing.

Reel's last several missions had all been outside the country. Robie could travel to each of them, but he wasn't convinced it would benefit his investigation.

He would have to go back the two years in her life that he had set as the outside time parameter. The only problem was, that would take time too.

How many more people would she kill in the interim?

If she kept the body count going, Robie could imagine himself being dismissed from the task of finding her. And maybe that would be perfectly fine with him.

He had called the number DiCarlo left him, but it had gone to voice mail. He wondered about the rose petals and what they might mean. He doubted Reel had left them as symbols of her pious lifestyle. Had she left them as symbols of bloody deaths with funerals certain to follow? That also didn't make sense to him, which meant he was looking at the issue in the wrong way.

So what was the right way? he asked himself as he poured out a cup of fresh coffee. He checked his watch.

Two a.m. He poured the coffee into the sink.

It was time to go to sleep. Without some shuteye he was going to be of little use to himself or anyone else.

Five hours later he awoke reasonably refreshed. He spent several hours going back over the files he had been given. Even with the redactions he felt there might be something in them that could help.

Again he didn't find much. He made some calls that were similarly unproductive. He worked out for a quick thirty minutes in the gym in the basement of his apartment building and then snatched a meal, eating it standing up in his kitchen. That's when he got the call from the agency. They had something for him that might help his search, but he needed to come and get it. He showered, gunned up, and was on his way.

He arrived at a CIA facility that Reel had used during her mission before killing Doug Jacobs. It was about an hour outside of D.C. There was a locker there with a few possessions that Reel had left behind. Considering the redactions and the policed crime scenes,

Robie held no hope that the locker would offer any useful details, but he had to check them out regardless.

He was processed through the facility's security and escorted to the locker. It was opened for him and he was left alone with the contents. They were few, and Robie had no way of knowing if these were the only ones that had been in the locker. Right now he trusted no one.

There were only three items: a photo, a book on World War II, and a nine-millimeter Glock 17 semi-automatic pistol with custom sights. The photograph was of Reel standing next to a man whom Robie did not recognize.

He collected all the items and made the hourlong drive back to his apartment to go over them.

Robie was feeling out of his depth. His specialty was preparing, in a scorched-earth way, to kill another human being and then successfully exiting that situation to live to kill another day. Sleuthing, painstakingly going over minutiae looking for clues, traveling here and there, questioning people simply wasn't his thing. He wasn't a detective. He was a professional trigger, but they were expecting him to investigate and so he would.

He laid the photo, the book, and the gun on the table and looked at them one by one as the rain once more picked up and banged against his window.

He disassembled the gun and found it to be simply

a gun. From the ease with which the elements came apart and went back together, Robie concluded that the agency had already taken it apart looking for clues as well. He had already checked the mag. It was a super-high-capacity configuration, thirty-three rounds. It was standard ammo that Robie had seen a million times, although the elongated mag wasn't typical.

Thirty-three rounds to do the job, Reel? Who would have thought?

There was also a titanium safety plunger. It reduced friction, made the trigger pull lighter, and increased your accuracy. Robie used one on his own weapon, although it was probably overkill.

Still, Reel clearly paid attention to the details.

The grip was stippled for better tackiness. It wasn't merely a slip-on; the frame had been altered with the embossed pattern etched right into the hardware.

Robie figured a soldering iron had been used to make the stipple on the Glock's polymer frame. He had done the same with his weapons early on. In fact, he and Reel had learned how to stipple from a senior field agent named Ryan Marshall, who swore by the process.

He next looked at the customized sight. It was a nice piece of engineering. Robie squinted to see the name on it. It bore the initials PSAC.

He Googled it and came up with the Pennsylvania

Small Arms Company. He'd never heard of them, but there were lots of such companies. Obviously, Reel had not been happy with the Glock sight for some reason. Again, details.

He laid the gun aside and studied the photo. Reel was standing next to a large man, easily six-four. He looked about fifty, built like an athlete going to pot. There was an edge of red next to the man. It might have been another person dressed in that color or a sign or a car, Robie couldn't be sure. And unless he had the negative or the photo card it came from he couldn't see if there was anything there that could be enlarged.

He studied Reel's image. She was tall even in flats. And unlike her companion, there was not an ounce of flab on her. Her gaze was pointed straight at the camera. This was of course not the first image Robie had seen of the woman. But each time he did see her picture, it was like he was looking at a different person.

We were all chameleons to a certain extent.

Yet he felt like he was coming to understand Reel better each time he saw her likeness or learned a new bit of information about her. It was like layers of an onion being peeled away.

She appeared calm, self-assured without being overconfident. The limbs were held loosely, but Robie could sense an inner tightness, signaling that they could be deployed as needed in a second. She seemed to balance herself on the balls of her feet, her weight equally distributed, whereas most people stood either too far forward or back on their feet. This would delay them maybe a second or two in movement. In most people's lives that wouldn't matter.

In the lives of Reel and Robie it mattered a lot.

The lips were fuller in this picture. The lipstick was red, nearly as red as that edge of something in the photo. Robie turned the photo at various angles to see if it helped him to discern what the thing could be.

It didn't.

He put the photo down and turned to the book, a history of World War II. He paged through some of it looking for marginalia that Reel might have left there, but found none.

And even if there had been something left in the book, Robie had to assume that the agency would have already deleted it somehow. That they had left the book, gun, and photo told Robie that they had found nothing in them. Otherwise the items wouldn't have been left in the locker for Robie to examine. He was convinced that they wanted him to find and kill Jessica Reel. But he was beginning to doubt whether they wanted him to find out the truth behind her actions.

He laid the book aside, rose, and looked out the window. Reel was out there somewhere, probably working out the details of her next hit. Julie was out there somewhere, probably doing her homework. But maybe she was also thinking of their encounter yesterday.

And Nicole Vance was out there trying to find Reel, though she didn't know it. That situation was only going to get more complicated.

Two hours later, while he was still staring down at the items he'd taken from Reel's locker, his phone buzzed. He looked at the message on the screen. Janet DiCarlo wanted to see him. But not at the last place they met. It was out in Middleburg. Probably her house, from the look of the address.

Robie responded to the message, pulled on his jacket, locked up Reel's gun, book, and photo in his wall safe, and headed out.

He hoped DiCarlo was ready to give him some answers. If not, he wasn't sure what his next step would be. But he could sense Reel pulling farther and farther ahead of him.

CHAPTER

29

IT WAS GROWING DARK AS he set out, and the drive took over an hour with traffic. Robie picked up speed but then had to slow down as he wound his way through some small towns on the way to DiCarlo's house. He wondered how the woman enjoyed the commute every day from here. He assumed she didn't. Most Washington-area commuters spent years of their lives sitting in traffic plotting intricate ways to kill their fellow rule-breaking motorists.

Robie slowed as he approached the turnoff. It was a long, winding gravel road that split two tall pine groves. The house was brick, old, and there were three cars parked in the front motor court.

Considering what had happened to Jim Gelder, Robie had expected to be stopped before now, but maybe they had seen who he was on long-range surveillance. He turned off the car and got out, making no sudden movements because he didn't want to be shot.

Two men appeared from the shadows. They were Robie's height, hard and muscled like tree knots. They checked his ID, let him keep his weapon, and escorted him into the house. They led him down a narrow, dark hall to a door and then departed.

Robie knocked and a voice inside told him to enter.

He opened the door and walked in. DiCarlo sat behind her desk. She looked worried and disheveled.

That was the first thing Robie noticed.

The second thing he noticed was the pistol resting on top of the desk.

He paused at the doorway. "Everything okay?" he asked, although he knew it clearly wasn't.

"Please sit down, Mr. Robie."

He closed the door behind him, walked across a small square oriental rug, and sat in the chair opposite her.

"Your security perimeter is a little soft," he noted.

Her expression told him that she was aware of this. "The two men out there I would trust with my life," she said.

Robie quickly read between those lines. "And they're the *only* ones you trust?"

"Intelligence is not a simple field in which to work, it's always changing."

"Today your friend, tomorrow your enemy," translated Robie. "I get that. I've actually lived that." He put his hands over his stomach. He did so to allow his right hand to inch closer to the gun in his holster. His gaze went to her weapon and then to DiCarlo's face.

"You want to talk about it?" he said. "If the number two is worried about her security and can't trust folks outside her immediate protection circle, that's probably something I should know about."

DiCarlo's hand went to her pistol, but Robie got there first.

"I was going to put it away," she said.

"Leave it where it is," said Robie. "And don't reach for it again unless someone is shooting at you."

She sat back, clearly upset at what she probably deemed insubordination on his part. But then her features cleared.

"I guess if I'm paranoid, why shouldn't you be?" she said.

"We can agree to agree on that. But why the paranoia?"

"Gelder and Jacobs are dead," she replied.

"Reel did it. She's on the outside."

"Is she?"

"What do you know that makes you think she isn't? When we spoke last you were more her advocate than anything else."

"Was I?"

DiCarlo rose and went over to the window. The

drapes were closed and she made no move to part them.

Robie began to wonder if there *was* long-range surveillance out there.

"You tell me," he said.

She turned back to him. "You're probably too young to remember much about the Cold War. And you're certainly too young to have worked for the agency during it."

"Okay. Is that what we're back to here, the Cold War? Where people are constantly switching sides?"

"I can't answer that definitively, Mr. Robie. I wish I could. What I can tell you is that there have been troubling developments over the last few years."

"Like what?"

She blurted out, "Missions that never should have been. Missing personnel. Money moved from here to there and then it disappeared. Equipment sent to places it should not have been sent to and it also disappeared. And that's not all. These things happened in discreet quantities over long periods of time. Taken singly they didn't seem to be all that remarkable. But when one looks at them together..." She stopped talking, seemingly exhausted by her outburst.

"And are you the only one who's done that?" asked Robie. "Looked at them collectively?"

"I'm not sure."

"Missing personnel. Like Reel?"

"I'm not sure."

"What are you sure of?"

She sat back down. "That something insidious is going on, Mr. Robie. I don't know if it has anything to do with Jessica Reel. What I do know is that it's reached a crisis point."

"Does Evan Tucker share your concerns?"

DiCarlo passed a hand over her forehead. She was about to answer when Robie heard the sounds. He pulled his gun with one hand and hit the table light with the other, knocking it off the desk and plunging them into darkness.

He reached across the desk and grabbed hold of DiCarlo's arm. "Get under the kneehole of your desk and stay there."

He groped on the desk, found her gun, and handed it to her. "Kept up with your certifications?"

"Yes," she gasped.

"Good," he said tersely. "Good."

The next moment Robie was on the move.

He knew exactly what the sounds had represented. He had heard them many times over his career.

Two muzzle blasts equaled two long-distance rifle shots.

This was followed by the sonic signatures of the rounds in the air.

Two thunks represented the impact of those rounds hitting flesh. The last two thunks were the dead bodies of DiCarlo's trusted security team hitting the dirt.

Her secure perimeter was gone.

Now it was just Robie between DiCarlo and whoever else was out there.

He thumbed a number on his phone but the call didn't go through. He looked at the bars. He had four. But the call wouldn't go through.

Because they were jamming the signal. Which meant there was more out there to confront than a single sniper.

He opened the door to the room, shot through the opening, and moved down the hall.

CHAPTER

30

ROBIE PEEKED OUT THE FRONT WINDOW. Lying face-down in the motor court were the two guards who had admitted him to the house. He backtracked down the hall, through the kitchen, found a hard-line phone, and punched in Blue Man's number. It rang twice and was picked up.

"Ms. DiCarlo?" said Blue Man, who was obviously seeing the number on his caller ID.

"It's Robie. I was meeting with DiCarlo at her house when shots were fired. Her security team is dead. I'm the only thing between her and whatever is out there. I need backup now."

"Done," said Blue Man, and he clicked off.

Robie put down the phone and looked around. He was debating whether to go back and stay with DiCarlo—to form an inner hardened circle around her—and wait for help to arrive. That seemed like a sound plan, only they were in the middle of nowhere and help would take some time in coming.

If he retreated to DiCarlo he would give a clear tactical advantage to the opponent. They could encircle them, close in, and with superior firepower it would quickly be over. A grenade tossed through the window would be enough.

So other things being equal, that meant Robie had to go on the offensive. That was okay. He was more comfortable attacking than defending.

Dead men out front meant the shooter had to be positioned there. But with the men dead that position could have changed.

Robie put himself in the mind of the shooter.

What would I do?

It was what Robie would call a plus-one situation. You think one tactical step ahead but you don't try to be too cute about it.

Dead out front. Use the rear. They do the plus-one analysis and conclude that Robie would think that far ahead and opt to go out the front.

So Robie did the plus-two and headed out the rear.

Of course, if there were two snipers, front and back, his chess playing was useless and he was dead.

No shots came as he exited the house. He moved away from the door and behind a tree where he could gain a bit of surveillance time while being somewhat shielded. It was dark, so he wouldn't be able to see much except for perhaps movement. Yet even if he did see the shooters it would be nearly impossible to hit them with a pistol shot if they were any real distance away.

After seeing nothing out there he slipped out from behind the tree and made his way to the right side of the house. In his mind he fixed the dead men's positions. From there he reverse engineered the trajectory lines necessary to kill them.

The only spot was the knoll about a quarter mile away. He had seen it when he'd driven up. There was a break in the trees there.

High ground was good ground for long-distance murdering. Any competent sniper could have made those kill shots.

He peered up toward the knoll, looking for any sign of the shooter.

Could it be Jessica Reel on the other end of that sniper rifle?

He got down on his belly and slid forward until he was behind his car. From there he could see the two bodies. He was able to grab the leg of the closest dead man and pulled the body behind the car. Robie saw that the round had gone right through the man's neck, severing the spine on the way out.

Instant kill.

He only glanced over at the other body, but he knew the man had probably suffered the same sort of mortal wound.

Hitting a torso at this distance was not hard if you knew what you were doing. Nailing the spine on an in-and-out was a little more problematic, especially at night. Whoever was out there knew his way around a long barrel and scope. Which meant he could nail Robie just as easily.

He opened the car door and slipped inside.

A plan had hit him in the last few seconds.

He intended to execute it in the next few seconds.

Keeping low, he slid over to the driver's seat, started the engine, and put the car in gear.

Then what he thought might happen did.

A round slammed through the driver's-side window, sending shards of glass over him.

They were waiting for him in front. Which meant they had stopped at the plus-one analysis. That lifted his spirits a bit. Now if he could only survive the next few minutes.

He revved the engine and popped it into reverse.

A round hit the front tire, exploding it.

The car backed up, bumping along with the ruined tire, which quickly shed rubber until he was basically running on the rim.

But he didn't have to go fast. He just needed to go.

Using his side mirror as a guide, he made the turn and sped along the side of the house. At the same time he was dialing the number in DiCarlo's house, which he had memorized from the hard-line phone's screen.

"Yes?" DiCarlo's voice was shaky and Robie could hardly blame her.

He told her the situation and what he was attempting to do. "The signal will be me blowing the horn," he said.

With the shooters out front, probably at the knoll, he had some time. He backed the car to the rear door of the house, shielding it from the sight line of any gunner who might be back here.

He blew the horn. The back door instantly opened and DiCarlo appeared. As Robie had instructed her, she kept low and scuttled over to the car, getting in the rear door and slamming it shut behind her.

"Stay down," Robie called out.

He put the car in gear and drove back around to the front. He was exposing himself to fire here, but he had no choice. There was only one road in and out.

The rounds started pinging off the car's frame and shattering windows as soon as they reached the front. Robie heard DiCarlo gasp and then groan. He poked his head over the seat.

Blood was pouring from a wound in her chest. She'd been hit, probably by a ricochet.

Another shot tore up his left rear tire. Now he had two bad wheels.

He also sensed the shots getting closer and more

accurate. That meant the shooters had left the knoll and were moving in for the kill.

Robie pulled up next to the Range Rover and parked beside it. He got out, searched the body of the guard lying next to it, and found the keys. He looked at the Rover's frame, glass, and tires.

Armored, bulletproof, and run-flats, he concluded.

He opened the rear door of his car and managed to drag out DiCarlo. Her breathing was ragged. He lifted her into the Rover's backseat as shots started clanging off the vehicle's frame.

He pulled his pistol and fired some shots back. He knew he couldn't hit anything at this distance, but it might slow their advance a bit.

He climbed in the passenger side, slid over to the driver's seat, and started the truck.

Rounds were coming fast now, hitting everything. Robie was tempted to roll down his window and fire back when the most remarkable thing happened.

Counterfire started up.

He looked a hundred meters in front of him. There was a figure behind a tree, holding a rifle that was balanced on the lowest branch. The rifle must have had an auto feed, because the shooter was rapid-firing.

Robie looked at where the shots were hitting. In the distance he now saw lights. As he watched, one of the lights exploded. Then the other lights scattered.

The countershooter had stopped the advance in its tracks.

Robie watched in fascination as the shooter out-guessed his opponents on the grid. They were trying to flee his shots by zigzagging. But the shooter was correctly guessing their movements and Robie saw another light explode as presumably another shooter hit the dirt for the last time.

Finally, the shooters headed the other way, in full retreat.

And the countershooter kept firing, chasing them all the way.

DiCarlo's moaning in the backseat brought Robie out of this observation. He put the truck in gear and hit the gas. Just as he made the turn to head back down the gravel road and to the main road, he saw it.

Or rather, he saw the countershooter.

Well, all he actually saw was the long hair.

And then the countershooter disappeared into the darkness.

His savior had been a woman.

And Robie was pretty sure that woman was Jessica Reel.

31

ROBIE DESPERATELY WANTED TO GO back to confirm that his ally in this firefight had been Reel. But he had a badly wounded woman in his backseat and he had no idea where the nearest hospital was.

He hit the main road, gunned it, and called Blue Man.

The man answered right away and Robie told him what had happened, leaving out, however, the information about the female countershooter.

Blue Man told Robie help was on the way and directed him to the nearest hospital; he indicated that a team would meet him there. They were also sending a response unit to DiCarlo's house.

Robie took two minutes to pull off the road, examine DiCarlo's wound, and stop the bleeding as best as he could. DiCarlo was going in and out of consciousness. She alternated between gripping his arm and then letting it go.

Robie said, "You're going to be okay, ma'am. I'm not going to let you die. You're going to be fine."

He didn't know if any of this was true, but she needed to hear it.

He arrived at the county hospital twenty minutes later. Agency personnel were already there, and they took over when Robie screeched to a halt in the parking lot. They stabilized DiCarlo at the hospital, and then she was loaded into a medevac chopper and flown off to a hospital better equipped to handle a trauma patient.

Robie stayed behind to debrief Blue Man, who had shown up about ten minutes after Robie. They sat in a small cubicle outside the emergency room sipping lukewarm vending machine coffee.

"So what's her condition?" asked Robie.

"She's stabilized, but in critical condition. From what I heard she lost a lot of blood and was in shock. Don't know if she's going to make it or not. Someone has obviously declared war on the agency." He paused. "Jessica Reel." It really wasn't a question.

Robie hesitated. Part of him wanted to tell Blue Man what he had seen tonight. The countershooter had been a woman; he was certain of that. He was also convinced that it had been Reel. That wasn't a fact; it was just his speculation. Yet who else could it have been?

In the end he decided to keep it to himself.

"There were multiple shooters," said Robie. "I think Reel is more of a loner."

Blue Man threw his coffee into a trash can, wiped off his hands, and sat back down next to Robie in a scratched plastic chair. The room reeked of antiseptic and stale food.

"Multiple shooters? You're sure?"

"Maybe four or five. Maybe more."

Robie wondered if they would find any bodies out there other than DiCarlo's guards. He was certain Reel had nailed at least two of them.

Blue Man wiped sweat from his forehead with his hand. "Do we have a full-fledged conspiracy going on here?"

"But why target DiCarlo?" asked Robie.

"She was number two."

"So the conspiracy is directed at top agency personnel? Then why go after Jacobs? He was nowhere near the inner circle."

"I don't know, Robie. But if it was multiple shooters and Reel is working with them, they must have some goal in mind."

"It's funny that DiCarlo's security team was so light," Robie said. "Particularly after what happened to Gelder."

Blue Man was nodding before Robie finished speaking. "I know."

"She comes out here with two guys and no perimeter. Multiple points of attack. You wouldn't have to be good to get to her. You just have to show up."

"It was her home."

"That's not a reason. The agency has lots of safe houses. She never should have been allowed to even go to her house, given what happened to Gelder."

"You're right, Robie."

"And the guy who should've told her that is Evan Tucker, the number one. One trumps two, right?"

"I'm not privy to the dynamics of their relationship or what might have transpired between them."

"So there's nothing you can tell me that might help?"

Blue Man looked up at him, the mental battle clear in his features. "I don't know what to tell you, Robie."

"That actually tells me a lot."

Robie went over with Blue Man the details of the meeting with DiCarlo. But again he didn't tell all. He could vividly recall the anxiety in DiCarlo's voice as she spoke to him:

Missions that never should have been. Missing personnel. Money moved from here to there and then it disappeared. Equipment sent to places it should not have been sent to and it also disappeared.

And her last comment had been even more troublesome, that *something insidious is going on, Mr. Robie. I don't know if it has anything to do with Jessica Reel. What I do know is that it's reached a crisis point.*

He didn't tell Blue Man this because, ever the dutiful agency man, he would have reported it up his chain of command. And right now Robie didn't want that.

"Anything else?" asked Blue Man.

"When will we know if DiCarlo will make it or not?"

"Last I heard it may take a couple of days."

"Has she given any sort of statement?"

Blue Man shook his head. "None. She was unconscious. They're hoping to get a statement from her in the next few days. If she survives."

"So who's going to be the new number two?" asked Robie.

"I'm not sure anyone would take the job right now," replied Blue Man.

"Is Evan Tucker coming here?"

"Don't know. He's been briefed, of course. And I'm sure he'll want to hear what happened directly from you."

"Nothing more I can tell."

"So you didn't see anyone else out there?"

Robie didn't hesitate. "Just the shooters. And they were at a distance. I was more concerned about getting DiCarlo out of there. I didn't have time to observe much."

"Of course." Blue Man stood. "You need a ride home?"

"Yeah. The Rover is officially evidence and my car is wrecked."

"I'm going to stay around here, but I'll have one of my men drive you back into town."

Before either of them could start toward the exit several men in suits appeared.

"Will Robie?"

Robie looked at them. "Who are you?"

"We'd like you to come with us."

"Who is 'we'?" said Blue Man.

The speaker looked at him. "This doesn't concern you."

"The hell it doesn't. Robie is with me." Blue Man showed them his creds.

The same man spoke. "Right, sir, we know who you are." The man held out his own creds. Their magnitude made Blue Man blink in surprise and take a step back.

Robie had also seen the ID card and badge. He wasn't surprised that Blue Man had stood down.

When the country's national security advisor wanted you, well, you went.

Robie walked outside, climbed into the waiting SUV, and was driven off.

He didn't expect to be home anytime soon.

CHAPTER

32

JESSICA REEL SAT IN HER CAR, which was parked at a curb on a normally busy street in D.C. However, it was late and the traffic had ebbed even on this main artery.

Her rifle was in the trunk. She had fired more than forty rounds at the shooters. She might have saved Will Robie's life; she wasn't sure. And while Janet DiCarlo might still die from her wounds, she would have assuredly died without Reel's intervention. And Robie's.

That gave a lift to Reel's spirits, something that hadn't happened a lot lately.

It had been stupid on DiCarlo's part to have such limited security that far out. Reel had been to her home before, years ago. A friendly meeting to discuss Reel's future.

She smiled grimly at this memory.

My future?

She'd had an epiphany after leaving Gioffre. She

knew that DiCarlo had been appointed the number two. She still had electronic back doors into the agency. Until these were all shut down—and they would be soon—she had utilized them to the maximum. She'd figured that in DiCarlo's position as the new number two, she and Robie would have to meet. Reel didn't know that this meeting was actually their second face-to-face.

She and DiCarlo went way back, farther than anyone else she knew at the agency. She had always been able to count on DiCarlo to cover her back. But now that was no longer possible. Reel had not only crossed the line, she had obliterated it.

She'd followed Robie out to DiCarlo's house. Initially she didn't know where he was going, and as the roads became more and more rural and the traffic less and less plentiful, she was afraid Robie would spot her. But at one point she deduced where he must be going and broke off her tail, only to circle back and take up position. She had no idea that an attack was coming.

But then again, she had no reason to assume that an attack *wasn't* coming.

She was certain she had hit some of the shooters. If she had, she expected that the mess would be cleaned up before anyone else arrived at the scene. There would be no leave-behinds.

Robie had exercised sound skills in using the armored

SUV to make his escape. He was resourceful and worked well under pressure. She remembered this from her brief time working with him. Reel had sized up her competition early and often at the agency. The only serious competition she'd had was Will Robie. They took turns topping the grading system in all their early missions. But Robie had eventually come out ahead. She'd never thought she would ever be pitted against him.

Her thoughts turned back to DiCarlo: Why target her? What did she know?

Reel had long suspected that DiCarlo was better informed than many people inside the agency thought. They probably had believed she would make a competent if temporary number two.

No, a *safe* number two, she corrected herself.

They obviously didn't know DiCarlo as Reel did.

They likely thought this because she was a woman. They failed to realize that she had worked three times as hard and had to be twice as tough as a man to reach the level she had.

The area had had a brief respite from the inclement weather, but the broad low-pressure system had anchored itself over the city, and when the clouds grew heavy with moisture the rains had commenced once more. The wind picked up and one of the gusts buffeted Reel's rental car. She started the engine and turned the heat on but did not put the car in gear. The rain-slicked streets had driven the few pedestrians to drier locations and she had an unobstructed if rain-soaked view of the pavement. If only her thoughts could be as clear. But they were as cloudy as a mountain hollow on a cold morning.

Judge Samuel Kent and the other person on her list had not only been forewarned, but were also now on the offensive. Reel had little doubt that this group had orchestrated the attack on Janet DiCarlo. This was troubling, because they obviously knew something about DiCarlo that Reel didn't. It was an extraordinary move and an extraordinary move had to have extraordinary justification.

She took out her phone and studied the screen. It was easy enough to text Robie. They couldn't trace her, of that she was sure. But Reel also knew that the agency could read every text she sent him. So she had to be careful, not just for herself but for him. A funny thought, she was aware, to be concerned about the well-being of a man that she had very nearly turned into a burnt husk. But now certain possibilities were opening for her and she meant to take advantage of them.

She tapped the keys on her screen and sent her text. Now that that was done, she would just have to see how it played out. A lot would depend on Robie.

The rain picked up as she drove faster.

Reel had never worn a uniform and yet she'd

probably killed more people than even the most decorated of professional soldiers. She risked her life every time she did so. Yet she'd taken her orders from those at a safe distance from the battle. She had never questioned those orders. She had executed them faithfully for nearly all of her adult life.

And then had come the time when she couldn't do that anymore.

Her father had been a monster and had nearly beaten her into an early grave. Those scars were permanent. Not the ones on her body—the ones in her mind. Those never really healed.

Her career as a sanctioned killer had given her something she thought she would never have.

Clarity of action.

Good versus bad.

Good wins. Bad loses.

It was like she was killing her father over and over. It was like she was extinguishing the neo-Nazis for eternity. And every other demon that dared try to walk among humankind wreaking havoc.

And yet it had never been and would never be that simple.

And it had finally dawned on Jessica Reel that the best arbiter of what was good and what was evil was her own moral compass, tarnished as it was by what she'd done in the past.

Her break with complete obedience to her employer

had not come easily. But once it had come it was surprising to her how exhilarating it had been to think once more for herself.

As she drove on, Reel wondered what Robie would make of the little present she'd left for him.

33

HE WAS NOT OFFICIALLY KNOWN as the NSA, because that would have confused him with the National Security Agency. Technically he was the assistant to the president for national security affairs, or APNSA. He was not Senate-confirmed, but was selected directly by the president. His office was in the West Wing near the Oval Office. The APNSA had no authority over any government agency, unlike the secretary of homeland security or the defense secretary.

Given those limitations it would be easy to conclude that the APNSA wielded little authority or influence. That conclusion would be patently wrong.

Anyone with the direct ear of the president had enormous authority and wielded staggering influence. In times of national crisis the APNSA operated directly from the White House Situation Room, with the president usually right next to him.

Robie knew all of this as he was driven to 1600

Pennsylvania Avenue. The tank-stopping gates opened and the SUV motorcade swept into arguably the most famous address in the world.

The walk was short once they left the vehicles. Robie was not taken to the Situation Room. That was reserved for a national crisis. Well, he thought, if things kept going the way they were, it might become a very busy place.

He was taken to a small conference room and told to sit. So he sat. He knew there were armed men right outside the door.

He wondered if the president was in town today. He was certain the man had been briefed on all this. What he had made of that briefing was anyone's guess.

Robie sat alone for five minutes, long enough to show that the man he was waiting for was very important and that Robie's matter, though critical, was only one of many the APNSA was juggling.

The world, after all, was a very complicated place. And America, as the only remaining superpower, was right in the middle of all the complications. And no matter what the United States did, half the world would hate it and the other half would complain that the Americans were not doing enough.

Robie refocused when the door opened. The man entering the room was largely unknown to a public that would have a hard time naming any cabinet member and sometimes even tripped over the vice president's name.

Robie assumed he preferred the anonymity.

His name was Gus Whitcomb. He was sixty-eight years old, a little soft in the gut, but he still had broad shoulders carried over from his days as a linebacker at the Naval Academy. He must not have taken too many hits to the head, because his brain seemed to be working on all cylinders. He had the reputation of going after America's enemies with a potent mixture of passion and ruthlessness. And he was thoroughly relied on by the president.

He sat down across from Robie, put on wire-rimmed spectacles, and glanced down at the e-tablet he had carried in with him. The White House, like the rest of the world, was going paperless. He read down the screen, took off his glasses, slipped them into his jacket pocket, and looked up at Robie.

"The president sends his best."

"I appreciate that."

"Well, he appreciates you."

The niceties over, Whitcomb shifted gears. "Tough night for you."

"Unexpected, yes."

"Last update on DiCarlo looks better. They think she'll pull through."

"I'm glad to hear that."

"I've read your account several times. But it gives no indication of who the attackers could have been."

"I never got a clear look at any of them. They were firing from long range. Forensics on the ground provide anything?"

"Lots of shell casings."

Robie nodded. "Any bodies?"

Whitcomb looked at him sharply. "Why would that be? You could hardly have hit them with your pistol from that range."

Robie had walked right into that one. He never should have offered anything other than what was in his official report. He must be more tired than he thought.

"They were advancing on us when I got us out of there. But I fired some shots right at them. You never know if you're going to get lucky or not."

Whitcomb didn't seem to be listening to this, which was troubling to Robie. That made it seem as though Whitcomb had already made up his mind about something. Then what the man had said registered in Robie's brain, and he tried hard to keep the realization off his features.

Shell casings. Lots of them.

As though he had actually read Robie's mind, Whitcomb said, "More than forty shell casings were found by a tree to the left of DiCarlo's home. The way most of the casings were positioned when they were found on the ground indicates that the shooter was firing toward where you reported the other shooters to be and also where blood and different shell casings were discovered. Also found there were glass shards that have been identified as being from both sniper scopes and flashlights. So the question becomes, who else was out there?"

He stared pointedly at Robie.

When Robie said nothing, Whitcomb said, "You could hardly have missed seeing the person who fired over forty high-powered rifle rounds at a target that was firing on you. So who was your guardian angel? That's the first question. The second question is, why wasn't that information already in your report?"

"It's an issue of trust, sir."

From his slack expression, this was not the response Whitcomb was expecting. "Excuse me?" he said sharply.

"Ms. DiCarlo expressed to me that things were not as they should be at the agency and other places. Things that troubled her. She indicated that a crisis was approaching. She only had two men guarding her because they were the only two she trusted."

Whitcomb put his glasses back on, as though doing so would make him see more clearly what Robie had just said.

"Am I to believe that the number two at the agency

didn't trust her employer? Meaning the CIA?" He shook his head slowly. "That is very, very difficult to comprehend, Mr. Robie."

"I'm just telling you what she told me."

"And yet that extraordinary assertion also was not in your report. And Ms. DiCarlo unfortunately is not available to corroborate your statement."

"She invited me to her house, sir. To tell me these things."

"Again, your word only."

"So you don't believe me?" Robie said.

"Well, you apparently don't believe anything either."

Robie shook his head but didn't respond.

Whitcomb pressed on. "My briefings indicate that we have a rogue agent killing agency personnel. You were assigned to come on board, find, and terminate said rogue agent. It does not seem to me that you are any closer to finding her. Indeed, it seems that you are starting to believe that the true enemy is located on the inside instead of on the outside."

"When one's own side withholds information from me I think it only natural that my confidence in my side goes down. And it also makes it a lot harder to do my job."

"Withholds information?"

"Redacted files, corrupted crime scenes, cryptic

meetings where more is left unsaid than said. Agendas that seem to keep shifting. Not an ideal platform for success in the field."

Whitcomb stared down at his hands for a few moments before looking up and saying, "Just answer this simple question. Did you see the person who fired off those rounds?"

Robie knew if he hesitated with his answer it would be calamitous. "It was a woman. I didn't see the face clearly. But it was definitely a woman."

"And you didn't attempt to confirm who it was?"

Now Robie had a ready answer that not even a hardass like Whitcomb could dispute. "I had a badly wounded person in the backseat who could expire at any time. There were shooters zeroing in our location. I had no time to do anything other than leave the scene as quickly as possible. My paramount concern was Ms. DiCarlo's survival."

Whitcomb was nodding even before Robie finished speaking. "Of course, Robie. Of course, completely understandable. And your prompt actions have, hopefully, resulted in DiCarlo's survival, for which you are to be commended."

He paused, seeming to marshal his thoughts while Robie waited for the next query.

"Do you have any idea who this woman might have been?"

"Sir, it would only be a guess on my part at this point in time."

"I'll take that, at this point in time," Whitcomb shot back.

"I think it was Jessica Reel, the rogue agent I've been assigned to hunt down."

34

GameStop would not be open for several more hours. Yet she knew he always got in early. So Reel sat in her car outside the mall entrance that he would use. She flicked her lights when she saw him drive up and park his vintage black Mustang.

He walked over to her car and got in.

She drove off.

Michael Gioffre wore an unzipped hoodie, baggy jeans, and his "Day of Doom" T-shirt. Reel assumed he had dozens of them.

"Where are we going?" he asked. "I've got inventory to check."

"Not far. And it won't be long if you have what I need. Just time for a cup of coffee."

She pointed to the coffee sitting in the cup holder. He picked it up, took a sip.

"You didn't give me much time," he mumbled.

"My recollection of you is that you never needed much time. Am I wrong?"

Gioffre took another sip and then wiped his mouth. "I could get in a lot of trouble doing this."

"Yes, you could."

"But you still expect me to help you?"

"Yes, I do. If the positions were reversed, wouldn't you?"

Gioffre sighed. "I hate it when you're logical."

"You're a gamer. I thought you lived by logic."

"I also appreciate fantasy. I kill guys on the screen. You kill them for real."

They drove in silence for a while.

"Stupid comment, sorry," Gioffre finally said.

"It's the truth, so how stupid can it be?"

"Logic again," he said. "You have an endless supply."

"I've always chosen that over chaos. When I had a choice, that is."

For Reel they could have been in a time tunnel, ten years ago, in a car, driving in some foreign land, her seeking information and Gioffre providing it. But then again, every place seemed foreign to her now. Even the one she used to call home.

They drove in silence for another mile. Each plunk of a raindrop on the windshield seemed to Reel to represent a second of their lives draining away.

"Did they deserve it?" Gioffre asked, quietly breaking the silence.

Reel didn't answer.

He shifted in his seat. "Because knowing you the way I know you, I think they must have."

"Don't give me credit for something I didn't earn."

"What do you mean?" Gioffre said sharply.

"I've terminated lots of people I never even met because someone higher up in the pecking order told me it was not only the right thing to do, it was my duty. Whether they actually deserved it or not never entered into the equation. *That's* what I mean."

"But that's what you signed up for. That's what I signed up for way back when. We were on the side of right and justice. At least that's what we were told."

"It was mostly true, Mike. But just mostly. You have human beings in the cycle so nothing is perfect, in fact everything is de facto imperfect."

"So did they deserve it? This time, I mean."

Reel made a quick turn, pulled to the curb, and put the car in park. She turned sideways in her seat and looked at him.

"Yes, they did deserve it. But it's both simple and complicated. The simple part is done. Or at least it's in progress. The complicated part will take a long time. And it may never get done."

"So there's more to come?" he asked.

"Do I look like I'm done?"

"No."

She put the car in gear and pulled off. "And if I tell you any more you become an accomplice for everything I do. So let's cut to the end. Do you have what I need?"

He pulled a flash drive from his pocket and handed it to her. Reel put it in her pocket.

"I've haven't looked at it," he said.

"Good."

"How did you know it even existed?"

"Because they're executing on it. You don't do something like that without planning. Without a map to go forward. Someone had to white paper it. That's not a puzzle you can reverse engineer. Every piece needs to be in place with every upside and downside considered beforehand."

"Who's 'they'?"

She shook her head. "Not going there."

"Guess you'd have to kill me too."

"Guess so," said Reel. She was not smiling even a little bit.

Gioffre rubbed a hand though his straggly hair and looked away.

"Your coffee the way you like it?" she asked.

He gripped the cup. "Perfect. You have a good memory."

"When you're always two seconds from dying violently you remember the little things. One cream put in before the coffee, then one sugar. Don't stir it. What kept me sane. Probably the same for you, right?"

"What else do you remember from those days?"

Reel stared out the windshield. In her mind's eye lots of images popped up. Most she would never forget no matter how hard she tried.

"The wind was always blowing. The sand hurt my skin and kept jamming my weapons. I could never get enough to eat or enough water to drink. But most of all I remember wondering what the hell we were all doing there. Because it was going to look exactly the same once we left. And all we were really going to leave behind was a lot of blood, much of it ours."

Gioffre turned and looked out the windshield. He drank his coffee slowly, methodically, like it would be his last cup ever.

"Mike, you did close the path back to you on this, right?"

"I did the best I could. They would have to be better than me to get to me. And I don't think they are. I know sixteen-year-old punks who've never even kissed a girl who can program circles around the best the NSA has out there."

"All the same, watch your back. No room for overconfidence on this."

He said, "Looks like it's going to rain all day."

"Looks like it's going to rain the rest of my life."

"How long might that be?" he asked. "Your life, I mean?"

"Your guess is probably better than mine. I'm no longer an objective observer."

"You shouldn't go out this way, Jess. Not after all you've done."

"It's because of what I've done that I have to go out this way. Because there's no other way to go and be able to look at myself in the mirror. If people did that simple test they wouldn't do three-quarters of the crap they end up doing. But at the end of the day people can justify anything they want. It's just how we're wired."

"They must have really hurt you."

They really hurt someone I cared about, thought Reel. *They hurt him so much he's dead. And when they hurt him, they hurt me. And now it's my turn to hurt them back.*

"Yeah, I guess they did," she replied.

She drove him back to the mall, parked near the GameStop, and let him out.

"I appreciate the assist, Mike. No one will ever know where it came from."

"I know that."

He started to leave but then ducked back inside the car as the rain pelted him.

"I hope you make it."

"We'll see."

"Who do they have coming after you?"

"Will Robie."

Gioffre sucked in a breath and his eyes grew wide with fear. "Shit. Robie?"

"I know. But he might cut me some slack."

"Why the hell would he do that?"

"Because I saved his life last night."

She drove on, leaving Gioffre standing in the rain watching her. She drove for some miles and then pulled into a parking garage, stopped the car, but kept the engine running. She popped the flash drive into her laptop and thoroughly read the contents.

This would require a plane ride.

And what would be would be.

She drove off.

35

THE SUV DROPPED ROBIE OFF in front of his apartment building. The men said nothing to him on the short ride over from the White House, nor did they speak as they opened the door and let him out. Robie watched the vehicle disappear into the early morning rush hour traffic.

Whitcomb hadn't said much after Robie had told him he believed that Jessica Reel had come to his and DiCarlo's aid the night before. He had written some things down in his electronic tablet, given Robie a few suspicious glances, and then risen from his chair and left.

Robie had remained sitting until a guard came and retrieved him a few minutes later. It was both a memorable and disturbing visit to the White House.

Now he stared at his apartment building and couldn't remember feeling this tired before. That was saying a lot, because he had gone days without sleep and not much to eat, laboring under the most intense conditions.

Maybe I really am too old for this anymore.

It was not a concession he wanted to make, but his aching body and tired mind were two stark reminders that there was probably more truth in that statement than not.

He took the elevator up to his apartment, opened the door, turned off the alarm, and closed the door behind him. He had turned off his phone while at the White House because they had asked him to. He now turned it back on and the text popped up on the screen:

Everything I do has a reason. Just open the lock.

Robie sat down in a chair and stared at the screen for a full five minutes. Then he laid his phone down on the table and took a twenty-minute shower, letting the hot water pound the exhaustion out of him. He dressed and had a glass of orange juice. Then he sat back down with the text.

Everything I do has a reason. Just open the lock.

Reel had done many things. Which ones was he supposed to focus on? What was he supposed to unlock?

The killings?

Her coming to his aid?

Her sending this latest text?

All of the above?

He expected to get another phone call from the agency. They would have already read this text and probably had a dozen analysts trying to decipher it. But no call came. Maybe they didn't know what else to say to him. He thought about texting Reel back, asking her what she meant. But she knew as well as he that the agency would be able to read every word. He decided not to bother answering.

He slipped the phone into his jacket pocket, stood, and stretched. He should try to get some sleep, but there was no time for that.

He suddenly realized he needed to rent a car. His was lying shot full of holes at some secure government evidence lot.

He had run through quite a few vehicles in the past year. He was glad the rental fees were deductible. Sanctioned assassins didn't get many tax breaks.

He took a cab to a car rental outlet and signed the papers on an Audi 6. The last one he'd driven had gotten shot up too. He wondered if he was on some rental car company watch list of bad-risk clients. If he was, the place he'd just done the deal with hadn't gotten the message to stay the hell away from him.

He drove off in his new vehicle, toward the hospital where Janet DiCarlo was currently a patient. He'd gotten the necessary info from Blue Man in an email that morning. He arrived there forty minutes later after the weather and rush-hour traffic took their toll on his journey.

He expected DiCarlo's floor to be surrounded by security. It wasn't. Robie took that as a very bad sign. That the intensive care unit was practically empty when he walked in was an even worse sign.

When he asked one of the nurses where DiCarlo was, she looked at him blankly.

Okay, Robie thought, they hadn't been given her real name.

He looked at the room numbers and pointed to one. "The woman in that room," he said. Blue Man had been very clear: ICU, Room 7.

The woman still said nothing.

"Did she die?" he wanted to know.

Another woman came up to him. She looked like a supervisor of some sort. Robie put the same questions to her.

The woman took him by the elbow and led him over to a corner. Robie showed her his creds, which she scrutinized.

She said, "That patient's condition and current location are unknown to us."

"How can that be? You're a hospital. Do you just let people take critically injured patients out of here?"

"Are you the woman's associate?"

"Why?"

"Because I've been working in this area for a long time. And we get all types. And the type that this woman was, I believe, is highly classified. They gave no name. And they came and took her early this morning. They didn't tell us where. I assume that they have appropriate medical care for her."

"Who took her?"

"Men in suits with badges and ID cards that scared the hell out of me, if you want to know."

"What did the badges and ID cards say?"

"Homeland Security."

It was Robie's turn to stare blankly.

DHS was involved. CIA and DHS did not play nice together, that was just how it was. But for DHS to get DiCarlo out of this place they had to do so with Langley's blessing. So the two federal behemoths had defied all odds and *were* working together.

Robie refocused on the woman. "And they didn't say where they were taking her?"

"No."

"Was it safe to move her?"

"As a nurse with twenty years' experience in the ICU, I would say emphatically no. But they did it anyway."

"How badly injured was she?"

"I can't get into that with you. It's confidential."

"I was with her last night when she got shot. I was

the one who got her away from the people trying to kill her. I was sent here by my agency to check on her condition. You can understand that I'm surprised that she's not here. I know there's confidentiality involved, but you don't even know her name. She was just the woman in Room 7. I don't see how you would be violating any HIPAA regs."

The woman mulled over this and said, "It *is* an unusual situation."

"No truer words have ever been spoken."

She smiled briefly. "She was in the ICU. And she wasn't going to be leaving here anytime soon. The wound she suffered had done a lot of internal damage. The surgery removed the bullet, but it had hit a lot of things inside her. She's going to have a long rehab. If she pulls through. That's all I can tell you."

Robie thanked her and left.

On the way to his car he called Blue Man and relayed this news. He was listening carefully to Blue Man's reaction. Robie wanted to know—no, he *needed* to know—if Blue Man was already aware of this.

The man's next words made Robie feel confident that he wasn't.

"My God, what the hell is going on?"

"I'll let you know if I find out," answered Robie.

He clicked off and got into his car.

There were a number of ways he could pursue this,

but only one was the most direct. And right now, Robie needed to be direct.

He punched the gas and cleaned out the fuel injectors on the Audi.

When you wanted real answers, sometimes it was best to go straight to the top.

CHAPTER

36

EVAN TUCKER'S MOTORCADE PULLED OUT from his house and headed down the street. The lead SUV suddenly screeched to a halt and men with guns jumped out.

Blocking the road was an Audi 6. Standing in front of the Audi 6 was Will Robie. In an instant, he was encircled by five security agents.

"Hands up, now!" shouted the lead agent.

Robie did not put up his hands. "Tell your boss that unless we have a chat right now, my next stop will be the FBI, where I will tell them all I know about everything. And he won't like that. Trust me."

"I said to get your hands up. Now."

Robie turned to look at him. "And I'm telling you to go get your boss. Now."

The agents moved in to tackle Robie. One ended up on the hood of the Audi. A second was thrown flat down on the pavement. A third agent was about to try his luck when a voice shouted, "Enough!"

They all turned to see Evan Tucker standing next to the middle SUV.

"Enough of this ridiculous behavior."

The fallen agents picked themselves up, stared grimly at Robie, and retreated.

Tucker focused on Robie. "Is there a problem?"

"Yes, actually there is. And her name is Janet DiCarlo. "

Tucker glanced around at several of his neighbors, who were standing openmouthed in their yards or next to their cars, or holding their young children's hands.

"Robie," he hissed. "We are out in public."

"Not my problem. I told your guys I wanted to talk to you. In private. They didn't seem to get the message."

Tucker eyed one of his neighbors, a young mother gripping the hand of her five-year-old, who looked ready to pee in his pants at the sight of all the men with guns.

Tucker smiled. "Just a little misunderstanding. We'll be leaving now. Have a nice day." He pointed at Robie. "You, come with me."

Robie shook his head. "I'll follow you in my car. It's a rental. Don't want to lose it. You know what happened to my last ride."

Tucker chewed on that answer for a few moments

and then got back into his SUV and slammed the door. Robie climbed into his Audi, backed it up, let the motorcade pass him, and then followed.

When they reached a major street, Robie saw what he needed. He did a quick right turn and pulled into a parking lot. He got out of the car, and before he went inside the IHOP he saw out of the corner of his eye the motorcade stop and start to back up. Cars all around started honking in protest.

Robie walked inside and up to the hostess stand. A young woman approached him, a menu in hand.

"Will it be just one for breakfast, sir?"

"No, actually it'll be two. But we'll need room for about five large men to surround the table."

The young woman's eyes widened. "Excuse me?"

"And if you have a private room, that would be great."

"A private room?"

Robie pulled his creds and flashed them to her. "It's okay, we're the good guys."

Robie had ordered two cups of coffee by the time Evan Tucker stormed in with his entourage. The hostess escorted them back, looking terrified.

"It's okay," Robie said to her. "I've got it from here."

The hostess had sat Robie in the back and around a corner, which was about as private as it was going to get at the IHOP. Luckily, the place wasn't very busy.

The closest customers were at least a half dozen tables away.

Tucker snapped, "What the hell game are you playing?"

"I didn't take time for breakfast. And I'm hungry. And I ordered you coffee."

"We cannot discuss the matter here."

"Well this is the only place I'm prepared to discuss it."

"Do you want me to have you arrested?"

"You have no arresting authority in the United States, Director. And I don't think you want to get the local cops involved. Way above their pay grade. They might arrest us all and let someone else figure it out. So why don't you sit down, have your guys surround the table, eyes outward, deploy their anti–electronic surveillance devices that I know they carry, and we can talk about this."

Tucker finally marshaled his fury, took a deep breath, and sat. He motioned for his men to do exactly what Robie had suggested. A low hum emanated from a device one of the guards held in his hand.

"You take cream and sugar in your coffee?" asked Robie.

"Black is fine."

A timid waiter barely out of his teens approached. In a shaky voice he said, "Uh, are y'all ready to order?"

Before the guards could shoo him away Robie said, "I am. Director?"

Tucker shook his head and then glanced at the menu. "Uh, wait a minute, I haven't eaten yet either." He asked the waiter, "What do you recommend?"

The young man looked like he would rather be eaten by sharks than open his mouth. But he stammered, "Uh...we're sort of known for our pancakes."

Tucker aimed a small smile at Robie. "Well, I'll have two eggs sunny side up, bacon, a stack of your recommended pancakes, and some grapefruit juice."

"Make that two," said Robie.

The waiter nearly ran away and Robie settled his gaze on Tucker.

Tucker said, "Now, can we get down to it?"

"One question. Do you know where Janet DiCarlo is?"

"She's in the hospital, Robie," Tucker snapped.

"Okay, which hospital? Because the one she was in last night has no idea where she is now."

Tucker froze with his cup halfway to his mouth. He set it back down.

"You really didn't know," said Robie incredulously.

"That's impossible. Where could she have gone? She just got out of surgery. She's in critical condition."

"So you're telling me that your men at that hospital didn't tell you that guys from DHS came and took her away to God knows where? Now, I would have said *that* was impossible, but I guess I'd be wrong."

Tucker licked his lips and took a sip of coffee, slowly setting the cup back down.

Robie watched this, thinking, *He's just buying time because his brain is racing.*

Tucker finally said, "DHS? You're sure about that?"

"That was the creds they flashed to the nurses to cut DiCarlo loose."

Tucker said nothing.

Robie said, "While you're mulling that over, Director, I should tell you that I also had a chat with the APNSA."

"Gus Whitcomb? Why?" Tucker said sharply.

"They came and got me. Mr. Whitcomb was blunt, to the point, and not very happy with what I told him."

Tucker took another sip of coffee. This time it was a tactical mistake on his part, because Robie could see his hand trembling.

"What exactly did you tell him?"

"You really want to know?"

"Of course I want to know."

"There was a good reason that I was able to get DiCarlo out of that ambush alive last night."

"What was that?"

"We had a guardian angel who came to our rescue."

"What angel?"

"Her name I think you know. Jessica Reel?"

Tucker's lips parted, but no words came out at first. Finally, he blurted out, "That's ridiculous."

"I would have thought so too, since I've been tasked to find her because she's a traitor to her country. At least that's what I was told."

"What did DiCarlo want to meet with you about?"

"She had some interesting things to tell me about past missions."

"Like what exactly?" demanded Tucker.

"Like missions that shouldn't have been, missing personnel and equipment. Dollars into the abyss." Robie went on to tell Tucker in greater detail what DiCarlo had shared. After he was done, Tucker was about to say something, but Robie held up his hand and pointed to his left.

Their food was here.

The circle of men parted and the plates were set before them.

"Anything else?" squeaked the waiter. "Coffee freshened up?"

"I'm fine," said Tucker, and he glanced at Robie.

"Little more coffee, thanks."

The waiter filled Robie's cup and fled.

Robie started eating but Tucker just sat there.

"Did DiCarlo give you exact details of these missions, personnel, equipment, and money?"

"No. But if I were you I would try to find out."

Tucker slowly shook his head. Robie couldn't tell if it was to indicate disbelief or frustration or both. "Are you certain it was Reel?"

"Same height, same build. It was a woman."

"So you can't be sure?" said Tucker.

"How many women do you have on the payroll that could take on a half dozen trained killers in a gun battle and win?" said Robie. "Hell, how many guys do you have who can do that?"

Tucker started cutting up his eggs. The two men ate for a few minutes in silence.

Robie put the last bite in his mouth, drained the rest of his coffee, and sat back, tossing his paper napkin on the table.

Tucker did the same. "If it was Reel, why?" he asked.

"That's what I was hoping you could tell me."

"Why would I have the answer to that?"

"You're the DCI. If you don't have the answer, who the hell does?"

"Maybe DHS."

"Are you still not playing well with your big brother?"

Tucker shrugged. "For decades the FBI was the eight-hundred-pound gorilla everybody else hated. Now DHS is the nine-hundred-pound grizzly we hate even more than the Bureau."

"It's not like you guys go out of your way to cooperate with anybody."

"More than you think, Robie."

"Then pick up the phone and call your counterpart at DHS and ask nicely for the return of your employee."

"It's not that easy."

"Why?"

"It's complicated."

"Explain it."

"I don't have time to explain it. I have important meetings I'm already late for."

Robie stood. "Okay. Then I'll let you get on to your *important* meetings. But if you can find the time you might want to see if DiCarlo is even still alive."

"I care very much about Janet, Robie, don't make it seem like I don't. She's a friend as well as a colleague."

"Actions, Director. They always trump the rhetoric."

"What's your next step in finding Reel?"

"There is no next step. Until someone explains to me what the hell is going on, I have officially retired from the field."

"You would be disobeying a direct order," barked Tucker.

"So arrest me."

Robie pushed through the shield of guards and left the IHOP.

When Tucker started to leave, the trembling waiter sidled over and handed him the bill and then fled. The CIA director stared down at it for a moment and then slowly pulled out his wallet.

CHAPTER

37

ROBIE SAT IN HIS APARTMENT, thinking that he needed information in a way that was discreet. Such information was often hard to come by when people were watching you.

Yet he did work in the clandestine division. And thus he had resources and a certain skill set. He intended to employ some of them right now.

He drove to a mall, parked in the covered garage, and went shopping. In one hour he had visited three different shops and carried three different bags.

He got some coffee, sat at a table, and drank it all down. He also had a muffin, even though he wasn't really hungry.

He got up, threw the empty cup away, and walked on.

He wasn't certain he was being followed, but he had to assume he was.

He had to believe his interest marker at the agency had gone up significantly. And there were other agencies that might be involved now too.

DHS apparently had Janet DiCarlo. They had a lot of resources available to them, including satellites. Satellites were hard to beat. But there were ways to do so. They could only spy on what they could see. And sometimes what they thought they were seeing wasn't what it really was.

He checked his watch. As good a time as any. They were really going to have to hustle now.

He didn't go back to his car. He took an escalator down to the Metro.

He was instantly surrounded by a horde of commuters scrambling to make trains. He wedged in with a group trying to board the train just entering the station. He got on and dropped his bags, which caused a scrum at the entrance to the train.

A voice announced that the train doors were closing. Robie kept walking, down the aisle of the train car. He looked back as he reached the end of the car. Two men were fighting their way onto the car by forcibly pushing the scrum out of the way.

Robie didn't know them. But he did know what they were.

They were his tail. The signs were unmistakable.

Right before the doors closed, Robie stepped out of the other door.

The train slid away from the station while Robie walked to the exit, invisible within a wall of other travelers.

He didn't go up the escalator. He slipped through a door that was nearly hidden in the wall. It led to a maintenance area.

Robie ran into two men in the hall inside this area. When they asked him what he was doing there, he flashed his creds and asked for the nearest exit. They told him and he was through it in under a minute.

He flipped his jacket inside out, turning his brown jacket blue. He slipped a ball cap from his pocket and put that on. Sunglasses covered his face.

He hit the street, found a cabstand, and within twenty minutes was on his way out of the city.

He got out of the cab well short of his destination. He walked the rest of the way.

The shoe repair shop was in a blighted area of run-down homes and businesses. The bell tinkled when Robie opened the door. It automatically closed behind him.

He paused, took off his hat and glasses, and looked around. It contained everything that one would expect to see in a shoe repair shop. The only difference was that the gent who owned it did not count on resoling shoes for all of his daily bread.

The man came out from behind a curtain set in a doorway behind the counter. "Can I help—" When he saw Robie he stopped.

Robie came forward and put his hands on the counter. "Yeah, I hope you can help me, Arnie."

The man was in his fifties with gray hair, a trim beard, and ears that stuck out. He automatically looked over Robie's shoulder. Robie shook his head. "Just me."

"You never know," said Arnie.

"You never know," agreed Robie.

"You working?" asked Arnie.

"Something different."

"Gelder?"

Robie nodded. "Could use some help."

"I'm mostly retired."

"That's mostly a lie."

"What do you need?"

"Jessica Reel," answered Robie.

"Haven't heard that name in a while."

"That status might change. Who were her contacts?"

"Inside you should know, you're still with the agency," said Arnie.

"I don't mean inside."

Arnie ran a hand along his chin. "Reel is good at what she does. Maybe as good as you."

"Maybe better."

"What's this about?"

"She's in a bit of a jam. Maybe I can help her."

"You two worked together," noted Arnie.

"A long time ago. I'd like to find her."

"And do what?"

"My job."

Arnie shook his head. "I'm not going to help you kill her, if that's what this is about."

"What this is about, Arnie, is making sure this country is secure. I thought that was the only thing this was about."

"I haven't seen her in a long time."

"But her contacts?"

"You swear to me that you want to help her?" said Arnie.

"If I did swear would you believe me?"

"You have the rep of a straight shooter, Robie. And I'm not just talking at the end of a rifle. But you level with me, maybe I can help you. Those are my terms. If you don't like them and you don't have shoes that need repair I'll have to ask you to leave."

Robie thought this over and decided he didn't really have a choice. "They think Reel killed Gelder and another operative."

"Bullshit."

"Actually, I think she did kill them. But it's not that simple. Something is going on, Arnie. Something internally that stinks to high heaven. I knew Reel. I trusted her with my life."

Arnie said, "But if she killed the number two?"

"And in the interest of full disclosure I've been tasked to get her."

"But you're having doubts?"

"If I weren't I wouldn't be here," replied Robie.

The two men stared at each other across the width of the scarred and stained countertop. It seemed to Robie that Arnie was trying to assess, as best he could, his sincerity. And Robie couldn't blame him. Sincerity in this business was hard to come by. When you found it you were almost always surprised at your good fortune.

"You might be in luck," said Arnie.

"Why's that?"

"It's a small world I operate in. Not too many players in that world. I won't say we have reunions, but we do keep in touch. One of us needs help, we call in chits or sometimes we do favors for one another, hoping when the time comes you get a favor in return."

Robie said, "And how does that help me?"

Arnie said, "Got a call, from another person who does what I do. No names, but he knows Reel. And maybe he just had recent contact with her."

"What did she want from your friend?"

"A document and an address."

"What sort of document and whose address?" asked Robie.

"Not sure. I actually couldn't help him. But I referred him to someone who I thought could."

"Again, Arnie, I'm not seeing any daylight here for me."

"There was a name attached to the address."

"What was the name?"

"Roy West."

"Who is he?" asked Robie.

"He was with the agency. Small fry, but Reel was interested in him. Interested enough to take a risk in contacting my friend. If she did kill Gelder, they would be putting markers on her known circle."

"Any idea why Reel is interested in West?"

"No. But the request was pretty urgent."

"Do you think your other friend was successful in getting this document for her?"

Arnie shook his head. "No way of telling. And don't bother to ask me to do the same for you. The friend does a favor maybe once every five years. He's gone back underground. No way to reach him."

Robie scrutinized the other man. Part of him thought this was bullshit, but part of him thought it actually made sense. Clandestine folks were not exactly retail vendors. Their shops were not open just because you wanted them to be.

"Well, I guess I'll have to track West and this document down another way."

"West is in Arkansas."

"How do you know that?"

"I couldn't help with the document, but I get a name, I get curious. I checked him out." Arnie pulled out a pair of glasses and put them on. He turned to his computer, which sat on the counter, hit some keys, and a piece of paper fell into the printer tray.

He pushed it across to Robie, who didn't glance at it before slipping it into his pocket.

"It's not an address, it's directions. Complicated ones from what I could see. Just that kind of a place, I guess."

"I appreciate this," said Robie.

"I won't appreciate you, if you've been bullshitting me. Reel goes down at your hand, don't ever come back here."

"I take it you like her?"

"If she killed them I know one thing. She had a damn good reason."

"Let's hope you're right."

Robie left and grabbed another cab for the next leg of his journey. It dropped him off two miles from his destination. He hoofed it the rest of the way.

The woods were on his right. He ducked down the gravel drive that cut between the trees and accelerated his pace. The house was a mile back.

His hideaway. His safe haven that the agency didn't know about.

But Julie knew where it was. So did Nicole Vance. But that was it.

Robie actually regretted their knowing about it, but there was nothing he could do about that now.

He disarmed the security system, ran upstairs, packed a bag, and went out to the old barn next to the house. He unlocked the door and slipped inside.

In the single bay of the barn was a pickup truck. It was fully gassed.

Robie pushed aside the hay that covered the floor, revealing a square panel of wood. He lifted this up and hurried down the exposed set of stairs.

He had not built this room under the barn. The farmer who owned it originally had done so back in the fifties, no doubt hoping that a veneer of wood and hay would somehow protect him against a Soviet thermonuclear strike. Go figure.

Robie had stumbled onto it by accident one day while looking through the barn after buying the property under an alias. He had outfitted it with things that he might need from time to time. This was one of those times.

He packed the gear in a large duffel and slid it into the bed of the pickup truck, which had a locking cover. He opened the barn door, drove the truck out, and locked the barn door. He drove out onto the main road and hit the gas.

He hoped for many things from this trip. Most of all he hoped he would run into Jessica Reel. And if he did, he hoped he was ready for whatever she threw at him.

CHAPTER

38

THE OLD WOMAN SHUFFLED THROUGH the security line at the airport. She was tall and thin, her hands covered in age spots. Her back was bent and she seemed to be in pain with each step. Her hair was white and cut short. She stared at the floor as she passed through the magnetometer without it making a beep.

She recovered her bag and kept shuffling.

She rode in coach in a window seat. She stared out the window and didn't engage in conversation with the passenger sitting next to her. The flight was smooth, the landing unremarkable.

When they arrived the sun was shining and the sky clear. It was a welcome change from wet and cold D.C.

She deplaned and shuffled to a restroom.

Twenty minutes later she reappeared, younger and straighter, and she no longer shuffled. Her disguise was carefully packed away in her carry-on.

She had one bag to claim at baggage. It was a large

roller bag, and inside were two metal boxes, both locked tight.

One held two different sets of ammo.

The other held her Glock.

She had lawfully declared it at check-in in her old-lady disguise.

The airline personnel at check-in had merely assumed she was an old woman who liked to protect herself.

There were also a lot of plastic parts and other pieces of metal and springs strewn throughout the nooks and crannies of her luggage.

She picked up her bag and rolled it to a car rental counter. Twenty minutes later Jessica Reel was driving out of the airport in a black Ford Explorer.

Her Glock was in a belt holster, fully loaded and ready to go.

She hoped not to have to use it. Or the other weapon she had brought.

Most of the time those hopes were not realized.

She had perhaps a dozen disguises that her former employers were completely unaware of. She had made certain it stayed that way even when she was working for them. She was not a trusting person—particularly with an employer who would disavow all connection to her if she failed on a mission.

She found the right road and headed west. It was not a populous area. It became even less inhabited with every mile she drove. Following the GPS, she turned off the main road, and ten miles of curves and switchbacks later the GPS failed her. Fortunately she had manually mapped this area previously, and in her mind's eye she followed the turns on her internal compass until she was about a mile from her destination.

She passed the turnoff she would later take and kept going.

It was time to do some necessary recon.

She followed the road around and then saw another turnoff, which she took. She rode it up as far as she needed to. She had to engage her four-wheel drive to do so, but she came away satisfied. She retraced her route and took the turnoff she had earlier passed. She drove up the dirt and gravel road for about three-quarters of a mile and then stopped.

This was as far as she would go by car. The rest would be on foot.

She opened her luggage and took out all the pieces of plastic and metal and springs. Some pieces were fairly large, others small.

She laid out all the items in the cargo area of the Ford. Her fingers moving with dexterity and precision, she assembled the MP5 submachine gun in a very short time.

She attached the box mag containing thirty-two rounds to the subgun and lifted the strap over her head so the weapon rested comfortably in front of her. She covered up the gun with a long leather duster that reached nearly to her ankles. She put on a cowboy hat pulled low, sunglasses, and gloves.

She could be the female version of a gunslinger going to do battle in the street.

She stared ahead of her, studying the topography, then she started walking. Her pace was unhurried, her gaze swiveling in all directions. Up and down. Side to side. And behind her, all the while listening for any sound that would herald a threat.

She covered the quarter mile, cleared a bend in the road, and stopped. She looked right and left and once more behind her.

She moved forward another fifty feet and then squatted down, took in the lay of the land. Potential threat points were numerous and all fully visible to her.

The house was really a cabin. Felled logs shaved down, their ends tapered, the filling in between solid and new-looking. The door was a sturdy piece of wood. She assumed it would have multiple locks and probably a security system.

No electrical lines out this far. Her gaze swiveled and she saw the diesel generator. But it wasn't on. It was a backup, clearly.

So where was the primary power?

She drifted to her right to get a better look behind the cabin.

That's when she saw where a large field of solar panels was arrayed. That was overkill, she thought. Enough energy to power a place ten times this size. There would be underground lines taking the power to the cabin.

To the left of the cabin and fifty yards back was a barn. Solar probably fed that too.

Totally off the grid. Makes sense.

Reel didn't think there were cows or horses in that barn.

A dusty, late-model four-door Jeep sat in front of the cabin. Local plates. Gun rack in the back with a rifle and scope hanging on it.

She started to move forward, then thought better of it. Keeping behind a tree, she lifted a slender metal object from her pocket, fired it up, and pointed it in front of her at near ground level. The invisible laser lines became visible. Trip field. Alert only? Or maybe booby-trapped.

There could be IEDs all over this place, with the owner the only one knowing where they were.

Reel stayed where she was, contemplating how she was going to pierce this perimeter. There were ways; she just had to come up with the right one.

As she watched, the front door of the cabin opened.

Maybe the problem would solve itself.

CHAPTER

39

I<small>T WAS AN EIGHTEEN-HOUR DRIVE</small> to Arkansas where Roy West had taken up residence. Robie only stopped for gas and to use the bathroom. He ate from provisions he had taken with him from his safe house.

The sun had risen as he pulled to a stop at what he calculated to be five miles from his final destination.

He looked around. He had passed civilization about two hours ago and was officially in no-man's-land. He hadn't even seen another house in a half hour. The terrain was both rocky and lush. The roads—well, there didn't seem to be many of them. And the ones there were had gone from asphalt to gravel and now to dirt.

Robie checked his watch. He had gained one hour by entering the central time zone. He hoped it was worth it. He was tired, but not exhausted.

He rolled down the window and breathed in the crisp air.

He had traveled over mountains and flatlands.

He was back in the mountains.

Arnie had said Roy West had worked at the agency. Reel had apparently been interested in a document that Robie assumed West had authored. This meant something to Reel. Something important.

And where was Reel? Already here?

He looked around again. Lots of places to hide. If the place he was going to was this remote, there was no way he could get to it unseen if he just continued to drive.

So he had to leave his truck behind.

He liked to be on foot better.

A truck was a big target at which to shoot.

Robie parked his vehicle well off the road, changed into cammie gear, and also blacked his face. He slung his gear pack over his bag and set off. He had memorized the directions to West's house. He was going to treat this like any other mission.

But unlike every other mission, he didn't have a clear goal when he got to his destination. He didn't know if West would turn out to be a friend or foe. He had no idea if he had just driven into a trap somehow orchestrated by Jessica Reel.

The terrain was rugged, but he traversed it easily. He had trained for years for missions like this. And even at age forty he floated over the rock and through the hilly terrain with the agility of an elite athlete in his prime.

He counted down the miles in his head. As he

drew closer to what might be ground zero his grip tightened on his primary weapon, his sniper rifle.

He had two other weapons in his pack, with enough ammo to take on a lot of guns on the other side. The weapons had been chosen for different scenarios.

His MP5 was for close-quarters battle against superior numbers. Its auto-fire selector could lay down opponents at a ferocious rate.

His Ka-Bar knife was for killing hand-to-hand. He could use it to slice or gut with equal efficiency.

His Glock rode in the shoulder holster. He never went anywhere without the weapon. It was like his third arm.

And he had a special type of ordnance in his gear pack. It was his fail-safe.

He reached a clearing and took the opportunity to snag his binoculars from his gear pack and take a good long look around from the vantage point of high ground.

There was not much around here that he could see other than nature. Then he spied it. A chimney poking out from a break in the trees. There was a dirt road full of switchbacks running up to it. He couldn't see the house attached to it.

Robie saw no smoke coming from the chimney, but the temperature wasn't that cold, so someone could still be there without needing to build a fire. And in his mental map that house was his destination, the abode of Roy West.

He kept looking in a wide arc through his optics. He finally set his binoculars down and looked through the scope on his sniper rifle, which was far more powerful than the binoculars.

He wasn't just looking for West or whoever else might be with him. He was looking for Reel. For Robie was now certain of one thing.

The woman was here.

He could just feel it.

CHAPTER

40

THE MAN STEPPED OUT OF the cabin.

Roy West was around forty, a wick under six feet, and a sturdy two hundred pounds. His fingers were long and leathery, his face the same. A mustache and beard covered his lip and jaw respectively. He had on Army combat boots, jeans tucked into them, a flannel shirt, and a corduroy vest with built-in shotgun shell holders.

He drew a remote from his pocket and hit the button. The laser trip field powered down and disappeared. He had parked his Jeep in a spot that the laser field would not intersect.

From her hiding place Reel watched him approach the vehicle, following every step he took. She had been right, the place was booby-trapped. West was carefully pacing out a zigzag path to the Jeep.

As he touched the door of the vehicle Reel said, "We need to talk, Roy."

He whirled, the gun appearing in his hand seemingly from thin air.

The MP5 fired on full auto before he could point his pistol at her. The rear door of the Jeep was shredded by the barrage, which pierced the metal and tore up the inside of the vehicle.

West threw himself on the hood of the Jeep.

"Next burst goes into you," said Reel. "Gun, down. Now. Not asking again."

West dropped the gun.

"Turn to me, hands over head, fingers laced. Eyes down. You look up, a bullet goes into your right eye."

He turned, his fingers wrapped around his head, his gaze down.

"What do you want?" he said, his voice shaky.

"Walk over here. Just don't trip on an IED."

He looked startled at this comment, but walked toward her, clearing the minefield and stopping two feet from her.

"Can I look up?"

"No. Get on the ground, facedown, arms and legs spread."

He complied.

She stood within a foot of him but still behind cover.

"I've got a guy in the cabin with a rifle trained on you," he said.

"Don't think so."

"You can't take that chance."

"Yes I can. I'm standing behind a tree. And if your 'guy' didn't show himself after my bullet barrage, he's a chickenshit and not worth my time worrying about."

"Who the hell are you and what do you want?"

"Who I am is irrelevant. What I want to know is this." She pulled a sheaf of papers from her duster and tossed them in the dirt next to him.

"Can I look at it without you shooting me?" he asked.

"Just move your arms very, very slowly."

He did so and gripped the pages. He pulled them close and read down the first page.

"So what?"

"You wrote it?" she asked.

"What if I did?"

"Why?"

"It was my job. My old job."

"I checked into your new job. You run your own militia."

West snorted. "We're not a militia. We're freedom fighters."

"Who are you fighting for freedom from?"

"If you have to ask you wouldn't understand the answer."

Reel frowned. "The big bad government? You live

in the middle of nowhere. You have your guns. You've got your own place. You're off the grid. No one's bothering you that I can see. So what's the problem?"

"It's only a matter of time before they come for us. And believe me, we'll be ready."

"You know what your paper said. Do you believe it?"

"Of course."

"You think it could actually happen?" she asked.

"I *know* it could. Because we're so lackadaisical about security. Only they didn't have the balls in D.C. to admit that. It seemed to me that the higher-ups *wanted* the assholes to attack us. One of the reasons I quit. I was disgusted."

"So you think this is the path to a peaceful future?"

"I never said a peaceful future was the goal. Our *having* a future is the goal. You lead by force. You kick the shit out of them. You don't just sit around and wait for them to attack you. Clusters of powder, we called them. They think security is impenetrable. Well, my paper showed them how impenetrable it was. It was bullshit."

"So you were tasked to do doomsday scenarios?" asked Reel.

"We had a whole office doing nothing but. Most of the others did the same old crap. Nothing outside the box. They were worried about ruffling feathers. Not me. You give me a job, I do it. I don't give a shit about consequences."

"Who did you submit the white paper to?"

"That's classified," retorted West.

"You're not with the government anymore," countered Reel.

"Still classified."

"I thought the government was the enemy."

"Right now, *you're* the enemy. And if you think you're going to get away from here alive, you're beyond stupid."

"You the law out here? You and your freedom fighters?"

"Pretty much. Why do you think I moved here?"

"Who did you submit it to?" she asked again.

"What are you going to do, torture me?" he sneered.

"I don't have time to torture you. Although you would find it memorable. If you don't tell me I'll just shoot you."

"In cold blood," he scoffed. "You're a woman."

"That should tell you all you need to know to be afraid."

West laughed. "You think a lot of your gender, don't you?"

"You were a desk jockey your whole career. You never fired a shot and never had a shot fired at you. The closest you ever got to danger was watching the video feed from a thousand miles away. Did that make you feel like a real man instead of the ball-less punk you really are?"

He started to jump up, but Reel placed a round an inch from his right ear, so close that bits of the hard dirt kicked up and struck his ear, which started bleeding.

He screamed, "You stupid bitch, you shot me!"

"Dirt, not metal. You'd feel the difference. Now spread your legs wider."

"What?"

"Spread your legs wider."

"Why?"

"Do it or I promise dirt will not be the next thing you feel."

West spread his legs wider.

Reel moved behind him and lined up her shot with her Glock.

"What the hell are you doing?" he cried out, panicked.

"Which testicle do you want to keep? But I have to tell you, at this angle, there's no guarantee I won't nail both of them with the one shot."

He immediately snapped his legs together.

"Then you'll get it right up the ass," she said. "I don't think it'll feel any better."

"Why the hell are you doing this?" he screamed.

"It's pretty simple. I asked for a name. You didn't give me one."

"I didn't officially submit it to anyone."

"Unofficially, then," said Reel.

"What does it matter?"

"Because it seems that some folks took you at your word and are going to try to do it."

"Really?"

"Don't sound so happy. It's insane. Now the name. I won't ask again."

"It was only a code name," said West.

"Bullshit."

"I swear to God."

"Why submit unofficially to a code name? And your answer better make sense or you're going to need a new way to evacuate your bowels."

"The person came to me."

"What person?" she asked.

"I meant electronically they came to me. They somehow found out I had written a comprehensive, groundbreaking scenario. It was vindication."

It disgusted Reel to see how animated he suddenly was in talking about his "accomplishments."

"When did this happen?"

"About two years ago." He added, "Are they really doing it? I mean who?"

"What was the code name?"

He didn't answer.

"You have one second. Now!"

"Roger the Dodger," he shouted.

"And why submit to Roger the Dodger?" she asked calmly, keeping her finger on the Glock's trigger guard.

"His electronic signature showed he had top-top-secret clearance and was at least three levels above me. He wanted to know what I had come up with. He said the scuttlebutt was my plan was revolutionary."

"How would he have known that if you hadn't even submitted it to anyone yet?"

The man hesitated and said sheepishly, "Maybe I talked a bit about it at the bar we would go to for drinks after work."

"No wonder the government kicked your ass out. You're an idiot."

"I would have quit anyway," he snapped.

"Right. To come to a little cabin in the middle of this craphole."

"This is *real* America, bitch!"

"Your doomsday paper was pretty specific."

He said proudly, "Country by country, leader by leader, step by step. It was all in the timing. It was a perfect jigsaw puzzle. I spent two years figuring it out. Every contingency. Everything that could go wrong. Everything was accounted for."

"Not everything."

"That's impossible," he snapped.

"You didn't account for me."

Reel heard the noises before he did. But when he did he smiled.

"Your time is up, little lady."

"I'm not little. And I've never been a lady."

Her boot came down on the back of his head, bouncing it off the hard dirt and knocking him out cold. She grabbed the pages and stuffed them back into her duster.

Reel retraced West's safe path to the cabin and gave it the quick once-over. There were stacks of weapons, ammo, grenades, packs of C-4, Semtex, and other plastic explosives. Through a window looking out on the back porch she saw fifty-gallon drums of what looked to be gasoline and maybe fertilizer. She doubted they were for the generator or to grow crops. She figured the barn was probably full of those containers as well.

She also glimpsed detailed plans of attack on major cities in the United States. These folks were domestic terrorists of the worst kind. She grabbed anything that looked like it might be important, including a USB stick plugged into his laptop, and stuffed them in her coat pockets.

She also snagged a couple grenades. A "lady" could never have too many grenades.

She ran back out, raced over to his Jeep, threw open the rear door, and pulled out the scoped rifle and a box of ammo in the cargo pad.

She hustled back to her Explorer, jumped in, and peeled out. But before she got to the main road, she realized it was too late. When she saw what was coming at her, she had no option other than turning around and heading back toward the cabin.

It looked like a few precious seconds were going to end up costing Reel her life.

CHAPTER

41

REEL PUSHED THE GAS PEDAL to the floor and the Explorer roared up the twisting gravel drive. In her mind she was planning her attack. When outnumbered, retreat wasn't always an option. Superior forces rarely expected an outgunned opponent to charge at them.

Reel wasn't going to exactly do that. She was going for a modified version of an all-out assault.

She checked the rearview mirror and gauged the distance between her and the massive Denali chasing her. It was full of what she presumed were wackos posing as freedom fighters, and she presumed they were all heavily armed.

Well, she would find out exactly how heavily armed they were in a few seconds. And how well they handled their weapons. She just hoped the feint she was planning worked.

She gained the separation she needed, lowered the window halfway, and skidded the Ford to a stop, leaving it blocking the road. She grabbed the rifle, rested the barrel on top of the half-lowered window, took aim, and shot out the front tires on the Denali. For good measure she put a round through the front grille. Steam started to pour out and the Denali ground to a halt.

The doors opened and men jumped out gripping a variety of weapons.

Pistols and subguns did not concern her. They didn't have the range to hurt her.

They opened fire but nothing came close to her.

She shot three times and three of the shooters fell, all with nonfatal wounds, which was intentional on her part. She just wanted them out of the action. And there was a sense of fairness as well. She didn't have to kill them and so she let them live but in no condition to fight.

She shifted her attention to another man who jumped out on the left side of the Denali. He was holding a scoped rifle.

That could reach her. So Reel put him down with one shot to the forehead. He fell backward and the rifle spun out of his dead hands. No one went to retrieve it.

The men, probably wondering what the hell they had gotten themselves into, retreated to the back of the Denali, using the big vehicle as a shield.

But through her scope Reel could see some of them pulling cell phones out.

They were calling in reinforcements.

Ironically, that was what she wanted. It would give her the time to proceed with part two of her plan. She gunned the engine and headed toward the cabin.

A few moments later she skidded to a stop a good distance from the cabin behind a stand of trees and leapt out. She pulled the grenades from her pocket, ran toward the cabin, pulled the pins, and threw the grenades through the structure's front window.

She was turning back to run to the Explorer when Roy West plowed into her.

Reel managed to keep her feet, but he had one hand wrapped around her throat. He assumed that with his superior size and strength the battle was over.

West could not have been more wrong.

Reel twisted her body to the left, breaking his grip around her throat. At the same time she brought her knee up between his legs, with devastating results. West's face turned purple, his knees buckled, and he grabbed his crotch. She slammed her right elbow into his left temple. He screamed, gasped, and started to fall away from her. But his foot accidentally hooked her leg and Reel fell too, him on top of her.

Before they hit the dirt the grenades detonated. And so did every other explosive and flammable material in the cabin. The roof blew twenty feet in the air and pieces of wood, metal, and glass became deadly shrapnel flying out in all directions at super-sonic speed.

Reel felt the impact of some of this debris collide with West's thick body. Hundreds of dull thuds, actually. His face turned white, then gray, and then blood started to pour from his mouth and nose.

Ironically, he had become her shield.

Reel rolled to her right, throwing the now dead man off her. She staggered up and looked at the flames and thick plumes of dark smoke rising up into the sky. She looked down at her clothes. The duster was shredded and covered in West's blood. Reel had not escaped unscathed either. She had cuts on her face and hands, and there was a dull pain in her right leg from where West had fallen on her. But she was alive.

She looked at the barn. The flames would reach that structure very soon. She didn't want to be around to witness or feel that flame ball.

She jumped into the Ford, backed up, and gunned it.

She heard vehicles racing up the road. The reinforcements had come. And with the explosion they would concentrate all their attention on the cabin.

That had been her intent when she had blown it up.

She knew exactly where she was headed next. When you built a cabin in the middle of nowhere and filled it with explosives and plans of mass destruction, you would never be content with simply one road in and out. If the authorities came, you had to have another form of escape.

And Reel, who had been looking for just such a route, had spied it on the way in when she had done her recon.

A logging road to the east. That was her exit. Unfortunately, two vehicles were blocking her path out. Along with a dozen men with enough firepower to tangle on equal footing with a fully equipped Army squad. They had outflanked her.

So this was it.

CHAPTER

42

REEL SAT IN THE FORD and stared down at the men. They were arrayed in two defensive positions that could quickly be modified to offensive scenarios. They were dressed in makeshift uniforms, cammie pants, muscle shirts. Most were large, with fatty, bench-press-swollen chests and shoulders and bulging guts.

They were pointing sniper rifles, shotguns, pistols, and MP5s at her. When they opened fire, which they looked prepared to do right now, the first volley would wipe her out.

This was not how Reel imagined dying. Not at the hands of jerks who looked like they were barely one evolutionary step removed from cavemen.

In the distance there was an explosion. That must have been the barn going up, she thought. She fingered her pistol. She could hit the gas and make a run at them, but the odds of her breaking through the blockade were not good. A quick calculation in her head put her survival rate at less than five percent.

Then she heard vehicles moving in behind her. She glanced at the rearview mirror and saw two more trucks and ten more militiamen slide in less than a hundred yards behind her.

Now she was outgunned *and* outflanked.

My survival rate just dropped to zero.

She pulled her gun and stepped from the truck. She had decided she was not going down without a fight. They would never be able to say that about her.

The men took careful aim and their fingers went to their triggers. They would have her dead center in a lethal field of fire.

She gave a small shake of the head, and even managed a smile.

"*Finito*," she whispered to herself.

"Go to hell!" she shouted at the militiamen as she raised her gun for what would certainly be the last time.

That's when the first explosion hit.

Caught off guard, Reel instinctively ducked and rolled under the truck. Her first thought was that one of the idiot militia guys had dropped a grenade and blown himself up.

When she looked back it seemed that this was indeed the case. The trucks on her forward flank were on fire, the men there dead, dazed, or scattered.

But then from the corner of her eye she saw a shot originate from a ridge to her left. It impacted with the side of one of the trucks on her rear flank. Its fuel tank ignited and lifted the two-ton truck three feet into the air, scattering lethal bits of metal in all directions.

Six of the men there were gutted where they stood and dropped, never to fight again. Then the gunfire opened up. But they weren't firing at her. They were firing up at the ridge.

Reel looked out from under the truck. The sunlight was in her eyes, but she slid a bit to the right and the glare vanished. She grabbed her binoculars from her pocket, clapped them to her eyes, and spun the focus lever.

She saw the muzzle of a sniper rifle. And not just any sniper rifle. She had one just like it. A customized job that only had a few patrons.

The gun fired once, twice, three times.

Reel looked back and saw three men drop to the dirt, dead.

She stared back up the ridge. The man was moving so fast and so low to the ground that he resembled a cougar going after prey.

Her jaw sagged. It was Will Robie.

She marveled at his ability to maneuver so fluidly through the rough terrain. Then she wondered why he was giving up the high ground.

She stopped wondering with what he did next.

He fired a round into the fuel tank of the second

truck on her rear flank. He'd had to move to get a sight line on the tank. He must have been chambering incendiary rounds, because this truck exploded too. Three more men died and the survivors ran for it, disappearing down the road in full retreat.

Robie stopped, pivoted, and then rapid-fired with his sniper rifle at the remaining men on the forward flank.

Acquire a target and fire. Acquire a target and fire. It was like taking breaths, as natural and seamless as could be. Reel counted off each shot and with each round fired, a man fell. Robie never once missed. It was a man against children.

They took cover and fired back. But even though he was outgunned it was like Robie had the superior firepower. While the militia shot wildly, their adrenaline and fear making it unlikely they would hit anything, Robie aimed and fired with such calm efficiency that it was like he was playing a video game and could hit reset anytime he wanted.

After another minute of this slaughter the remaining militia on the forward flank were in full-scale retreat.

That left just the two of them.

Reel looked back at Robie. He stood on a small knoll staring down at her.

She came out from under the truck and held her pistol loosely at her side.

He had dropped his rifle. His Glock was in his right hand. He held it loosely too.

Reel looked at the burning carnage and the dead bodies and then back at Robie.

"Thanks."

Robie took a few more steps forward and then stopped. He was nearly at level ground, sixty yards from her.

They both knew the same thing.

Twenty more yards of closure and their Glocks would easily be in kill range.

"You could have just let them kill me," she said. "More than twenty to one, inevitable. Keep your hands clean."

"Wasn't on my option board." Robie glanced at one of the dead men. "Who are they?"

"Militiamen. And not very capable ones."

He nodded. "Did you kill Jacobs and Gelder?"

Reel drew a few yards closer and stopped. She glanced at Robie's hands. They hadn't moved. But it would only take a second for that to change and the Glock to fire.

"How did you know to come here?" she asked.

"Friend of a friend. Didn't know if you'd be here or not. I was looking for West."

"Why?"

"Because you were looking for him."

Reel said nothing. She just stared at his gun hand.

"You don't have to send any more cryptic texts, Jessica. I'm here. So tell me what the hell is going on."

"It's complicated, Will."

"Then let's start out simple. Did you kill them?"

Robie walked forward another five yards. They were now right on the cusp.

Neither of them was holding their Glocks loosely now. The muscles in their trigger hands were flexed tight. But the fingers were still on the trigger guards.

"You haven't changed much, Will."

"Apparently you have," said Robie. "Roy West? Where is he? With the pile of bodies?"

She shook her head. "Not those piles. But he's still dead."

"You killed him too?"

"He did himself in. It's dangerous to fill your house with explosives. Like living with rattlesnakes."

"Why did you need to find West?"

"He had something I needed."

"A document?" asked Robie.

Her face flashed concern. "How did you know about that?"

"Did you get it?"

"I already had the document and I've read it. I wanted more info, but I didn't get it."

"So all this was a waste?" he said.

They both glanced sideways. In the far distance a sound could be heard. Sirens. Even in the middle of

nowhere explosions and gunfire drew the police eventually.

She looked back at him. "I know what you've been
tasked to do," she said.

"And I'm giving you a chance to explain."

"So explanation before execution?"

"That depends solely on the explanation."

The sirens were drawing closer. Each singsong
screech burst the quiet like artillery rounds.

He added, "And we're running out of time."

"I'm not a traitor."

"That's good to know. Now prove it."

"I don't have proof. Not yet."

Their fingers slipped near their respective triggers.
They each took two steps forward. It was simultane-
ous but not choreographed. They were now squarely
in their Glocks' kill zones.

Robie frowned. "You're going to have to do better
than that. I've got a dead number two and another
agency grunt on a slab. Under normal circumstances,
that would be enough, so this is taking me out of my
comfort zone. So talk to me. Now."

The sirens sounded almost on top of them.

"Gelder and Jacobs were the traitors."

"How?"

"They killed somebody. Somebody that meant a
lot to me."

"Why?" asked Robie.

"Because he was going to expose their plot."

"Which was?"

The sirens were deafening now. It seemed like every cop in Arkansas had been called in.

"I don't have time to explain now."

"I'm not sure you have a choice, Jessica."

"What does it matter? You have your orders, Will."

"I don't always follow them. Just like you."

"You almost always follow them."

"You sent me the texts. You said everything you did has a reason. I just had to open the lock. So tell me what you meant! But there are no guarantees, Jessica. None. Not even if your explanation makes sense. That's just the way it has to be."

They were no longer looking at each other. Their gazes were on each other's hands. Hands with guns were what killed, while eyes were just points of deception; it was a lesson learned too late for the fool who stopped looking at the fingers.

"How do I know I can trust you?" she said. "Sending you texts is one thing. But it troubles me greatly that you were able to find me and this place so fast." She glanced up at him, daring to take her gaze off his gun hand. "It makes me think you had help. Agency help. So it comes back down to, how do I know I can trust you?"

"You can't know that, not for sure. Just like I don't know if I can trust you."

"I'm not sure that gets us anywhere, Will."

He saw her gun hand tighten just a bit.

"It doesn't have to go down like this, Jessica."

"You'd think, wouldn't you? But it probably will go down just like this."

"Roy West was an analyst who got canned. What's so important about him?" There was more urgency in Robie's voice, because the sirens were growing so close that he was afraid they would have to engage in a gun battle with the cops just to escape. "And talk fast."

She said, "He's a bad guy but a good writer."

"What exactly did he write? The document?"

"The apocalypse," she replied.

They could now hear the screech of tires in addition to the sirens.

"The apocalypse? Explain that."

"Not enough time, Will. You'll just have to trust me."

"That's asking a lot. Too much."

"I didn't ask for your help."

"Then why the texts?"

She started to say something but then stopped. "I guess I didn't want you to think I'd gone bad." She paused, but only for a second. "I'm sorry, Will."

Before he could answer Reel fired. Not at Robie, but at one of the militiamen, who wasn't quite dead yet and was set to shoot at them. He dropped back to the ground for good with one of her rounds in his head.

When Reel turned back Robie had his pistol aimed at her head, with both hands wrapped around the Glock's butt. His finger hovered over the trigger. She had no chance now. Her pistol dangled uselessly at her side.

The sirens were screaming in their ears now.

"Close your eyes, Jessica."

"I'd prefer to keep them open."

"I said close your eyes. I won't ask again."

Reel slowly closed her eyes. She braced herself for the impact of the round. Robie would only need one shot. She could count on him for that. Her death would be instant. But she still wondered how it would feel.

Seconds went by but there was no shot.

She finally opened her eyes.

Will Robie was gone.

43

REEL JUMPED INTO HER TRUCK, gunned the engine, and made her way back to the main road on a route that took her away from the sirens and screeches.

She finally hit firm asphalt, slammed down the gas pedal, and the Ford hurtled down the road. She was twenty miles away and could no longer see the smoke plume above the tree line before she slowed the vehicle to under eighty.

She pulled off the road, disassembled her weapons, stowed them away in her bag, and drove back toward the airport. Along the way she slipped into a car wash and got most of the dirt off the Ford, although there were some scratches and dents that hadn't been there before. She drove on and reached the airport.

When she turned the rental back in the attendant didn't even look at the vehicle. He noted her gas and mileage and printed out her receipt.

"Fast trip," he said.

"Yeah."

"Hope you enjoyed your time here. We're known for our slower pace and peace and quiet."

"Better rethink that," said Reel as she walked toward the bus that would take her to the terminal.

She changed back into her old woman's disguise in the restroom and boarded the next flight east.

When they were wheels up and the sun was burning down into the horizon, Reel put her seat back, closed her eyes, and thought about what she had learned.

Someone with top-top-secret clearance, at least three levels above Roy West, had read that white paper.

That was two years ago. The level and clearances could have changed. In fact, they most certainly had changed. The person would be higher-placed now. That was both instructive and problematic.

Had it been Gelder? Two years ago he would have been easily at least three levels above someone like Roy West, if not more.

But that was assuming West had told her the truth. She had no way to verify that there even was someone with the code name Roger the Dodger.

But she knew the white paper existed. She knew the plan set forth in that paper was being executed. She knew some of the people who were trying to execute it.

She had killed two of them and tried to kill a third.

But I don't know all of them.

And if she didn't know all of them there was no way she could truly stop it.

She looked out the window.

An hour later, as they flew east, it was dark. And in that vast blackness all Reel could see was hopelessness.

She had gone all that way, nearly been killed, and really had nothing to show for it. But she did, actually. She turned her mind to what was really important about this trip.

It was the man.

She still couldn't quite comprehend what had happened out there. The killing that had taken place was, for her, routine. Dead bodies, explosions, devastation. That was her world. But this was something different.

She closed her eyes and the image of Will Robie instantly appeared. He was pointing his gun at her head. He was telling her to close her eyes so he wouldn't have to face her for the kill shot.

But he hadn't fired. He had let her live.

He had let her escape.

She had been surprised by this. No, she had been stunned by this.

Exactly what she had been surprised by was an emotion she had never encountered in her work.

Mercy.

Will Robie, the most accomplished assassin of his generation, had shown her mercy.

When she had seen Robie killing her enemy for her, Reel had thought it just possible that he would become her ally. That they would finish this together. That had been a ludicrous thought. This was her fight. Not his.

And yet he had let her live. And escape.

His mission would have been complete. The agency would have lauded his performance. Maybe he would have been promoted out of fieldwork, or been given extensive time off. He would have bagged their number one problem, in record time.

And he had just let her walk away.

She had always admired Will Robie. He was the calm, cool professional who did his work and never talked about a single triumph. And yet she saw an infinite sadness in the man, which she could never quite get her arms around. She saw that very same emotional state in herself.

They were a lot alike, she and Robie.

And he had let her live.

Killers didn't do that. Killers never did that. Reel wasn't sure, if the positions were reversed, that she would have let Robie walk away.

I probably would have shot him.

And maybe she had lied to Robie. About not wanting his help. She actually did want his assistance, because it had finally struck her that she couldn't possibly accomplish this alone. So she had failed.

And now something happened that had not happened to Jessica Reel since she was a young girl.

Tears slid from her eyes and down her cheeks.

She closed her eyes again. And didn't open them
until the plane touched down.

When she did open them, she still couldn't see
anything very clearly.

CHAPTER

44

TWO HUNDRED MILES. Robie drove this distance without stopping. He headed directly east, which was the direction he needed to go. But finally, even his iron will broke down and he had to stop because he could no longer see the road.

He checked into a motel right off the highway, paid for his room in cash, and slept for eighteen straight hours to make up for a week of barely being able to sleep at all.

It was the heaviest sleep he'd had in years.

When he woke it was fully dark again. He had lost nearly a day of his life.

But he could have easily lost his life a day earlier.

He found a diner and ravenously ate two meals in one. He couldn't seem to get enough to eat or drink. When he set his coffee cup down for the last time and rose from the table he felt his energy returning.

He sat in his truck in the parking lot, staring at the dashboard.

He'd had Reel lined up in his gunsight. One trigger pull and it would have been over. Reel dead. His mission accomplished. All worries gone.

His finger had actually slipped to the trigger. Every other time in his entire professional life when his finger had gone to that point he had fired.

Every single time.

Except that time.

Jessica Reel.

He had ordered her to close her eyes. When he had done so Robie was fully committed to making the kill shot.

And walking away.

To let someone else figure this whole thing out. He was just the triggerman. All he had to do was pull the damn trigger.

And I didn't.

Once before in his life he had failed to make the shot. It had turned out to be the right decision.

Robie didn't know if that would be so in this case.

Reel looked different. Not totally, just subtly. But that was enough. Most people were terrible observers. And even those good at observing were not very adept at it. Reel had done just enough to beat the odds that someone would spot her. Not too much. Not too little. Just enough.

Robie would have done the same thing in her position.

And by not pulling the trigger maybe I am in her position now.

He drove back to the motel, went to his room, stripped down, and stood in the shower, letting the water wash off the grit he felt over every part of his body.

But the water couldn't get to his brain, where it felt like muck a foot deep had gathered, dulling his senses, obstructing his ability to think clearly.

He dried off and dressed. He leaned against the wall and slammed both hands into it so hard he felt the drywall crack. He dropped fifty bucks on the bed to repair the wall and grabbed his bag.

He had a long drive ahead of him. He had better get to it.

He switched on the radio when he reached the interstate highway. The news was full of it. A massacre on a lonely ridge in the middle of nowhere, Arkansas. No one was talking, but apparently rival militias had had a go at each other. A cabin had been blown up. Trucks too. Men lay dead.

One of them was identified as Roy West, a former intelligence analyst in D.C. When and why he had headed to Arkansas and taken up his new life of guns and bombs was as yet unknown. There were intimations that folks from D.C. were heading to the site now to begin an investigation.

Robie looked up, almost expecting to see a government jet fly over en route to the crime scene.

As the news went off in other directions, Robie thought more about what Reel had told him.

West had written the apocalypse. What exactly did that mean?

West had worked at the agency. His official title had been "analyst." That could cover lots of different things. Most analysts whom Robie had encountered spent their days on real-time issues. But there were some who didn't.

Robie had heard that the agency had papers written on lots of different scenarios. They took into account the changing geopolitical landscape. These white papers would almost all end up on the shredder pile, unexecuted and largely forgotten. But maybe West's hadn't ended up on that pile. Maybe someone was taking it seriously.

Writing the apocalypse.

Reel had risked a lot to come out here. If Robie hadn't been there too she would be dead. Reel was a first-class killer with few peers. But she had been outgunned more than twenty to one. Even the best trained person could not survive that.

If she knew that West wrote the apocalypse, this meant she had either read the paper or knew of its contents. In fact, she'd said she had the document. So she probably hadn't come out here to ask West about it. Robie doubted she cared what his inspiration or reason was for doing it.

So what then?

He drove on for fifteen more miles before the answer hit him.

She wanted to know who he'd given the report to.

If it hadn't gone through official channels, then it could have gone to someone who wasn't official. That must have been what Reel wanted. The name of the person or persons who had seen the apocalypse paper.

More miles went by. Robie stopped for gas and another meal. He sat at the counter, his attention focused on the food in front of him, but his mind racing well beyond the confines of the roadside diner.

There was her shot list.

Jacobs first. Gelder next. She said they were traitors.

She also said there were others.

But she had killed Jacobs and Gelder before she'd come out to see Roy West. So she had to know they were part of the apocalypse paper before she'd confronted West.

That could only mean one thing.

Robie had lifted the glass of iced tea to his lips but then slowly set it down without drinking.

There had to be someone else out there. Maybe more than one who knew about the paper, who were perhaps actively pursuing its goals but were still unknown to Reel.

She was methodically killing off these conspirators—that was how Robie naturally started to think of them—but her list was incomplete.

So many more questions assailed him now, chief of which was why and how Reel had become involved in all this. What was the catalyst that had prompted her to risk everything to do what she was doing?

He had looked the woman in the eyes. He had come away with a definite conclusion.

This was not simply another mission. This was personal.

And if Robie was right about that, there had to be a reason. No, there had to be a person involved who made it personal for her. She said they had killed someone who meant a lot to her. And he or she had been killed because they were going to expose the plot.

Robie had lots of questions and no answers. But he knew one thing.

An apocalypse was never how you wanted it to end.

CHAPTER

45

CHILDREN WHOOPING. Balloons all the colors of the rainbow. Presents that each cost well into three figures.

Judge Samuel Kent looked around the room and smiled at the antics of the elementary school–age kids in the large sunroom where the birthday party was taking place. Kent had married later in life, and his youngest child was a guest here at the home of a well-heeled lobbyist who made his money by selling whatever needed selling on Capitol Hill.

Kent's wife, nearly twenty years younger, was not in attendance. A spa trip to Napa Valley with her girlfriends had taken priority over her son's friend's party. Yet Kent was happy to fill in. It gave him certain opportunities.

He scanned the room once more and nodded his head.

The man walked briskly toward him.

He was taller than Kent, running to flab, and his

hair was receding rapidly. And though it was a party, he wasn't smiling. He looked, in fact, like he was going to be sick.

"Howard?" said Kent, holding out his hand, which the other man quickly shook. His skin was clammy.

Congressman Howard Decker said, "We need to talk."

Kent smiled and indicated a large piñata hanging from the ceiling in one corner of the room. "I don't want to be here when they start attacking that thing. Shall we take a walk outside? The garden is very impressive."

The two men went out the French doors and started strolling through the elaborate gardens that covered the better part of three acres. There was a pool, a guesthouse, an outdoor stone pavilion, a reflecting pond, benches and gates and side gardens, and a potting shed. Both men were wealthy and thus felt right at home in such a palatial setting.

When they were well away from the house in an isolated stretch of the property, they stopped walking.

Kent said, "How're things on the Hill?"

"That's not what I want to talk about and you know it."

"I do know, Howard. I'm just trying to keep your nerves from running away with you. Poker faces are important."

"And you're not concerned? I understand she nearly got you," said Decker.

"We were prepared. The only problem was she was more nimble than we thought."

"You know Roy West is dead."

"Neither significant nor relevant," replied Kent.

"Reel?"

"Again, neither significant nor relevant."

"I think she is very significant and relevant. Jacobs, Gelder, you? She has a list. How?" he demanded.

"It's obvious," said Kent. "I trusted Joe Stockwell when I shouldn't have. I thought he was one of us. He wasn't. He fooled me and it cost us."

"So he told Reel?"

Kent nodded, looking thoughtful. "That seems to be the case. Too bad we didn't kill him sooner."

"Why? What's the connection between Stockwell and Reel?"

"I don't know," replied Kent. "But there must have been one. He was with the U.S. Marshals at one point and had good connections. I tried to find what those were after we learned he was spying on us instead of working with us. But a lot of it is classified. I couldn't push too hard without raising suspicions."

"Then we're all compromised. *I'm* probably on that list. He knew about me."

"Yes, you very well could be on the list."

"Reel got to Gelder. He was the number two, for God's sake. What chance do I have?"

"A very good chance. We almost got *her*, Howard.

She has to know the targets are hardened by now. She'll be on the defensive. She'll have to pull back."

"If she killed West, she's hardly on the defensive," countered Howard.

"West wasn't really a hardened target. And we still don't know all the facts. If she did kill him she went there to gain more information."

"And if he gave it to her?"

"He had none to give. She was grasping at straws. That shows how weakened her position is."

"Someone had to tell her about West."

"We're looking into that. But I don't see it as especially important. We have bigger fish to fry."

"West went psycho militia. I would hardly call that not hardened. He had guns and bombs and a bunch of men as crazy as he was. And she still killed him."

"I never said she wasn't capable or dangerous. She is."

"So she could get to me."

"She could get to me too. But we have to play the odds, Howard. And the odds are with us. But at the same time, when we entered into this 'opportunity' we knew it came with risks. You don't set out to do something on this grand a scale without risks."

"What if she knows everything?"

"She doesn't. If she did there are other channels she could have pursued. She knows who is involved. She may know generally what we want to do. She doesn't know the specific target. I would know if she did, trust me."

Howard passed a hand over his forehead, which was wicking off sweat though the day was cool. "It didn't seem as risky when we were planning it."

"Planning something never seems risky. It's in the execution where all the risk comes."

"And that's what Reel has been doing, executing people."

"That's what she does. And she's good at it."

"How do you know so much about it?"

"I wasn't always a judge, Howard."

"Intelligence?"

"Not something I can talk about."

"How did you end up on the bench?"

"A law degree and friends in high places. And it allows me great cover and latitude for other endeavors. But I know what I'm talking about. We'll get through this. Don't for a second think that I'm not counterpunching against Reel. She's good, but she's alone. She can't match our resources."

"She's still out there. She's still alive."

"For now." Kent looked toward the house. "I think they must be getting close to cake and ice cream. We should probably head back. Don't want to disappoint the kiddies."

As the two men walked back to the house, Kent thought about the next move on the game board.

He had not been entirely honest with his nervous congressman.

Reel was a force to be reckoned with; that was certain.

But Kent had bigger problems.

The fact of Jacobs's and Gelder's murders didn't bother him so much. Now that the plan was being executed, it was to his advantage that principal players started dropping. If the plan went awry it was always fellow conspirators who turned and brought you down.

Gelder probably would have held up, but he also had a lot to lose.

Jacobs was a weak link. He was a necessary part of the operation on the ground, but he came up short when real pressure was applied. He would have turned on them. If Reel hadn't killed him Kent would have.

When they were back at the party, Kent glanced sideways at Decker as the ten-year-old birthday boy blew out his candles.

Decker was another weak link.

Kent should have known better than to enlist a congressman, but Decker had his value—his chairmanship of a committee that was of particular use to Kent. Now that value had been utilized and Decker's importance had declined correspondingly.

And there was one other person on board.

He was not a weak link.

Kent, in fact, had to take precautions against this person arriving at the decision that he himself was a liability.

That was his bigger problem. If he was deemed to be a weak link by this partner, then his life was in grave danger. More danger, in fact, than having Reel on his trail.

Kent left the house with his youngster in tow. He watched Decker get into a Town Car with his son. The driver looked capable and was no doubt armed.

But there was only one of him.

Right before Decker climbed into the car he stopped and looked back at Kent.

The judge smiled and waved.

Decker waved back and then got into the car.

Kent climbed into his Jag. He had no guards with him. But he had his son. And from what he knew of Jessica Reel, she wouldn't kill him in front of his boy. That moral compass of hers was his best protection.

Now if he could think of a way to glue his child to him, he'd be fine.

Absent that, he had to find Reel and kill her as quickly as possible.

And he thought he had a way to do just that.

And that plan involved a man named Will Robie.

CHAPTER

46

Robie parked across from the school and waited.

He had returned to the D.C. area, put his truck back in the barn at his isolated old farmhouse, and taken a cab to retrieve his car from the mall.

He hadn't heard from Evan Tucker since he had left the IHOP.

He hadn't heard from anyone since he'd left the IHOP.

He didn't take that as a good sign.

But he hadn't been arrested. He took that as a plus.

He stiffened when Julie came out of the school building and walked to the bus stop. He sat lower in his car and watched her.

She was dressed in her typical kneeless jeans and floppy hoodie and dirty sneakers and carried the same overstuffed backpack. She tucked her long hair behind her ears and stared around.

She wasn't listening to her music on her phone.

She wasn't texting.

She was being observant.

Good, thought Robie. *You have to be, Julie.*

The bus came and she got on. When it pulled off Robie followed. He followed all the way until the bus stopped and Julie got off. Then he watched her make it safely into her home. When she walked inside and the door clicked behind her Robie drove away.

He knew he couldn't do this every day. But right now he just wanted to keep Julie safe. He just wanted to be accomplishing something positive.

He stared down at his phone and decided to just do it. He hit his speed dial.

Two rings later she answered.

"Unbelievable," said Nicole Vance. "Did you misdial?"

He ignored her sarcasm. "You have time to meet?"

"Why?"

"Just to talk."

"You never want to just talk, Robie."

"Today I do. If you don't have time, no worries."

"I can make seven o'clock, not before."

They made arrangements to meet and Robie clicked off.

He had time to do something and he decided to take full advantage of it. He made another phone call and arranged to meet with the man.

He really didn't know what to expect, but he felt it was the path of least resistance. And to the extent that he trusted anyone, he trusted this person.

Thirty minutes later he was sitting across from Blue Man.

"I understand that several days ago you waylaid the director while he was being driven to work," Blue Man said.

"Is that the scuttlebutt here?"

"Is it true?"

"I needed some answers."

"Did you get them?"

"No, that's why I'm here."

"This is all above my pay grade, Robie."

"That's not an excuse I can accept."

Blue Man fiddled with his tie and wouldn't make eye contact.

Robie said, "Are we being recorded here?"

"Probably."

"Then we need to go somewhere else."

"Another IHOP? I heard about that. It's now the stuff of agency lore, in fact," said Blue Man, and he wasn't smiling.

"Let's make it a Starbucks."

Twenty minutes later they walked into the Starbucks, ordered, got their coffees from the barista, and sat down at a table outside that was well away from all the other coffee drinkers. The wind was picking up, but for once it wasn't raining and the sky didn't look overly threatening.

They sipped their coffees and Blue Man huddled in his trench coat. To Robie he looked like a banker out for a cup of expensive perked coffee beans. He didn't seem like a man who made life-and-death decisions. Who dealt with issues of national security as readily as other people made choices for lunch.

Look who's talking, Robie. You may not decide who lives or dies. But you actually pull the trigger.

Robie and Blue Man spent a silent minute looking around at people getting into and out of cars. Going into shops. Coming out with bags. Holding their kids' hands.

Blue Man caught Robie's eye.

"Ever miss it?"

"What?" asked Robie.

"Being part of the normal world."

"Not sure I ever was."

"I was an English lit major at Princeton. I wanted to be the William Styron or Philip Roth of my generation."

"So what happened?"

"I went to a government recruitment session with a friend of mine who was interested in going to work for the FBI. There were some men there at a table with no sign on it. I stopped by to see who they were. Fast-forward well over thirty years and here I am."

"Sorry you didn't end up writing the great American novel?"

"Well, there's some consolation. My world is full of fiction."

"Lies, you mean."

"A difference of no real distinction," said Blue Man. He glanced at Robie's arm and leg. "Have you been back in to get those looked at?"

"Not yet."

"Do it. The last thing we need is you dying from an infection. Do it today. I'll set it up. Same place as last time."

"Okay. Any word on DiCarlo?"

Blue Man frowned. "I understand she has been taken under DHS's jurisdiction."

"That I know. Can you explain to me how that is possible? Because even Tucker wasn't aware of that until I told him."

"I'm not sure I can. Because I'm not sure I understand it either, Robie."

"Is she alive?"

"I would think it inconceivable that DiCarlo would have died and we would not be informed."

"What is DHS's role in all this?"

"They protect the homeland. We, on the other hand, have no authority to operate in this country."

"And that, as you well know, is a long-standing piece of fiction."

"Maybe it was. Maybe it's not anymore."

Robie could see that Blue Man was serious. "That bad?"

"Apparently."

"And the reason?"

"What did DiCarlo tell you that night? Why did she want to meet in the first place?"

"She only had two guards with her. What does that tell you?"

"She felt compromised inside her own agency?"

"Something like that."

"What else?"

Robie drank some of his coffee. "Isn't that enough?"

"Not unless there's more."

"Maybe I'm feeling compromised too."

Blue Man looked away, his features unreadable. "I guess I can understand that."

"Different dynamic, like you said."

"The problem is if none of us trust each other the other side has already won."

"That would be true, if we were sure who was on the other side."

"Jessica Reel?" asked Blue Man.

"What about her?"

"Whose side is she on?"

"I'll tell you what I told Gus Whitcomb. I think it was Reel who saved my ass and DiCarlo's life."

"I thought you were going to say that."

Robie was surprised by this comment and his features showed it. "Why?"

"Because I think Jessica Reel might be on our side."

"And yet she's killed two of our people."

"Follow that out logically, Robie."

"So you're saying that Jacobs and Gelder were not on our side." Reel *had* called them traitors, and Robie was surprised to see that Blue Man was entertaining this possibility. He was usually an agency man through and through.

"That's right. If Reel is actually on our side."

"And you're saying that's true?"

"I'm saying it's possible."

"Then the number two at the agency is a traitor?"

"Possibly. But then a traitor can have many different definitions. And agendas."

"Who else thinks this?"

"I haven't talked to anyone other than you about it. If you hadn't suggested leaving the office I was going to. These are not statements I make lightly, Robie. I hope you know that. This is probably not a lone turncoat who does it for money like Aldrich Ames or Robert Hanssen. This might be systemic, and I don't think the motivation is simply money."

"So if they are traitors, who were they working for? And what were they working on? And how did Reel find out?"

"All good questions, and I have no answers for you."

"And DHS's involvement?"

"Others must suspect there's a problem. They might have taken DiCarlo for safekeeping."

"And Evan Tucker?"

"He must be a very worried man about now. Did you tell him about Reel being at DiCarlo's?"

Robie nodded.

Blue Man took a long drink of coffee. "Then he's probably more worried than I thought."

"You heard about Roy West?"

Blue Man nodded. "Apparently he went way off the grid and into the world of paranoid lunacy."

"He was an analyst. What exactly did he analyze?"

"Why do you want to know? You don't think it has anything to do with—"

"I can't afford to discount anything right now."

"He was nothing special. Had a rep for writing nonsense scenario papers. Probably why he was let go. I don't see how he plays into this."

Robie wanted to tell him exactly how West and Reel played into this, but he didn't. "Tucker wanted me to keep going after Reel."

"And what did you say to that?"

"I said no."

"No one will ever have to tell you to grow a pair, Robie."

"The question is, what do I do now?"

"You did not hear this from me," replied Blue Man.

"Okay."

"If I were Will Robie, I would think about going off the grid."

"And do what?"

"Find Jessica Reel. And if you do, you might just find all the answers."

I did find her, Robie thought. *And I let her go.*

Blue Man finished his coffee and rose. "And then you can do something else, Robie."

Robie looked up at him. "What's that?"

"Isn't it obvious? You can thank Reel for saving your life."

After Blue Man walked off, Robie muttered, "Too late. I already returned the favor."

CHAPTER

47

Robie sat on the exam table, his shirt and pants off while Dr. Meenan checked his burns.

"They look better. But it's good you came in. There was some drainage and infection. I'm going to clean the areas and put in some sutures to stabilize the affected areas and just to make sure we don't have any problems. And I'll give you another shot and more meds."

"Okay."

She removed some of the dead skin, cleaned the areas thoroughly, and then sutured some portions where the skin had pulled apart. Once finished with that, she brought over a syringe, rubbed alcohol on his left arm, stuck him, and then placed a Band-Aid over it. "So you did come back in one piece."

"I did, yes."

"I'm glad."

Robie glanced at her. "Why?"

"We lose enough good people. You can put your clothes back on."

Robie slipped his pants back on.

She said, "I'll have the meds bagged up. They'll be available for you out front in about five minutes."

"Thanks."

Robie buttoned up his shirt as Meenan made some notes in her file. Without looking up she said, "Did you hear about that crazy stuff in Arkansas? Did you know the guy used to work here?"

"Roy West?"

"Yeah. I actually knew him. Well, I examined him once."

"What for?"

"Sorry, patient confidentiality. It even applies here. It wasn't for anything serious. But I can tell you he was a strange guy."

"Lot of strange guys here."

"No, I mean really strange." She paused and finished writing, closed the file, and put it away in a rack on the desk.

"Can I tell you something in confidence?" she asked.

"Sure."

"I mean, really?"

"I mean really, sure."

She smiled at this, but then her smile faded to a frown. "He was creepy. And he seemed like a holier-than-thou type. Like he had this big secret he was just bursting to tell me."

"Probably lots of people here like that."

"Maybe. But he stuck out."

"Well, in the end it didn't help him."

"Killed in a militia war, I heard on the news."

"So they say."

"You know different?" she asked sharply.

"No and I've got my hands full with my own stuff." He laced up his shoes and slipped off the table. "I appreciate you patching me up."

"It's what they pay me for."

"So this West guy was kind of a psycho. Heard he got canned from here."

"I'm not surprised. I can't believe he passed the psychological vetting. He just seemed too unstable."

"What else do you remember about him? He ever mention anyone to you?"

"Anyone like who?"

"Just anyone."

She smiled slyly. "I thought you said you had your hands full."

"I'm naturally curious."

"Well, he did mention that he had friends in high places. Very high places, he said. I thought he was just blustering. He was pretty low-level at the agency." She blushed.

"What?" asked Robie.

"Well, I thought he was saying all that to impress me."

"You mean he was hitting on you?"

"Yeah, I think he was." She slapped him playfully on the arm. "And don't sound so surprised."

"You think he was serious?"

"I've thought about that. If I had to guess, I think he did have someone higher up who had his back."

"Not that high up. He got canned."

"You're right. Anyway, I'll just leave it that he was trying to hit on me." She slipped a business card from her pocket. "Just in case you lost my other card, here's another one with all my contact info, including my personal cell. If you have any problems with the injuries please don't hesitate to call."

As Robie took the card, her fingers grazed across his. She didn't meet his eye but her cheeks were slightly red.

Robie had a strong feeling that she was hitting on *him*.

CHAPTER

48

NICOLE VANCE WAS WAITING FOR him this time. And she wasn't wearing any makeup. The woman was all business tonight.

Robie sat down.

"I already ordered you a drink," she said.

He eyed her glass. "Gin?"

"Ginger ale. I'm still technically on duty."

"Long day."

"Long life. At least I hope." She eyed his right arm. "You're carrying that a little stiffly. What gives?"

The burns were healing, but slowly. And the arm *was* stiff, the new sutures Meenan had put in making it even stiffer. He wondered how fast he could draw his weapon. Maybe not fast enough. Yet he had done okay out in the hinterlands of Arkansas. Adrenaline made pain manageable. It was only later that everything hurt.

"Old age."

She smirked. "Nice try."

"Why are you still on duty?" asked Robie.

She sipped her ginger ale; her gaze held a faraway look. "When an investigation is going nowhere I tend to work overtime. Whole world's going to hell, Robie."

"What's new?"

"You heard about this stuff in Arkansas. With Roy West?"

"Saw the news," he replied.

"He was with your agency."

"Never knew him."

"He didn't last long, apparently. Then he went off half-cocked and turned into some antigovernment freak. Don't you vet your people better?"

"Not my job," said Robie.

His drink came and he tasted it.

"Just how you like it?" asked Vance.

He nodded. "Yeah, thanks."

"Good, we can drink to the world going to hell."

"So what part of the world exactly is going to hell?"

"Pick any spot you want. No leads on Jacobs. Nothing on Gelder. The shit in Arkansas. And the ATF is going nuts too."

"About what?"

"An explosion at a remote place on the Eastern Shore. Very sophisticated device used. And someone had even put accelerant in a pond on the property. There wasn't much left in the way of evidence. I'm not on that case. We *do* have other FBI agents. The

Bureau got called out on the Arkansas case too. This militia crap is getting really scary. There used to be just dozens of these groups. Now there are thousands of them. Maybe more."

"So how did this Roy West guy die?"

"Don't really know. Like I said, I'm not working it. And to top it off there was a shooting over near the federal court in Alexandria."

"I didn't hear about that," replied Robie.

"Several cars involved. No one got a license plate, of course. Some gal in a sedan driving like Jeff Gordon. Shots fired from the vehicles. And the kicker is a federal judge just happened to be strolling down the street at the same time."

"You think he was the target?"

"Don't know. I sort of doubt it. It was in the report because he's a judge. We have to cover that angle."

"Which judge?"

"Samuel Kent."

"Maybe it was just a street gang thing."

"That part of Alexandria is very upscale. No gang activity there."

"So no sign of the 'gal'?"

"Nope. Nifty piece of driving by all accounts, and then she was gone."

"And the shooters?"

"Gone too. Amazing how that can happen on a crowded street, but it did." She finished her ginger ale.

"You asked to meet and I've done all the talking. Now I'm shutting up and putting on my listening ears."

Robie nodded, trying to assimilate all that she had told him and wondering if the "gal" was who he thought she was. It seemed both ridiculously impossible and extremely likely that it was Jessica Reel, particularly after Arkansas.

"It was good to see Julie," said Robie.

"Really? I didn't think it went all that well from my point of view."

"She was upset," replied Robie.

"And shouldn't she be?"

"Yes, she should. But we talked on the drive to her house."

"And?"

"And she was still upset."

"Your personal skills must've been exceptional on that drive."

"My goal is to keep her safe. You warned me too."

"I know, Robie. But you don't have to completely shut her out of your life. You two went through a lot together. Hell, she and I went through a lot together."

"You and I went through a lot together," noted Robie.

This comment caught Vance off guard. She sat back, her posture relaxed. "Yeah, we did. You saved my life and risked your life to do it."

"I was the reason you were in danger in the first place. Which brings me back to my point about Julie.

And you. Every time I meet with you I could be putting you back in danger. I don't take that lightly, Nikki. It would probably have been better if I hadn't called and asked you to meet tonight."

"But you can't protect everybody all the time, Robie. And I'm an FBI agent. I can take care of myself.'

"In normal circumstances, absolutely. I'm not normal."

She snorted but caught his deeply serious expression and said, "I know what you mean, Will. I get that. I really do."

"And what chance would Julie have? I'm involved in things right now." He stopped talking and looked away.

She reached out tentatively and touched his hand, wrapping her long fingers around it and squeezing. "What things?"

He looked back at her as she removed her hand, looking embarrassed at having performed this intimate gesture. "In order to cover my back, I have to look in all directions at the same time," he said.

She blinked, obviously trying to decipher this. "Meaning you can't trust anyone?"

"Meaning there are things going on that no one can explain." He paused. "Did you hear about Janet DiCarlo?"

"A vague story about something at her house."

"I was there. It wasn't vague. It was actually pretty straightforward on certain levels."

"What the hell happened?"

Now Robie gripped her hand, hard. It was not an intimate gesture. "If I tell you, it can go no further. I'm not talking about professional courtesy. I'm talking about you staying alive."

Vance's mouth opened slightly and her eyes widened. "Okay, it goes no further."

Robie took a sip of his drink and set the glass back down. "DiCarlo was attacked. Her guards were killed. She was wounded. I got her out. DHS took her for safekeeping."

"Why couldn't her own agency protect—" Vance stopped.

Robie nodded. "Exactly."

"Are you talking rogue or systemic?"

"It's not one traitor running around."

"So systemic?"

"Could be."

"What are you going to do about it?"

"I'm thinking about going off the grid."

Vance sucked in a breath. "Are you sure about that?"

"You went off the grid for me."

"I'm FBI, Robie. You going off the grid is a whole other thing."

"I think it's the only way I'm going to get to the truth."

"Or get killed."

"That could easily happen if I stay where I am." He slowly raised his right arm. "It's already nearly happened twice in the last few days."

She glanced at Robie's arm and then looked back at him. The strain was etched on her face. And that same level of strain was clear on Robie's features.

"What can I do?" she asked.

"You've done plenty already."

"That's bullshit and you know it."

"I may contact you at some point."

"Robie, isn't there any other way to handle this? You can come in to the FBI. We can protect you and maybe…" Her voice trailed off.

"I appreciate that. But I think my way is better."

"What are you going to do?"

"I've got some leads to follow up on."

"Can you even get off the grid with all this crap going on?"

"I can try. That's all I can do." He rose. "Thanks for meeting with me."

"Why *did* you want to meet? Not just to tell me you're going off the grid?"

Robie started to say something but then couldn't get it out.

She rose and stood next to him. Before he could move, Vance had put her arms around him and squeezed so tightly it was as though they had become one body. She went up on her tiptoes and kissed him on the cheek.

She said, "You will come back. You will get through this. You're Will Robie. Hell, you perform the impossible on a regular basis."

"I'll do what I can."

Robie turned and left.

Vance walked to the front of the restaurant and watched him head down the street until he disappeared into the darkness.

When she got back to her car she just sat there staring off and wondering if that was the last time she would ever see him.

CHAPTER

49

OFF THE GRID.

Robie was sitting in his apartment thinking about taking this step.

The last time he had gone off the grid it had not been pleasant. In fact, it had nearly cost him his life and the lives of several other people, including Julie and Vance.

Jessica Reel was off the grid right now. She seemed to be employing a complex strategy that had her on both sides of the chessboard at the same time. What advantage she hoped to gain by this was lost on Robie. It only meant that both sides had incentives to find and kill her.

Doubling your opposition made no sense. Yet Reel didn't strike him as lacking in the brains department. So if she was doing it her strategy had to make sense somehow.

A former agency analyst in Arkansas turned militia nut. He'd written an apocalypse paper. She was there to find out whom he had sent it to.

Then there was a federal judge in Alexandria.

If Reel had been the one in Alexandria too, what the hell was the connection?

A judge, Gelder, Jacobs, and Roy West.

Were they all in on this apocalypse?

If so, exactly what was it?

If West had a copy of it, Robie had no way to get to it. The police would be crawling all over his place, or what was left of it. Reel probably had a copy, but again, he had no way to get it from her.

Robie stared down at the text Reel had sent him previously.

Everything I do has a reason. Just open the lock.

He suddenly groaned and slapped the table with his palm. How could he have been that stupid? Literally staring him right in the damn face.

He went to his safe, opened it, and pulled out the three items that had been left in her *locker.*

Right, her locker. All I had to do was open it.

Okay, now that the simple part was over, it got complicated really fast.

The gun.

The book.

The photo.

The gun he had already ripped apart and found nothing. It was just a pistol with some specialized parts that pointed him in no specific direction at all.

The book had no notes in it. No marginalia. Nothing to point him to a specific part.

The photo meant nothing to him. And he didn't know who the man standing next to Reel was.

Everything I do has a reason.

He said in exasperation, "Great, lady, next time don't make it so damn complicated. It's adding up to something impossible for mere mortals to figure out."

Robie locked the items back up and stared out the window.

What Blue Man had told him was only one more disquieting piece of information on top of many others. It seemed like the agency was imploding from the top level on down. How this state of chaos could be happening to the premier intelligence organization on earth was astounding.

The world was a truly dangerous place right now. It was far more dangerous even than during the Cold War. Back then the opponents were clearly delineated and aligned across the world. The stakes were just as clearly understood. The destruction of the world was a possibility. But not really. The theory of mutual assured destruction was a great catalyst for peace. You couldn't take over the world if there was no world left to take over.

Today's situation was far more fluid, far subtler, and the sides kept changing with alarming frequency. And Robie didn't know if the element of mutual assured destruction was enough anymore. Apparently some people didn't care if there was a world left

afterward. That made them dangerous at an unprec-
edented level.

DiCarlo's comments came back to him: *Missions that never should have been. Missing personnel. Money moved from here to there and then it disappeared. Equipment sent to places it should not have been sent to and it also disappeared. And that's not all. These things happened in discreet quantities over long periods of time. Taken singly they didn't seem to be all that remarkable. But when one looks at them together.*

To Robie's mind, missing personnel alone should have been enough of a warning, much less everything else that DiCarlo had described.

How had that can gotten kicked down the road?

Tucker had been director long enough to have taken care of such significant issues. Or at least addressed them.

Unless Tucker was on the other side of the chessboard. But that seemed impossible. It was hard enough to envision Jim Gelder being a traitor. But if Reel was to be believed, he was. Yet both top slots corrupted? How likely was that?

However, what other explanation was there for so many things to go awry and not be addressed by the management?

He took out his wallet. Inside the compartment where he kept his cash was a small sealed baggie. In it were the rose petals.

That was the other clue Reel had left behind.

Someone had taken the roses and who knew what else, but had missed these items. What had Reel meant by this?

If everything she did had a purpose, there had to be some explanation. And it might be significant.

The lady at the florist shop had said the pink-ish marks on the rose were sometimes interpreted as blood. Well, there had been a lot of blood spilled over this. Was that the simple meaning that Reel had intended? But if so, how did that help him?

Blue Man had postulated that Reel might be on the side of right in all this. What that actually meant in the spy business Robie wasn't sure. Right and wrong switched sides all the time. No, perhaps that was unfair. There were core elements of right and wrong.

Terrorists who killed innocent people with hidden bombs were on the side of wrong, without question. In Robie's mind they were also cowards.

He killed from long distance, but he also risked his life to do it. And he didn't target innocent people. All those he went after spent their lives bringing pain to others.

Does that make me permanently on the side of right?

He shook his head to clear it of these troubling thoughts. Nice fodder for a philosophy class discussion. But it was bringing him no closer to the truth.

Or to Jessica Reel.

He had told Tucker he was not going to look for her.

In part his answer was truthful.

He wasn't going to look for her anymore. At least not on behalf of Tucker and the agency. But he was going to find her, and this time he was going to make her tell him what was going on.

Whatever else happened, he was going to get to the truth.

CHAPTER

50

THE MEETING WAS NOT SCHEDULED.

It really didn't have to be.

Sam Kent sat on one side of the small oval table. Across from him was another man, younger, fitter, shorter, with hands like bricks and a torso like a wall.

His name was Anthony Zim.

He did not go by Tony.

"They picked Robie for obvious reasons," said Kent.

Zim nodded. "Good choice. He knows what he's doing."

"And he's not off the grid like you."

"I'm not off the grid, Mr. Kent," Zim corrected. "I'm offline. There's a difference, a big one."

"I realize that," said Kent quietly. "I was instrumental in putting you there. Where we could maximize your talents."

Zim said nothing. He placed his palms on the tabletop. Even sitting he kept his weight balanced on the balls of his feet. He could move in an instant if he needed to. And over the years he had needed to on many occasions.

"Jessica Reel," said Kent.

Zim just sat there, waiting.

Kent continued, "She's out there and she's growing more troublesome by the minute."

"She was always good at that."

"I take it you knew her well?"

"No one knew Reel well. Just like no one knows Robie. They kept it all inside. Just like I do. Goes with the territory."

"But you worked with her?"

"Yes."

"And Robie?

"Twice. Both in support roles. Turns out he didn't need the support."

"Can you take out either or both of them, if it comes to it?"

"Yes. If the conditions are right."

"We can try to make sure they are."

"I need you to do better than try."

Kent frowned. "I came to you because I understood you were one of the best."

"You're asking me to go after two people who may be as good as me. Singly I can probably take them. Together, there are no guarantees."

"Then we have to make sure they never get together."

"Robie is tasked to go after her. Maybe he'll get there and save you the trouble."

"There have been recent developments with Robie that give me some concern about that happening."

Zim shifted his weight slightly. "Such as?"

"Reportedly he's starting to think for himself on this rather than following orders. And it's more than that."

"I need to know it all."

"Reel has been communicating with him. Telling him things."

"Manipulating him, you mean. She's good at that."

"I didn't think you knew her well?"

"I knew her enough to know that." Zim leaned forward an inch. "Can I make a suggestion?"

"I'm listening."

"Let it play out. Robie kills Reel. Or vice versa. Or they kill each other."

"That was the original plan. It may still happen," replied Kent. He leaned forward until he was only a few inches from Zim. "You're the fail-safe. And if I'm reading things correctly you're going to be deployed to get the job done. I can't count on an ideal world. That's a sucker's bet and involves an element of luck that I simply can't depend on."

"Then the conditions better be right."

"As you suggested, I will do better than try."

"How?" said Zim.

"Jessica Reel isn't the only one who can manipulate."

"Not as easy as it might look."

Kent said, "I don't think it's easy at all. It's very difficult, in fact."

"So how?"

"I'll take care of that. You take care of your end."

"That's all I get?"

"Compartmentalize. It's the best protocol all around."

"You're not the sort I expected."

"You mean a judge?"

Zim shrugged.

Kent smiled. "I'm a special kind of judge, Mr. Zim. My time behind the bench is limited to a very few cases. The rest of the time is spent doing other things for my country. I like doing these other things far more than my infrequent rulings from the bench."

"You must have pull. Otherwise I wouldn't be sitting here with you."

"I have more than pull. I'm often the one doing the pulling."

"When will I be deployed?"

"The exact timing is unknown. But if I'm reading the tea leaves correctly it will be very soon. You're to be ready twenty-four/seven. Move at a moment's notice."

"Story of my life," replied Zim.

"Let's hope it's not the story of your death."

"Goes with the territory."

Kent sat back. "You keep saying that. I might start believing it."

"I don't expect you to understand it, Mr. Kent. It's a small club I'm a member of."

"I actually can understand that."

"I don't think so. Not unless you've killed as many people as I have. And there aren't many in the world who have."

"How many have you killed?"

"Thirty-nine. That's one reason I'm interested in Reel. She'd make an even forty."

"That's impressive. And of course Robie would make it a very uneven forty-one."

"Not something I would lose sleep over, I can assure you."

"Glad to hear that."

Kent smiled. The muzzle was against Zim's forehead before he had time to react.

Zim's eyes widened as the metal pressed against his skin.

Kent said, "As I mentioned, I wasn't always a judge. I checked your file. You've been working for eleven years. Is that right?"

When Zim didn't answer Kent pushed the muzzle harder against his face. "Is that right?'

"Yes."

Kent nodded. "I pulled an even twenty. That was before they put a cap on time in the field to fifteen.

I think people these days have gotten a little softer. I never even had decent night optics. Did four kills in the dead of night with a flashlight and a piece-of-shit Vietnam-era sniper rifle. But I still got the job done. And by the way, I never bragged about my kill total."

Kent pulled the gun's hammer back. "One more thing: did I mention that there was a test involved in your selection?"

"Test?" asked a bewildered Zim.

"If an old man could get the drop on you, I don't think you're much use to me. You're not even qualified to wipe Robie's or Reel's ass. Which means this interview is officially over."

Kent pulled the trigger, the gun fired, and the round destroyed Zim's brain. He fell backward out of his chair.

Kent rose, wiped the blood blowback off his face with a handkerchief, and then holstered his gun.

He looked down at the body. "And for the record, I finished with sixty kills. There's only one person out there with more. He's old-school. Just like me. I never would've gotten the drop on him like I did you. Asshole."

Kent walked out the door.

CHAPTER

51

REEL WAS STARING AT HER PHONE. On the screen was a familiar face, at least from a distance.

Will Robie looked back at her.

She knew she should have told him more during the standoff in Arkansas. But in truth she had been stunned to see him there. She had convinced herself that somehow the agency had been able to follow her and sent Robie in for the kill. That had rocked her, made any faith she had in him disappear. That faith had been restored when he hadn't killed her, of course. But now she was afraid for him.

If the agency found out he had the shot but hadn't taken it, Robie would be in serious jeopardy. And if she tried to communicate with him again and he agreed to work with her, something she had thought she wanted, then he would be in even graver danger. Killers would be sent after him. And he hadn't prepared to go on the run like she had. As good as he was, he wouldn't survive. They had too many resources.

I have to go this alone.

She pulled the white paper from her bag and read through it again.

Having now met Roy West, she would have hardly expected the man to be capable of piecing together a plan of such complexity. Unfortunately, his decision to plot mass murder against his fellow citizens to fuel his bizarre rage against the government was entirely in keeping with the essence of his white paper. It and he were insane.

And anyone who subscribed to what was in that paper was insane as well. And dangerous.

West was dead. He couldn't harm anyone ever again. But there were others out there far better placed to execute the Armageddon outlined in his paper.

Country by country.

Leader by leader.

The perfect jigsaw puzzle.

If death and misery on a massive scale had a face, it could be West's perverted masterpiece.

And then there was the unknown. The person who she felt certain had to be out there. The three levels above West. The top-top-secret clearance. The person who had wanted the paper. Who had wanted to know the master jigsaw puzzle.

Roger the Dodger. Who was he? Where was he? And what was he planning right now?

The attack against Janet DiCarlo was predictable, but Reel had never seen it coming until it was too late. DiCarlo was alive, but for how long? Reel would have loved to sit and talk with her old mentor. To find out what and how she had discovered something that had led to her nearly dying.

But that wasn't possible. Reel had no idea where DiCarlo was. And she would be heavily guarded. And yet if the attack against her had come from the inside, how safe would she be wherever the woman was?

Reel looked down at her phone again. Should she chance it?

Without stopping to think about it anymore, she pecked the keys and the message was sent to Robie, despite her having just decided not to communicate with him again. But it was a different sort of query, one that they couldn't hold against him.

She didn't know if she would get an answer. She didn't know if Robie trusted her or believed her. She remembered being part of his team early in her career. He had been the most professional among a group of consummate pros. He had taught her things, without really saying much. He sweated the little details. They were the difference, he told her, between making it or not.

She had learned some of what had happened to him earlier in the year. He had done the unthinkable for people in their profession. He hadn't pulled the trigger. He had disobeyed orders because he believed them to be wrong.

The average citizen would think there was nothing special in that. If you thought something was wrong, why not disobey? But it wasn't that easy. More even than regular soldiers, Robie and Reel had been trained to follow orders without question. Without that unbreakable chain of command, without that devotion to authority, the system simply didn't work. Nothing could interfere with that.

But each of them *had* disobeyed orders.

Robie had refused to pull the trigger. Twice. The second time was the only reason Reel was still alive.

But she *had* pulled the trigger. She had killed two men who worked for the government. Both constituted crimes punishable by long imprisonment or even death.

Reel wondered if Robie was still coming after her. She wondered if right now he regretted not killing her.

Her phone buzzed. She looked down at the screen. Will Robie had just answered her.

52

Robie looked at his screen. His fingers had just finished typing. He wondered how long before people from the agency would contact him.

Or kick down his door.

Alive. For now.

That's what he had typed and sent her in response to her simple question:

DiCarlo?

Robie continued to stare at his phone screen, part of him hoping that she would text again. He had many things he wanted to ask her. Things he hadn't had time to ask when he had seen her in Arkansas.

He had just about given up when another text from Reel dropped in:

GPB.

GPB?

Robie was certainly not up to date on the latest Internet acronyms. And he had no idea if GPB was one of those or was a coded message from Reel. If it was coded he had no idea what it meant.

But why would she think he would?

He sat back in his chair and thought back to the last mission they had done together all those years ago. It was about as routine as you could expect in their line of work. But something had gone wrong, which sometimes happened.

Robie had gone to the left and at the same second Reel had darted to the right. If they had gone in the same direction, they both would have been dead. As it stood, they neutralized the threats coming at them from two sides.

Robie had thought about it later and even asked Reel why she had gone the opposite way, because there was no visible threat on either flank yet. She really couldn't answer him other than to say, "I knew you were going the way you did."

"How?" Robie had asked.

She'd asked a question in answer to his. "How did you know which way I was going to go?"

And he couldn't answer her other than to say that he had just felt it. It was that simple. Not that he could literally read her mind. But he knew what her reaction would be in that exact situation. And she knew what his would be.

That had never happened to him again. Only with

Jessica Reel. He wondered if that had been her last time too.

When the call came he looked at the screen and then put his phone away. It was Langley. He didn't feel like explaining to them why he had done what he had. In one sense he didn't feel it was any of their business. If they could keep secrets from him, he could keep secrets from them. They were all spies, after all.

And that's when a totally unrelated thought entered his mind. Well, part of his mind must have been thinking about it as he took this walk down memory lane.

Reel had told him few things about herself, but one had struck him.

"I'm a linear person, Robie," she'd said after they returned from their last mission.

"Meaning what?" Robie had asked.

"Meaning I like to begin at the beginning and end at the end."

With this thought inspiration occurred. He jumped up, ran to his wall safe, took out the three objects again, and looked at them.

Gun.

Photo.

Book.

GPB.

He sat down with renewed energy and interest. He

had unconsciously laid them out in the correct order when he'd looked at them last. But at least now he had confirmation that there was an order to them.

He held the gun. He had already taken it apart and found nothing. But actually he had found something.

Everything I do has a reason.

That's what Reel had written him. Everything she did had a reason.

He looked at the gun. Well, Glock had built this gun. She hadn't.

His eyes narrowed.

But she *had* done some alterations to the gun.

He looked at the weapon's sight. Pennsylvania Small Arms Company. An add-on by Reel, though the standard sight that had come with the gun was perfectly fine.

The titanium plunger. Nice add-on, but again not necessary.

He examined once more the stippled grip that Reel had presumably put on the weapon. Again, although polymer frames like the Glock could sometimes be slippery, the original grip was perfectly fine.

So why had Reel taken the time to manually reengineer the factory grip when she didn't really need to? Etching a stippled surface onto the frame would have taken time. And if you didn't know what you were doing or made a mistake, it could make the weapon

nearly unusable, at least so far as the grip was concerned.

And most of her killing would be done at long range
anyway when the weapon's grip really wasn't an issue.

And then there was the thirty-three-round mag.
That had bugged him from the first. In their line of
work if you had time to fire off thirty-three rounds at
something, that meant you had screwed up and were
most likely going to die. One or two or possibly three
shots and you were supposed to be out of there.

Seventeen rounds were pretty much standard in
this Glock model. Yet she had nearly doubled her
capacity in an extra-long mag that, in truth, was a
little cumbersome.

Reel didn't strike him as someone who enjoyed
clutter.

He looked at the model number: Glock 17.

He was going to have to do this methodically. He
imagined that Reel had come up with it in the same way.

Robie knew he was on the right path because of
the text she had sent him. It had to mean Gun, Photo,
Book. There was no other possible explanation. And
it was a pretty shrewd way to go about it. Reel had
known that the agency would allow him to search
her locker and take her things once they had assigned
him to hunt her down. And the only reason they had
allowed him access to her locker was because they had
searched through the items and found nothing useful

in them. So she must have assumed that he would at some point gain access to the items and would examine them for a clue of some kind.

He took out a pad of paper and a pen and fired up his laptop. He opened a search engine and started looking, feeding the facts he had gleaned from the gun into the search. He had to go through quite a few false starts until what he saw finally started to make sense. Not complete sense, but enough to get him moving in a fresh and possibly rewarding direction.

He wrote it all down, closed out his search, and shut down his laptop.

He jumped up and went to pack a bag. He had somewhere to go. And he had to make sure he got there without someone tailing him.

Vance's words came back to him. Could he successfully go off the grid?

Well, I'm about to find out.

53

It was a fine, stately chamber, full of dark woods, mitered-perfect moldings, plush carpeting, large, ornate doors, massive lighting fixtures, and an air of sublime prosperity.

It was federal money spent just right. A true rarity.

At least that was Sam Kent's humble opinion.

He sat in his office at the courthouse. He closed the book he was reading and checked his watch.

Just about time.

A minute later his clerk came in and announced the arrival of Congressman Howard Decker. The man walked in and shook hands with the judge as the clerk left them to their private meeting.

Besides chairing the House Permanent Select Committee on Intelligence, Decker had once been on a judiciary subcommittee, so his meeting with Kent would raise no eyebrows. Plus, the men had been friends for years and shared a commonality of thought and ambition. As the chairman of the Intelligence

Committee, Decker had congressional fingerprints from the CIA to the Treasury Department and lots of federal real estate in between.

They sat at a table laid out with crystal and linen napkins and a cold lunch prepared by the court chef. Kent poured out glasses of white wine for them both.

"A nice treat," said Decker. "The Congressional Dining Room gets a little old."

"Well, we needed to talk, so why not here, in comfort and privacy?"

Decker chuckled and lifted the wineglass to his lips. "Not worried about someone listening in on the court that authorizes people listening in?"

Kent's features were impassive. "We need to talk, Howard."

Decker put the glass back down and his expression became serious. "It's about Roy West, isn't it?"

"It's about a lot more than that," said Kent.

"You think Jessica Reel did all that? It looked like a war zone on the news."

"I've been to war, Howard. It didn't look anything like a war zone. They look a lot worse than that."

Suitably put in his place, Decker sat back in his chair and licked his already chapped lips. "What do we do now?"

"Our plan hasn't changed, has it?"

"Which plan? To get Reel? Of course not."

"Good, just checking. I wanted to make sure we are still on the same page."

Decker grimaced. "But what steps have you taken? It doesn't look like this Robie person is going to get the job done."

Kent took a sip of wine and considered this. "He may get a job done. Just not the one we want."

"I'm not following you."

"I have received a very detailed report of what happened out in Arkansas. A very detailed report, from the highest sources."

"And?"

"And that level of carnage could not have been perpetrated by one person, not even someone as skilled as Jessica Reel."

Decker sat forward. "Are you telling me that she had help?" he blustered. He paused, then added, "Robie!"

"I have no definite proof of that. But it would be a coincidence of immense proportions to believe that someone else wandered into that little drama with a skill set perfectly designed for survival against what should have been overwhelming odds." He put his glass down and took a forkful of salmon. "And I for one do not like coincidences."

"If Robie and Reel have teamed up..."

"I didn't say that."

"But you just said it had to be the two of them."

"But that doesn't mean they've teamed up, Howard."

"What the hell else could it be? You just as good as said they killed all those men together."

"Mutual survival does not mean you're on the same side. I could be wrong, but it might simply be that conditions on the ground led to a temporary alliance."

"But that's still not good for us."

"Of course it isn't. But it might mean it's manageable."

"If Robie joins Reel?"

"Then he will be dealt with. I have people in mind for the task."

"If it's the same people you have going after Reel I'd say don't bother."

"And your alternative?"

"It's your job to have the answers in this particular area, Sam, not me. Our division of labor was explicitly laid out. I helped get you the assets you needed. And the target. That was my job. I did it."

Kent took a mouthful of rice and broccoli and washed it down with some water from a cut-crystal glass. "You're right, it was. I apologize."

Mollified, Decker sat back and started to eat.

Kent said, "I actually anticipated Reel locating West. I thought they were prepared to take care of her. I was obviously wrong. I won't make that mistake again."

"I would hope not."

"I also tried to recruit someone to deal with Reel and possibly Robie, but he didn't work out."

"Will he be a problem?"

"I doubt it." Kent picked up his glass of wine.

"How can you be sure?"

"Because I shot him in the head." Kent took a sip of the wine.

Decker dropped his fork. It clanged off the china plate and fell to the floor.

"You don't like the salmon?" asked Kent as he wiped his mouth.

His hands shaking, Decker bent down and picked up his fork. His face ashen, he said, "You shot him?"

"Well, there wasn't a viable alternative, really. And he was an arrogant prick. Thought way too much of himself. Hell, I believe I would have shot him regardless." Kent settled his gaze on Decker's frightened features. "I don't like arrogant pricks, Howard. I don't like people who think too much of themselves. I tend to shoot them. I tend to shoot them in the head to make sure they're dead."

Decker licked his lips. "I know you're under a lot of stress, Sam."

Kent shook his head. "This isn't stress, Howard. Living in a hole in the ground in the middle of a snake- and mosquito-infested jungle for months on end wondering what was going to get you first, the dysentery eating your insides away or the Viet Cong who kept picking your guys off one by one—now *that*, my friend, that was stressful."

"I'm under a lot of pressure too."

"Right. You get elected and you have your big office and your driver and your staff and the fancy dinners and you go back home and raise money by kissing rich asses and then you come here and occasionally actually do your damn job and vote on something. Lots of pressure. Politics is hell. Glad I never went there. I just wore a uniform and got my ass shot up. You, on the other hand, never wore the uniform."

"I was too young for Vietnam."

"So you would have volunteered, like I did?"

"I'm not saying that."

"And nothing was stopping you from joining over the years."

"Not everyone is cut out for the military. I had other goals in life."

"I earned two Purples and a Bronze and would've gotten the Silver but my CO didn't like the fact that his troops would rather follow me than him. After the war I got my college and law degrees. Uncle Sam helped pay for it. No complaints there. I did my time. I got my quid pro quo. You did shit and now you *serve* the people from a nice, safe office."

Kent suddenly reached across and gripped the back of Decker's fleshy neck and jerked him forward until their faces were barely an inch apart. "So the next time you seek to lecture me on anything will be the last time you lecture anyone about anything. Are we crystal clear on that? Because I don't intend to repeat it."

Kent let Decker go and sat back. He picked up his fork. "Try the rice. It's a little spicy, but it goes well with the seasoned broccoli."

Decker didn't move. He just sat there staring across at Kent.

Kent finished his lunch and rose. "My clerk will show you out. I hope you have a productive day up there on the Hill serving your country."

He walked out of the room, leaving Decker trembling in his chair.

CHAPTER

54

Robie drove slowly down the narrow streets of Titanium, Pennsylvania. It was a small town with the usual assortment of homes and businesses. People ambled down the street, window-shopping at the mom-and-pop stores located there. Cars puttered along. Folks waved at each other. The pace was slow, comfortable.

He had done everything possible to avoid being trailed here. He felt it would have been impossible for even the best agents out there to keep him under surveillance. And if they had, they deserved to put one in the win column.

He eyed his GPS. He was looking for a certain street, and he hoped it was the right one. The computer told him it was a mile or so out of the downtown area.

Marshall Street. As in Ryan Marshall, the senior field agent who showed me and Reel how to stipple our pistol grips. Something only the two of us would know.

Robie had loaded in a specific number address on Marshall Street. It could have been one of two possibilities. He had inputted the one he'd chosen on the flip of a coin back at his apartment. However, in such a small place he figured Marshall Street couldn't be that long if he had to run down the second choice.

He slowed the car after he'd left the town and reentered a rural area. He made the right on Marshall and drove straight back until the road cut sharply to the right. There didn't seem to be any street numbers here, because there were no houses. He had just started to fear that his trip had been for nothing when he cleared another curve and saw it up ahead. It looked like a motor court of some sort, dating back to maybe the fifties.

Robie pulled his car to a stop in front of a small office that had a large plate glass window in front. The building formed a horseshoe with the office at the center. It was two stories high and dilapidated.

Robie didn't focus on that. His gaze went first to the street number painted on the front of the building.

Thirty-three.

The same number as the rounds in Reel's Glock's oversize mag.

The other number that Robie had considered was seventeen, the model number of the Glock.

Thirty-three had obviously been the correct one. His coin flip was a winner. But it also made sense.

The 17 model was standard. Reel had modified it with the extra-long mag.

His gaze next went to the sign in front of the motor court. Its background was painted white, with narrowly drawn black concentric circles emanating from the center, and the perimeter painted a bold red. The name of the motor court was the Bull's-Eye Inn; the sign represented the bull's-eye.

Cheesy, thought Robie, but maybe it had been original and catchy when the place was first built.

The red edge was what had drawn his attention, however.

He held up the photo he'd found in Reel's locker. The picture of Reel and the unknown gent. The edge of red on the right side of the photo could be from the sign, if they had been standing next to it. More confirmation that he was in the right place.

Robie parked the car and got out and headed to the office. Through the plate glass he could see an elderly white-haired woman sitting behind a waist-high counter. When he opened the door a bell tinkled. The woman looked up from her computer, which was old enough not to be a flat-screen but still had the bubble butt the size of a small TV. She rose to greet him.

Robie looked around. The place didn't appear to have been changed since opening day. It looked frozen in time from well before a man had walked on the moon or JFK had been elected president.

"Can I help you?" the woman said.

Up close she looked to be in her eighties. Her hair was delicate, cottony, her shoulders rounded and bent, and her knees didn't look all that sturdy. The metal nameplate on her blouse read "Gwen."

Robie said, "I was just driving through and saw this place. Quite something."

"Original owner built it right after WW-Two."

"Are you the new owner, Gwen?"

She grinned, showing capped teeth. "Honey, there's nothing 'new' about me. And if I were the owner, I wouldn't be sitting here trying to use a computer. I'd hire someone to do it for me. But I can always phone my great-granddaughter. She tells me what button to hit."

"You have any rooms available?"

"Yes, we do. Not exactly the busy season for us. Most people come here to get closer with nature. But it's a little cold to be with nature right about now. We do the best in the summer months, and late spring is pretty good too."

"Is Room 17 available?"

She looked at him with a quizzical expression. "Room 17? We don't have a Room 17."

"But it looks like you have more than seventeen rooms."

"Oh, we do. But it was the quirk of the original owner. He started with room 100 and worked up from there. Guess he wanted the place to sound a lot bigger than it was. We have twenty-six rooms, thirteen on each floor. That's unlucky, come to think of it. Thirteen. But we've been here a long time, so I guess no harm, no foul."

Robie had taken a shot in the dark with the number 17. If Reel had left him hidden clues he wanted to try all of them.

"Well, then give me whatever room you have available."

She slid out a key for Room 106 and handed it to him after he paid for two nights in cash.

"There's a pretty good place to eat in town called Palisades. That's the nice restaurant anyway. You know, tablecloths and napkins made of something other than paper towels. They got stuff on the menu I've never heard of and couldn't cook myself to save my life. But it's real good if you got the money to spend, which most folks around here don't. Now, if you're economy-minded you can try the Gettysburg Grill one block over from Palisades. It's just plain comfort food. Burgers, pizza, and fries. I'm partial to the Neapolitan shake they do. It's real nice and only costs a buck."

"Thanks."

Robie was turning to go back to his car and get his bag when her words made him stop.

"Of course, there is a Cabin 17."

He turned to face her. "A Cabin 17."

"Guess I forgot to tell you about our cabins."

"I guess so," said Robie, looking at her expectantly.

"But it wouldn't have done you any good."

"Why is that?'

"Well, if you had your heart set on Cabin 17, I couldn't have rented it to you."

"Why not?"

"It's already rented. Has been for a long time."

"A long time. By who?"

She pursed her lips. "Well, that's confidential, isn't it?"

"If you say so," replied Robie with a smile. The last thing he needed was her calling Titanium's police on him for being overly curious. "Thing is number 17 is the one I wore when I played football in college. Best years of my life. So wherever I go, I always try to stay in number 17. Stupid, I know, but it's important to me."

"Hell, honey, I play the same numbers on the lottery every week because they're my wedding day, 11, 15, and 21, my age when I got married. My big ball Lotto numbers are the year I was born, which I won't share with you because you'd know I was over twenty-one. Hard to know just by looking at me, right?"

"Right," said Robie, with another grin.

"So I don't begrudge you your 17."

"Thanks," answered Robie. "So where are your cabins?"

"Oh, we have twenty of them. I know, almost as many as the rooms we have. But that was the original owner's idea again. Let you get communal with nature. They're set back in the woods. Very rustic. That means one room with a bed and a toilet and sink, a woodstove that's also a cookstove, and running water when the pump's working. So, R-U-S-T-I-C."

"How about a shower?"

"You can use the one here. We have it designated for cabin renters. Or you can just use the sink in the cabin for a quick one. Most folks renting cabins don't have personal hygiene high on their priority list. Hell, I never see most of the folks. They come and go as they please."

"Other than Cabin 17, any others rented?"

"No."

"Anyone in Cabin 17 now?"

"I wouldn't know. Like I said, they come and go."

"They. Two people?"

"Well, aren't you the curious one?"

"Always have been. Gets me in more trouble, so I'll just stop right now." Robie gave her another grin, which he hoped was disarming. He had the sense he had just pushed too hard. He hoped he didn't regret it.

She eyed him. "Look, honey, you want to trade in your room for a cabin? Number 14 is all ready to go. It's got a nice view and a new toilet. Well, new in the sense that it's less than five years old and works more often than not."

"Hey, why not?" said Robie. "I like communing with nature as much as the next person. How do I get there?"

"About a quarter-mile walk from here. The cabins are spread out in the woods, but there're signs posted telling you where each one is. You can leave your car in the lot out front and walk back there. The trail starts right behind the center of the motel."

A few minutes later Robie was walking on the trail toward Cabin 14 with his knapsack over his left shoulder.

And his Glock in his right hand.

CHAPTER

55

CABIN 14 WAS EXACTLY AS Gwen had described it. Rustic. He set his knapsack down on the bed that was barely more than a cot. It was shorter than Robie was tall.

Woodstove in the corner. A table. A chair. A toilet and sink behind a makeshift enclosure. Two windows on opposite walls. He went to one window and looked out.

There was no cabin in sight, just trees. People who rented them must want their privacy. He would have to do a walk around to get the lay of the land.

He had seen the sign for Cabin 17. It was to his left. He just didn't know how far. He was so deep in the woods now that he could hear no cars, no people talking. No TVs or radios.

He could be alone with nature.

Only maybe he wasn't alone.

He sat in the one chair, facing the door, his Glock

in his right hand. With his left hand he slid the book on World War II out of his knapsack. It was the last unsolved clue.

Everything she did had a purpose.

She was linear.

I like to begin at the beginning and end at the end.

He opened the book. He had looked through it before, but not all that carefully. It was a long book and he just hadn't had the time.

Now he felt like he had to make the time.

The light was rapidly diminishing and the cabin was not wired for electricity. As he slowly turned the pages and it drew darker, he put his gun aside and used a small flashlight to illuminate the page.

However, he kept glancing at the door and windows. The latter had curtains, but he was aware that his light made him a target. He had moved the chair to a point in the room where he was in no direct sight line from outside.

He had pushed the table in front of the door after locking it. He figured if someone burst in he would have enough time to douse the light, grab his weapon, aim, and fire. At least he hoped so.

He slowly turned the pages, taking in every word. When he came to the middle of chapter sixteen he stopped.

The section was entitled simply "The White Rose."

Robie read swiftly. The White Rose was the name taken by a resistance group of mostly college students in Munich during World War II who worked against the tyranny of the Nazis. The group had taken its name from a novel about peasant exploitation in Mexico. Most of the members of the White Rose were executed by the Nazis. But pamphlets they had printed were smuggled out of Germany and dropped by the millions from Allied bombers. After the war the members of the White Rose had been hailed as heroes.

Robie slowly closed the book and set it aside.

Once more adopting Reel's obsession with order and logic, he went through the ordeal of the White Rose and tried to graft those elements onto her situation.

The White Rose had fought against Nazi tyranny.

They had felt betrayed.

They hadn't killed anyone, but they had attempted to stoke anger against the Nazis in order to see them stopped.

They had been killed for their troubles.

Robie slowly turned this over in his mind and then moved forward in time.

Reel had been fighting against something.

She had felt betrayed.

She had taken action to stop whoever was against her, and that included killing. But that's what she did. The woman was no college student writing pamphlets.

The jury was still out on whether she would sacrifice her life or not.

Then Robie thought back to DiCarlo's words.

Personnel missing.

Equipment moved.

Missions that never should have been.

And Blue Man. According to him a different dynamic seemed to be in place.

DiCarlo had been distrustful of people within her own agency. She'd had only two bodyguards with her because of this. And she'd been both proved right and paid the price for such limited protection.

Allegedly, Reel had gone off the grid and murdered two members of her own agency. If she'd done so, again according to Blue Man, it might have been because they were on the wrong side and Reel was on the side of right.

If all that was true, then the agency was full of traitors, and they went very high in the pecking order. At least as high as Gelder and maybe higher.

And then there was the matter of Roy West.

He had been with the agency. He had written some sort of apocalypse paper. He had joined a militia. He was now dead.

Robie picked up his gun and checked his watch. He had not come here simply to read a book.

It would soon be dark, and darker still where he was, with no source of light other than the stars, which were now hidden behind a gauzy veil of clouds.

He opened his knapsack and pulled out his night optics. He put them on and fired them up. They worked fine, turning the invisible to visible.

Robie's plan was simple.

He was going to visit Cabin 17.

The darkness would be both a benefit and danger to him.

If it wasn't occupied, Robie would find what he could. If the cabin yielded no clues he would have wasted a lot of time and come away with nothing.

He wondered what his next step would be if that turned out to be the case. Go back to D.C.? Go back on the grid? After what he suspected? That his agency was compromised and corrupted?

His last text exchange with Reel had without doubt been picked up by others. They would want to know what Robie had deduced. They would want to know where he had gone. They might want him dead, depending on his answers.

Well, then I just won't give them any answers until I know which side folks are really on.

He had relied on a moral compass that by some miracle he still had inside him, despite what he did for a living. That meant he couldn't walk away from this one. That meant he had to confront it at some point.

He waited until after two in the morning before setting out. He opened the door of Cabin 14 and stepped out into the pitch black.

Next stop, Cabin 17.

IT LOOKED JUST LIKE CABIN 14, except there was a flowerpot out front on the porch with a single drooping flower. The first frost would kill it off. The flowerpot also had a cat painted on it.

Robie was standing back at the tree line. His gaze went to the door of the cabin, to the flower, and then to the surrounding darkness.

Through his night optics, the world was presented in sharp relief. But it couldn't show him everything. There could be something else out there that he didn't see.

So he studied that flowerpot for a long time, wondering why it was there. Just one droopy flower. And it was one that needed sun, as many flowers did. Yet there was no sun here. Which meant there was no reason to plant it in a pot and put it on the steps.

It made no sense. And thus it made perfect sense. Everything Reel did had a purpose.

He went back over the Eastern Shore fiasco frame

by frame in his head. He had fired at the door and the porch, trying to set off booby traps from a safe distance.

He twirled a suppressor onto the muzzle of his Glock, aimed, and fired twice. The pot cracked, and dirt and flower parts flew up into the air.

There was no explosion.

But through his night optics Robie did see the remains of some device whirling off into the darkness.

He moved closer and examined some of this debris: the shattered parts of a surveillance camera. He picked up a piece of the clay pot. A hole had been bored into it and then hidden by the picture of the cat.

The pot had been Reel's eyes.

And Robie had just blinded her.

It felt good.

And he also now had confirmation that the renter of Cabin 17 was indeed Jessica Reel. She had given him the clues to get here.

But that didn't make him trust her.

He slipped his thermal imager out of his knapsack, fired it up, and pointed it at the cabin. Nothing living inside registered on its screen.

But that had happened last time and still Robie had almost fried.

Ultimately, he decided he just had to get it done. He moved stealthily toward the cabin, knelt, and fired at the door and the porch floor.

Nothing happened other than metal ripping through old wood.

He waited, listening for sounds.

A scampering in the trees was a squirrel or deer. Humans couldn't move like that.

He crab-walked forward some more, squatted, and studied the structure.

There wasn't much remaining to deduce from the outside. He hoped the inside would be a lot more informative.

He moved toward the porch and hurried up the steps to the door. One kick and the wooden door flew back. Robie was in the room in the next second and had cleared it five seconds after that. He shut the door behind him, pulled his flashlight, and shined it around.

What he saw was not what he had been expecting. There was no *SORRY* stenciled on the wall.

There could be a firebomb in here somewhere, but he didn't focus on that. There was a woodstove, a table, chairs, and a bed. And a small toilet and sink. Just like his cabin. On the table was a battery-powered lantern. He examined it for booby traps, found none, turned it on, and the room became dimly illuminated.

Also on the table were two pictures set in frames.

One was of Doug Jacobs.

The other was of Jim Gelder.

Black slashes had been drawn across the pictures of the dead men.

There were three other frames lined up next to them. There were no pictures in them. In front of the frames was a single white rose.

He picked up the pictures of Jacobs and Gelder and checked to see if anything was hidden behind them. There was nothing. He did the same with the three other frames.

Robie wondered whose pictures Reel intended to insert in these when and if the time came. And he still didn't know why, other than that for some reason she thought these men were traitors to their country.

Robie still had no proof of that.

But what had happened to Janet DiCarlo made him realize that something was off. He touched the white rose. It felt moist. Perhaps it had recently been placed here.

He whipped around so fast, he heard her gasp at the speed of his reflexes.

His gun was pointed right at her head, his finger past the trigger guard and near the trigger itself. One twitch of his finger and she was dead from a third eye between her other two.

But it wasn't Jessica Reel.

It was Gwen from behind the counter at the Bull's-Eye Inn who stared back at him.

CHAPTER

57

"WHAT ARE YOU DOING HERE?" demanded Robie.

He did not lower his pistol. She was old but she could still be a threat.

She said calmly, "I could ask you the same question, young man. This is not Cabin 14. This is Cabin 17. As I told you, it's already rented."

"Doesn't seem to be anyone here. Doesn't look lived in at all. Just photos and a white rose on the table."

Gwen looked past him to the photos and flower then drew her gaze back to him. "Doesn't matter. They paid, and it's theirs to do with what they want."

"Who exactly are 'they'?"

"Like I said before, confidential."

"I think we're well past confidences, Gwen. I think you need to tell me right now."

"She won't but I will."

Robie swung his pistol around to take aim at the newcomer.

Jessica Reel was standing in front of him.

What surprised him was that she had no gun. Her arms were down by her sides. Robie ran his gaze quickly over her.

Reel said, "No weapons, Will. No throwing knife. No tricks."

Robie remained silent as she took another deliberate step into the room. He kept swiveling his gaze between both women.

Reel had said she was unarmed, something he didn't believe. But she hadn't said the old woman wasn't packing. And at this short distance even an eighty-year-old could shoot and kill him.

"You two know each other?" he asked at last.

"You could say that," replied Reel. "She was my security blanket."

Robie cocked his head questioningly at her.

"I thought if she was here you wouldn't put a bullet in my head."

"I didn't in Arkansas."

"I appreciate that more than you'll ever know. But circumstances change."

"Yes, they do. But why would you think her being here would stop me from killing you now?"

"Because if you kill me, you'd have to kill her. And you don't kill innocent people. It's not how you're wired."

Robie shook his head. "How do I know she's innocent? She doesn't seem surprised by any of this."

Gwen said, "But I was. Didn't think you could move that fast. Scared me."

"He always did move fast," said Reel. "But no unnecessary movement. Everything calculated for maximum efficiency. I saw that in Arkansas vividly. A one-man army."

"So where does that leave us?"

"With you pointing a gun at me. Like back in Arkansas."

"Doesn't really answer the question."

"What do you want the answer to be?"

"You killed two members of the agency in cold blood. Under normal circumstances that would be enough of an answer for me. That's what I told you in Arkansas, and that's what I'm telling you now. Back there I asked for an explanation. I'm asking again."

She took another step forward. "Under normal circumstances?" she said.

Robie let his finger slide past the trigger guard and close in on the trigger. Reel noted this and stopped moving. They both knew he was close to the point of no return.

Gwen hovered in the background looking tense, her gaze focused on Reel.

Robie said, "DiCarlo? She made it clear to me that the situation was not normal." Robie gestured over his shoulder to the table. "White Rose? Resistance group in

World War II. Fought against what they considered the traitorous Nazis."

"I was afraid they'd police the roses I left."

"They did, only they missed a couple of petals. Probably the only reason they left the book in your locker for me to look at. They didn't think I'd have any evidence of the flower."

"Good to know they make mistakes."

"My problem, though, is that maybe you're the traitor and all this is a smokescreen."

"Maybe I am."

"Jess!" snapped Gwen. "You know that's not true."

Robie let his gaze flicker over the old woman. He had already noted she was fully dressed, though the hour was very late.

This was all planned.

Robie asked Gwen, "Who exactly are you?"

Gwen looked at Reel but said nothing. Reel slowly turned to look at her. Robie thought he saw her smile, though it was hard to tell in the poor light.

Reel said, "An old friend of mine. A very old friend. Family, actually."

"I didn't think you had any. Your mom's dead. You old man's in prison for life."

"Gwen was the only decent foster parent I had."

"When they took you away..." Gwen began, but her voice faltered.

"If you were a good foster parent, why was she taken away?"

Reel answered, "There is no logic in foster care. What happens happens."

"Okay, but that doesn't explain why she's here."

Reel said, "I bought this place four years ago. Under an alias, of course. I brought Gwen up to run it."

"You own the motor court?" said Robie in surprise.

"I had to put my money somewhere. And while I wasn't that concerned about turning a profit, I did want a place where I could get away."

"Literally get away?" said Robie.

She glanced past him to the photos on the table. "Aren't you going to ask me about them?"

"I thought I already did. I don't remember hearing an answer other than they were traitors but you had no proof."

"I walked in here with no weapon. What does that tell you?"

"That you want to talk, so talk. I especially want to hear about the apocalypse."

"It's a very long story."

"My calendar is clear for the rest of the year."

"Can you lower your weapon?"

"I don't think so."

She held out her hands. "You can cuff me if it'll make you feel better."

"Tell me what you need to tell me. Explain to me

why you put a bullet in Doug Jacobs when you were supposed to be planting a round between the eyes of a man who has sworn to destroy our country. Tell me why Jim Gelder had to die. And tell me why you killed an analyst turned militia freak. I'm really looking forward to the answers. It might save your life. *Might*," he added.

"I told you, I didn't kill Roy West. He tried to kill me and I defended myself. He died from shrapnel wounds when his house blew up."

"Why go out there at all?"

"He had something I needed."

"Yeah, you told me that in Arkansas. But what? You told me you'd already read the paper he'd written."

"Confirmation."

"Of what?"

"Of which people had seen the paper." Reel watched him expectantly. "You had figured that out. I can tell by your expression."

"You killed those people over think-tank bullshit?"

"It wasn't a think tank. And it wasn't bullshit. At least to certain people it wasn't. The paper was not widely circulated. But a few key people read it. People in a position to make the plan contained in the paper a reality. And if that happens, Robie..." Her voice trailed off.

He was just about to ask what specifically the paper said when they both heard it.

People were coming.

Not deer. Not squirrels. Not bears.

People. For it was only people who moved with stealth like that. And both Reel and Robie recognized the movements.

Reel snapped her head around at Robie. The accusation in her face was clear. "I didn't expect this of you, Robie. You led them right here."

In answer Robie reached behind his back, slid his spare gun out of its holster, and tossed it to her. She caught it, racked the slide, and held it loosely in her hand.

Now it was Reel's turn to look surprised.

"They're not with me," said Robie.

"Then you were followed."

He turned off the lantern, plunging the cabin into darkness. "Looks that way. I just don't know how. Is there another way out of here?"

Reel said, "Yes, there is."

58

REEL WENT TO THE CORNER of the room, shoved the table aside, knelt down, and lifted up a section of the floor, revealing a three-foot-square opening.

"Where does that go?" asked Robie, who sounded chagrined that he hadn't noticed it before.

"Away from here."

She sat on her butt and dropped down into the hole. "Let's go. They won't be waiting out there long."

"Then let me persuade them they should exercise some caution," said Robie.

He moved to the window and fired five shots through it. He placed his rounds in a wide enough array that anyone approaching would be forced to take cover. Then he moved to the hole and dropped through. He stood up and motioned to Gwen. "Come on."

Gwen shook her head. "I'll just slow you down."

Reel stood next to Robie. "Gwen, you're not staying behind."

"I'm old and just worn out, Jess."

"This is not open for discussion. Come on."

Gwen slipped a revolver from the front pocket of her dress and pointed it at Reel. "You're right. This is not open for discussion, Jess. Go."

Reel looked at her in disbelief.

Robie pulled on her arm. "Not much time."

They heard footsteps approaching from all sides.

"Go!" snapped Gwen. "I didn't raise you to die like this. You're going to go and finish this, Jess. Now."

Robie slung his bag over his shoulder, pulled Reel down into the hole, and then moved the piece of flooring back into place. Gwen scuttled over and repositioned the table back over the opening. Then she turned to the door to face what was coming.

Robie and Reel had to crawl on their bellies. At one point in the tunnel there was a large knapsack. Reel snagged it, slung it over her shoulder, and kept crawling.

"Where does it come out?" asked Robie.

"In the woods," she whispered. Her voice was strained.

Robie knew where her mind was. On Gwen. On what was about to happen to her. But maybe they wouldn't hurt the old woman.

The gunshots they both heard moments later settled that question. Barely inches behind her in the tunnel, Robie ran up the backs of Reel's legs as she stopped at the sound.

They just lay there for several seconds. Robie could hear Reel breathing fast.

"You okay?" he finally asked.

"Let's go," she said in a husky voice, and she started crawling again.

What they heard thirty seconds later made them accelerate their movements. Other people had dropped into the tunnel. Robie and Reel whipped their bodies back and forth, performing a hyper-speed version of the Army crawl.

A minute later Reel stood, pushed against something, and then her legs disappeared from sight. Robie scrambled up after her, gained purchase on the dirt, and looked around.

They were in the middle of the forest.

The cover for the tunnel had been well designed: a fabricated tree stump made of lightweight materials.

Reel unzipped her bag, slipped out a grenade, counted to five, pulled the pin, bent down, and tossed it as far down the tunnel as she could.

Then they both ran for it, Reel in the lead because she knew where to go, Robie right behind. His gun was out and he was alternating between following Reel and covering their rear flank.

The explosion wasn't loud, but they could both hear it clearly.

"That was for Gwen," Robie heard Reel say as they

raced through a barely discernible path between the trees.

Up ahead was an old shack. Reel headed right for it. She unlocked the door, darted inside, and a few moments later came out, rolling a dirt bike behind her.

"I wasn't expecting company. It'll be a tight fit."

They could barely sit on the seat together. Reel drove and Robie clung to her. He was now carrying both bags over his shoulders. As they wound through the trees he was nearly thrown off several times, but just managed to maintain his seat.

Twenty minutes later they finally hit asphalt after clearing a cleft in the trees and then a broad ditch that Reel simply jumped. They landed so hard that Robie thought he would leave his privates behind. But he gritted his teeth and clung to the woman. She rotated the throttle to maximum and roared off down the road.

"Where to?" Robie shouted in her ear as the wind whipped them both.

"Not here," she yelled back.

They drove for what seemed like hours, and finally ditched the bike behind an abandoned gas station on the outskirts of a small town. They walked into the town, which was made up of decrepit buildings and mom-and-pop stores.

The sun was starting to rise. Robie looked over

at Reel, now revealed in the coming dawn. She was dirty, disheveled. As was he.

She looked straight ahead, the anger on her face almost painful to see.

"I'm sorry about Gwen," said Robie.

Reel didn't answer him.

An Amtrak train station loomed ahead. It was just a tired-looking old brick building on a raised platform with a slender ribbon of track next to it. A few people were sitting on wooden benches waiting for their early morning ride to somewhere.

Reel went inside and paid cash for two tickets. She came back out and handed one to Robie.

"Where to?" he asked.

"Not here," she said.

"You keep saying that. But it doesn't really tell me anything."

"I'm not prepared to have this discussion yet."

"Then get prepared as soon as this ride is over," said Robie.

He walked down the platform and leaned against the wall, looking in the direction from which they had come.

How did they follow me? How did they know?

There wasn't anybody. I could swear there wasn't anybody who could have known.

In his pocket was his Glock. He gripped it with one hand. He had a strong feeling that things were not safe yet.

He was still holding both the bag from the tunnel and his knapsack. He glanced over at Reel. She was just standing there next to the tracks.

Robie assumed she was thinking about Gwen lying dead back there.

Ten minutes later he heard the train coming. It came to a stop with a long screech of brakes and release of hydraulic pressure. He and Reel boarded the middle car.

This was not the Acela bullet train. The car looked like it had been in service since Amtrak was created in the early seventies.

They were the only passengers on this car. There was a single attendant, a sleepy-looking black man in a uniform that didn't fit him very well. He yawned, took their tickets, stuck them to the back of their seats, and told them where the café car was located if they were hungry or thirsty.

"The conductor will be along at some point to take your tickets," he said. "Enjoy the ride."

"Yeah, thanks," said Robie, while Reel just stared straight ahead.

As the train rolled out of the station the attendant walked up the aisle and disappeared into the next car, probably to make his spiel to the few passengers there.

Robie and Reel settled down in their seats, he at the window, she at the aisle. Robie had put both bags at his feet.

Minutes passed and he said, "So where are we going?"

"I've booked us through to Philly, but we can get off at any stop in between."

"What's in your bag besides grenades?"

"Things we might need."

"Who was the old guy in the photo with you?"

"Friend of a friend."

"Why not the friend?"

She glanced at him in mild reproach. "Too easy. If I'd done that, do you think they would have left the photo for you to see? They're an intelligence agency, Robie, so you have to assume they have *some* degree of it to exercise."

"So the friend?"

"Give me a few minutes. I'm trying to deal with the loss of another friend, maybe my last one."

Robie was about to push her, but then something told him not to.

The loss of a friend. I can relate to that.

"Did you dig that tunnel?"

She shook her head. "It was already there. Maybe bootleggers. Maybe some criminal owned it and that was his escape hatch. When I bought the place and found it I made Cabin 17 my hideaway for that very reason."

"Good thing you did."

She looked away. She obviously didn't want to talk anymore.

"You want something to eat or drink?" he asked a few minutes later as the train started to slow. They were probably approaching another podunk station where a few more sleepy people would climb aboard.

"Coffee, nothing to eat," she said curtly, still not looking at him.

"I'll get some stuff, just in case you change your mind."

He walked up the aisle and kept going until he reached the café car. There was one person ahead of him, a woman dressed in a jean skirt, boots, and a tattered coat. She gathered up her coffee, pastries, and a bag of chips and headed on her way. She stumbled as the train slid into the station and stopped.

Robie helped right her and then stepped up to the counter. The uniformed man behind it was about sixty with a full gray beard and small narrow eyes behind thick glasses.

"What can I get you, sir?" he asked Robie.

Robie looked at the offerings on the menu board behind the counter. "Two coffees, two muffins, and three packs of peanuts."

"Just brewing a fresh pot. Coming up."

"No hurry." Robie turned and looked out the window. This station looked even smaller than the one at which they had boarded. He couldn't even see the name of the place, although he assumed it had to be posted somewhere.

The next moment he forgot about that.

At the far side of the station, its bumper hanging out just far enough that he could see it, was a black Range Rover.

Robie looked at the few passengers getting on. One was an old woman carrying her belongings in a pillowcase.

Another was a teenage girl with a battered suitcase.

The last passenger was a black man in his forties. He was dressed in not overly clean bib overalls and falling-apart work boots, and he had a dirty knapsack slung over one shoulder.

Robie did not like to stereotype, but none of the new passengers looked like patrons of the Range Rover brand.

When the man behind the counter turned to him with two fresh cups of coffee, Robie was gone.

CHAPTER

59

GUN OUT, Robie reentered the train car. He looked down the aisle. Reel was still in her seat, but she looked stiff, unnatural.

Robie looked around. He saw no obvious breach points.

He looked back at Reel, squatted low, and moved forward, prepared to fire in an instant. He cleared each row of seats until he got to Reel and looked up at her.

Only it wasn't her.

It was a man.

With his throat cut.

Robie glanced down. Her bag was gone.

Where was Reel?

A voice called out softly, "Robie, over here."

He glanced up. Reel was at the rear of the train car.

"We have company," she said.

"Yeah, that one I'd figured out," replied Robie. "Where did he come from?" he asked, gesturing to the dead man.

"Rear door. Advance guard, I guess."

"They should have sent more guards," noted Robie.

"He was tough to kill. Very well trained."

"I'm sure." Robie looked around. "The train's not moving. Station's not that big. All passengers should have gotten on by now."

"You think they've commandeered the train?"

"Wouldn't bet against it. They'll do a car-by-car search."

"The dead guy was trying to call in that he'd spotted me. But he never made it." She looked around. "Got a plan?"

Before Robie could answer the train started to move.

"What do you think that's about?" asked Reel.

"Too many questions in the station, maybe. They want to be rolling through the country when they hit us."

"Toss us out on the fly?"

"After they make sure we're dead."

"So, again, got a plan?"

Robie looked behind him. The attendant who had greeted them hadn't come back. He might be dead too.

Robie raced up the aisle to a small storage closet located at one end of the car and grabbed a large metal bowl from inside it. He rushed into the small bathroom compartment, turned on the water, and filled up the bowl. Then he emptied half the bowl of water in front of each of the connecting doors into their train cars. He rubbed the slickened metal floor with his foot and came away satisfied.

Then Robie looked at the dead man.

Reel joined him and said, "He had no creds. No ID, nothing."

"Missing personnel, missing equipment."

"Is that what DiCarlo told you?" asked Reel.

"Yes."

"The apocalypse scenario has been a long time in preparation, Robie."

"I'm starting to see that."

He climbed up on a seat and squatted down.

Reel did the same.

"You left, me right," said Robie, and Reel replied, "Copy that."

A few seconds later armed men came racing in from both directions. It was a designed pincers move, to trap Reel and Robie between two flanks and catch them in a crossfire they could not withstand.

Only they had not counted on a slippery floor.

Three of the men went down hard and slid along the floor, while a fourth staggered around trying to regain his balance.

Reel and Robie popped out from the hidden spots and opened fire, Robie right, Reel left. Nine seconds later four men lay dead, their blood turning the floor and walls crimson. The other men retreated to the cars bracketing this one.

Robie looked at Reel. "How fast do you think we're going?"

She looked out the window. "Fifty, maybe a little more. These old bangers don't get much above sixty."

Robie looked at the terrain outside. All trees. "Still too fast," he said, and Reel nodded.

Robie glanced to his left and then back at her. "Where's your bag?"

"I stashed it here." She pulled it out from between two of the seats.

"Got any flash-bangs in there?"

"Two of them."

He looked at one of the connecting doors between the cars through which the men had retreated. It was metal but with a glass window. Then he ran over to a control panel built into one wall in the car's vestibule. He ripped it open and took a few seconds to see what was available.

While he was doing that Reel snagged both flash-bangs from her bag.

"You ever jumped off a moving train before?" he asked, looking up from his work.

"No. You?"

He shook his head. "I figure at sixty, we have no chance. At thirty our odds improve some."

"Depends on what we jump into," said Reel, who was already clicking keys on her phone. She brought up their current location.

"Body of water coming up on the left in about two miles."

"Could be harder than dirt depending on how we hit."

"We stay here we die."

Robie hit a button and the left-side door slid open. Cool air rushed in.

"They won't be waiting long," said Reel, looking at each doorway.

"No. We need to take care of that."

She handed him a pair of earplugs, which he pushed deeply into his ears. She did the same with her ears. Then she passed him one of the flash-bangs.

"Give me a countdown," she said.

Reel went to the middle of the car, drew her pistol, and waited.

"Five-four-three-two-one," called out Robie.

Reel fired to the left, shattering the glass on the door leading to the train car in front of them. She gripped the flash-bang, engaged it, and threw it through the opening. She whirled and shot out the glass in the window to the rear. The bullet was followed by the second flash-bang, which Robie tossed through the new opening. Robie crouched down and covered his face and his ears as both flash-bangs detonated within seconds of each other.

Screams came from the other train cars.

Reel, who had ducked down a split second before

the flash-bangs went off, raced back down the aisle and joined Robie.

He engaged the emergency braking system. They were thrown forward as the train's brakes caught. They righted themselves, faced the open door, and looked at each other. They were both breathing hard.

"How fast are we going?" Reel asked.

"Still too fast."

He glanced out the door. "Water's coming up."

The train was slowing, yet it took a long time for something that big to reduce its speed. But they were out of time.

Shots were starting to rip through the train car as their opponents recovered.

"Gotta go." Robie gripped her hand as the train slowed even more.

"Robie, I don't think I can do this."

"Don't think, just do."

They jumped together.

It seemed to Robie that they stayed in the air a long time. When they landed, they hit soft mud, not water. The one thing they couldn't have accounted for was a summer drought that had extended into fall and had lowered the lake's water level by about four feet. When they hit the wet dirt, Robie and Reel rolled and tumbled along about twenty feet past their first impact.

The train was already out of sight around a bend.

But at some point the brakes would bring the million-pound-plus behemoth to a stop.

Robie slowly sat up. He was covered in mud and slime. His clothes were ripped and he felt like an entire NFL team had jumped on him.

He looked over at Reel, who was starting to slowly get up. She looked as bad as he did and probably felt worse. Her pants and shirt were torn too.

Robie managed to stand and stagger over to the knapsack, which had separated from him on impact.

Reel groaned. "Next time I'm staying and just shooting it out."

Robie nodded. There was a pain in his right arm. It felt funny. He worried that he had broken it, but it didn't feel broken, just...funny.

As Reel walked over to him he rolled up his shirtsleeve, exposing his burn.

What he saw surprised Robie. But it also solved the question of how the people had been able to follow them.

Robie looked at Reel and smiled grimly.

"What?" she said.

"They just made a big mistake."

CHAPTER

60

SAM KENT WAS AT HOME when the call came in.

"Believed to be dead," said the voice.

Robie and Reel had jumped off a train going nearly forty miles per hour. It was thought unlikely that they could have survived.

The fail-safe tracker had gone silent.

It was over.

Kent didn't believe that for a second. But he had confirmation that his greatest fear had been realized.

Robie and Reel had teamed up. And despite the report, his gut was telling him that they were alive.

Kent was sitting in his study in his exquisite home set among many exquisite homes in a section of Fairfax County that was home to the unassailable "one-tenthers," the people in the top one-tenth of the one percent. Average income per year: ten million dollars. Most of them made far more than that. They did it in myriad ways:

Inheritance.

Gaining the ear, for a fee, of those in power.

And many, like Kent, actually worked hard for a living and provided things of value to the world. Though his wife's money had certainly come in handy.

Now Kent sat in his castle and contemplated the phone call he was about to make. It was to someone of whom he was understandably afraid.

His secure phone was in his desk drawer. He pulled it out, hit the required numbers, and waited.

Four rings and a pickup. Kent winced when he realized it was the person and not a recording. He had been hoping for a bit of a reprieve.

He reported the latest news in terse, information-packed sentences, just as he had been trained to do.

And then he waited.

He could hear the other person breathing lightly on the other end of a communication line that not even the NSA could crack.

Kent did not break the silence. It wasn't his place.

He just let the man breathe, take it in, think. The response would be forthcoming, he was certain of that.

"Has a search been made?" asked the person. "If they're believed dead, there have to be bodies. That will be the only confirmation. Otherwise, they're alive."

"Agreed," said Kent, who let out a nearly inaudible sigh of relief. "I personally don't think they're dead."

"But injured?"

"After that sort of a jump, most likely yes."

"Then we have to find them. Shouldn't be too difficult if they are hurt."

"Yes."

"Cleanup on the train?"

"The train was stopped. Everything has been removed. All witnesses have been dealt with."

"Explanation?"

"We can place the blame on whomever we want."

"Well, I would place it on two rogue agents who have obviously lost their way. That will be the official line."

"Understood."

"It's still an enormous mess. And one that should have been avoided."

"I agree."

"I didn't ask for your agreement."

"No, of course not."

"But we're near the end."

"Yes," said Kent.

"So don't create any more obstacles."

"Understood."

"Robie and Reel together. A cause for concern."

Kent didn't know if the person was asking a question or stating a fact.

"I would not underestimate either of them," said Kent.

"I never underestimate anyone, least of all my *allies*."

Kent licked his lips, considered this statement. He was an ally. And this person would not underestimate him. "We'll make a major push."

"Yes, you will."

The line went dead.

Kent put the phone away and looked up when the door to his study opened. For one panicked moment he thought his time had come and the open door would reveal a person like Robie or Reel dispatched to give him his final punishment.

But it was simply his wife. She was in her nightgown.

Kent's gaze flicked to the wall above the door where the clock showed it was nearly eight in the morning.

"Did you even go to bed?" she asked. Her hair was tousled, her face bare of makeup, her eyes still weighted with sleep. But to Kent she was the most beautiful woman in the world.

He was lucky. He had never deserved a life of simple domesticity. But that was only half his life. His other half was decidedly different. Equal parts perfume and gunpowder. But right now, all gunpowder.

"Grabbed a few hours in the guest room. Didn't want to disturb you, honey," he said. "I finished up work late."

She went to him, perched on the side of his desk, ran her fingers through his hair.

Their kids looked more like their mother. That was good, thought Kent. He wanted them to be like her. Not him.

Not me. Not my life.

He wanted his children to have exceptional lives. But also ordinary ones. Safe ones. Ones that did not involve carrying weapons or shooting others while being shot at. That was no life. Just a way to an early death.

"You look tired," said his wife.

"A little. Burning the candles at both ends lately. Things will even out."

"I'll go make you some coffee."

"Thanks, sweetie. That would be great."

She kissed him on the forehead and left.

Kent watched her go every step of the way.

He had a lot.

Which meant he had a lot to lose.

He looked around his study. None of his awards, his military medals, his records of professional accomplishments were displayed here. Those things were private. They were not meant to impress or intimidate. He knew he had earned them. That was enough. They were kept upstairs in a small, locked storage closet. Sometimes he would look at them. But mostly they just sat up there gathering dust.

They were records of the past.

Kent had always been a forward thinker.

He unlocked a safe that sat on a shelf behind his desk and drew the paper out. It was Roy West's white paper. A thing of intellectual beauty from a man who had become a paranoid militia nut. It was hard to believe that he could have concocted something that powerful. But perhaps from the forming depths of paranoia sometimes sprang genius, if for only a few frenetically productive moments.

Yet they had taken his original vision and turned it into something very different that suited their own purposes.

He walked over to the gas fireplace set against one wall. With a flick of a remote that he kept on the mantel, Kent turned on the fireplace. Then he dropped the white paper on top of the gas logs and watched it quickly disintegrate.

In less than thirty seconds it was gone.

But the ideas in there would remain with Kent for the rest of his life.

Whether that was to be a short or long time he couldn't tell right now.

He was suddenly beset with doubts. His mind raced ahead to one catastrophic scenario after another. Such thoughts were never productive. But finally his military training took over and he calmed rapidly.

His secure phone, still on the desk, buzzed.

He hurried over to it.

The message was from the person with whom he had just talked.

It was a text. It was only three words.

But to Kent it proved his superior was indeed a mind reader.

The text read, *No going back.*

CHAPTER

61

THE CAR WAS PARKED OUTSIDE of a grill pub across from a bank. It was late, the darkness deep and broken only by the exterior light of the building.

There were only four other cars in the parking lot. One car's lights came on as the owner hit the unlock button on her key fob.

She walked toward the car, staggering slightly. She had had more to drink than she probably should have. But she lived close by and was confident she could navigate the roads to her home safely.

She climbed into the car and closed the door behind her. She started to put the key in the ignition when a hand clamped over her mouth.

Her right hand went to her purse, to retrieve the pistol she kept there. But another hand encircled her wrist and held it inches from the purse.

The passenger door opened and the woman climbed in.

She had her gun pointed at the driver's head.

The woman with the gun was Jessica Reel.

The woman in the driver's seat did not seem to recognize her. She started, though, when the man's voice from the backseat said, "I might need you to sew me up again, Doc. The tracking device in the sutures got broken."

In the rearview mirror Karin Meenan looked at Will Robie.

He said, "Start the car. Then we'll tell you where to go."

"I'm not going anywhere with you," said Meenan.

Reel pulled the hammer back on her gun.

"Then she's going to put a bullet in your head right now," said Robie.

Meenan glanced at Reel, who was staring directly at her. The look in the woman's features was clear. She wanted to pull the trigger. She was hoping for any chance, any opportunity provided by Meenan, to do so.

Meenan started the car, put it in gear, and drove off. Robie directed her to a dilapidated motel about five miles away. They parked in the rear and Reel and Robie bookended Meenan as they walked to their room.

Robie closed the door behind them and directed Meenan to sit on the bed.

She stared up at them. "I don't know why you're doing this, Robie. You're in a lot of trouble. You've kidnapped me at gunpoint."

Robie sat in a chair and seemed not to have heard her. Reel stood with her back to the door and her gun pointed at her.

Meenan snapped, "Who the hell are you?"

"You know who she is," said Robie calmly.

Meenan turned to look at him.

"And you might want to watch your drinking and driving," noted Robie. "Two beers and a shot of tequila. You're officially shit-faced. That could cost you your clearance and your job."

"You were watching me?"

"No, we just happened on you by accident. I feel so lucky right now, I'm going to play the Lotto."

"You're cracking jokes?" she snapped. "Do you realize what you've done? You're going to prison for this."

"Is that the same bar where you met Roy West?" Robie asked.

"I never met Roy West at a bar. He was briefly a patient of mine. I already told you that."

"You want to reconsider that answer?"

"Why should I?"

Robie slipped a photo from his pocket. "I had a friend at the FBI pull this off the surveillance camera from the bank across the street from the bar."

He held it up. On the image were Roy West and Meenan getting into her car.

"I've done nothing wrong. So I had a drink with Roy West. So what?"

Robie slipped off his jacket and rolled up his shirt-sleeve, revealing where the sutures had been.

"I took out these and the ones you put in my leg. Pretty ingenious stuff. Communication filaments and an internal power source disguised basically as stitches. GPS locator. Satellite up- and downlink. Probably electronically lit me up like the Eiffel Tower at night. The agency has really made great strides in the surveillance business."

Meenan looked at Reel. "Robie, if that is Jessica Reel you should be arresting her. Or killing her. She's the enemy. Not me."

"Who told you to put those sutures in me?" asked Robie. "Sam Kent?"

Meenan made no reaction to this.

"Howard Decker," said Reel.

Again, no reaction from Meenan. She kept her gaze on the far wall.

"Somebody else up high," Robie barked.

Now, there was the barest of flinches from Meenan. But it was enough.

She must have realized that she had given herself away. She looked at Robie with an ugly expression. "You have no chance."

"I was about to say the same thing to you."

This came from Reel, who had placed her muzzle against the back of Meenan's head.

The doctor looked at Robie with pleading eyes. "You're just going to let her murder me?"

Robie's look was impassive. "I don't know, Doc. People have been trying to murder us. Why should you be any different?"

"But...but you're one of us."

"One of us? I don't really know what that means anymore."

"Please, Robie, please."

"I'm not sure what to do with you, Doc. Can't really let you go."

Meenan was crying now. "I won't say anything. I swear to God."

"Yeah, I'm sure," said Robie.

He glanced at Reel. "What do you think?"

Meenan shrieked, "Don't ask her! She's crazy! She's a traitor!"

Reel looked at Robie. "Okay?"

"Okay by me."

"No!" screamed Meenan.

Reel dropped her muzzle to the base of Meenan's neck and pulled the trigger.

62

Robie carried Meenan over his shoulder and down the steps into the bomb shelter. They were under the barn at his hideaway. At the far end of the underground shelter was a makeshift cell that Robie had constructed. It was easily strong enough to hold someone like Meenan.

She was starting to come around after Reel had shot her in the neck with a tranquilizer dart.

Robie lay Meenan down on a cot in the cell. Stacked against one wall were enough provisions to last the woman two weeks. Robie assumed that by then he would have worked things out or else died trying.

He locked the cell door about the time that Meenan slowly sat up, rubbed her neck, and looked at him. "You didn't let her kill me?"

"We never had any intention of killing you."

"Why not?"

"You may be corrupt, but you were defenseless."

"You're an assassin, that's what you do."

"Did you read the apocalypse paper?"

"The what?"

"The white paper that Roy West wrote. Reel told me he used to brag about it to people. Maybe you were one of them. Over pillow talk? At the bar?"

"I don't have to answer that."

"Did you believe it?"

"Roy talked about a lot of things. And many of them made sense."

"So you're for an apocalypse?"

"For real change to happen, certain people have to be sacrificed."

"Wasn't that what the Nazis said?"

She snapped, "Don't be ridiculous. That's not even a close analogy."

"Really? You got led around like a lemming by a nut who loaded up his cabin with explosives and had plans to blow up half the government? How does that make sense? You *work* for the government."

"We all fight for liberty in different ways."

"I'll stick with my way. You can keep yours."

"You go and kill the people they tell you to. Talk about a lemming."

"Well, the difference is now I understand that. You apparently don't."

She gave him a condescending look. "You can't stop this from happening."

"I can if you help me."

"Not a chance in hell."

"So you just stand by and watch all those people die? Doctors are supposed to preserve life, aren't they?"

"I'm not just a doctor. I care about my country. Our enemies are trying to destroy us. We have to kill all of them first."

Robie said, "Care to tell me who is really behind this?"

She folded her arms across her chest and looked at him dully. "Just give it up, okay?"

He held up her phone. "Got your laptop too. They should tell us a few things."

She looked suddenly panicked.

"Don't ever go to Vegas," he advised. "Your poker face is seriously lacking."

"They're password-protected."

"You had your phone on a five-minute auto lock. You must have just used it before you got into the car. The lock hadn't reset yet, so I got everything I needed. As for your laptop, next time use a password more difficult than your name spelled backwards and your date of birth."

"Robie, you're on the wrong side of this. Trust me. Reel is a murderer. She killed two defenseless men. In cold blood."

He pointed to the provisions. "There's enough food and water to last you at least two weeks, maybe more if you ration."

"And if you're not back by then?"

"Start yelling. Somebody might hear you. Oh, and while you were knocked out Reel stripped you down and checked every possible place for a transmitter. You might be sore, but you're definitely tracker free."

"Robie!" She jumped up and ran to the cell door. "Think about this very carefully. You won't get a second chance."

"Funny. That's what I was going to tell you."

"You're being stupid. Please let me go."

"This is the safest place for you."

She looked at him with a stunned expression. "Safe? Are you insane?"

"They didn't find our bodies, Doc. And they can no longer track us. Which tells them we're onto how we were tracked. You put the sutures in. We found you. You're out of the loop for a while. If we let you go, you go back to them."

"I won't say anything. I promise."

"That's not the point."

"So what is the point?"

"They'll know you were with us. They'll interrogate you. And then they'll kill you."

Meenan took a step back. "Why would they kill me? I'm on their side."

"Because they'll believe you helped us. That would be the only way we would've let you go. And your price for that is you die. It's really that simple. See, to them, you'll have become the enemy. And like you said, the goal is to kill all of the enemy. And now that includes you."

"But—"

"It's not an either/or proposition. So you stay here, you live. You go out there, you die. I'll let you decide. What's it going to be?"

Meenan stared up at him and then took a few hesitant steps back before plopping down on the cot and studying the floor.

"Good choice," said Robie, and then he walked out.

CHAPTER

63

REEL WAS WAITING FOR HIM outside the barn in a new rental. He climbed in, snagged Meenan's laptop from the backseat, opened it, and started clicking keys as Reel drove off.

"How did it go?" she asked.

"I think she's starting to see the light. Not that it matters."

"Just so you know, I'm down to my last fake ID," said Reel.

"Let's hope it's enough."

"Where to?"

"I've got a contact at the FBI I want to work. I got the photos of West and Meenan from her."

"Special Agent Nicole Vance?"

Robie shot her a glance. "How did you know that?"

"You started out as my enemy. I find out all I can about my enemies."

"How much did you find out?"

"Julie Getty."

She looked at him.

"That makes you angry?"

"It doesn't make me happy. What if someone was following you?"

"Someone *was* following *you*. Vance. And me."

"Okay, let's just call a truce on that. We need some info that we can't get on our own."

She said, "Don't be too sure about that. And the more people we involve, the more potential pitfalls we face."

"We face pitfalls everywhere we turn."

"Proves my point. What do we need to know?"

"Lots of things."

"Find anything interesting on Meenan's computer?"

"I got into her email. She has a varied correspondence. Multiple boyfriends, from the content of some of the emails. A little racier than I would have given the doc credit for. West was probably one of them, but he's not on there now." He refocused on the screen. "This might be something."

"What?"

"Give me a sec."

He read some more emails, scrolling down the screen.

"What is it, Robie?"

"Cryptic one-word messages. Without context they

don't mean anything. 'Yes,' 'no,' 'now,' 'tomorrow'—things like that."

"Who's the sender?"

"The address looks generic, and is probably untraceable. But there are three letters at the end of the messages, like the writer's signature. RTD. Mean anything to you?"

Reel was silent for a long minute. "Roger the Dodger," she said.

"Who?"

"It was the code name of the person West said had requested the white paper. He said the person was at least three levels above him at the time."

"Did he say anything else that might lead us to the person?"

"Unfortunately, that was about the time I had to knock him out."

"Roger the Dodger? Odd moniker."

"I thought so too. But he's been able to dodge us pretty effectively. So it does fit. What do you think Vance can help us with?"

"Finding the apocalypse. Before it happens."

"The white paper was pretty explicit. Country by country. Leader by leader. Simultaneously. It's dazzlingly complex and brutally efficient. It's all in the timing."

"But what are the exact details? You never said."

"Targeting all G8 leaders, except the U.S. president, on the same day at the same time using a coordinated attack, and intelligence–sharing, and buying whatever resources are needed on the inside. They're all killed. What follows is chaos in the civilized world. The paper goes on to detail what steps the perpetrators of the attacks should take to press their advantage."

"Okay, but who are the perpetrators?"

"West papered various ones. Not surprisingly, they were mostly radical Islamic fundamentalists. He broke it down to include factions of al-Qaeda, the Taliban, Hamas. I have to admit, it was well thought out."

"Why leave out the U.S. president?" asked Robie.

"Probably because the agency didn't want to pay its people to think up plausible ways to kill POTUS. If that got out there would be hell to pay."

"And what was the purpose of such an attack, at least according to West?"

"Power vacuum in the civilized world, chaos in financial markets, upheaval across the globe, 9/11 on steroids."

"And why would we want a paper out there that tells people how to do that?"

"They probably didn't believe it would be circulated. And maybe they wanted to see the scenario to know how to counter it so it didn't happen or deal with it if it ever did. Roy West wasn't too clear on that."

"Did we come up with counters?"

"I doubt it. The paper apparently didn't go anywhere within the agency hierarchy."

"You know what that strategy reminds me of?" said Robie.

"What?"

"The scene in *The Godfather*. Where Michael Corleone is having his child baptized. And then they intercut to the scenes of the rival bosses who tried to kill Marlon Brando's character being assassinated. It was Michael's revenge."

"Maybe that's where West got the idea. From a movie. He didn't strike me as an original thinker."

"But for it to work they have to have personnel in all those different countries ready to move at the same time."

"So who on the inside of the U.S. government would want to see that scenario played out?" asked Reel.

"I would hope no one. But that apparently isn't the case."

"So America gets thrown into the apocalypse. In a scenario like that, nobody wins."

They were both silent for a while, each probably contemplating what the world might look like after such an event.

"Feeling pretty hopeless?" asked Reel.

"Aren't you?"

"I've never forgotten one thing. It might seem stupid to you."

"I'm listening."

"There is always hope in *hope*less."

They exchanged a brief smile.

"Tell me something. Who was the friend of the friend?"

Reel looked away. Robie saw her fingers tighten on the steering wheel but she didn't answer.

"The guy in the photo with you. You said he was a friend of a friend because putting the other guy in there would guarantee I never would have gotten the picture."

"Why do you need to know who he is?"

"If you didn't want me to know, why leave the photo in the locker?"

"Maybe I didn't have a reason."

"You told me there is a reason for everything you do."

A minute later Reel said, "The friend was a mentor. A guy who cared about me way back when. When no one else did."

"How did you know him?"

"I just knew him."

"Witness Protection, maybe?"

She glanced at him in surprise.

"DiCarlo told me about your past."

"But that's still a big deductive leap."

"The guy in the photo looked like a retired cop to me. So maybe his friend was a cop too."

Reel slowed the car and pulled off the road, putting it in park and turning to look at Robie.

"His name was Joe Stockwell. He was a U.S. marshal. And you're right, he looked after me when I was in Witness Protection. When I joined CIA, I kept in touch. He retired a number of years ago. But after that he stumbled onto what they were planning."

"How was that possible?"

"Joe knew Sam Kent from way back. They served in Vietnam together. He even went to Kent's wedding. Kent approached him about some things over time, innocuous things, but taken together it made Joe suspicious. But he played along and learned more. I guess Kent trusted him, and when he believed Joe wanted to be part of the plan he told him more. Then Kent found Joe was actually working against him, collecting evidence. So he had him killed, although his death was officially ruled an accident. But I knew better."

Robie said, "I'm sorry about that. Sounds like Stockwell was really trying to do the right thing."

She nodded. "He was able to get me the list of people and some details about what was going on. That's how I got Jacobs's and Gelder's names. That's why I killed them."

"But if Stockwell had enough info to put together a list, why not go to the cops?"

"The people on that list were pretty powerful and he apparently didn't believe he had enough evidence to convince the authorities. Joe knew what he was doing. He was a real pro. He wanted a slam-dunk case, apparently. He just didn't live to get it."

"Yet you had enough belief in Stockwell to kill two of them and try and take down a third."

"I know what they're planning to do, Robie. I know that they killed him. He was a good, decent guy trying to do the right thing. He could have been enjoying his golden years, but he was trying to bring this scum down. He failed. I won't."

"I hope you're right."

"You had your proof on that train, didn't you? And what Meenan told you? Don't tell me you need more convincing."

"It's complicated."

"So you're telling me you wouldn't have taken out these guys given the chance? You know that if our agency knew what was up we would have been sent to put a bullet in their brains. I just didn't wait for orders."

"We have a justice system complete with judges and jails for things like that."

"You really think these guys would have been charged, much less convicted? There is no way a case could have been made against them. No way."

"Which means under our system they're presumed innocent."

"So was everybody we've ever pulled the trigger on, because none of them had the benefit of a trial."

Robie sat back. She was absolutely right about that, he thought. "Talk to me about Judge Kent. He served in Vietnam. What else?"

"I researched him. Got into databases I probably shouldn't have."

"And found what?"

"He used to be one of us, way back when. After he left the Army."

Robie slowly nodded. "That makes sense, actually."

She continued, "And now he's a judge on FISC."

"Who else besides Jacobs and Gelder?"

"Congressman Howard Decker was also on the list."

"Chairman of House Intelligence?"

"Yep."

"Is that the complete list?"

"No. There's somebody else out there. Somebody else that even Joe couldn't uncover. But he's out there. I know he is. And he's highly placed, Robie. Very highly placed."

"At least three levels above our boy West?"

"I think far more than three. I think that was just a subterfuge."

"Roger the Dodger."

"Could be. I certainly don't think it was Gelder. He's dead but this thing is still going full torque."

Robie looked up ahead. "So let's see what we can do."

Reel drove off.

CHAPTER

64

Evan Tucker looked across the width of his substantial desk at the man who sat there. Blue Man's features were haggard, his clothes not nearly as impeccable as they normally were.

"It's a total screwup," snapped Tucker.

"Yes, it is," agreed Blue Man.

"Robie's gone off the grid. Reel is God knows where. This event on the train? I know it has something to do with them. I know it."

"There's no proof of that. No witnesses."

"Because they killed them," exclaimed Tucker.

"There is something else going on here," said Blue Man.

"Care to elaborate?"

"DiCarlo?"

"Old news."

"I disagree. Firmly."

Tucker sat up in his chair. There was a dangerous look in his eyes. "Based on what?"

"Based on reality, sir."

"You're very close to insubordination, Roger."

"That of course is not my intent. But we still don't know about DiCarlo. Why DHS took her. Why she was attacked. We do know that Robie saved her life. That's very telling."

"And he believed that Jessica Reel was also there. Also saving DiCarlo's life."

"Correct."

"But we only have his word for that."

"The shell casings were there, sir. You can't get around that."

Tucker put his fingers together and stared at the ceiling. "Reel murdered two of my people. Robie has gone underground. For all we know he's teamed up with the woman somehow. That means he's joined a killer."

"They're both killers, sir. They've been deployed in the field for years eliminating people."

"Killing our enemies, Roger."

"Maybe they're still killing our enemies."

"You will never get me to believe that Jim Gelder had been turned. It would have been impossible. He wasn't even in the field, for Godsakes. No one could have approached him."

"I don't think anything is impossible. We've certainly seen that. Men in high office who ruined careers and jeopardized legacies because of an affair."

"I'm very happily married, thank you very much."

"I'm sure, sir."

"And we're not talking about a romp in the bed here. How could Jacobs and Gelder have been turned? Do you have an ounce of proof?"

Blue Man shrugged. "The only proof I have is that I know Will Robie. And I would trust him with my life. I *have* trusted him with my life. He has sacrificed everything for his country."

"Do you know what you're saying?" Tucker's voice became strident. "If they could turn the number two man in our agency?"

"I clearly understand the ramifications, sir. And any such conspiracy may have spread farther than here. In fact, it may have its origins elsewhere."

"Robie conveyed to me some of what DiCarlo told him."

"I would be glad to hear it."

"Missing personnel. Missing equipment. And money. Missions that never should have been. I have people looking into it. But it's troubling, Roger. Very troubling."

"It would be nice to hear it from DiCarlo's lips," said Blue Man.

Tucker fiddled with a pen on his desk and made no response.

"Sir?" said Blue Man. "Did you hear what I said?"

"It *would* be nice to hear it from DiCarlo's lips,"

Tucker said. "The problem is she took a turn for the worse, is currently in an induced coma, and is not expected to live." He glanced up. "I pushed hard at DHS and finally got them to listen to me. We're now providing her protection along with the FBI. Had to go all the way to the APNSA."

"Gus Whitcomb?"

Tucker nodded. "Whitcomb sided with me. Which meant the president sided with me. Which means I saw Janet." He paused. "It really doesn't look good for her, Roger."

Blue Man looked down. "I'm very sorry to hear that. She's been a great asset to the agency."

"We seem to be running out of those."

"A few bad apples, nothing more."

"I do care about my people, you know."

"Yes, sir."

Tucker doodled on a piece of paper. "Where do you think Robie is?"

"He's certainly gone off the grid." Blue Man paused, seeming to choose his next words with great care. "In fact, I was the one who encouraged him to do so."

Tucker looked stunned. "You advised him to go off the grid?"

"I also advised him to find Jessica Reel."

"His initial task was to do that," snapped Tucker.

"I didn't mean to find and kill her. I meant to find

her and thank her for saving his life. And then to team up."

Tucker's face turned red and a vein near his temple swelled. "Team up to do what exactly?" he barked.

"To do what needs to be done. There is something going on, sir. I realized it even before Jacobs and Gelder were killed. We've had infiltrations at the agency. Robie knew this too. Trusted people who it turned out were working against us."

"We believed that to be isolated. And resolved, Roger," Tucker said in a calmer tone.

"Maybe we believed wrong."

"So you're saying it's something more than a few bad apples, then?"

"Conspiracies are supposed to be relegated to popular fiction. However, it's surprising and a little distressing how often they show up in real life."

Tucker suddenly looked tired. "We are ill-equipped to handle broad-based conspiracies, Roger. Particularly from inside our own tent."

"Which is why perhaps Robie and Reel have a shot at this. By working from the outside in."

"If they do that, we have no way of deploying assets on their behalf. They're on their own."

"With all due respect, sir, that's exactly how they've been operating their whole careers here. On their own with no cover, no backup."

"So maybe they're ideally suited to crack this thing," Tucker said slowly.

"I wouldn't bet against them," said Blue Man with confidence.

"So you really think Gelder and Jacobs were traitors to their country?"

"I can't say they're not."

"And there are others?"

Blue Man shrugged. "Things are still happening and Gelder and Jacobs are dead. They could have had nothing to do with the attack on DiCarlo."

"What about the attack on Roy West in Arkansas? What was that about?"

"I don't know, sir. But from the carnage I wouldn't discount the possibility that both Reel and Robie were there."

"What could possibly be the connection? I've looked at West's record. He was a nothing. Hardly left a mark here. And then he was canned for what amounted to being stupid and lax with security measures. Do you think Reel and Robie know of some connection?"

"If they don't I think they can find out."

Tucker sat back, looking doubtful. "I hope you're right."

"Me too," said Blue Man under his breath. "Me too."

CHAPTER

65

"HELLO, CONGRESSMAN," said the woman as she walked past, her small dog straining on a leash in front of her. "I saw you on TV the other night."

Howard Decker stood on a path at the park near his home. He was dressed casually in jeans and a button-down shirt, loafers and no socks. He had donned a light windbreaker because the evening skies promised rain. He held a leash with his big Labrador Bruin tethered to the other end.

He nodded and smiled at the pretty woman as she walked past. "Thanks. Have a good evening," he said. He liked being recognized. It was a nice taste of celebrity that fed his ego.

He watched her go, appreciating her tall, slender figure, tight skirt, and the way her blonde hair swirled around her shoulders. He was very comfortable with his wife, but he had never been able to cure himself of his roving eye. And his exalted position in

Washington made him a plum target for a variety of sophisticated, accomplished, and attractive women.

He sighed contentedly. Not a bad life. He was wealthy from his past business successes, in relatively good health, with many years in politics ahead of him. His wife was suitably supportive but not eager to grab the limelight from him. She didn't often travel with him, which allowed him the latitude for the occasional dalliance in his hotel room with a young staffer.

His children were young and well behaved. They would have good lives. They looked up to their father. He was popular with his constituency and his district had been redrawn to make him election-proof. That allowed him to spend less time fund-raising and more time plotting his political aspirations. Yes, all in all, he led quite a satisfactory life.

There was only one major problem, but it overshadowed all of the positives. He had long since regretted becoming a part of a plan that was spiraling out of control. But his position as chairman of the Intelligence Committee had made him a pivotal player in a scheme so grand it had taken Decker's breath away the first time he was approached about it.

He was an old-school believer in national security. Nothing trumped that. He had been in New York during 9/11 and had seen the towers collapse. He had run along the streets with thousands of other terrified people as the dust and debris and bodies rained down. He had told himself never again would something like that happen to his country. Not if he had anything to say about it. And he did, more than most people.

And that was why he'd agreed to be part of this colossal plan that, if successful, would right the power balance in the world, bringing it back to where it needed to be to create global peace. He'd thought it a huge, perhaps career-ending risk, but a goal well worth that risk. He had worked behind the scenes to secretly authorize the movement of personnel, equipment, and funds to enable this to happen. Just about everything the Intelligence Committee did was secret, from the funds deployed to the operations on which the members were briefed. Thus he had been in a unique place to assist the plan. He had felt honored to be part of it. He had felt immensely patriotic, particularly as he watched brave young Americans die every week in foreign lands, many of them killed by the very people they were fighting to protect and training to defend themselves. It was a horrendous situation that couldn't be allowed to continue.

But things hadn't gone smoothly or cleanly. Problems had cropped up almost immediately. His partners in this venture, principally Sam Kent, had handled these far better than he had. They were used to mistakes resulting in the loss of human life. But Decker was not accustomed to such things. They scared him. And the more they occurred, the more scared he became.

He had come to the park tonight to walk his dog simply to get away from these thoughts, if only for a few minutes. But he couldn't escape them, not even with big, happy-faced Bruin licking his hand and wanting to play.

Decker was especially afraid of Kent. When the man had said he'd killed a potential assassin, Decker knew that the man was not exaggerating. He *had* killed the man. And it had been a clear warning to Decker not to step out of line.

He had no intention of crossing such men. He'd seen what they were capable of doing. As the chair of the Intelligence Committee he was far more privy to clandestine operations than the average congressperson.

He knew about the Special Activities Division within CIA that utilized the resources provided by people like Jessica Reel and Will Robie. He knew how skilled they were at their work. He'd been briefed on their missions. He'd seen photos of the bodies that resulted from those missions.

His phone buzzed.

He looked at the screen and groaned. It was him.

He hesitated, thinking he wouldn't answer, but he did. He was afraid not to.

But then his courage bucked up.

He was the chairman of one of the most powerful

committees in Washington. He had leverage. He had strength. He could play hardball with these folks.

He clicked the button.

"Hello?"

Sam Kent said, "We need to meet."

"Why?"

"You've seen the story about the train?"

"What about it?"

"It was Reel and Robie."

"How?"

"That's not important. They've teamed up. Without a doubt."

Decker swallowed nervously and held tightly to the leash as Bruin started to go after a squirrel. "The last time we spoke you didn't think that was a real possibility. You said they might have been at the center of what happened in Arkansas, but you weren't convinced they were in this together."

"Well, the simple answer to that is, I was apparently wrong."

"That is not a good enough answer, Sam. I've risked everything for this. Everything."

"And you don't think I have?"

"You as good as threatened me the last time we met."

"I know. I apologize for that. I'm under unbelievable pressure."

"And you don't think I am?"

"We have to stick together on this. I've been given

an ultimatum. I have to find Reel and Robie and eliminate them."

"Okay. But how?"

"I'll need your help."

"Me? What can I do?"

"You're the chairman, Howard. There's a lot you can do."

"Okay, okay, just calm down." He thought for a minute. "I certainly can get information about the agency's reaction to this recent development. They may have a line on the two."

"That's exactly what we need, Howard. We have to piggyback on the agency's pursuit of Reel and Robie. If you're not read in over there on it, get read in on it. Push for answers. Push for the ultimate solution. Tell them you want to be kept apprised of every step. If they're located and a strike team is sent in you want to know ahead of time."

"So you can send in your team?"

"Exactly."

"But why not just let the agency personnel do it? It's cleaner that way."

"Because they might just take them alive. And then they can talk, Howard."

"You...you think they know things that might lead—"

"That might lead right back to us. Yes, I do. We're on Reel's list. At least I am. And I would be stunned if you weren't. We've talked about this before. Neither of them can be allowed to come in alive. You have to get the agency to lead us to them. That way we can end it quick and relatively clean."

"But if I tip you off they might suspect my involvement."

"Think, Howard, think! They want this put to bed as much as we do. This is a black eye for them. They will cover this over with so much dirt no one will ever get to the truth of it. Now, can I report back that you're in?'

Decker didn't hesitate. "Yes. Absolutely. I'll do whatever it takes."

"Thanks, Howard. You won't regret this. Let's meet at my office tomorrow morning around seven. We can discuss further details. Time is really of the essence."

Kent clicked off and Decker slowly put the phone back in his pocket.

He was shaking. He was actually shaking with fear and doubt.

But I will get through this. I will survive this.

The little dog was running toward him, its leash trailing behind it. Decker saw the same young woman racing to catch it. He shot out a hand and snagged the leash.

Breathless, the woman ran up and stopped next to him.

He held up the leash. "That's your exercise for tonight," he said.

"Thank you so much."

"What's your name?" He ran his eye over her figure. He couldn't help himself.

"Stacy. The little guy there is Darby."

"Hello, Darby," said Decker, bending down to pet him. "Do you live around here?" he asked, rising back up.

A gun was pointed at his face.

"No," said Stacy. "And neither do you anymore."

She fired and the suppressed round slammed into Decker's face. He dropped where he stood, dead before he hit the dirt.

The woman walked off with her dog.

CHAPTER

66

Robie stood on the crowded Metro train holding on to an overhead handrail. He wore sunglasses, a ball cap pulled low over his forehead, and a hoodie for extra concealment.

The train pulled into the next station and stopped. Robie didn't react when the woman boarded. He kept his gaze partially downcast, but his peripheral vision was firmly on her.

For her part, Nicole Vance didn't react when she saw Robie. The only reason she recognized him was because he had told her what he would be wearing, which train car he would be on, and where he would be standing in that car.

She took her time working her way over to him. Most people around them were reading e-books, surfing on their electronic devices, listening to music through earbuds, or simply dozing in their seats.

She stopped next to him and grabbed a handrail. In a low voice she said, "How are you?"

"A little stressed."

"I can understand that. The stuff that happened on that train?"

He nodded.

"How did you get away?" she whispered.

"Jumped."

She flinched. "Alone?"

He shook his head.

"Who?"

He shook his head again.

She looked at him stubbornly. "I'm trying to help you."

"And I'm trying to keep you safe. Do you have it?"

She gazed at him sternly for another moment and then took the newspaper out of her bag. She pretended to read the front page. As the train picked up speed she unfolded the paper. Taped to it was a USB stick. The way it was positioned, only Robie could see it. With a swipe of his hand he slipped the stick into his pocket.

He turned to leave, but Vance gripped his elbow. Robie looked at her cautiously. He was afraid she was about to blow everything.

She mouthed two words:

Kick ass.

He nodded curtly, turned, and weaved his way through the passengers. As the train entered the next station he drew close to the door. As he was exiting he looked over at Vance. She was staring off. But Robie could read her mind.

She doesn't believe I'm going to survive this.
And if I'm honest with myself, neither do I.

Robie rejoined Reel in her rental car. As she drove through the streets, he used a laptop to scroll through the files Vance had given him.

"Anything?" she asked.

"Vance got me all she could find on suspicious movements overseas, heightened threat alerts. Upgraded military preparedness. Unusual chatter in the usual places."

"And?"

"There's some strange sub activity in the Atlantic. We're sending a few more ships to the Persian Gulf, probably to do with Iran. And there was a surprise naval exercise in the Pacific. But that's all on our side. I'm not finding anything that might be what we're looking for, meaning unusual movement by our enemies."

"Nothing?"

"Wait a minute," Robie said sharply.

He scanned down a page. "I remember seeing this on TV a while back, but that was before I knew about any of this so I didn't make the connection."

"What is it?"

"The president is going to Ireland for a conference on terrorism."

"So?"

"It's not just the president."

"Okay, who else will be there?"

He looked up. "All the leaders of the G8. The God-father scenario is a lot easier to play out if all of them are in the same place."

"But, Robie, think of the security they'll have there. Locked down tighter than anything else on the planet. There is no way they can hit that. No way."

"After 9/11, I refuse to say anything is impossible."

"But you said the president will be there. He's not part of the target."

"According to West's paper he wasn't. That doesn't mean they're sticking to the paper in every detail. Maybe they want to nail him too."

"I get the bad guys coming after us. But why in the hell would people inside our government want to kill the president? And I still don't understand why they would want to kill the G8 leaders."

"They're traitors. Maybe they were just paid off. It happens."

Reel didn't look remotely convinced. "But this is not some gun-down in the street, Robie. This is global meltdown. If they are being paid off, where are they going to spend their money? They have to live on the planet too. It makes no sense."

"You're the one who believes that this white paper

West wrote is at the center of this whole thing. If you no longer think that, I need to know, right now."

"I do still believe it."

"Because of Joe Stockwell?" he said.

She nodded, blinking slowly. "Yes."

"Who did he get close enough to in order to figure this out?"

"I don't know. I wish I did. He sent me enough details for me to know what was going on. He sent me the names on the list. He told me what they were planning to do based on that paper, at least as much as he knew of it."

"Did he send you the paper?"

"No. I got that from another friend of mine who tracked it down."

"Nice to have friends."

"So do we go to Ireland?"

"If that's where the hit is going to take place, I don't see an alternative."

"How about we tell Vance our suspicions? She can send word up the line."

"They're not going to take any action without meeting her sources. And she can't tell them it's us without getting herself arrested. Same reason we can't do it. So that's a no-go," said Robie.

"You have a fake passport the agency doesn't know about?"

"Of course," said Robie.

"Then maybe it's time to head to Ireland."

Robie looked down at the screen once more. "Maybe it is."

"I would like to check one other thing, Robie."

"What's that?"

She picked up her phone. "The friend."

"Where is this friend? And can he or she be trusted?"

"Yes, he can. And he works at the mall."

"The mall? Doing what?"

"He's a whiz at video games. Among other things."

"What can he find out for us?"

"The real name of Roger the Dodger. Because that son of a bitch is going to die and I'm going to pull the trigger."

67

THERE WERE FIVE MEN IN the room:

Evan Tucker.

Blue Man.

Gus Whitcomb, the APNSA.

The director of the FBI, Steve Colwell.

And the president of the United States.

The president said, "Any leads on who killed Howard Decker?"

Colwell shook his head. "Not yet, sir. It was an execution-style hit. We've recovered the bullet, but we have no gun to match it to."

The president looked incredulous. "And no one saw anything? They were in a damn public park."

"We've made inquiries," said Colwell. "Unfortunately, we've turned up no witnesses yet."

Tucker said, "There might not be any witnesses. If it was a professional hit they would have made sure there was no one around."

"But for what purpose?" asked the president.

Blue Man said, "It might be tied to Decker's Intelligence Committee activities."

"Is it also tied to the deaths of Gelder and Jacobs?" asked the president. He leaned back in his chair and studied the other men in the room, looking them over one by one, awaiting an answer.

Tucker said, "Well, they all were involved in the intelligence field. At least it's a common theme."

The president gazed at Colwell. "And we're no closer to solving those murders, are we?"

"We're making some progress," said Colwell lamely.

"Good to hear," said Tucker. "*Some* progress is always welcome, whatever minimal form it might take."

The two directors shared a nasty glance.

Whitcomb said sharply, "And there is the matter of the Amtrak train. Casualties and what looks to be a considerable cover-up." He paused and gave a sideways glance at the president. "And there is of course the outstanding issue of Jessica Reel. And now, apparently, if I'm reading the tea leaves correctly, Will Robie." He gazed at Tucker. "Is Robie still off the grid?"

Tucker nodded before glancing at Blue Man and then quickly looking away.

"And what might Robie be doing off the grid?" asked Whitcomb.

Tucker shrugged. "I wish I knew, Gus."

Whitcomb continued, "When I spoke with Robie— before he went off the grid," he added in a contemptuous tone—"he told me several troubling things." He glanced at the president, who seemed to be aware of what Whitcomb was about to say.

The president nodded encouragingly. "Go ahead, Gus. We need to get all this aired."

Whitcomb said, "Robie told me that Janet DiCarlo was troubled by unexplained incidents at the agency." He looked sharply at Tucker. "Your agency."

"What sorts of things?" Colwell wanted to know.

Whitcomb looked at his tablet. "Missing personnel. Missions that never should have happened. Missing money. Missing equipment."

Colwell looked surprised but also somewhat pleased by this revelation.

"Serious allegations," said the president.

"Serious allegations indeed," echoed Colwell.

The president continued, "I am well aware that we had some enemies of this country placed very close to home." He shot a glance at Colwell. "And it wasn't simply at CIA. It was at your agency as well." Colwell immediately lost most of his cocksure manner.

The president returned his gaze to Tucker. "I thought it an isolated incident. I am sitting here almost entirely due to the courage and skill of Will Robie. If he thought something was still wrong, then so do I. If he said that DiCarlo was worried, I believe him."

"And yet he's gone off the grid," said Colwell.

"That could be explained any number of ways," said Whitcomb.

"If he's teamed up with Jessica Reel, and she was responsible for the deaths of Jim Gelder and Doug Jacobs, then any explanation would be highly problematic," noted Tucker ominously.

Blue Man glanced at him, but Tucker continued, "I have heard theories that Gelder and Jacobs were traitors to this country. I am aware that a former analyst to the CIA, Roy West, was recently killed. And that Reel and Robie might have been there."

"That's the first we've heard of such speculation," snapped Whitcomb.

"Because that's what it is, speculation," countered Tucker. "I don't know where people stand on this thing. I don't know if Reel and/or Robie are on our side or not. What I do know is that people are dying and there has to be a good reason for that. The stakes surrounding this matter must be astronomically high. But no one has been able to figure out what they are or where the motivations lie."

"And Decker?" said Whitcomb quietly. "Could he also be involved somehow? Perhaps a traitor too? Might Reel have killed him too?"

"I don't know," said a clearly frustrated Tucker. "I just don't know."

Whitcomb said, "Robie told me that he believed it was Jessica Reel who saved his and DiCarlo's life that night. That she was the countersniper who left all the shell casings. If that is the case then I am hard pressed to see how she could be a traitor."

"If she shot and killed Jacobs and Gelder, she is at the very least a *murderer*," snapped Tucker, but then he seemed to regret his loss of temper. He went on more calmly, "If they were traitors, that's why we have courts. You don't go around and just shoot people because you suspect them of some wrongdoing."

"Yes, but be that as it may," said Whitcomb, "I'm not prepared to come down so hard on Reel if the men had turned against their country. There is nothing in her record, or Robie's for that matter, that would suggest either of them have turned traitor."

"Well the same holds true for Jim Gelder and Doug Jacobs," interjected Tucker.

"Duly noted," said the president. "But we'll cross that bridge if and when we come to it. For the time being, we have to put every resource we have into solving this thing. And that includes finding Robie and Reel, as quickly as possible. If they are working for us somehow, they could be invaluable in clearing up this matter."

"And if they're working against us?" asked Tucker.

"Then their fate is completely predictable." The president looked around. "Any disagreements there?"

Every other man in the room shook his head.

The president rose. "I'll be leaving for Ireland shortly.

But keep me informed. Highest priority. No major decisions without briefing me. Clear?"

The others nodded.

The men all stood as the president disappeared through a door held open for him by a Secret Service agent.

When the door closed behind him, Whitcomb sat. So did the others.

"So where do we really stand on all this, Gus?" asked Tucker.

"I thought the president was perfectly clear on it, Evan," said Whitcomb in mild surprise.

"With the things he said, yes. I mean the things that were left unsaid."

"I think you can deduce what they are. But I'll give you a hint. If this isn't resolved satisfactorily then there will be ultimate accountability."

He looked at Tucker, then at Colwell, and finally at Blue Man. "Ultimate accountability," he repeated.

"How much time do we have?" asked Colwell.

Whitcomb rose, signaling an end to the meeting. "Apparently almost none at all."

68

Reel and Robie separated after they got out of her rental car and entered the mall through different doors.

They were communicating via earwigs on a secure frequency. Robie had insisted on treating this like an op, and Reel had quickly agreed. She apparently didn't expect any trouble, but she also never expected everything to go perfectly either.

That was a good rule to live by, Robie knew, because perfection was rarely the case in the field.

She walked down the main corridor of the mall. It was in the afternoon and there weren't as many people around as there would be later in the day. Still, she did her best to blend in.

She approached the GameStop from the east side of the mall. She spoke in a low voice. "Ten steps from target. Giving a signal and then heading west and down the hall to the restrooms."

"Copy that," said Robie.

He was on the upper level of the mall, hidden in

his hoodie, looking down at her as she passed by. He watched as she strode past the GameStop. She slid her finger along her chin and then kept going.

Robie smiled at this. He had used that very same signal once. He watched her turn down the hall to the restrooms.

A minute later, Robie keyed on a short, skinny man wearing a black silkscreened T-shirt who came out of the GameStop and followed the path Reel had taken.

The next second Robie had his hand around the gun in his pocket.

There were two teams out there.

One coming east, the other west.

He had seen dozens of such configurations over the years. They all looked a little different, but to someone like Robie they all also looked the same.

They obviously hadn't accounted for Robie. He was the wild card. He intended to make the most of that status.

He spoke into his mic. "Two bogie teams headed your way. East, west. Pair of deuces. Armed and commed so they can coordinate."

That had been one way for Robie to ID the hit teams.

Their earwigs.

He had covered his with a hoodie. They had not seen fit to do that.

Their mistake.

"Copy that," was Reel's calm response. "Do what I can."

"On your six."

"Copy that."

She was seconds from having to fight her way out of here, and she sounded like she was simply going to use the bathroom to relieve herself.

Robie would have expected nothing less.

He took the escalator three steps at a time. When he hit the first floor he was already at a full sprint.

One of the bogie teams had already gone down the hall toward the restrooms. The second team was two steps from there.

"FBI, freeze!" called out Robie.

The men did not freeze. Robie had called out on the off chance that they might be the authorities.

They weren't.

It was burned into law enforcement folks to ID themselves when possibly confronted by fellow lawmen. Creds came out and people started screaming who they were with. The last thing a cop wanted was to get shot by another cop. Or shoot another cop.

These men said nothing, and the only things that came out of their jackets were guns.

Before they could fire on him, Robie shot one man in the knee. He screamed and dropped immediately, his gun flying from his hand. Robie wasn't worried about him reentering the fight. Destroyed knees were so painful that even the toughest men could only lie there and sob like babies.

The second man fired at Robie, shattering a large planter that a moment earlier Robie had been standing in front of. Robie crouched and turned to the side. He tasted acid in his mouth as bile was shoved up his throat. No matter how many times you did this, being shot at was not natural, and your body reacted in consistent ways. Robie had fear; anyone would in that situation. But he didn't have panic, which was the key difference between those who lived and those who didn't.

The man would not get another chance to shoot. No knee shot this time; Robie dropped him with a round between his eyes.

Robie raced down the hall. He ran even harder when he heard the shots.

He spoke into his mic. "Reel? Reel, you copy? You okay? Reel?"

He slowed, turned the corner prepared to fire, and stopped.

There were three bodies lying in pools of blood.

When Robie saw they were all men, he let out his breath.

But three?

Then it hit him. The friend. From the GameStop.

Reel stepped from around the far corner, her gun in her right hand.

He looked at her. "You okay?"

She nodded, but said nothing. Her gaze was on her friend.

Robie heard screams behind him. Feet running. Mall cops probably.

That was the last thing they needed. He was not going to fire on an unarmed young punk or retired geezer posing as the authorities.

"We've got to get out of here."

"I know," she said dumbly.

"I mean now."

Robie looked past her. There was a set of exit doors there. Had to be a way out.

When he looked back at Reel, she was bending down next to her dead friend, wiping a lock of hair out of his face.

Robie heard her say, "I'm so sorry, Mike."

He ran forward, grabbed her arm, and pulled her down the hall. He kicked open the exit door and the two raced through it.

Robie looked around. They were in a storage area.

"You know which way is out?"

Reel didn't seem to have heard him.

He turned. "Jessica, do you know the way out!" he barked.

She focused, looked embarrassed, and pointed to the left. "That way, doors let out on the east side. Come on, follow me."

They reached the outside and fast-walked back to

the parking garage. They got to Reel's car. It looked like they had made a clean exit.

Until they heard the screech of tires coming fast.

The dead men had backup.

And they were coming fast.

Robie only had time to say, "Look out."

CHAPTER

69

REEL SMOKED HER WHEELS AND drove in reverse right at the larger vehicle. Robie braced for impact, but it never came.

He saw the front grille of the SUV for an instant. It seemed to swallow up the whole of the back glass of their car. Then somehow Reel had turned just enough to slide through a gap between the SUV and a concrete support column.

She cut a J-turn and rammed the car into drive before she had even finished the 180-degree maneuver. She left a quarter inch of tire rubber on the concrete floor of the garage and the car careened through the exit and out into traffic entering the mall.

Reel cut her wheel to the left, jumped the median, and punched the gas. The car shot to the right. She slammed into a line of orange traffic cones, cut the wheel to the right, and slid into another turn.

Robie barely managed to buckle his seat belt. His gun was out but there was nothing to shoot at.

There was traffic up ahead, but it was only on one side. Unfortunately it was on their side. Reel solved this problem by going British and driving on the opposite side of the road.

She cleared the logjam, didn't bother to stop at the red light, slashed into oncoming traffic, managed to somehow bend the car's path into a left-hand turn, losing a hubcap in the process, and pushed the gas pedal to the floor as she got back on the right side of the road.

Sirens were coming from all over the place now.

Robie looked behind them. "We're good. Dial it back so the cops don't get a clue."

She eased off the gas, held for a second at a yield sign, and then merged into traffic. A few minutes later they were on a highway going seventy with the traffic flow.

Robie put his gun away. "Sorry about your friend."

"I'm sorry you keep having to say that," she replied.

"Who was he?"

"His name was Michael Gioffre. And I'm the reason he's dead."

"Really? I thought it was the guys shooting at you."

"I didn't check for an observation team, Robie. I knew there used to be one there. A legit one. I always checked. But I didn't today."

"How did it go down?"

"Shot from one of them ricocheted off a trash can

and caught Mike right in the eye. He was dead before he hit the floor."

"Then what?"

"I shot the guys. One round each. They weren't very good. Came running in like I wasn't going to even fight back. Stupid."

"My guys weren't that good either, actually," said Robie.

She looked at him sharply. "I wonder why not?"

"Maybe their best guys are already in Ireland."

Robie turned the radio on. "I want to hear if there's anything on the news about the mall yet."

There wasn't. But there was another story that captured their interest. The news anchor was succinct with the details, although right now there weren't that many of them.

When the anchor went on to another story Robie turned off the radio and stared over at Reel. "Someone murdered Howard Decker," he said.

"They're cleaning up loose ends, Robie. These sons of bitches are planning to pull this off and then get away scot free. But they're not. I'm going to put a round into every single one of them. I'm going to keep shooting them over and over until I run out of bullets."

He placed a hand on her arm and gripped it.

"What are you doing?" she said.

"I'm sorry about Mike. We can go somewhere and you can grieve for him. And for Gwen—"

"I don't need to grieve for anybody—"

"I think you do."

"You don't know anything about me. So leave your damn grieving sermon for somebody who cares. I'm a killer, Robie. People are usually dying all around me."

"But not usually your friends, Jessica."

She started to say something, but then the words seemed to catch in her throat.

Robie continued, "I'm not playing grief counselor. Once we get to Ireland, there will be no time for you to get right in your head. So you're either in this a hundred percent and I know I can count on you, or you're useless to me and you can drop me at the next exit."

Reel blinked. "You used that ploy on me once before, Robie."

"Yemen. We lost Tommy Billups. You blamed yourself. More to the point, you checked out on me for about half an hour."

"Until you kicked my ass."

"Because a team is a team, Jessica. And there're only two people currently on our team. A house divided is screwed. Which in our case means dead."

She took a long, calming breath. "I'm good, Robie."

"Turn the anger into something that will guarantee we beat these pricks, Jessica. That's all I'm saying."

"I know. You're right."

They drove in silence for a few miles.

Reel broke it by saying, "That's why you always were number one."

He turned to look at her.

"You never let your emotions get the better of you, Robie. Never. You were a machine. Everybody thought so."

He stared down at his hands. He actually felt embarrassed by her words.

By how wrong they were.

He reached into his jacket and rubbed the stock of his pistol. Not for luck. It was never about luck.

This was his talisman. This was his tool of choice. This was what he did.

I am a killer.

I am also a human being.

The only problem is, I can't be both.

Reel glanced at him. "What are you thinking?" she asked.

"Nothing important," he answered.

CHAPTER

70

THE TRI-ENGINE DASSAULT FALCON COULD carry a dozen passengers comfortably.

It only held two tonight.

Reel sat in the rear seat of the cabin.

Robie was next to her.

No one was behind them. That was how each liked it.

"How did you score this ride?" he asked.

"Fractional share ownership. A lot less security. And a lot more privacy." She looked at him. "What do you spend your money on?"

"Remember my little house in the woods? The rest is in the bank earning negative interest."

"Saving for your retirement? Your golden years?"

"Doubtful. You know, they could trace your ownership of the plane."

"It's not under my name. It's under the name of a Russian billionaire who doesn't even know how many planes and yachts he owns. I just get my little piece and no one's the wiser."

"That was clever."

"We'll see how clever I am when we get to Dublin."

"I've done some recon."

"Your friend Vance again?"

"Never hurts to have the Bureau's research muscle behind you."

"Didn't she ask questions?"

"She was thinking them, but she didn't ask them."

"So what did she find out?"

"The protection bubble is much like past years, with a couple of new wrinkles."

"Such as?"

"Apparently, in a show of global cooperation, they have invited some non-G8 leaders for a day event. It actually opens the conference."

"Which non-G8 leaders?" asked Reel.

"Several from desert climates."

"Are they idiots?"

"Apparently they don't think so, no."

"You know what comes with leaders."

"Their security details."

"And those details are internally vetted. We have to trust that they are what they say they are."

"That's right."

Reel looked out the window at forty-one thousand

feet where the dark sky sat there, vast, empty, and apparently brooding.

"Do you want a drink?" asked Reel. She rose to head to the bar at the front of the cabin.

"No," responded Robie.

"You might change your mind about that."

A minute later she settled back in her seat cradling a vodka tonic.

They hit some modest turbulence and she held the glass up to avoid spilling the contents. As the air smoothed out she took a sip and looked at Robie's laptop screen.

He said, "We've got a bag full of weapons back there. How about customs?"

"Russian billionaires don't go through ordinary customs and neither do their ride-share partners. The process is very streamlined and private for the most part."

"Tell me again how you managed that?"

"I didn't think I told you in the first place."

"You sure your Russian billionaire's not a security issue?"

"He loves America. Loves free markets. Loves capitalism. He's an ally. No issues there. And he gets us private wings and an arsenal through customs."

"I'm impressed with some of the firepower you have."

"Don't think it'll be enough. Too many of them. Not enough of us."

"We just have to be more clever and more nimble."

"Easy to say. A lot harder to do."

He stared at her drink.

"You want one now?" she asked.

"Yeah. I'll make it."

"No, I got it. It's my one chance to be domestic."

He watched her walk down the aisle. The last thing he could ever envision was Jessica Reel domesticated.

When she returned, she clinked her glass against his. She said, "When this is all over, it still won't be all over."

Robie nodded. He knew right where she was going.

He sipped his drink, thought about his response. "I guess it won't be."

"Would you believe me if I told you at this point I didn't care?"

"But that doesn't necessarily change anything."

"So kill or capture me?"

"I received conflicting orders, actually. Some were kill. Some were capture."

"But with capture I could make public statements. I could say things they don't want to hear. I have the right to freedom of speech. I'm entitled to a legal defense. So I don't see an option other than kill, Robie."

Robie sipped his drink and ate some nuts she had brought back in a bowl. "Let's see if we survive Dublin. If we do, we can revisit the question."

She swallowed the rest of her drink and set it down. "Yeah," she said. "I suppose we can."

He stared at her. He knew this was a lie and so did she. They flew for another hundred miles in silence. Down below, the Atlantic frothed and churned as an ornery low-pressure system drifted farther out to sea.

Reel finally said, "When I pulled the trigger on Jacobs, you know what it felt like?"

He shook his head.

"No different from any of the other trigger pulls I've made. No difference at all. I thought I would feel something new because he helped kill Joe. I thought there would be some sense of revenge, of justice even."

"And Jim Gelder? How did you feel when you killed him?"

She looked at him. "How do you think I should have felt?"

Robie shrugged. "I'm not the person to ask."

"You're the perfect person to ask. But let me ask you something."

Robie waited, his eyes narrowed, wondering where this conversation was going.

"You didn't pull a trigger when you were supposed to. How did that feel to you?"

"The target died anyway."

"That's not what I asked. How did you feel?"

Robie didn't answer right away. The truth was he had tried not to think about that very thing.

How did I feel?

Reel answered for him. "Liberated?"

Robie looked down. That had been the exact word forming in his mind.

Reel seemed to sense this but did not push the point. "Another drink?" she asked, noting his empty glass. When he hesitated, she said, "Remember the domesticity, Robie? I sense I'll become bored with it before we land. So strike while the iron is hot."

She took the drink out of his hand but set it down on the tray. She looked at her watch. "We have exactly three hours and forty-one minutes to landing."

"Okay?" asked Robie, looking confused and dropping his gaze to the empty glass.

Then it occurred to him that she was not talking about a second drink. His eyes widened slightly.

"You think the timing sucks?" she asked in response to his look.

"Don't you?" he said.

"This is not the first time I've thought about it with you. Those youthful hormones, in close proximity in life-and-death situations with lots of guns. Recipe for something to happen. How about you?"

"It wasn't supposed to be part of it. Never, in fact."

"Supposed to be doesn't equal what could be."

"About the timing?"

"It's perfect, actually."

"Why?"

"Because both you and I know we're not going to live past Ireland. They know you've sided with me. They're not going to let you survive this. There are a lot more of them than there are of us. Doesn't take a roomful of analysts to decipher that one. Now, I'll die with many regrets. But I don't want *that* to be one of them. What about you?"

She rose and held out a hand. "What about you?" she said again. "The bed in back is very comfortable."

Robie stared at her hand for another moment and then looked away.

He didn't get out of his seat.

Reel slowly drew her hand back. "See you in Dublin." She started to walk down the aisle to the private quarters in the plane's aft section.

"It has nothing to do with you, Jessica."

She stiffened and stopped walking, but didn't look back.

"There's someone else?" she said. "Vance?"

"No."

"I'm surprised you found the time for someone."

"She's no longer alive."

Now Reel did turn.

"It was recent," said Robie.

Reel came back and sat down next to him. "Do you want to talk about it?"

"Why? I'm a machine, right? That's what you said."

She put her palm against his chest. "Machines don't

have heartbeats. You're not a machine. I shouldn't have said that. I'd like to hear about it. If you want to talk."

"Are you sure?"

"I've got nowhere else to go for the next three hours and"—she glanced at her watch—"thirty-eight minutes."

The plane flew on.

And Robie talked about a young woman who had stolen his heart and then nearly his life, because she turned out to be the enemy.

And in response he had done the only thing he was really good at.

He had killed her.

It was something that only a person like Jessica Reel could understand.

CHAPTER

71

SAM KENT WAS ON the move.

He had taken two weeks off from his duties as a judge. The FISC didn't have a backlog. They were swift in their judgments. They could spare him.

He packed a bag and kissed his wife and children goodbye.

This was not unusual. He often went away without a lot of explanation. His wife understood it to be part of his past life that he did not talk about.

Well, this wasn't really about his past life. It was about his future. Precisely speaking, whether he was going to have one or not.

Jacobs, Gelder, and now Decker were dead.

Kent knew that he would have to dance nimbly not to end up like the other three men. He had foes on both flanks now.

Reel and Robie were formidable. He was less concerned about them, though, than with the opponent on his other flank. But the clear way out was to make sure that the plan succeeded. At least his part of it. After that, it was out of his hands. But he also couldn't be blamed for that part failing.

It was also an opportunity for him to get back out in the field after years of sitting behind a desk. That inactivity had been a slow death for him, he could see that now. It had been a luxury killing that idiot Anthony Zim. He had missed that.

He drove to the airport and checked his car into long-term parking. The night was a fine one. Clear skies, many stars, light winds. It would be a good flight. He would have to hit the ground running. There was a fair amount of prep work that needed to be done.

Success or failure was always defined largely during the preparation. With good planning all one had to do was execute. Even last-second changes could be made with greater ease if the planning in the first place had been precise.

Kent carried no weapons in his bag. That was not his job this time around. He was a thinker, a processor, not a doer.

Part of that pained him, but at his age, he also knew it was the most realistic option for him. Once this was over, the future was both uncertain and crystal clear. Clear for those who knew what was about to happen. A little murkier for everyone else. Flowing up his spine was an electrified charge of excitement mixed with dread. It would certainly be a different world after this. But a better one, he truly believed.

He took a bus to the terminal, showed his passport, checked his bag, passed through security, and walked to the lounge to await his international flight.

The wild card or cards were obvious.

Robie and Reel.

The attack at the mall was conclusive proof in Kent's mind. Four pros wiped out by two pros who were far more professional.

The battle lost, but not the war, of course.

Eliminating Reel's source of information was the primary objective. The cleanup had been messy. Cover stories had been deployed and the FBI and DHS would be led round and round the merry-go-round until they were so dizzy the truth could bite them in the collective ass and they would fail to see it.

Kent sipped on a bottle of orange juice and had some crackers and cheese in the airport club to which he belonged. Ordinarily he would fly on private wings to his destination, but this time commercial was just as good. He looked out the window and watched jet after jet pull back from their gates, taxi off, and a few minutes later lift into the clear night sky.

Soon it would be his turn.

He wondered where Robie and Reel were right now.

Perhaps on the way to the same place he was?

Could they have figured it out considering what they had to work with?

The white paper was a key piece, but it listed no specific target. It just gave a scenario of players. The other pieces they might have put together, but to make sense out of it all—that was a stretch even for the likes of them.

And if Reel had gotten what she needed from Roy West she wouldn't have had to turn to the late Michael Gioffre. It was lucky that Kent's superior had remembered that connection and quickly posted a team on him.

The only misfortune was that his men had not picked up on Robie. But for him they might have gotten Reel. But they hadn't and that was that.

His flight was called an hour later. He boarded after watching the other passengers crowd into the small gate area. The flight would be full. That was okay. It was a popular route.

He would try to sleep.

But he doubted that he would be successful. He had too much to think about.

As he was sitting down in his seat, his phone buzzed.

He looked at the text. *Good luck*, it read.

He put it away without texting back.

What was he supposed to say? Thanks?

He buckled up and reclined the seat. He pulled out his wallet and slipped the photo out.

His other life. His family. Beautiful young wife, adorable children. They lived in the perfect home in the perfect neighborhood and had all the money they would ever need to be happy. He could be with them right now. Tucking his kids in. Making love to his wife. Having a scotch in his study while reading a good book. He could do that for the rest of his days and be extremely content, euphoric even.

But here he was on a plane that would be flying to yet another destination where he would risk life and limb for the greater good.

Kent ran his finger against his wife's picture.

A female passenger sitting next to him, who had observed what he had done, smiled. "I know. I miss my family every time I leave too," she said.

He smiled and then turned away.

A few minutes later the plane zipped down the runway and lifted into the air.

Kent had been on many flights, from patched-together choppers in the jungles of Vietnam where every tree seemingly provided cover for Viet Cong trying to take the aircraft down, to 747s that had whisked him across the globe in luxury. But in each instance when he'd gotten on the ground he had been prepared to kill. And quite often did.

He unfolded the paper and looked at the front page.

Howard Decker was still alive—in the photo, that is. His eyes were open. He was smiling. His wife was by his side at some social function that required outrageously expensive formal gowns for the women and cookie-cutter penguin suits for the men.

In reality Decker was on a slab at the D.C. morgue with part of his head missing. He would never smile again.

Kent had known nothing of the hit but he agreed with its execution. Loose ends tied up. The weak separated from the rest of the herd.

They were near the end of this and nothing and no one was going to interfere with the desired result. Too much time in the planning. Too many obstacles avoided. Far too much at stake.

It was Super Bowl Sunday. All the hype was over.

It was time to play the damn game.

72

DUBLIN, ROBIE AND REEL HAD to admit, was a fortress. They had been here less than twenty-four hours and they could already tell. They had done every possible recon and feint to test the security perimeter around the G8 conference, and there was not one weakness to be found.

They were in Robie's hotel room overlooking the river Liffey. He was at the window with a pair of binoculars, staring across at the hotel center where the conference's main events were taking place. It seemed as if there were more security personnel than G8 attendees.

"What about the non-G8 elements?" asked Robie as he lowered the optics and looked over at Reel, who sat in a chair by the door.

"Basically sequestered. And Vance didn't have it exactly right. The security for those folks is being provided by the G8. Their own security details were not invited."

"And they were okay with that?"

"If they weren't okay with it they didn't get to come."

"So if the hit is coming it's an inside job coming from Western resources," noted Robie.

"Not necessarily. There's nothing preventing a terrorist attack coming separate from the conference. Or there could be a terror cell in Dublin right now."

He shook his head. "I'm telling you, something is definitely not right."

"I have the same feeling."

He sat on the bed, faced her. "We're missing something."

"I get that, I just don't know what."

He rose.

"Where are you going?" she asked.

"To find what we're missing."

Robie left the hotel. Within fifteen minutes he was outside the area where the G8 conference was being held. The security perimeter was dense and multilayered. He had no chance of getting inside it without the proper credentials.

As he was standing there, two men came out of one building inside the security perimeter. They had on suits, but also were wearing traditional Muslim headwear. They did not get into a car or cab. They simply walked. Robie assumed they were part of the non-G8 delegation.

He looked at them as they passed by and decided to follow them. It might pan out or it might lead to nothing. But nothing was what he had right now.

He slipped in behind them. They eventually entered a hotel and went straight to the bar. They were forbidden by their religion to drink, but for some Muslims that edict disappeared while they were in Western lands. And there were few places on earth better suited to satisfy one's thirst for alcohol than Dublin.

They took their drinks and sat at a table by the window. Robie bought his pint and took up a chair at a table next to them. He put his earbuds in and set his smartphone on the table but did not turn on any music. He sipped his beer and eavesdropped on their conversation, all the while swaying his head as he pretended to listen to a tune.

The men talked in low tones in Arabic. They had no reason to think that a westerner would understand a word they were saying. They would be right in almost every instance except this one.

They were attendees of the conference, but they weren't talking about the G8. There was another conference commencing shortly. It was to take place in Canada at a small town well outside of Montreal. Robie had seen a brief news report about it a while back. It seemed a strange place for an Arab summit, but the Canadians had offered and there indeed was some logic to it. By meeting in a neutral place far removed from the violence and conflict that seemed to permeate the Middle East, it was hoped that meaningful progress could be made. At least that was the official story. And the Canadians were picking up the tab for the whole thing. It also showed goodwill from the West to try to work with the Arab countries. And while the United States, for political reasons, was not involved, the Canadians were such close allies to America that everyone knew the nexus—and implicit support—was clearly there.

At the conference would be the leaders of the major Arab nations, all clustered together in one place to discuss ways to move forward peacefully instead of violently, as much of the recent Arab Spring had done. These men were not attending, but knew many who were. They didn't seem to think that any major breakthroughs would happen during this conference. One man laughed and said that Muslims, like westerners, couldn't really agree on much when it came to sharing power. They talked about certain leaders who would be there. Some they liked, others they wished dead.

The men finished their drinks, got up, and left. Robie could have followed them, but saw no real need to. It was far better for him to sit here and try to think this through. He sipped his drink and stared at the wall opposite.

The attack described in Roy West's apocalypse paper had the G8 leadership as its target. Robie and Reel had assumed that people working inside the United States had assisted enemies of the G8 with planning an attack at this conference, wiping out the G8 leadership and causing a global panic. That made sense. But what the Muslim men had been talking about made him rethink this.

A conference in Canada of leaders from numerous Muslim countries.

Then his thoughts turned to the hit that Jessica Reel had never made.

Ahmadi. In Syria. Blue Man had said they wanted to derail Ahmadi's coming to power and they had a more palatable choice in the wings, waiting to take over.

Robie put his beer down. As the liquid cleared his throat and settled into his stomach, his thoughts crystallized.

That's where he and Reel had gotten it wrong. They had assumed that whoever was behind this was following West's doomsday scenario to the letter. But that was just speculation, not fact. There *was* going to be an attack, only not on the G8; the security nut was too hard to crack.

But all those leaders clustered together in a small town outside of Montreal? They were fish in a barrel. Eliminating them in a single stroke would result in complete pandemonium in one of the already most chaotic regions on earth. Regime after regime falling. Power vacuums. Elements fighting to take control. But maybe there were folks waiting to take power. And maybe they'd have help. And maybe whoever was behind this thought a better future would look a whole lot like the past.

And perhaps Roy West's apocalypse paper would be played out in force, only not in the way its author, with all his paranoia, ever imagined.

Robie rose and walked back to his hotel.

The answer was not in Dublin. It was three thousand miles away.

73

IN TWO HOURS, Robie and Reel were packed, gone from the hotel, and at the airport outside Dublin.

"Are you sure about this, Robie?" Reel asked for the fifth time.

"If you want a guarantee I can't give it. But otherwise I'm pretty damn sure."

Reel looked out the window of the terminal. "If you're wrong? If we leave here and something happens?"

"Then it happens," he said flatly. "I'll take full responsibility."

"I'm not worried about who takes responsibility."

"Neither am I. I'm just looking to stop it."

She said, "So instead of killing the G8 leadership they're planning to knock out the Middle Eastern heads of state? That's quite a leap."

"I didn't plan it, so I can't really account for the logic."

"It's still a terrible risk."

"Yes, it is."

"Even if everything goes according to plan we're still talking about a catastrophic scenario."

"The West used to pick their puppet and put him in power. The puppet kept everyone in line and the area was peaceful. Look at the shah of Iran. And Saddam was our friend until he stopped being our friend. I'm sure the people they want in power have been carefully selected. Remember Ahmadi? That was one guy and one country. Just hitting singles. They're going for homers now by inserting puppets all at one time."

"But there'll be security in Canada too."

"Not like in Dublin. And it'll be a different sort of security."

"But it still comes down to how do just the two of us stop it?"

"We have a plane ride to come up with a plan," said Robie.

"You really think we can map this out in seven hours?"

"No."

"What, then?" persisted Reel.

"We have eight. I checked the flight time. There's a stiff headwind."

"Robie, cut the crap!"

"An extra hour is an extra hour. But all I know is we have to try. Because if we don't try it will happen."

They boarded their flight. Thirty minutes later the private wings took off heading due west.

From the Internet Robie had assembled all the information he could on the event to which they were heading. After reviewing it, Reel finally sat back and said, "We don't have enough intel to pull this off, Robie."

"Well, Janet DiCarlo said something that could help us. Missing personnel. Missions that never should have been. So we might see some old friends on this one."

"We might," Reel said doubtfully.

He stretched out his tight shoulders. "We won't have much time when we hit the ground. It starts tomorrow in the morning."

"If they hit today, while people are still just arriving, we won't even get a shot."

"They won't. They have to make it look like the real thing. Otherwise people will get suspicious. Terrorists always go for the symbolic blow. The summit will have to be up and running before they hit it."

"So the opening ceremony?"

He nodded. "That's what I think."

He rose and poured two cups of coffee from the small bar set up against a bulkhead. He set one down for her and retook his seat.

"I have a question for you," said Robie. "And it has nothing to do with what's coming up."

Reel sat back and stared at him. "What?"

"You saved my butt at DiCarlo's, right?"

"Yes."

"You didn't have to do that. It was a big risk, in fact."

"Everything we do has big risks."

"That's not an answer, Jessica."

She took a sip of coffee. "I figured I got you into this mess, it was my responsibility to look after you."

"Like you did on the Eastern Shore?"

"Nothing is absolute, Will. That was early on. I just wanted to survive to finish this. Later, my thinking changed."

"Changed about me?"

"It would have given me no pleasure to see you die." She looked away for a few moments. Robie saw her hand tremble.

When she turned back her features were calm. "Are we done with that? Good to go now?"

"Good to go," said Robie.

For the rest of the flight they did nothing but troubleshoot what they had to do, looking for any weakness, any advantage. As they neared landing in Canada, Reel sat back, rubbed her eyes, and looked at Robie.

"So let's assume we actually survive this," she said. "What's next for you?"

He shrugged. "Have you been thinking about your future?"

"I'm just tired, Robie."

He nodded. "I can see that."

Reel studied him. "Do you miss her? The woman who hurt you?"

"No," he said, but his tone was unconvincing.

Reel sat back. "Okay."

"I blame myself."

"What, for being human?"

"For not doing my job."

She settled her gaze on him. "Which requires you to not be human."

"A job is a job."

"And a life is a life. You only have one of those."

He shook his head. "So call it quits?"

"How many out there have lasted as long as we have?"

"Not that many, I guess."

"You must have thought about life after."

"I have. But I guess I never thought about it seriously."

"I would respectfully suggest that you do. Because we might get really lucky and actually survive this."

CHAPTER

74

THE PRIVATE WINGS LANDED IN MONTREAL. That was where all the planes had come through on the way to the event.

After that Reel and Robie drove.

For a long way.

"Why here?" asked Reel. "Why have a summit for the Middle East all the way out here?"

"Where should they have held it? In the middle of Manhattan? On the National Mall in D.C.?"

"It's not easy to get to."

Robie said, "That's one reason they chose it. Restricted access. They can more easily check people coming and going."

"Who's moderating the event? The UN?"

"The Canadians. The PM left the Dublin summit early to deliver the keynote at the opening ceremony."

"Odd choice."

"Odd everything," agreed Robie.

*   *   *

The town's main street wasn't large, but it was well stocked with shops. To Robie, it looked like a place you might find inside a snow globe.

Trapped inside a snow globe, actually. Foot traffic was far higher than normal, as was the number of cars. But heavily armed checkpoints had been set up at all entry points. Cars were searched, the IDs of each vehicle's occupants checked.

Because of this, Robie and Reel didn't drive through any checkpoints. They were staying at a hotel outside of town. They had to leave their weapons behind when they separately entered the town on foot.

Robie walked the streets front to back, committing to memory all landmarks, the location of the major event—the town's old city hall—and the security personnel who roamed the area. He knew that Reel was making the same sort of canvas of the area.

He had concluded that the multihit Godfather scenario was less plausible. It would require pinpoint timing and a lot of luck. And most professionals knew that neither one was, realistically, in ample supply during these sorts of missions.

It would be one hit, an all-out assault with concentrated fire or explosives on a central target. This included several leaders who headed up what amounted to terrorist organizations masquerading as governments. But then again, crazies had been allowed to address the UN in New York, so he supposed this wasn't such a stretch. And some of them had been elected by a majority of voters exercising their democratic right to install whomever they chose to lead them.

Even if it was to oblivion.

He bought a cup of coffee and watched a group of turbaned and bearded men cross the street and enter another shop. There were many such groups here. All men. No women, at least that he could see. That was just how things were. And that was a big part of the problem, he felt.

Despite the chill he sat at an outdoor table and drank his coffee. His gaze kept wandering and he finally keyed on a group of men walking down the far side of the street.

He spoke into his mic. "Group of five guys on the east side of the street heading toward the hotel at the end of the street. Do a pass and tell me what you see."

A few seconds later Reel emerged from an alley. She wore a hooded coat and sunglasses. She passed the group. Robie was the only one who noticed that she slowed down just a tad as she passed them. Her gaze seemed to be fixed straight ahead. But it wasn't. It roamed over the men, taking in all relevant details.

That was what years of training got you, an almost supernatural talent for observation.

Over his earwig Robie heard, "Nothing."

She kept walking and he heard her say, "Hold on a sec. Let me check something."

She kept walking down the street. Robie watched as she passed a guy wearing a black warm-up suit, with a ski cap pulled low. He was looking down at the pavement but Robie could tell his gaze was also roaming.

Reel passed him. A few seconds later over his earwig Robie heard her say, "Bingo. Tag, you're it."

Robie immediately rose and took up the tail on the guy. As he walked he mumbled into his mic, "Talk to me."

"That was Dick Johnson. Remember him?"

"Dropped out of the clandestine service about two years ago, or so I heard."

"Disappeared was more like it."

"You sure it's him? I didn't know him that well."

"He's changed. But what he didn't change was a tat on his shooting hand."

"What of?"

"Oh, pretty routine. A scorpion holding a gun with its stinger and the word 'Mom' inked on the scorp's back."

"Okay, that sounds about as good as a fingerprint for ID."

"See where he goes."

"You think he's part of the missing personnel DiCarlo was talking about?"

"I doubt this village is a hot destination, particularly in winter. No place to ski."

Johnson turned down one corner and a few seconds later so did Robie. He said into his mic, "Parallel us on the next street over. Then take up the tail after the next intersection. I'll drop off and dogleg it over to the next street. We'll keep up that rotation all the way to where he's staying so he doesn't get suspicious."

"Copy that."

They exchanged the role of trailing Johnson three times. The streets were crowded, which helped. Robie was behind him when Johnson went into what looked like a hostel. Robie went to a café across the street. He sat down at a table and waited.

A few minutes later Reel's voice came over the mic. "Room 21, second floor. I saw three other guys in there I could swear were just like us."

"I wonder how many they have."

"More than four, that's for sure."

"Anybody pay you any attention?"

"One guy looked at me a little too long, so I turned around and started speaking German to the guy behind the desk in the lobby. He didn't understand me, but the guy lost interest and walked off. Good thing I had a little plastic surgery done. But you didn't, so keep low and your hat down and don't talk much unless it's in a foreign language."

"Right," said Robie.

"So what now?"

"We sit on Johnson and his team. Let them lead us where they'll lead us. You know what they're going to do?"

Reel said, "They'll have to recon the site and do a walk-through."

"That's probable."

"Do we hit them then?"

"Love to, but we have one problem."

"Our weapons are outside the checkpoints," she noted.

"Right. Now, Johnson wasn't wearing any security badges like the other grunts we've seen, so I'm wondering how they're getting their firepower. Because it has to be here somewhere. They're not going to beat these guys to death with sticks."

"Maybe it's waiting for them inside the security checkpoint," said Reel.

"Along with whatever else they're going to need to do this."

"Which might just solve our dilemma."

"And kill two birds with one stone."

"Would be nice," she commented.

"Yes, it would."

Dɪᴄᴋ Jᴏʜɴsᴏɴ ᴡᴇɴᴛ ᴏɴ ᴛʜᴇ move late that night. And Robie and Reel, who had changed clothes and looked as different as possible from earlier, were right there with him.

The town was actually larger than it looked, and there were many streets and back alleys off the main roads. Johnson took one of these and kept going for about fifteen blocks until the snow globe town turned into something a little less picturesque.

As before, Reel and Robie took turns trailing Johnson. They were wearing layers, and when one broke off from the tail they would shed a layer and stuff it in the knapsack each of them carried. With different clothes and staggering their surveillance, even someone as trained Johnson would have been hard pressed to spot them.

But he was taking steps to make sure he wasn't followed. He continually crossed the street. And occasionally when he would pass a darkened plate glass window he would stop in front of it and pretend to look at the merchandise while he used the reflective surface to check who was around. Sometimes he would simply stop, turn around, and start walking in the opposite direction, his gaze swiveling in all directions. Robie and Reel knew all of these tricks but still had to hustle to keep their cover.

The trail finally ended at a large old building on the outskirts of town, far away from the scheduled event and security perimeter.

Johnson went inside and Reel and Robie stood next to each other in the deep shadows of a nearby alley.

"Warehouse?" said Robie.

"Or operations center more likely," said Reel.

"Then we need to get in."

"Tricky. It's probably better guarded than the Middle East event."

"And yet here we are just a few feet away with a target under surveillance."

The front door of the place opened and a man came out.

Robie lifted his night optics to his eyes and took a peek. He handed the optics to Reel, who watched the man slowly walk down the street.

"Judge Samuel Kent," said Reel.

"They brought in the big gun for the finale."

"That validates our decision to come here."

"Validates, but that's all."

"We need to split up," said Reel. "I'll take Kent. You take the warehouse."

She started to head off, but he gripped her arm. "Follow, don't kill. We need him alive. For now."

She pulled free from his grip. "Do you really think you need to tell me how to do my job?"

"I'm thinking about your lost friends. Sometimes the temptation can be too great."

"I don't want just him. I want them all, Robie. And if he needs to keep breathing in order to do that, so be it."

"Just so we have it straight."

"We have it straight."

She headed off into the darkness.

Robie watched her until she and Kent disappeared into the night.

He turned his attention back to the building. Slowly he made his way around its footprint, checking out all entry and exit spots as he went along. Most of the windows were dark, but not all.

Three lighted windows, and he saw movement at two of them. They were all on the lower level.

He figured perimeter security was posted 24/7 if this was really their command center. And because Kent had been here, Robie had to assume it was. So how to get in and then out with what they needed but no one the wiser?

"Pretty much impossible," he told himself as he

crouched in the alley staring up at the building. But then another idea struck him.

He spoke into his mic. "Progress report?"

"Very little, actually. Still walking," answered Reel. "Don't think he's staying at the same place as the hired help. You?"

"Gonna try something."

"What does that mean exactly?" she said, sounding a little startled.

"It means exactly that I'll let you know when I'm done."

"Robie, if you're going to go in there I'm coming with you."

"I didn't say I was going in there."

"You didn't say you weren't either."

"I've been doing this sort of thing solo for a long time, okay?" he said harshly.

"Right, okay," she said, sounding sheepish. "Report back when you can."

Robie took a few careful steps out of the alley and peered upward. The front and rear doors were out. They would be guarded. The lower-level windows were out for the same reason.

That was why Robie was peering upward. He figured this strike team didn't have unlimited manpower. They would have to conserve what they did have and utilize it optimally. That meant not wasting it guarding portals that were literally out of reach.

But few things were truly out of reach. And this building was old. And the veneer was brick. Uneven brick.

That meant there were handholds.

The back of the building faced an abandoned structure. Robie gripped an edge of brick with fingers that were nearly as strong as steel. Handling a fifteen-pound sniper rifle, pulling triggers, and bracing for recoil to immediately fire again had made his grip one of the strongest things about him.

It would come in handy tonight.

He had to make the climb in darkness, because even a penlight would seem like a ship's beacon. But there was a dull glow of moonlight. That was both good and bad. Good if it made him see a handhold he ordinarily wouldn't have seen. Bad if they had a patrol passing around the outside of the building and one of them happened to look up.

He kept going, slipped twice, nearly fell once, but his hand finally gripped the ledge outside a darkened window and he lifted himself up and perched on the narrow space. The window was locked.

He pulled out his Swiss Army knife, which the security checkpoint had missed, and a few seconds later passed through the open window and dropped noiselessly to the floor. Now he used his penlight to see, because the darkness was nearly complete in here.

The room was empty except for a few odd pieces

of furniture, some old paint cans, tarps, and rusted tools. It seemed someone was going to renovate the space and then thought better of it.

He moved to the door very slowly. The floors were wooden and old, and such floors creaked. He didn't take actual steps. He slid his feet along the floor to minimize the noise. He reached the door and put his ear to it.

He could hear sounds. But they all seemed to be coming from downstairs.

He shined his penlight on the hinges. They looked old and rusty. That wasn't good. They might sound like a fighter jet shrieking in when he opened it.

Robie looked around and his gaze lighted on the stack of paint cans, tools, and tarps. He slid over there, quietly rummaging around until his hand snagged a can of oil.

He went back over to the door and soaked the hinges with it. He let the lubricant seep deeply into the metal joints and then he slowly opened the door.

Thank God for small treasures, he thought as he peeked between the door and jamb.

The hall was clear.

He moved out into the corridor. There were three doors facing him across the hall, with stairs heading down in the middle of the landing.

He shuffled across the hall and over to the other doors. He pulled his knife, a poor weapon against guns, but all he had. The hall was thankfully dark, so he used his penlight to examine the lock and floor in front of the three doors.

Bits of rust were in front of only one door, the one obviously that had been opened. He noted that the hinges had been lubricated.

The door was locked. But with his knife it was unlocked ten seconds later.

He opened it, the hinges moving silently, and stepped in. He shut the door behind him and locked it.

He shined his light around.

In one corner, on pegs, was a long line of clothing items. He examined some of them. Now the other side's plan started to take shape for him. It actually made sense. In fact, it was a tactic that had worked well for terrorists in other scenarios.

As he continued to look around he realized he had hit the jackpot. It looked like the armory at a military base. There were so many weapons here that Robie wondered how they could possibly miss a few. They were stacked haphazardly and weapons of different capabilities were mixed together. He could sense from this disorganization that the team here either lacked military precision or deemed their opponents too weak to put up much resistance. From what he had seen in the town so far, Robie opted for the latter explanation.

These weapons hadn't come in through the checkpoints. The people who had missed Robie's knife couldn't possibly have missed this. Either people had been paid off or, more likely, the weapons had been placed here before the checkpoints were set up.

Robie grabbed a few pistols, two subguns, and as much ammo as he could carry in his knapsack. Ideally, he could sabotage the rest of the weapons by knocking out the firing pins. But he didn't have the tools to do so. And it would take too much time and make too much noise.

But as he looked down at the weapons an idea occurred to him. He took photos of all of them with his cell phone.

What he was planning to do with these photos was incredibly risky, but in the end, he deemed the risk of not doing it far greater.

CHAPTER

76

REEL WAS WAITING FOR ROBIE at a small inn they had chosen as their rendezvous point. They had taken one room, and when Robie knocked on the door, she peeked through the peephole and let him in.

From under his coat and his knapsack he pulled out the weapons he'd taken and dropped them on the bed.

Reel picked up one MP5. "How much did they have?"

"Enough to take down this entire town and then some."

"How many men you figure?"

"At least two dozen, going by the amount of firepower. What happened with Kent?"

"He's staying at the finest hotel in this little hamlet. I left him having a glass of sherry by the fireplace."

"What do you think his role is? He won't be in the attack itself. You said he was one of us, but that was a long time ago."

Reel shook her head. "I think he was sent here to oversee things. He was at the building where the weapons were. He probably went over the plan with the troops and their respective assignments."

"What do you think their exit plan is?"

"With the sort of firepower you saw, I would say they could easily shoot their way out of here. Private wings lifting off a private runway and they're out of the country."

"And Kent?" asked Reel.

"He probably has some official role here as a representative of the U.S. He'll act as surprised as everyone else. He goes home, glad to be alive and properly mournful for all of the dead." He paused. "So we still think the opening ceremony is where it will happen?"

"It's in one big room, Robie. Open spaces, multiple firing lines once the security perimeter is pierced. No place to hide."

"So they exit, fly away, and Kent goes home to report the success."

"But if we stop it here?"

He said, "We *have* to stop it here. We're the last line of defense."

"A damn thin line."

"I figure if they have two dozen guys nearly as good as we are, we can take out at least half of them, maybe two-thirds if luck and the element of surprise are on our side. That may be enough to save the day."

She gazed up at him, a smile playing across her lips. "Not a bad legacy. 'Robie and Reel; they saved the world.'"

"At the sacrifice of their own lives?"

"Nobody's that lucky, Robie, not even the good guys." She picked up a pistol, checked the mag, and stuck it into her belt.

"We'll have to figure out where and how to hit them for maximum effect."

"The tactic they're going to employ will make that a little difficult." He explained what he had found in the room along with the guns.

Before he'd finished Reel was nodding. "I get that. But it allows some opportunities for us as well."

"Yes, it does."

"So it's a waiting game?"

Robie said, "Patience is a virtue. And tomorrow it'll be the only thing keeping us alive."

"You know we'll have two sides gunning for us as soon as we show our hand."

"We concentrate firepower on the target. They'll show their hand and we can only hope the official security understands what's going on."

"When shots are going off all around and people are running and screaming? It'll be mass confusion."

"That's why I said *hope*. We're going to have to split up."

"Two targets to shoot at."

"Right."

"But that means we dilute our fire concentrations."

"Can't be helped. Benefit outweighs the downside."

"Then let's pick our spots well." She paused, studied him. "If we manage to survive this, I've got another set of problems. I'm a wanted woman."

"Not by me. Not anymore. I'll help you, Jessica."

"You can't do that, Robie. What you've done so far could be construed as treason. If you stop this, all will be forgiven. But not if you keep consorting with the enemy. And that happens to be me."

"Extenuating circumstances."

"Not proved. And probably won't matter even if they were. You know how the system works."

"You mean how the system *doesn't* work."

"Let's just see how tomorrow goes. Things might just take care of themselves," she added ominously.

"Okay," said Robie. "They just might."

CHAPTER

77

THE DAY BROKE CLEAR AND COLD. With each breath taken, tiny puffs of smoke rose into the air. The leaders of various Arab countries made their way to their official motorcades looking discomforted by the chill, their robes buffeted by the stiff breeze.

It was eight o'clock in the morning. People were tense. There was a collective feeling that the citizens of the town simply wanted this to be over. Their wish would come true shortly, but not in a way that they ever imagined.

There was only one way in and one way out of the building where the opening ceremony was taking place, which made it appealing from a security point of view. But it also had its disadvantages.

The motorcades drifted down the street with Canadian police providing the traffic security. There were a number of Canadian Mounties on their horses; they looked resplendent in their red uniforms. But they were also brightly colored sitting ducks when it came to an actual armed confrontation.

Reel's and Robie's plan had come together at five in the morning.

Neither of them felt the least bit tired. Adrenaline trumped exhaustion.

Reel was across the street from ground zero, just beyond the security checkpoint. That was a no-go for her because she was armed to the teeth.

Robie stood on the opposite corner, nearer the building but again beyond the checkpoint. Jersey barriers had been erected to prevent a truck bomb from getting close enough to drop the structure. Thus there was barely enough room to get a single car through at a time.

Bottlenecks like that could cause other sets of security problems, but on the whole Robie felt the plan had been well thought out.

He checked his watch. It was nearly time. He said into his mic, "Just about there."

"I've counted seven motorcades so far. From my list that makes five more to go."

"They'll want them all in place. Give it a few minutes and then they'll pull the trigger."

"Here we go," said Reel.

Here we go, thought Robie.

The last motorcade pulled through and disgorged its occupants. They walked into the building and the setting was complete.

The program was on a tight schedule. Opening

ceremonies and remarks would last forty-five minutes. After that the group would be dispersed to different places for other discussions and events. This
was one of the few times all of them would be in the
same place at the same time.

From the heightened looks of concern of the security arrayed around the place, this fact was not lost
on them either.

Robie moved to an alley and his hand closed around
the butt of his gun as he did so. He looked at his watch.
The program had been going on for twenty minutes.

Tactically the attackers wouldn't want it to get
close to the end on the off chance that any of the
attendees left early. It was critical to get them all.

He said into his mic, "I think—"

That was as far as Robie got.

Flames shot out from the front door of the building and all four front windows. The same thing happened at the rear entrance.

Thirty seconds later the front of the building was
engulfed in fire, blocking the entrance. The rear was
similarly cut off.

Robie braced himself as he heard it coming. Fire
trucks and ambulances raced down the street, sirens
blaring.

Security let them through and the emergency vehicles screeched to a stop in front of the building. Men
poured off the trucks and out of the ambulances.

Robie stepped out, his gun ready.

Reel did the same from across the street.

Robie fired and his shots blew out the front tires and windshield of an ambulance.

Reel killed one of the firefighters before he could deploy the subgun he had pulled from under his coat.

Both Robie and Reel opened fire directly on the group of men, forcing them to scurry for cover.

But before they could return fire someone shouted, "Freeze!"

Robie watched as an army of FBI and Canadian security agents charged forward from both ends of the street. They wore body armor and toted subguns. Emerging from hiding places along rooftops were snipers who pointed their long barrels at the fake first responders and fired shots close enough to the heads of the targets to make them realize any resistance would result in a slaughter.

So the targets did the only thing they could do.

They gave up.

A minute later more than twenty men were on their knees on the street, hands over their heads, with an array of pointed guns keeping them there.

Robie came forward and greeted her. Nicole Vance had on body armor and held her pistol in her right hand. Her smile was wide and welcoming.

She said, "Thanks for the heads-up last night. And the photos of the arsenal you found. Couldn't really believe it at first, but you were very convincing. And in turn, I was very convincing with my superiors. And I can't tell you what good things this will do for my career."

Robie looked over as two men came forward holding another man between them. Sam Kent didn't look very pleased at the sudden turn of events. But he wasn't saying anything either. No protests of innocence. No demands to know why he was being held.

Robie stared at the man. When Kent caught his gaze he stiffened. Robie thought he caught a hint of a resigned smile pass over the man's features.

"You can help us," said Robie quietly. "You know what we need."

"I highly doubt that I can help you or myself."

"Going to claim that you know nothing about this?"

"Not at all. It's just that dead men don't make capable witnesses."

"Come again?"

"Can I tell you something?"

"A name would do."

"No, the message is much simpler." He smiled and said, "Goodbye, Robie."

The two men stared directly at each other.

"Robie!"

Robie turned and saw Reel on the other side of the street.

She shouted, "Robie! Johnson isn't there. He's not there."

Robie looked over at the line of men on their knees in the street. He glanced down the faces one by one.

Dick Johnson *wasn't* there.

Robie started to move, but knew he was already too late.

The shot hit Kent full in the face and blew out the back of his head, taking a large chunk of his brain with it.

Robie had looked back at Kent a second before the round hit.

There had been no fear in the man's features. Just resignation.

78

ROBIE AND VANCE WERE SITTING in the lobby of the local police station. The fire had been put out and the event had been moved to another location. At first it seemed likely to be canceled. But after the FBI promised to help with security for the event, the participants had changed their minds and agreed to go forward.

The hit team was being held in cells under the eye of both Canadian special agents and the FBI. The joint mission had come together quickly. The FBI was taken seriously by everyone in the world. It also didn't hurt that the Canadians were such close allies. And the last thing they wanted was a slaughter of foreign leaders on their soil.

Sam Kent's body was lying on a freezer bed inside a mobile forensics unit.

Dick Johnson had so far eluded capture.

"Who was the woman who called out to you?" asked Vance.

Reel had disappeared into the crowd after warning Robie about Johnson.

"Someone who was working with me on this to stop it. I can fill you in on her later."

"Okay. So they were planning to take out all these leaders at one time?"

"Seems like it."

"Would've created a global nightmare."

"Probably their plan."

"How did you guys get keyed in on this?"

"Chatter, bits and pieces here and there that we followed up on."

"Always thought having this summit here was kind of weird. I mean, the G8 was having a conference on terrorism in Ireland at the same time. Did you know that?"

"Read about it in the papers," Robie said vaguely.

"I'm glad you called us in, don't get me wrong. But why wouldn't you have your own team in place for this? I mean, we're not in the U.S. The CIA can operate legally here."

"Not sure the Canadians see it that way. Some hard feelings between us over some past agency actions. We felt the FBI would be the right element to call in to provide the backup once we nailed down the target." None of this was true, but it was also the only explanation Robie could think of.

"I guess the important thing is it didn't happen, right?"

"That's the way I look at it."

"But the guy who was killed? We identified him. He's a federal judge. How does that figure into this?"

"Not sure yet. I think it'll take some time to dig through all of it. If I had to guess—and that's all it would be—he might have been paid off. And maybe he wasn't always a judge."

"Right. He seemed to know who you were," said Vance suspiciously.

"Just the way it worked out," said Robie, not meeting her eye.

"So this was what you were working on that you had to go off the grid?"

Robie nodded.

"And I'm assuming that this is somehow tied to Jim Gelder's and Doug Jacobs's deaths?"

"And Howard Decker's."

"Decker's? How does he figure into this?"

"I'm not sure, Vance. It's still pretty muddled."

She looked put off. "Don't think that I'm accepting all your answers at face value. I know you too well. You talk the bullshit really well, but at the end of the day, that's still all it is."

"I'm telling you all I know."

"You mean you're telling me all you *can*." She studied him closely and then apparently decided to change direction. "Robie, the men we've arrested. They... they look like..."

"There's a lot of freelance talent out there. And we trained a ton of it."

"So mercenaries?" she said.

"Probably so."

"Now we just have to find out who hired them."

"We might never know."

"No, we'll get there. I'm thinking that Gelder and Jacobs might have stumbled onto something. The other side found out and killed them. Maybe something with Decker too." She snapped her fingers. "He's head of the Intelligence Committee. There's the connection right there."

"You might be right."

"We'll see. Like you said, these things tend to get muddled."

Yes, they do, thought Robie.

"When are you heading back?" asked Vance.

"Got a few things to clear up here and then I'll be reporting in. I'm sure our agencies will be burning up secure lines hashing this one out. Sometimes the truth complicates things."

"I don't think so. Not here. Good guys officially kicked the crap out of the bad guys. They can't put any spin on that one. And the U.S. just scored some serious points with the Middle East. We just saved their collective ass. And I've seen a list of the attendees. There are some on there who are no fans of ours."

"No, they're not. But maybe they will be now." He rose. "I better get going."

"You see, Robie, sometimes communication is a very good thing."

Robie had not gone ten steps down the sidewalk when the voice in his ear said, "On your three."

He looked over to where Reel was staring at him from the far corner. He hurried over and they walked down an alley.

"Kent is dead," he said.

"That was easy to see. Most of his brain was on the street."

"Johnson is nowhere to be seen."

"He was the fail-safe. Kent knew everything. The other guys just had their piece. They won't be able to lead us anywhere. Firewalled out of the loop. Kent was the key, and Johnson was tasked to keep back and take him out if things went wrong."

"Agreed."

Reel's voice turned harsh. "But why didn't you tell me about the FBI?"

"Did you need to know?"

"I thought we were a team on this."

"I thought that if you knew the FBI was going to swarm in you might have done things differently."

"Meaning what?"

"Meaning you're a wanted person."

"What did you tell them about me, by the way?"

"That we were tasked to stop this by the agency."

"And Gelder and Jacobs?"

"They believe they were killed by the people behind the planned hit here. I told them I thought they were on the right track with that theory."

"I doubt that Vance is going to stop there. She doesn't seem the type to take anybody's word in place of an investigation and her own conclusion."

"She's not. What I did back there was just a stop-gap. Just to give us some time."

"Okay."

"But it can't end there, Jessica."

She looked over her shoulder. "I've been thinking about nothing except that ever since I started on this."

"There are ways," Robie began.

"There are no ways, Robie, not for this. It has one possible outcome and it's not a good one for me. But you'll be okay. In fact, if I were you I'd go back to Vance right now and just tell her the truth. The more you try to cover for me the worse it will be for you when the truth does comes out."

Robie didn't budge. "You really want to waste time arguing over something that stupid?"

"It's not stupid. It's your future."

"I'm not going anywhere, Jessica. That's my decision, and I'm sticking to it."

"You're sure?"

"Don't ask me again."

"But just so you understand the possible conse-quences."

"Someone gave the order to Johnson to take out Kent. I want that person."

"Loose ends, Robie. They'll be finding Johnson's body any minute now. That idiot was dead as soon as he pulled the trigger on Kent. No way they're going to leave him alive."

"We're loose ends too," he said.

"That's right, we are," she said, looking suddenly cheerful.

"What?" said Robie, noting her upbeat expression.

"Loose ends are a two-way street. They want to get to us. But to get to us they have to come to us."

"And that gives us a shot at getting them first," he said.

"I'm done hitting singles too, Robie. It's time to go for the shot out of the park."

"How exactly do we do that?"

"You just have to trust me. Like I've been trusting you this whole time."

"What exactly is your plan? We've got nothing."

"I'm not really into sports, but I've been doing some basic research," she replied.

"On what?"

"On Roger the Dodger."

"Do you know who it is?"

"Actually, I think I do."

"Proof?"

"A witness."

"Where can we find the witness?"

"We don't have to."

She walked off.

When he didn't follow she turned back and said, "Despite what you just said, if you're out I need to know, right now. I'll have to adjust my plan and fly this one solo. But either way, it's happening."

"Because of your friends?"

"Because I don't like getting crapped on. I don't like traitors. And, yeah, because of my friends."

"I'm in," he said.

"Then come on."

Robie followed her.

CHAPTER

79

The White House.

It was often a place of near chaos buffered by moments of intense calm, like the eye of a hurricane. One could tell that inches past the serenity lurked possible bedlam.

This was one of the serene moments. The precise location of the possibly hovering bedlam was as of yet unknown.

They were in the Oval Office. It was reserved for symbolic moments that often were attended by dozens of photographers. There were no photographers here today, but it was a symbolic moment nonetheless.

Robie sat in one chair. Across from him was DCI Evan Tucker. The president was perched on a settee. Next to him in a separate chair was National Security Advisor Gus Whitcomb. Completing the party was Blue Man, looking slightly awed to be once more in the presence of such august company.

"This is getting to be a routine, Robie," said the president affably.

"I hope it doesn't actually become one, sir," said Robie.

His suit was dark, his shirt white, and his tie as dark as his suit. His shoes were polished. Next to the others, with their colorful ties, he looked like a man attending a funeral. Maybe his own.

"The exact details of what was going on are still coming out, albeit slowly," said Whitcomb.

"I doubt we'll ever know the whole truth," said Tucker. "And you'll never get me to believe that Jim Gelder was involved in any of this." He glanced at Robie. "And the people responsible for his death, and that of Doug Jacobs, will be brought to justice."

Robie simply stared back and said nothing.

The president cleared his throat and the other men sat up straighter. "I believe that we dodged a very large bullet. This is not the time for celebration, of course, because we have tough times ahead."

"Agreed, Mr. President," said Tucker. "And I can assure you that my agency will do all it can to ensure that those tough times are met head-on."

Robie and Whitcomb shared a raised eyebrow over that comment.

Whitcomb waited until it seemed the president wasn't going to respond to Tucker's statement. "I agree that we have many problems ahead of us. If, as Mr. Robie believes, there were moles at the agency—"

"For the record that is a statement I highly dispute," interjected Tucker.

The president put up his hands. "Evan, no one is testifying here. Gus is just saying that we need to get to the bottom of this. As much as we can, at least."

Whitcomb continued, "If there are moles at the agency, then that needs to be resolved. We have four dead men who were all highly placed in various sectors of this country. We have a near catastrophe averted in Canada thanks to the actions of Mr. Robie and the FBI. What we have to do is connect the dots between the two."

"Of course," said Tucker. "I never said there shouldn't be an investigation."

"A thorough one," added Whitcomb.

"Do we have any new leads on who killed Gelder and Jacobs?" asked the president.

"Not yet," said Blue Man.

They all turned to look at him, as though they had forgotten he was even there.

He continued, "But we are hoping for that status to change."

The president said, "And this Johnson person?"

"Dick Johnson," said Whitcomb, looking at his notes. He glanced up at Tucker. "He once worked for the CIA."

The president shot a look at Tucker. "From one of ours to one of theirs, Evan? How is that possible?"

"Johnson was a washout, sir. If he hadn't disappeared, one day he would have been let go."

"He wasn't the only one, sir," said Robie. "Of the twenty-odd people the FBI arrested, half of them had ties to the agency. And that doesn't include Roy West out in Arkansas."

"Roy West was fired," snapped Tucker, "and I am well aware of the others, Robie. Thank you, though, for pointing it out," he added sarcastically.

"But the ultimate goal," began the president. "Obviously, taking out all those leaders would have led to great upheaval in the Muslim world. But was that the only reason?" He glanced around at the others with a questioning look.

Tucker shot a piercing look at Whitcomb, who did not seem to notice it. He glanced at Robie. There seemed to be an understanding between Robie and the APNSA. In fact, they had spoken before the meeting.

Whitcomb cleared his throat and said, "It could be that whoever was behind this had plans to replace the dead leaders with others who believed as they did."

"So it was internal?" said the president. "Meaning factions competing for power within the Middle East were behind the attack in Canada?"

"That appears to be the case," said Whitcomb.

"Well, thank God it didn't come to pass," said the president.

"Yes, thank God," added Tucker.

The door to the Oval Office opened and the president's "body man" looked in. It was his job to keep the president on schedule.

"Sir, two-minute warning before your next meeting."

The president nodded and rose. "Gentlemen, you will keep me posted on how this goes. I want to know about any new developments. We will maintain the status quo until such time as conditions on the ground dictate otherwise, but I want a full-court press on this."

They gave him their assurances, shook hands, and said their goodbyes.

On the way out, Robie cornered Blue Man. "We haven't spoken in a while."

"You've been off the grid for a while."

"I took your advice. It turned out to be good advice."

Blue Man drew closer to Robie and spoke in a low voice. "And her?"

Robie nodded. "As good as advertised."

"What will happen to her?"

"I don't know. If it were up to me she walks free."

"It's not up to you," pointed out Blue Man.

"Like the president said, we maintain the status quo until conditions on the ground dictate otherwise."

"And you really think the conditions on the ground are going to change?"

"Actually, they always do."

"But not here."

"Especially here," said Robie.

Robie caught up to Tucker as he was about to climb into his SUV outside the White House.

"Give us a minute," Tucker said to his aide as he glanced questioningly at Robie. The two men strolled a few feet away.

"Interesting meeting," said Robie.

"Why did I think I was being ganged up on?" Tucker said accusingly.

"What did you expect? Your agency is in the middle of this whole thing."

"You're really close to getting your ass canned."

"I don't think so."

Tucker snarled, "You work for me, Robie."

"I work for the guy in the White House. And if you want to get really technical, the American people are actually my boss."

"That's not how it works, and you know it."

"What I know is that people are dead. And not just the bad guys."

"Who are you talking about, exactly?"

"A woman named Gwen. And a guy named Joe. And a guy named Mike."

"I don't know who they are."

"They were good people."

"So you knew them?"

"Not really, no. But someone I respect vouched for them. So watch your back, Director."

Robie turned to walk away.

"Who do you respect, Robie? Would that be Jessica Reel? The person who murdered two of my people?"

Robie turned back. "They might have been people, Director. But they weren't *your* people."

Robie walked off.

Tucker stared after him for a few moments and then stalked to his vehicle.

Through the gates of the White House watching all of this was Jessica Reel.

She and Robie exchanged a glance and she turned and strode off.

80

ROBIE WAITED ON THE BENCH at Roosevelt Island, right across from the Kennedy Center in the Potomac River. In the middle of a million people the small island was heavily wooded, isolated, and private. It was not open to the public today, which made it even more private. There was a good reason for this.

It was a fine day, bright, sunny, and warmer than normal.

Robie looked up at some birds soaring by and then his attention turned to the man coming down the path toward him. He was walking slowly. He saw Robie and gave a small wave before taking his time heading over.

He sat, unbuttoned his jacket, and leaned back.

"Nice day," said Robie.

"It will be nicer when we nail the bastard," said Whitcomb.

"I'm looking forward to that too."

"You spooked Tucker after our meeting."

"He was definitely on the defensive."

"As he should be. Tucker is a disgrace, but difficult as it is to admit, I don't see how we do it, Robie. The proof just isn't there. No matter how hard we want it to be."

"The shooters had been with the agency."

"His motive?"

"With the world gone to hell the CIA would sky-rocket right to the top in budget dollars and turf. The twin holy grails of the intelligence sector."

Whitcomb shook his head. "Circumstantial only. His lawyers would tear that to pieces. Not one of the shooters had anything useful?"

"They were out of the loop. Hired guns only. Kent is dead. Gelder, Decker, Jacobs. All loose ends tied up."

"He was efficient, I'll give him that."

"One mistake, though."

"What's that?"

"We have one loose end that was forgotten."

"What?" asked Whitcomb eagerly.

"A who, sir. A woman. Karin Meenan. She worked at the CIA as a physician. She was the one who put the tracker device on me. She knew Roy West. And she knew about the white paper."

"White paper?"

"We called it the apocalypse paper. It diagrammed in meticulous detail an attack on the G8, country by country, assassination by assassination, executed by

Islamic terrorists. Then it outlined what would be done after the killings to maximize the global chaos."

"But the attack in Canada centered on Arab leaders, not the G8."

"Right. They took West's document and reversed it. An attack on Muslim leaders by—" Here Robie fell silent.

"Not by factions in the Middle East," said Whitcomb. "As we told the president. But by Tucker and those idiots at CIA who can't seem to get this nation-building crap out of their system."

"I'm afraid new evidence cuts against that conclusion, sir."

"New evidence?"

Robie waved his hand, motioning over the person who had just appeared on the entrance path. Whitcomb saw the woman coming forward, her steps hesitant.

"I had her locked up in a little hideaway," said Robie. "I was fearful for her safety."

Karin Meenan stopped in front of them. Robie said, "I'd introduce you, but you two already know each other."

Whitcomb stared up into the woman's frightened features. Then he turned to Robie. "I'm not sure what's going on here."

"A friend of mine did some research on you and had an epiphany. Did you enjoy playing football at the Naval Academy with Roger Staubach? He was a couple of years ahead of you and you played on the D-line and he was the QB. But it still must've been a thrill for you. Heisman Trophy winner, Navy's last one. Hall of famer. Super Bowl winner and MVP. Pretty awesome."

"It was, actually, but I think we need to get back to the matter at hand."

"He had a nickname too when he played. Quite the scrambler. The running quarterback. What was that nickname again?"

Meenan said in a small voice, "Roger the Dodger."

"That's it," said Robie. "Roger the Dodger. Same handle that the person gave Roy West. West sent him the apocalypse paper. That's where this all started. Now, I don't think it was Staubach." He pointed at Whitcomb. "I think it was you."

"I am very confused here, Robie. You and I have already discussed this. We put the blame squarely on Evan Tucker. You grilled him after the meeting with the president with my full blessing."

"Just done to throw you off your guard. To get you to come here and meet to discuss what you thought would be Tucker's professional destruction. Tucker's a prick, but he's not a traitor. You're the traitor."

Whitcomb slowly stood and looked down at him. "I can't tell you how disappointed I am. And I'm more offended than disappointed."

"I've spent my whole working life killing bad guys, sir. One monster after another. One terrorist at a time. I'm good at it. I want to continue to do it."

"After these accusations today, I'm not sure you'll be able to, quite frankly."

"Patience at an end? Didn't want to wait for people like me to keep pulling triggers? Wanted to clear the game board in one move?"

"If you have one shred of evidence, you better reveal it now."

"Well, we have Dr. Meenan here, who will testify that she worked with you directly to set this up. And that she put a tracker into my body on your orders."

Whitcomb stared menacingly at Meenan. "Then she would be lying and she will be charged with perjury and she will go to prison for a very long time."

"I just don't see this going to a trial."

"Once the president hears of this I am sure that—"

Robie cut him off. "The president has already been briefed. Everything I've just said, he's already been told. It was at his suggestion that I meet with you."

"His suggestion?" Whitcomb said blankly. Robie nodded.

"But there is no evidence tying me to any of this."

"There is evidence, beyond Meenan here. Sir, you might want to sit down before you fall down."

His legs shaky, Whitcomb sat back down on the bench. "You said you don't see this going to trial?"

"Too much of an embarrassment for the country. We don't need that. There are lots of terrorists out there. That would hurt our ability to go after them. You don't want that, right?"

"No, of course not."

Robie looked up at Meenan. "Thank you. There are people waiting for you over there." He pointed to his left where two men in suits hovered.

After she walked off, Robie said, "Your security detail has been dismissed, by the way."

Whitcomb glanced in the direction from which he had come. "I see."

"Your resignation might be in order."

"Did the president suggest that too?" Whitcomb said dully.

"Let's just say that he didn't object when it was raised." Robie looked at the man. "Did you know Joe Stockwell?"

Whitcomb slowly shook his head. "Not personally, no."

"Retired U.S. marshal. Good guy. Got in with Kent, gained his trust. Found out what was going on. You had him killed. And a woman named Gwen. Nice old lady. And a former agency guy named Mike Gioffre. They all meant the world to a friend of mine."

"What friend would that be?" But Robie could tell that Whitcomb already knew the answer.

Robie pointed to his right. "Her."

Whitcomb looked to where Robie was pointing.

Jessica Reel stood ten feet from them, her gaze on nothing other than Whitcomb.

Robie stood and walked down the trail to the exit. He never once looked back.

The island in the middle of a million people now contained only two people.

Gus Whitcomb.

And Jessica Reel holding a pistol.

To his credit, Whitcomb looked unafraid.

"I've been to war, Ms. Reel," he said by way of explanation as she drew close to him. "I've seen many people die. And I almost died myself a couple of times. You never get used to it, of course. But the shock level *is* diluted."

"Gwen Jones, Joe Stockwell, and Michael Gioffre did die," she replied. "You had them killed."

"Yes, I did. But the world is complicated, Ms. Reel."

"And it's also extremely simple."

"You look at it in different ways. You think you see an opportunity for improvement. Vast improvement. And sometimes you take it. That's what we did here. We were tired of the killing, the chaos, and always being at the edge of the precipice. We just wanted a more stable, peaceful world by having people we could actually deal with in power over there. A few lives to save millions? How can that possibly be wrong?"

"I'm not here to judge what you did. That's really not my concern." She raised her weapon. "There have to be others besides the ones we know. Who are they?"

He shook his head and smiled grimly. "Now, do you want me to kneel? Do you want me to stand? Whatever you say I'll do. You have the gun, after all."

"You have family."

For the first time Whitcomb looked concerned. "They knew nothing of any of this."

"I don't care."

"I would please ask you to not harm them. They're innocent."

"Gwen was innocent. And so were Joe and Mike. And they had families."

"What do you want?"

"Who else was behind this?"

"I can't."

"Then I'll start with your oldest daughter. She lives in Minnesota. And after that your wife. And then your sister, and I'll keep going until there's no one left." She pointed her pistol at his head. "Who else?" she asked.

"It won't matter. They're outside this country, completely untouchable."

"Who else? I won't ask again."

Whitcomb gave her three names.

She said, "Congratulations, you just saved your family."

"You give me your word that you will not harm them?"

"Yes. And unlike some people, I do keep my word."

"Thank you."

"One more thing. DiCarlo?"

"She was too close to figuring things out. It pained me, but there was too much at stake."

"You'se a bastard."

"So stand or kneel?" he said.

"I don't care, really. But I want you to close your eyes."

"Excuse me?"

"Close your eyes."

"I will have no trouble watching you kill me," Whitcomb replied.

"It's not for your benefit. It's for mine."

Whitcomb closed his eyes and waited for his life to end.

When no shot came and the minutes passed by, Whitcomb finally opened his eyes.

The island now contained only one person.

Jessica Reel was gone.

CHAPTER

81

"I COULDN'T PULL THE TRIGGER," Reel told Robie.

It was later that afternoon. They were sitting in Robie's apartment. Reel looked totally dejected.

"It was sanctioned," he said.

"I know it was sanctioned." She paused. "I told him to close his eyes. Like you told me to. When he opened them I was gone." She looked up at him. "Just like you were."

"It was your choice. But I have to say I'm surprised."

She let out a long breath. "You let me live, Robie, when everything you've done the last dozen years was telling you to pull the trigger on me."

Robie sat down next to her. "You didn't deserve to die, Jessica."

"I killed people. Just like Whitcomb."

"It's not the same."

She snapped, "At every important level it *is* the same."

Robie remained silent.

Reel wiped her face. "He was just an old, tired

man sitting there. And he wasn't afraid of dying." She rose, went to the window, and stared out, her forehead pressed to the cool glass. "I couldn't pull the trigger, Robie, even though I wanted to."

"He wasn't an old, tired man. He was quite the warrior on the football field and off. Special forces in Vietnam, killed his share of the enemy. Guy was quite the badass in his day. And during his tenure as the APNSA, he orchestrated the killing of more members of terrorist organizations than any of his predecessors. He always goes for the jugular. Not a guy you would want against you. Kent found that out. So did Decker."

"So why are you telling me all this?" Reel asked.

"To let you know that you have more compassion than he or I do. I would have shot him and not even thought twice about it. And he would have done the same to you."

"So what will happen to Whitcomb?"

Robie shrugged. "Not our concern. I don't see him going to trial, do you?"

"So...?"

"So just because you didn't pull the trigger doesn't mean that someone else won't. Or maybe they'll bury him in some cell at Gitmo."

"Pretty high-level guy to go out like that. Media will be all over it."

"The media can be controlled. But let's hope no more high-level guys attempt something like this."

"So what happens to me now?" she asked.

Robie knew the question was coming. It was certainly a legitimate one. And yet he wasn't sure he knew the answer.

"The fact that they sent you after Whitcomb tells me that things are back to the status quo." He looked at her. "Is that what you want?"

"I don't know. I'm not sure I'll ever know. If I couldn't pull the trigger on Whitcomb, who's to say I'll ever be able to pull the trigger again?"

"You're the only one who can ultimately answer that."

"I'm not sure I'll ever be able to answer it."

"There is some good news."

"What?"

"Janet DiCarlo came out of her coma."

Reel's eyes widened. "Robie, there might be others out there. If they know that, she'll be dead in—"

He held up his hand. "No she won't."

"Why?"

"Cerebral hemorrhage. She's not . . . she'll never be the same as she once was."

"And that's good news?"

"She'll get to live." He paused. "Would you like to see her?"

Reel nodded.

Two hours later they stood at the bedside of Janet DiCarlo. Her head had been shaved and deep suture marks were stamped on her scalp where major surgery had been performed to relieve pressure on her brain. Her eyes were open and she stared up at them.

Reel reached out and took her hand. "Hello, Janet," she said in a husky voice. "Do you remember me?"

DiCarlo stared up, but no recognition came to her features.

"My name is—" Reel broke off. "I'm just a friend. An old friend who you helped a long time ago."

Reel looked down when DiCarlo squeezed her fingers. Reel smiled.

"You're going to be okay," she said.

Reel looked over at Robie. "We're going to be okay."

No we're not, thought Robie.

A few seconds later his cell phone buzzed. He looked down at the screen. The message was short but definitely to the point.

They were being summoned.

And now it starts.

CHAPTER

82

THE CONFERENCE ROOM SEEMED TOO small to hold everyone who was there. On one side of the table sat Robie and Reel. On the other side were Evan Tucker, Blue Man, and the acting APNSA, Josh Potter, who was much younger than Gus Whitcomb, barely fifty. Robie didn't envy his coming into this situation.

Tucker slid a USB stick across the table. Robie and Reel looked at it, but neither made a move to pick it up.

Tucker said, "New mission."

"For both of you," added Potter.

Tucker said, "We're giving you a second chance, Reel."

"I never asked for one."

"Let me put it this way. We're giving you your *only* chance. You murdered two people from the CIA, for God's sake. You should be in prison. Do you know how unbelievably generous this offer is?"

Potter cleared his throat and sat forward. "Let me

just say that these are extraordinary conditions and that everyone here is under enormous stress. As the new man in the loop I also want to say that putting this behind us is a priority. I think we can all agree on that."

Reel said, "Gelder and Jacobs were traitors. I just didn't wait for the sanction order. I'm sure it would have been forthcoming."

Blue Man added, "And the agency has uncovered evidence tying both of them to the plot. Sam Kent left files behind. So what Ms. Reel did was serve her country."

"Bullshit!" snapped Tucker. "You are a murderer, Reel, nothing will ever change that."

"Your objection is duly noted, Director," said Potter in a calming tone. "But the 'offer' has been authorized at a level above any in this room. So let's just focus on that instead of exercising histrionics."

Robie was not looking at Tucker or Potter. He was looking at Blue Man.

And Blue Man was doodling on a piece of paper.

Robie did not take this as a good sign.

Robie said, "Can we get a preview?"

"Like I said, a second chance," replied Tucker. "Ahmadi? Syria? He's still there. We need him taken care of."

"Little dicey to go in now," said Robie.

"If she had done her job before instead of shooting Doug Jacobs in the back, we wouldn't be having this conversation," barked Tucker. "It's gotten to the critical stage. We believe that Ahmadi is partnering with al-Qaeda and will soon offer them training, resources, and official cover into other countries if he comes to power, which looks likely. That obviously can't be allowed to happen."

"So we both go?" said Reel, watching Tucker.

He spread his hands. "Like Robie said, it's dicey right now. We believe the odds of success are increased with both of you going in."

"Which of us takes the shot?" asked Robie.

Potter pointed at Reel. "She does. You're the spotter."

"She has to finish the mission, Robie," added Tucker. "That is the official deal. She does that, as far as this country is concerned, the slate is wiped clean."

"I'd like that in writing," said Reel.

"In writing?" Tucker scoffed. "Where the hell are you coming from asking for that?"

"From a place called 'I don't trust you,'" she answered.

"You don't have a damn choice," thundered Tucker.

Potter held up a hand. "Look, maybe we can accommodate you."

"Whatever you want to call it, I don't care. All I want is someone really high up's ass on the line that says you will honor the deal."

"We could put you in prison," said Tucker. "So how about you go kill Ahmadi and our 'agreement' is you don't rot in a jail cell?"

Reel looked at Potter. "So accommodate me."

"How high up do you want the signatory to be?" asked Potter.

"Way higher than either of you," she said.

"That is a short list."

"And don't I know it."

Potter looked at Tucker, who sat back, folded his arms across his chest, rocked back in his chair, and stared at the ceiling, looking for all the world like an overgrown child who had just had his crayons taken away.

"Okay," said Potter. "Consider it done."

Reel scooped up the USB stick. "Nice haggling with you."

She and Robie started to leave.

"Robie, hold up," said Tucker. "We have matters to discuss with you separate from this."

Reel looked at Robie and shrugged. "I'll be outside." She left.

Tucker motioned for Robie to retake his seat. "She's a liability."

"I don't see it that way," said Robie. "And why are you really sending me along? She doesn't need a spotter."

"Because you are to make sure that she comes back. She is going to be held responsible for her crimes," said Tucker.

"You mean for killing traitors?"

"I mean for murdering two of my people."

"And the deal you gave her?"

Tucker looked triumphant. "There is no deal."

Robie glanced at Potter. "You just told her there was a deal."

Potter looked uncomfortable. "I'm usually a man of my word, Robie. But this is out of my hands."

Tucker pointed a finger at Robie. "And just to be clear, if you tell her the truth your ass will be in a prison cell until the day you die. We've got you on all sorts of aiding and abetting the enemy, meaning Jessica Reel."

Robie looked over at Blue Man, who was still doodling on his paper. "What do you think about this?" he asked him.

Blue Man looked up, thought for a moment. "I think you should go. And do your duty."

Robie and Blue Man gazed at each other for a long moment. Then Robie rose. "See you on the other side," he said, before going out the door.

Blue Man caught up with him before he left the building.

"Was that bullshit back there from you?" Robie asked.

"It was actually the best advice I could give you under the circumstances." He put out his hand. "Good luck."

Robie hesitated and then shook it.

Blue Man walked off and Robie left the building.

Reel was waiting for him at his car. They got in.

Reel said, "What did they want with you?"

"Doesn't really matter, now that I know."

"Know what?"

Robie held up the piece of paper that Blue Man had slipped him while shaking his hand.

Reel looked at the two letters Blue Man had written on it.

They were both lowercase t's.

She gazed up at Robie. They both knew exactly what it meant.

"Double cross," said Reel.

"Double cross," repeated Robie.

THE OPERATIONS ROOM WAS SMALL and the company selected to sit in on this particular mission few in number.

Potter, the APNSA.

Tucker, the DCI.

The new number two at CIA, who looked slightly gun-shy, since his two predecessors had been killed and permanently incapacitated, respectively.

The director of homeland security.

A ramrod-straight, white-haired three-star from the Pentagon.

And Blue Man.

On one wall was a mass of giant TV screens on which real-time SAT downloads were streaming across. The men sat in comfortable chairs around a rectangular table. Bottles of water sat in front of each of them. They could be getting ready to watch every NFL game being broadcast.

Or another type of contest from a half a world away.

Potter checked one of the digital clocks on the wall. "One hour away," he said, and Tucker nodded.

"Everything in place?" asked the three-star.

"Everything's in place," replied Tucker. He had on a headset and was receiving communications from assets on the ground. This was hard to do in a place like Syria, but the United States had enough muscle to do just about anything just about anywhere.

He hit a button on the control console in front of his chair and one screen flicked to the sniper nest set up in an empty office building in downtown Damascus.

"It was fortunate that Ahmadi's people never learned of the assassination attempt," said Tucker. "In fifty-seven minutes he's going to find himself in the crosshairs once more."

"When does Reel arrive at the nest?" asked Potter.

"In ten minutes."

"And Robie?"

"His spotter site is set up on the street opposite where Ahmadi will be getting out."

"And their exit?" asked the director of homeland security.

"Planned and polished and we expect it to work," said Tucker vaguely.

"But everything is a risk," added Potter quickly. "Especially over there."

The three-star nodded approvingly. "It takes balls to do what your people do. Sending two in with light weapons and no backup. We send our guys into tough situations, but they have a lot more firepower and resources. And we don't leave people behind."

"They're the best we have," said Blue Man, drawing hard stares from Tucker and Potter.

"I'm sure," said the three-star. "Well, godspeed to them."

"Godspeed," mouthed Blue Man.

A voice spoke in Tucker's ear. He turned to the others and said, "Robie has just communicated in. He'll be in position in five minutes. Reel will be in the sniper's nest in seven minutes. Everything looks good. Ahmadi will be leaving the government building right about now. He will be out of target for the next forty-eight minutes. Then they'll have a two-minute window to—"

Tucker broke off speaking for a very understandable reason. On the TV screens, screaming people were suddenly running down the streets of Damascus. Guns were being fired into the air. Sirens were starting up.

"What the hell?" barked Potter.

Tucker was transfixed by what was happening on the screen.

Potter grabbed him by the shoulder. "What's going on?"

Tucker spoke into his headset, demanding an explanation for the sudden chaos on the streets.

"They're trying to find out. They don't know yet."

"Dial up Robie," demanded Potter. "He's right there."

Tucker attempted to do so. "He's not answering. He's gone silent."

"Reel, then. Get somebody, for God's sake."

"Look," said the three-star.

Syrian security forces were hanging out the window of the room where the sniper's nest was set up.

"How the hell did they get there so fast? Reel isn't even there. She hasn't fired a shot yet," added the DHS director.

"The whole operation has been compromised," said Tucker. "There's been a breach somewhere." He exchanged a glance with Potter. "This was not supposed to happen."

"And Ahmadi got away? Again?" snapped the three-star.

"He was not supposed to get away," Tucker muttered under his breath.

"For Christ's sake," said Potter. "Can't we get anything right?"

"Hold on," said Tucker. "Something's coming through now."

He listened to the voice in his ear. His expression went from stunned concern to absolute amazement.

"Copy that," he said.

"What is it?" screamed Potter when Tucker didn't say anything else.

Tucker turned to the others, his face white. "Ahmadi was just shot outside the government building, while he was getting into his car. He's dead. It's been confirmed through reliable sources."

"Thank God for that," said the three-star. "But I don't understand. Did the mission change? The hit was supposed to be outside the hotel."

"The mission didn't change. Not on our end," said Blue Man calmly.

The DHS director was staring at the Syrians swarming over the sniper's nest. "What I don't get is how they were onto the sniper's nest so fast." He turned to Tucker. "It's almost like they knew the hit was coming."

"A breach, like we said," Tucker responded, still looking ghostly pale.

"But Reel and Robie must've known about it. That's why they made the switch to the government building and did the hit there," explained Potter quickly.

"But that doesn't make sense," said the three-star.

"Why not?" asked Tucker.

"You said Robie just reported in. He was getting

into position as the spotter outside the hotel. And he also reported that Reel was expected to be in place in ten minutes. The hotel and government building are nowhere near each other. Why would he communicate to his own agency one thing and then do something else entirely? It was almost as though he didn't trust—"

The three-star stopped talking and turned back to the screen, where the Syrian security forces were still screaming from the balcony of the sniper's nest.

Then the three-star glanced back at Tucker with a suspicious look.

Tucker looked over at the DHS director and found his gaze boring into him as well.

Tucker started to say something and then stopped. All he could do was stare at the screens.

The three-star said, "But the kill was still made. Under the, um, unusual circumstances I'd say that was the finest hit I've ever, well, not seen."

"Same for me," said the DHS director.

"And me," added Potter lamely, which drew a long glare from Tucker.

"Robie and Reel deserve this country's thanks," said the three-star firmly.

The DHS director added, "And we'll see that they get it."

"If they get out of Syria," said the three-star darkly.

If they get out of Syria alive, thought Tucker.

84

OTHER THAN NORTH KOREA AND IRAN, Syria was arguably the most difficult country in the world to escape from for a westerner.

Foreigners were inherently suspect.

Americans were hated.

American operatives who had just killed a potential Syrian leader were good for only one thing: execution and then being dragged through the streets headless.

The only positive element was that Syria's borders were not secure. They were flimsy and ever-changing, just as the politics of the moment were, in one of the countries constituting the "cradle of civilization."

Robie and Reel understood this fully.

They had a chance, a slender one.

Reel had delivered the kill shot from a building across the street from where Ahmadi had been about to get into his limo. It would have been easier to don a full burqa face covering and escape that way. However,

Syrian women didn't wear traditional Islamic garb for the most part. And full facial veils had been banned in universities and other public settings by the increasingly secular government, who felt it was a security risk and promoted extremism. Thus putting one on would have been a red flag, not a disguise.

But she could still wear a hijab. This would reveal part of her face, but she had stained it darker and simulated wrinkles and sun damage. And in the long black robe she had incorporated a harness and padding that added about sixty pounds to her frame. She stooped as she walked and looked as though she were about seventy.

She picked up a market basket and left the room, waiting patiently at the elevator with another man who was standing there. The elevator doors opened and she got into the car. It headed down. When it reached the ground floor she stepped off.

She was swept to the side as police flooded the building. They grabbed the man who had been in the elevator car with her and pulled him, as well as several other Syrian men, along with them. They stormed into the elevator and up the stairwell.

Reel waited for a few moments and then continued on. When she got outside, police cars were everywhere. Swarms of people were screaming. People were crying. Others were marching in the streets, chanting.

A car caught on fire. Guns were racked back and

fired into the air. Shop windows were smashed. There was a small explosion down the street.

Reel followed another group of women down the street and into an alley.

Under normal circumstances, it would have been unthinkable for men to search a woman on a Syrian public street.

These were not normal circumstances.

Police swept into the alley and started grabbing everyone, pulling at their clothing, looking for weapons or other signs of culpability.

One man had a knife. The police shot him in the head.

A woman ran screaming. She was repeatedly shot in the back and dropped to the pavement with blood pouring from multiple wounds.

The police were now closing in on Reel. She didn't look like an assassin. She looked like a fat old woman. But the police apparently didn't care. They were only a few feet from her as she backed away.

Her hand reached inside her basket.

They were just about to surround her, their guns drawn and pointed at her.

Her back was against a brick wall. One of the police reached out to grab her arm. Once they saw the padding, it would all be over. They would shoot her right on the spot.

The loud voice reached to the alley.

The police stopped, turned.

The voice yelled out again and again. In Arabic it said, "We have the shooter! We have the shooter!"

The police turned and ran back down the alley toward the voice.

The crowd closed in on Reel. Sobbing people bent down to the dead bodies.

Reel pushed backward, away from the crowd, and managed to ease into a sliver of a side alley.

She walked quickly down it and reached another street, a busy thoroughfare. A taxi pulled up to the curb and she climbed in.

"Where to?" the bearded driver asked in Arabic.

"I think you know," she said in English.

Robie hit the gas and the cab sped off.

He glanced in the rearview mirror. "Close?"

"Close enough," she said.

She pulled the remote from her basket and held it up. "This came in handy. Once they find the source of the 'We have the shooter' voice they won't be happy."

"A little boom box in the street never hurts," said Robie.

As they rounded a turn she tossed the remote out the window.

He looked in the rearview mirror again and saw the crowds spilling into the streets behind them. "They'll know the shooter got away. So we're not free and clear yet."

"Face it, Robie, we'll never be free and clear again."

"They found the sniper's nest. Even though you didn't fire from it."

"Big surprise. But at least it validates what your guy told us about the double cross."

"I wonder how they felt back in the ops room watching?"

"One of my greatest regrets in life will be missing the looks on their faces. Especially Tucker's."

He turned right and then left and sped up again. Traffic was lighter now. But Robie could envision roadblocks being set up right this minute.

Damascus to Israel was a short trip, but that would be the exit the Syrians would be expecting. And also the one designed by the CIA. So that option was out.

The trip to Amman, Jordan, was a little over a hundred miles. But the border between the two countries had been strengthened, with limited crossing points. So that was also out.

Iraq was to the east. It was a long border with many ways across. But neither Robie nor Reel saw much advantage in sneaking across the northern border of Iraq. They would most likely die there.

That left one option. Turkey, to the north. It was also a long border, hundreds of miles. The closest major Turkish city was Mersin, about 250 miles distant. There was a shorter route they could take through a narrow section of Turkey that poked like a misshapen finger into Syria a little north of Al Haffah. But Mersin, though farther away, would have more options for their onward travel, and a large city was easier to hide in. Besides, Robie wanted to put greater distance between them and the Syrians than the finger of Turkish land provided.

But they had to get there first.

And though the border had many holes in it, Syria and Turkey were also informally skirmishing with each other. Bombs dropped from planes and guns fired by roving packs of soldiers were becoming the standard of the day around the border. Plus there was a lot of illegal activity involving the trafficking of drugs, immigrants, guns, and other contraband through the region. And the criminals typically had one response to pesky witnesses.

They killed them.

"On to Turkey," said Robie.

"On to Turkey," she parroted back.

She didn't take off her disguise. Not yet. She had papers, in case they were stopped. She had to hope they would be good enough.

As Robie looked up ahead, he knew they were about to be tested.

He had shaved his head, grown a trim beard, and stained his entire body darker. His blue eyes were hidden by tinted contacts. He could speak Arabic fluently, with none of the accent of a westerner. Reel, he knew, could as well.

The checkpoint had been set up quickly, faster than Robie had thought possible. He wondered if the double cross had anything to do with that.

Security checkpoints were far more frenetic in the Middle East than in other parts of the world, barely controlled chaos where guns were pulled at the slightest misstatement or an ill-timed glance.

Robie slowed his taxi to a stop. There were three cars and a truck in front of his. The guards were searching vehicles, and Robie saw one of them with a glossy piece of paper in his hand.

"They have our photo," he said.

"Of course they do. Fortunately, we don't look like that anymore."

The guards reached the taxi. One of them yelled at Robie. He produced his papers and the man carefully examined them. Another guard poked his head in the back window and yelled at Reel. She kept her eyes down, showed her papers, and spoke deferentially. He looked in her basket and found a chunk of bread, a bag of nuts, a jar of honey, and a bottle of spices.

The car was searched and nothing out of the ordinary was found.

The first guard gave Robie a searching look and even tugged on Robie's short beard. It remained firmly attached to his face. Robie cried out in pain and the man laughed and then yelled at him to continue through the checkpoint.

Robie put the car in gear and drove on.

They cleared Damascus and Robie pointed them north.

Nearly two hundred miles later they arrived on the outskirts of Aleppo, Syria's largest city by population. It was dark now and they managed to slip into Aleppo without incident.

They had arranged for a safe house there. They changed, ate, and rested up for the second leg of their journey.

The next morning they climbed aboard bikes and started off with a touring group that would cycle through northern Syria to the Turkish border fifty miles away. The trip would normally take three days, a leisurely affair through ancient ruins and beautiful countryside.

They reached the Church of Saint Simeon Stylites, where the biking group planned to bed down for the night.

Robie and Reel didn't choose that option. They left the group and biked on, past Midanki, made several exhausting climbs over poor roads, and then entered a downhill sprint to Azaz.

They continued on to Turkey, making their border crossing in the middle of the night. They watched military aircraft soaring overhead and dropping bombs, which destroyed targets on the ground. Gunfire also sounded during the night, but they ignored it, pushing ahead.

Two days later they biked into the outskirts of Mersin.

A day later they ferried across the Mediterranean to Greece, and from there they flew west. They landed in the United States a week after Ahmadi's bloodied body hit the pavement in Damascus.

As soon as they reached America, Robie made a phone call. "We're coming in," he said. "Get the champagne ready." And then he clicked off.

Evan Tucker slowly put down the phone.

CHAPTER

85

ALMOST ALL AWARDS CEREMONIES CONDUCTED by the CIA were held in secret. That was the nature of the beast. This one was particularly so.

It involved the Special Activities Division of the CIA's National Clandestine Service. Within that division was the SOG, or Special Operations Group. They were the best of the best, running around the world doing the bidding of the United States either with a gun or by inserting themselves in the riskiest settings for purposes of intelligence gathering. They were the most clandestine special ops force in America, if not the world. Most of the members came from the military elite.

Most, but not all.

The ceremony was held in an underground room at the agency's installation at Camp Peary in Williamsburg, Virginia. It seemed appropriate that the event was below ground, in the shadows, and unknown to the rest of the world.

In attendance along with about two dozen others were Evan Tucker, APNSA Potter, the three-star, and the DHS director, who had watched the events unfolding in Damascus. And Blue Man.

Robie and Reel were each awarded the Distinguished Intelligence Cross, the highest award given out by the CIA. It was analogous to the Medal of Honor and was usually given posthumously. It was only bestowed for extraordinary heroism in highly dangerous conditions.

Evan Tucker read off the citation listing their achievements not only in Syria but also in Canada. And then Reel and Robie came forward to accept their medals.

As Tucker presented the medal to Reel he hissed, "This is not over yet."

"Clearly not," she said.

When Potter gave the medal to Robie he whispered, "You need to choose sides on this, Robie."

"So do you," Robie replied. "And choose wisely."

Robie and Reel walked out of the ceremony together. Outside, they were greeted by Blue Man.

"Thanks for the heads-up," Robie said quietly.

"Just doing my duty."

"Tucker isn't taking this too well."

"Hard to say how much longer he'll be heading up the agency," replied Blue Man.

"Days numbered?"

"They might be. He hasn't been that stellar as a DCI."

"You might want to consider the job."

Blue Man shook his head. "No thanks. I'm broken down enough as it is."

Robie and Reel drove out of Camp Peary and headed north. Neither of them spoke because neither had anything to say. The last couple of weeks had pushed them right to their maximum. They were both physically and mentally exhausted.

When they arrived back in D.C., Robie surprised her by saying, "I've got someone I want you to meet."

He drove to the building and parked at the curb. About ten minutes later people started coming out of the building carrying large backpacks.

When Robie saw her he got out of the car and waved her over. Julie Getty approached cautiously.

"What are you doing here?" she asked.

"First you complain when I don't come by, and now you complain when I do?"

Julie glanced in the car. "Who's that?"

"Get in and you'll find out."

"Jerome is coming to pick me up."

"No he's not. I already phoned him and told him I was."

They climbed in the car and Robie said, "Julie, Jessica; Jessica, Julie."

The two women nodded at each other and then both looked questioningly at Robie as he steered the car into traffic.

"Where are we going?" asked Reel.

"An early dinner."

Julie looked at Reel but she merely shrugged.

Robie drove them to a restaurant in Arlington. As they sat down to eat, Julie said to Reel, "How do you know Will?"

"Just a friend."

"Do you work together?"

"Sometimes."

"I know what he does," she said bluntly.

Reel said, "So you know he can be a real pain in the ass, then?"

Julie sat back and a grin spread across her face. "I think I like you." She looked at Robie. "Where is super agent Vance?"

"Doing super agent things, I imagine," replied Robie.

Julie turned back to Reel. "So you do what he does?"

Reel bit into a roll. "We both do things a little differently."

Robie said, "How's school going?"

"Fine. What have you two been up to?"

"This and that," said Robie.

"I read the news. I know what's been going on in the world. Have you two been overseas lately?"

"Not lately, no," said Reel.

"You lie as well as he does."

"Is that bad?"

"No. I admire people who can lie well. I do it all the time."

"I think I like *you*," said Reel.

Robie put a hand on her arm. "I screwed up before, Julie. I won't again."

"So does this mean you'll come by sometimes?"

"Yes, it does."

"With her?"

"That's up to Jessica."

Julie looked at her.

"I can do that," Reel said slowly, glancing uncertainly at Robie.

After dinner, they dropped Julie off at home. She gave them both hugs. Reel awkwardly hugged her back and then watched Julie climb the steps to her house.

As soon as Robie drove off, Reel said, "What the hell was that all about?"

"What? Having a meal with someone?"

"People like us don't have meals with...normal people."

"Why not? Is that somewhere in the agency manual?"

"We just took down a terrorist leader, Robie. And barely escaped. We could just as easily be in a hole somewhere in Syria with our heads cut off. You don't just sit down to a meal with a teenager and shoot the shit after that."

"I used to think that too."

"What do you mean, 'used to'?"

"I mean I used to think that way too. But I don't anymore."

"I don't understand you."

Robie drove to the next intersection, took a right, braked hard at the curb, and got out. Reel did too. They looked at each other over the roof of the car.

"I can't keep doing this job and cut off the rest of the world around me, Jessica. It can't be an either/or. I have to live a life. At least a little bit."

"That thing back there with the kid? What if someone followed you there? What kind of life might she have then?"

"Our side already knows about Julie. And I take precautions. But I can't protect everybody every minute of every day. She could step out in front of a bus and be just as dead as if someone had shot her."

"That is a specious argument at best."

"Well, it's my argument. And my life." He paused. "Are you telling me you didn't enjoy meeting her?"

"No. She seems like a great kid."

"She is a great kid. I want to be part of her life."

"You can't do that. We can't be part of anyone's life. Our friends end up dead because of us."

"I refuse to accept that."

"It's not up to you, is it?" she snapped.

"Then let's walk away from this shit. Start over."

"Yeah, right."

"I'm being serious."

She looked at him, saw that this was true. "I don't think I can walk away, Robie."

"Why not?"

"Because this is who I am. This is what I do. If I stopped..."

"It seemed you were prepared to stop when all this happened."

"That was revenge. I never looked past that. If you want the truth, I never thought I would survive it."

"But you did. We *both* did."

They both lapsed into silence.

She rested her arms on the roof of the car. "I didn't think anything would ever scare me, Robie." She exhaled a long breath. "But this does."

"It's not like a hit where you cross the i's and dot the t's. You don't really think, you just execute. This, this you really have to think about."

"And one and one don't necessarily make two."

"Almost never make two," he amended.

"So how do you make sense out of it?"

"You can't."

Reel looked up. The rain had started falling after

several days of dry weather. It was gloomy, depressing; even objects in the near distance were hard to make out.

As the rain picked up, neither of them made a move to get into the car. In about a minute they were soaked, but they just stood there.

"I'm not sure I can live like that, Robie."

"I'm not sure either. But I think we have to try."

Reel glanced down at her pocket. She pulled out the Distinguished Intelligence Cross and looked at it.

"Did you ever in a million years think you would get one of these?"

"No."

"We got this for killing a man."

"We got this for doing our job."

She dropped the medal back into her pocket and looked at him. "But this is not a job you walk away from."

"There aren't many who have."

"I'd rather leave it all in the field."

"From the look of the world right now, you might get your wish."

She looked away. "When Gwen and Joe were alive I knew I had at least two people who would mourn me. Who were my friends. That was important to me."

"Well, now you have me."

She stared back at him. "Do I? Really?"

"Close your eyes," he said.

"What?"

"Close your damn eyes."

"Robie!"

"Just do it."

She closed her eyes as the rain continued to fall.

A minute passed.

She finally reopened them.

Will Robie was still there.

ACKNOWLEDGMENTS

To MICHELLE, for taking care of everything else in the way only you can.

To Mitch Hoffman, for always seeing the trees and the forest.

To David Young, Jamie Raab, Sonya Cheuse, Lindsey Rose, Emi Battaglia, Tom Maciag, Maja Thomas, Martha Otis, Karen Torres, Anthony Goff, Bob Castillo, Michele McGonigle, and everyone at Grand Central Publishing, who support me every day.

To Aaron and Arleen Priest, Lucy Childs Baker, Lisa Erbach Vance, Nicole James, Frances Jalet-Miller, and John Richmond, for always having my back.

To Anthony Forbes Watson, Jeremy Trevathan, Maria Rejt, Trisha Jackson, Katie James, Natasha Harding, Aimee Roche, Lee Dibble, Sophie Portas, Stuart Dwyer, Stacey Hamilton, James Long, Anna Bond, Sarah Willcox, and Geoff Duffield at Pan Macmillan, for leading me to number one in the UK.

To Arabella Stein, Sandy Violette, and Caspian Dennis, for being so good at what you do.

To Ron McLarty and Orlagh Cassidy, for continuing to astonish me with your audio performances.

To Steven Maat at Bruna, for keeping me at the top in Holland.

To Bob Schule, for always being there for me.

To Janet DiCarlo, James Gelder, Michael Gioffre, and Karin Meenan, I hope that you enjoyed your characters.

To Kristen, Natasha, and Lynette, for keeping me straight, true, and sane.

And to Roland Ottewell for another great copy-editing job.